Teen Valour

by

Alaric Adair

Published by Oaksys Tech Ltd

Publishers
Oaksys Tech Ltd
41 Chalsey Road
London SE4 1YN

Copyright © Oaksys Tech Ltd 2009
All rights retained
First published in Great Britain in 2009.

Alaric Adair has asserted his right under the Copyright, Designs and Patents Act 1988 to
be identified as the author of this work.

http://www.alaricadair.com

This first book in a series was published September 2009.
"Teen Valour People" is a companion book.
"Company Mole" the second in the series; published December 2009.
"Dangerous Donkey" the third in the series; published Aug 2010

Cover pictures artist - Nicola Ivison
Editor - Autumn Conley

British Library Cataloguing in Publication Data
Adair, Alaric.
Teen valour.
1. Hostages--Fiction. 2. Victims of terrorism--Fiction.
3. Heroes--Fiction. 4. Adventure stories. 5. Young adult
fiction.
I. Title
823.9'2-dc22

ISBN-13: 9781907250033

Edition 1.3.1

Contents

Foreword

This world is facing great problems such as global warming. Most of the problems arise from population growth. Many powerful people know that these problems have to be fixed. Waiting for governments to agree globally and to provide the answers will not work in time. Some people feel it is time for strong leaders to arise to take those tough decisions. Sometimes those leaders will feel that they have to use unlikely allies and tough methods. These impatient people are going to change the future world of our hero Adam.

The mind of a young person is limited only by what they he or she has been told is impossible. Many of the rules taught to young people are social rules to help people live together in society, but some rules arise from the limited imagination of adults. If we give a young person the support and opportunity to develop they can do amazing things. I have had the privilege in my life to lead people in a youth organisation. I've seen how teenagers can achieve amazing things once that they are released from the chains of other people's imaginations.

I've had the idea for the book Teen Valour for several years. It is time to release the story of what happens when you take the boy who lives next door and give him opportunity to develop. Adam Cranford, the hero of this book is one such boy. At the age of 13 he attracts the attention of an ancient and benevolent organisation called the Foundation of Honour. He gains the respect of the leaders of the Foundation and he shows them that he can lead other people. He is given the opportunity to develop. How will he cope in the world of the unlimited? The path is not easy for our hero. He finds real danger, deception and despair along his path.

This book is the first of a series, so be patient as I introduce you to the hero, his early development and his friends. You will see more of them in later books. If you are just seeking action, skip forward to chapter 21, but you will miss a lot of the history and insight of how the boy-next-door is able to gain access to power and money. For those who love this book there is an Adam Cranford club at my web site. Club members can ask questions about the plots and get early previews of the next books.

In this book series you will often see reference to gold bullion. The value of gold remains unchanged, but the price changes frequently as the bankers and politicians play their economic games. Consequently the sharp eyed reader will soon realise that the monetary amounts in the text may not match current day prices. We've done our best to make them accurate, but we do not control the price of gold.

Alaric Adair
August 2009
http://www.alaricadair.com

Acknowledgements

When I wrote this book I called upon a panel of teenage reviewers spread around the globe. The magic of the Internet made this possible. I pass my thanks to Trae, Candassaie, Chloe, Kinga, Josh and Saif for their forthright views.

I also thank members of the public who have taken the time to publish reviews of the early editions of this book. Their feedback is welcome even when they were critical of errors. We can all gain from mistakes. Autumn Conley, my patient editor, who re-edited this book, shocks me every time with the number of errors that she finds in my narrative.

Finally and not least I must pass my thanks to my ever patient wife and family who leave me undisturbed as I slaved away at this book.

Chapter 1   Disaster at School

Adam began to suspect this Monday was going to be very different from other Mondays. He didn't realise then that as a consequence of this Monday he would end up fighting to save the lives of thirty school children including his own.

His suspicions about this day were triggered when everybody in school started smiling at him when he entered through the school gates. Even some of the Year 7 boys and girls were pointing him out to each other. When he was walking to his normal place in the morning assembly, he could feel everyone watching him. Of course he had a pretty good idea of what had caused the excitement, but he hoped against hope it wasn't public knowledge—at least not so soon after the fact.

The day's lessons had started normally. He didn't even have to think of an excuse about his maths homework, as he had worked hard over the weekend to make sure that he gave the teachers no reason to pick on him. At the end of the second session during maths class, his fears were confirmed when one of the school secretaries entered the room and passed a note to the class teacher. Mr. Fulbright read the note and looked in the direction of Adam. A hushed whisper rushed around the classroom as the teacher leant forward and beckoned to him. Adam's heart sunk, and his face paled as he heard the fateful words from the teacher.

"Master Cranford, you are to report to the Headmaster's office immediately. Please go with Miss Wilkinson."

He was dimly aware of the rest of the class cheering and hooting as he gathered his school books and bag and headed to the front of the classroom. He felt pats on his back from the other boys as he walked past their desks and out through the door. The door swung to with a *squeak* and a *click* of finality behind him. He had to rush to keep up with Miss Wilkinson as she set off indifferent to his progress. The *click-clack* from the heels of her shoes remorselessly rattled along the dark wood floors of the poorly lit corridor. She said nothing to Adam en route. She paused only when she reached the tall, dark door of the Headmaster's office. A green light was showing on the control light box by the door. She knocked twice on the heavy oak door and, grasping the well worn brass door handle, swung it open. She stepped into the room and ushered the boy in with a single imperious sweep of her arm.

"You wished to see Adam Cranford, Headmaster?"

Wilkinson stalked out of the room, closing the door firmly behind Adam. He stood there awkwardly clutching his school bag of books to his chest, waiting for the storm to break. There was utter silence in the room save the heavy, slow *tick-tock* of a grandfather clock standing against the wall. The Headmaster's desk was positioned in front of a large window. The bright light from the window made it difficult to see the Headmaster's face from where he was sitting behind the desk. The rest of the room was quite dark and gloomy. An empty, worn, brown wooden school chair was positioned one metre in front of the desk. To the left of it were sat two men whom Adam did not recognise. To the right sat a man whom Adam had no trouble recognising; it was his father, and he did not look happy. The Headmaster impatiently gestured to the empty chair.

"Sit down, Cranford."

Adam walked over to the chair and sat down, glancing at his father who frowned at him. He clutched his school bag to his chest and sat with a straight back facing the Headmaster.

"This is Mr. Reece. He is from the local education authority. The other gentleman is Detective Inspector Norris from the local police. I think you know why you have been called here."

Adam felt blood rush to his face as he blushed. He could feel his heart thumping rapidly in his chest. "No sir, Mr. Stilson. I'm not sure. Is there something wrong?"

The Headmaster glanced at Norris and then back at Adam. "Perhaps you might like to look at this photograph and explain?" The man lifted a large photo print from a folder on his desk and slid it across the desk towards Adam. "Come on, boy. Take a closer look."

Adam pretty much knew what he would see in the picture before he rose to look at it on the Headmaster's desk. As his father would say, "Sometimes even the best laid plans go wrong." This was one of those times.

"Well, Cranford? Tell us what you see. Do you recognise anyone in the photograph? Don't be shy now."

Adam could see his own face grinning back at him from the photograph. He was sitting alone behind the steering wheel of a vintage Mini Cooper S car. His eyes were glowing red in the picture from the camera flash, making him look like some kind of demon. His hands were encased in fake hairy gorilla gloves, grasping the steering wheel like a crazy driver. Clenched between his teeth was one of Stilson's tobacco pipes. What was unusual about the picture was that the Mini was inside an office—clearly the Headmaster's Study. The distinctive pictures on the walls, oak door, and grandfather clock were unmistakable. After looking at the photograph, Adam sat back in the hard chair.

"We know there were other boys involved in this Cranford, but we are not sure how you got the car into the room. The doorway is too small for the car. You boys must have dismantled the car and rebuilt it in the room. Is this accurate?"

"No, Mr. Stilson. It is just someone playing a joke—using graphics software to make a fake photograph with my face in the picture. It's just been photoshopped, sir."

"Cranford, did you notice the time on the clock in the picture? The date marked on the calendar? At that time of night last Friday, I had reported to the police that the car had been stolen from outside my home. Look below the chair you are sitting on, and you will see a black motor oil stain on the floor. My car leaks oil. The licence disk in the picture is the same expiry as my car licence disk. When you people returned the car to my home, you unfortunately parked it facing the wrong way around. We found this photo pinned to the front doors of the school this morning. You may think it is highly amusing, Cranford, but we do not. We want to know who is involved and how you got the car into the room. We know the older boys must have been the ringleaders. We want to know how you avoided triggering the building alarm system. Pay attention and look at me when I'm speaking to you, boy."

Adam had been staring at the frame of the large window behind the Headmaster, hoping the temporary fix they had made last Friday night would be strong enough to hold the window in place if there was a storm. He guessed it was Hudson that had spread copies of the photographs around the school—a revenge for what he'd done to Hudson last year. Hudson was the photographer, after all, but they planned to release the photo's at the end of summer term. Mr. Stilson was a bad tempered school principal hated by most of the pupils, but he was very proud and protective of his vintage Mini car.

"Err... sorry, Mr. Stilson, but it was just a joke. We didn't do any damage to it, sir. I can't grass up my mates, sir."

"Adam, be sensible about this. You don't need to protect these other boys. They must have tricked you into sitting in the car. I've spoken with the Head, and he says you will only be suspended to a couple of weeks if you identify the ringleaders," his father urged from the side of the desk.

"It's not that simple, Mr. Cranford. There is the matter of 'taking without the owner's consent' and also the cost of a safety inspection of my car in a garage. There is no telling what damage they caused when they reassembled my Mini. They may have caused hundreds of pounds of damage to my car. I know you said you will pay for that, but it is the leaders of this crime who should pay."

Adam sat with a sick feeling in his stomach. He knew there had been no damage to the Mini because it had not been dismantled. A group of four seniors had slipped the insecure door lock of the Mini and silently wheeled it to a nearby trailer. At the school, they had assembled scaffolding and removed the whole window of the Headmaster's ground-floor office before the car's arrival. They had then pushed the car up and down scaffolding ramps with the help of some ropes and pulleys through the window void. The most difficult bit had been remembering to put everything back in exactly the right place after replacing the Headmaster's desk after removing the car.

He was well aware of who the ringleader was, considering it was himself. They had carefully rehearsed it all before at a farm that was the home of one of the seniors. There had been a few months of measuring and planning. He knew he should have supervised the return of the car. Even though there were eight other boys involved, there was no way he could betray them. He had to take the punishment himself, as nothing was to be gained by identifying his accomplices. He was a bit worried that the replaced window frame did look a bit shaky still.

"I'm sorry, Mr. Stilson, but I cannot tell you the names of the others. I was here on Friday night, and we didn't damage your car, but that is all I'm prepared to say."

"You refuse to tell me, boy? In that case, I will give you two days to reconsider your actions and refusal. If I do not hear from you with a full list of names, you will be permanently expelled from this school. As of this moment, you are on suspension. Mr. Cranford, the school secretary will write to you confirming this decision concerning your son and provide details of the appeal process. She will also provide you with contacts to arrange your son's continued education at another place if need be. Cranford Junior, I believe Detective Inspector Norris wants to talk with you down at the Police Station. This meeting is now over. Mr. Reece, if I might have a word with you before you leave?"

Adam stood and left the room followed by his father and the policeman. He could not help but notice that someone had pinned another copy of the photograph on the outside of the Headmaster's door. It was obvious the rest of the school knew about the joke-gone-bad.

"Mr. Cranford, I don't need speak with your son at the Station right now. If you could phone later and make an appointment, that would be much more convenient. On the basis of what I've seen so far, I don't think this is a matter that should trouble the police too much or lead to further action. There doesn't seem to have been any real damage, and you have offered to make good any damage that may have occurred. I just need to have a brief word alone with Adam before we leave."

Adam's father gave a sigh of relief and a gesture of acceptance as he walked away down the corridor, leaving the policeman with his son.

"This conversation is strictly off the record, Adam. If you mention it to anyone, I will deny it ever happened. Understood?"

"Yes, sir."

"Young man, it looks like you almost got away with that little prank of yours except for someone setting you up with the photographs spread around the school. Don't worry. We at the Police Station know all about Stilson and how the lads here hate him. Two of my sons went to this school, so we know how strict he can be with you all. It is very brave of you not to grass up on the ringleaders, but are you sure it is worth getting thrown out of school just to protect them? You should know we have CCTV footage of who was driving the Land Rover with the trailer that night. We can also guess where you guys liberated the scaffolding from a certain building site. Strictly speaking, what you did was breaking and entering which is a crime, but we are not going to follow up unless Stilson insists. I've seen the marks in the grass outside the window, so I have a pretty good idea of what you lads did. You need to think carefully about whether you need to protect those boys at the cost to you of expulsion from school."

"I was the ringleader. I planned the whole thing. The other guys just helped out. If I tell Stilson who it was, we will all get punished anyway, and that wouldn't be fair, seeing how it was my idea."

Norris stood back, looked at Adam, and grinned. "Just how old are you again? Thirteen, isn't it? Planned just by you?"

Adam nodded. "Yes, sir."

"Right. Well, you best go home with your father. I guess he is going have a lot to say to you about this."

He rested his hand on Adam's shoulder and led him out of the school, walking along with the boy's father. Adam looked back up at the school windows. Most were filled with boys' and girls' faces watching him leave. The grapevine worked fast in his school; it had to be efficient to beat the rigid discipline. He knew that while he may be a hero to them, he would not be coming back to the hated school. Regardless of what his parents might have to say to him back at home, he would not be changing his mind about that. While he had some good friends there that he didn't want to lose, there was no way he would go back.

Their trusty family car was parked in the visitors' car park. It was an old Ford estate car almost as old as Adam and had been in the family since his father had bought it brand new from the car showroom. Adam sought refuge in the back seat, carelessly dropping his school bag on the seat next to him.

Gordon Cranford was deep in thought as he drove his son home that afternoon. He knew it would be impossible to get his son to change his mind. His stubbornness was legendary in the family, even from when he was a baby. His son had not been happy at the school, but he still could not believe his son would get involved in prank of such proportions. It had not been the school they had chosen for him when the time had come to make a school selection; his place had been allocated by the local authority. They couldn't afford to send him to the really good private school nearby, so he knew Adam might have to go to Davison High, a large comprehensive school in the next town. That would mean a lot more travel for the boy. He wondered if there was some way they could get their son to back down and apologise to the Headmaster. The Headmaster had a reputation for strictness, so there was no way he would change his mind otherwise.

After twenty-five minutes of driving, they reached their home in Chalfont. It was a small country cottage that Gordon had inherited from his father. There was no way they would have been able to afford a house like that in such an area on the money from his current job as the manager of a local Garden Centre. It was a good area to bring up a family, as there was countryside nearby and a lot of social activities. He parked the car in the rose bush lined driveway, and they jumped out.

"Ok, Adam, you'd had best let me speak to your mother first, and then I have to get back to work in the Garden Centre. We'll all talk about this in the evening and decide what we can do with you. I'm quite angry with you now and need to cool down first."

"I'm really sorry about this, Dad. It shouldn't have gone wrong like this. We planned it real carefully so there would be no damage. It was just meant to get some stuff ready for the end of term."

"I know, Adam, that you probably meant no harm, but it hasn't turned out that way, has it? Now we've got a real problem on our hands. Go get changed out of your school things. Like I said, we'll talk about it tonight. Don't worry too much. I'm sure we'll find a way around this."

As they entered the house, Adam's mother Amanda was awaiting them, having been phoned by her husband before they arrived.

"Hi darling. We need to talk about our son a bit, and then I have to get back to work."

Gordon guided his young son up the stairs while he directed his wife into the kitchen. He would deal with the first questions and try to calm things down. There was no doubt there would be some tough questions and raised voices around the kitchen table tonight.

Adam slowly stomped up the dark stairs to his bedroom and dropped his bag on the floor. He tugged off his tie and school jacket and then slumped on top of his soft, comfortable bed. He lay back, closed his eyes, and sighed. He was almost in tears.

This must be the worst day of my life. How could it have gone so wrong? he thought to himself. He reached over to his bedside table and grabbed his mobile phone. They weren't supposed to take them to school because of the risk of mugging. Looking at the screen, he could see he'd missed a lot of calls and messages. He scrolled though the texts. There were a mixture of messages from his mates, some calling him an absolute nutter and others calling him a hero, saying it was so unfair he'd been expelled. It seemed like everyone had heard about it already. There was even a text from Hudson saying he was sorry to hear about what had happened. Adam typed a brief response to that one, asking Hudson if he'd had any luck in finding a father yet.

The voicemails were similar in nature, though one was from his best friend at the school and also the main co-conspirator on the Mini car photo incident. Bill had arranged the temporary liberation of the scaffolding necessary to hoist the Headmaster's Mini into his study.

"Adz, mate, I was really sorry to hear they got you. It's so cool you didn't grass on us. I will understand if you have to do that. Call me back, please?"

Adam clicked off the phone, making a note to call Bill back later in the afternoon when his friend was away from school. There was not much he could do at the moment, so he sat at his desk and cranked up his faithful PC and signed onto his favourite Internet multiplayer game. His normal crew wouldn't be on now, but he knew some of the players from US west coast who would be. He turned up the sound on his speakers and lost himself in the game as he battled against the other players. At this time of day, no one would be complaining about the noise. He played for a couple of hours, but his mind was really not in the game. He lost a couple of hard earned useful weapons and some armour. It was a relief really when his mobile phone rang, interrupting his game.

"Hi. This is Adam."

"Adz, you nutter, how did you manage to get caught then?" asked Bill, his best mate at school.

"It was Hudson, I think. He set me up with those photographs. Old Stilson didn't have a clue how we did it. The police worked out what we did, but they seem pretty cool. I don't think they like Stilson either. I'll be expelled from school unless I tell them by Wednesday who was involved."

"Expelled? Whoa! That's harsh. I guess you will have to tell them. We were all in it together and you can't take all the blame."

"I'm not sure what to do at the moment. If I tell, all of us get punished. I think it is best that I take the heat on this one. I hate the school really."

"Adz, that is plain crazy. You can't screw up the rest of your life over a stupid end-of-term prank, even if it was the best one ever. I'm going to talk to the others, and we'll all go talk to Stilson. We might even tell them where we buried Hudson."

"Bill, don't do that. Stilson has never liked me. I'm not really sure it was Hudson who gave me away anyway. Look... I'm going to take the heat on this. It's not the end of the world. Something will come up. I guess I can't hang out tonight 'cos I have to 'discuss the issues' tonight, but how about we go down to the Village Square tomorrow night at seven? You can tell the others what is happening."

"Adz, you are an absolute nutter. If you change your mind, just let me know. I've got no problem with taking my share of the blame on this. I have to go. Speak to you later, ok? Don't let this get you down."

After lunch, Adam spent the rest of the afternoon hanging around the house. He read books but could not settle into the stories. He tried watching television but found it really boring. His mother was around but was clearly trying to avoid much conversation about the events at school. She had promised Gordon those discussions would wait until the evening when everyone was available and had had a chance to cool down. The tense atmosphere was relaxed briefly when Gilly, Adam's younger sister, returned home from school.

"Hi, Addie. What are you doing home so early? You throwing a sickie or something?"

Adam wasn't quite sure what to say. Her mother swiftly hustled her into the kitchen where Adam could hear his mother explaining the events of the day to Gilly. Clearly, she had been told not to discuss it, but curiosity seeped out of her wide grey eyes when she came back to the lounge after changing out of her school uniform. However, before she could ask any questions, they heard their mother's voice floating through from the kitchen.

"Young lady, you have homework to do. Get your tail upstairs and get the work done... and keep your TV turned off."

She twirled a strand of her blond hair, pulled a face at her older brother, and smiled as she flounced out of the room, frustrated that she had not been able to get the full gossip.

Adam was bored. The waiting around for the big discussion in the evening was killing him. He grabbed a football and set off to find some school friends, but before he reached the front gate, his heard his mother call to him, "Just where do you think you are going, young man? You are grounded until we get this school thing sorted out. Now go upstairs and study or something. Heaven knows you will have to be working hard at school in the future."

"Aw, Mom!" was the automatic response from the boy, but he knew from the tone of her voice that she would not be taking any argument from him. He stormed up the stairs and slammed his bedroom door.

The evening meal was a quiet affair with the four of them gathered around the dining table. Though it was completely against her nature, Gilly had managed not to ask any questions about the possible expulsion but was clearly eager to find out the full detail. The meal seemed to last forever. The clock on the sideboard cupboard dragged its hands with deliberate slowness.

Finally, Gordon Cranford announced, "Gilly, clear the table and go get the dish-washing done in the kitchen. Your mother and I need to have a serious discussion with your brother."

Unusually, the girl did not protest and efficiently collected the dirty plates and cutlery. As she went into the kitchen, she made sure doors were left open so she could hear every detail of the conversation.

"Adam, you have had some time to think over what happened in school today. You have been expelled. You might even have to go to court if the police take action, and I might have to spend a great deal of money that I don't have to fix Stilson's car. I won't even ask what possessed you to get involved in such a prank, but we do need to know if you are going to do the sensible thing and apologise to Stilson?"

"Dad, there's no point. I hate the school, and I hate Stilson. He's never going to forget this. If I name the other boys, it just means we all get punished."

"Adam, you should listen to your father. You know how difficult it is to get into school around here. If you don't do what the Headmaster says, you are going to end up at Davison High. That's about an hour's journey each way, and it has a worse reputation than your current school."

Adam's eyes appeared to darken from a pale grey to a slate grey, and his expression hardened. "My 'ex-school', Mom. I'm not going back."

Both parents immediately recognised the stubborn expression of their son. They knew from long battles in the past that it would prove impossible to force their son to change his mind.

At that point, the house phone rang. "Gilly, can you stop listening and get that call please?" queried her mother.

They sat in silence for a moment, each pondering what should be the next move.

"Dad, the call's for you. Some guy called Mr. Robertson."

"Robertson? I've never heard of him, but I suppose I'd best talk to him. I'll be right back." He left the room to pick up the phone in the hallway.

"Adam Cranford," hissed his mother, "there is no point in getting stubborn on this foolishness. You are going to apologise and name the other people involved. I refuse to let you destroy your future in school—not to mention the cost of getting you a new uniform and fixing the Headmaster's car."

"Mum, there is no damage to the car. It won't cost anything. We wheeled it into the office without taking it apart. The uniform won't cost any extra. It is almost the end of school year, and I've just about grown out of all of my stuff anyway. I'm not going back, and that is final. Stilson is over reacting because he hates me, and the feeling's mutual."

Adam knew better than to turn his back on his mother, so instead, he sat in his dining chair, arms crossed, glaring defiantly at her. He knew this was going to be tough because, like him, she would never give in. She would chip away at him for weeks if necessary until she got her way. There wouldn't be any harsh punishment—just constant pressure and questions. This time, however, he was not going to give way. Gilly crept into the room and hugged her mother, trying to provide a break in the tension. She recognised the battle of wills that was starting.

"Adam, you know there is no point arguing on this apology. It is going to happen, and you are going back to the school. It is outrageous that you should be taking the blame for the other boys. What you did was wrong, and you know it. You should be punished for that, but you should not take the whole blame."

"No, Mum."

A tense silence reigned in the room, though they could hear Adam's father on the phone in the hallway.

"Adam, don't go silent on me. Tell me who was involved. Why did you leave the house late at night without telling us? I'll bet that Bill Hetherington was involved in this. You two are always getting into crazy things together. I'm going to go see his mother and get to the bottom of this."

"No, Mum."

"Don't you 'no, Mum' me! Your soft-hearted father might give in on this, but I will not. You are not going to ruin your life because of your stupid stubbornness."

"No, Mum. I'm not being stupid."

"Gilly, go to your room, please, and leave us alone. I need to have a serious chat with Adam."

The young girl left the room. She rarely saw her mother get this angry. She also knew Adam would never break. He was just as stubborn as their mother, so it would become a battle of wills between two masters.

"You can forget about going to another school. I am not going to make any arrangements for you to go to Davison High. You are going to apologise and get your place back. You can recover from this situation, and we will help you, Adam."

"No, Mum. If necessary, I'll call Davison High myself."

"You can't do that. They won't speak to you."

"Yes they will, Mom."

"Adam, you may be almost fourteen years old, but there are times when you have to do what your parents tell you to do. This is for your own good."

"No, Mom, I'm not giving in on this. I know it, and you know it."

Just then, they heard his father put down the phone. The tense silence was broken as his father emerged into the room with a puzzled look on his face. "It looks like we should postpone this discussion until tomorrow evening. Apparently, this Mr. Robertson works for an organisation that helps schoolboys who get into trouble. Somehow, they heard about what happened at your school, and they want to come and speak with us tomorrow evening at seven p.m. He said not to make any decisions just yet because he may be able to help out. I think he's from some type of law firm, but he wouldn't say what it was. As we are obviously not going to reach an agreement tonight, I suppose it won't hurt to wait another day, but we are going to have to talk to Mr. Stilson on Wednesday."

He glanced to his son. "Adam, I think you should go to your room now. Don't forget to put your clothes away tidily and have a shower." He gave his son a hug and led him to the door of the kitchen. Gordon smiled at Gilly, who was sat on the stairs trying to catch the details of the conversation. The two children walked up the stairs.

Gilly followed into Adam's room. "Don't think you are getting away that easily, Addie. Come on and tell me all the gory details."

"I told you not to call me 'Addie'..."

The door closed, and the rest of the conversation could not be heard.

Chapter 2   The Other Side of the World

It was just coming up to the end of a long night shift in the dimly lit laboratory. With just the one worker present, things were relatively quiet. The peace was only slightly disturbed by the rustle of her heavy protective suit and the wheezing sound from the exhaust air vent valve in her plastic full-head helmet.

Hea Gwon was tired, and the work was boring, but she knew she had to be meticulous. She was annoyed her country could not afford proper monitoring equipment and that this monitoring work had to be undertaken manually. Even the university laboratory where she had trained in Scotland had better equipment than here. The sanctions against her country had prevented them from importing what was needed. It was far too easy for foreign security services to track such devices, and then they would quickly guess what was being developed at this secret establishment hidden deep in the mountains of her country. Much effort had gone into the improvising equipment that could safely meet the needs of the project.

Despite the underlying complexity of the dangerous project, the monitoring work was simple to perform. It was not dangerous as long as all the temperatures and pressures were correctly maintained. Her suit would provide protection if there was a sudden leak. In several locations around the room were cages containing rats. If they started sneezing or stopped moving around, she would know there was a problem with a leak in the room. They could have used electronic biosensors, but those were expensive and difficult to source. The rats were cheap, effective, and self-replicating.

Hea moved from flask to flask in the long rows in the laboratory. She had to check temperature and pressure and ensure there were no leaks and that the agitators were working properly at the base of the flask. In the dim light of the laboratory, she had to use a head torch to make the readings. It was the type of task any unskilled person could perform, and it was rather boring to someone of PhD qualification, but she knew the whole thing had to be kept strictly secret. There was going to be a progress inspection by Headquarters inspectors later in the day. Everything would have to be spot on, or next week they could all be employed sweeping the streets of their capital city. Her superiors rewarded success generously but awarded harsh punishment for failure. Her boss, Mr. Gu, was already concerned about the poor yield from the existing installation.

The lights flickered on in the office next to the laboratory. She looked up and saw that Mr. Gu had arrived early. He came to the viewing window of the laboratory and signalled 'call me' by placing his hand against the side of his head.

She nodded and moved to the intercom set against the wall. "Ah, honourable Mr. Gu, how can I be of service to you?"

"I have come to tell you, Assistant Gwon, that we have decided to move the laboratory. We have found a location where there will be better results, and it will be safer for our nation. It will be your task to plan this move and set up the new laboratory. Come out from the containment laboratory now so we can discuss this in detail."

"At once, Mr. Gu, but what about the monitoring of the project?"

"It has been declared a success and will be dismantled. Other people will arrive to undertake that work. You must hurry now, for they have given us a very urgent project date. We have little time to waste. I am afraid it will be some time before you can meet with your family again. We will tell them you are safe and doing very important work."

Hea disconnected her air supply tube, turned on her portable air unit, and moved to the airlock exit of the laboratory. Passing through the airlock, she stepped under a power shower, which washed her protective suit with strong disinfectant. Once dressed in her outside clothes, she went to a bare office where her boss was waiting.

"Assistant Gwon, you must prepare yourself for a long journey. You are going back to Scotland to continue this research. You do not need to pack any clothes. They will be provided to you on the journey. You will leave now."

Hea Gwon remembered the country with some affection. After a tough selection programme, she had at the age of twelve been trained in the English language by her mother country. Disguised as a refugee from the Vietnam War, she had been smuggled into Britain and had finished her education as a doctor in Scotland.

They left the building, passing through three separate solid steel security doors along the route. Outside the laboratory building with Mr. Gu, she stepped into a waiting car. The car drove them to the conference centre located outside the double layered security wire fences of the laboratory compound. To exit the compound, the car had to pass through two security gates, thirty metres apart. Each gate was manned by armed guards, who, at each gateway, carefully checked the identity papers for each person in the car. Looking back against the early morning sun, Hea Gwon saw for the last time the large mound of earth that disguised the laboratory building from American spy satellites.

Chapter 3   The Foundation Calls

A loud knock at the front door jolted Adam from his daydream. Looking out from his bedroom window, he could see that a postman was waiting. He realised his mother must be out of the house that morning. After a restless night, he had slept through his alarm. Throwing on a dressing gown, he rattled down the stairs to get to the door before the postman left. He could see the man turning away through the glass panel of the front door. "Hang on! I'm coming!" he yelled.

The postman turned back as the boy swung open the door.

"I've got a special delivery letter for Mr. and Mrs. Cranford. Someone needs to sign for it."

"I'm their son. Is that ok?"

"I guess that will be ok if they are not in. Sign here and print your name here." The postman pushed forward a clipboard and a pen. As Adam signed the receipt, the man dug a letter out from his bag. Removing a bar code label from the letter, he stuck it onto the receipt and handed the thick brown envelope to Adam.

Adam stood with the door ajar, turning the letter over and over. He heard the man jump into his post van to drive off with the clatter of a diesel engine. He recognised the postmark on the letter as having been sent from his school. He closed the front door with a soft *click* and wandered into the kitchen, then dropped the envelope on the kitchen table. It all suddenly seemed so real now: he had been expelled. The ordeal the day before was a bit like a dream. Everything had happened so fast, and in some way, it seemed like if he just woke up, everything would be back to normal. The letter jolted everything back to reality.

He dropped vacantly onto a kitchen chair alone in the house. *What am I going to do now?* It was a relief not to have to rush to catch the school bus, but he knew it couldn't last. He just didn't know what to do next. Everyone was at school or work. For Adam, it was as if the world had rushed by, leaving him in some kind of isolated time bubble. After some time, he realised there was already another letter on the kitchen table. It was addressed to him in his mother's handwriting. He opened the letter.

> *Dear Adam,*
>
> *You will not be feeling good this morning. Don't worry, darling, for we will look after you. I'm sure we can sort out this whole problem before too long. I've left you lunch in the fridge. Please wash up the breakfast things and put them away after you have eaten.*
>
> *I'll be back from work at two o'clock this afternoon. If you need to contact me, call me on the usual number.*
>
> *Lots of love,*

Mum

P.S. If you get bored, please clean out all the junk in the garden shed.

He absentmindedly poured himself a bowl of cereal and added milk. Sitting quietly, he wondered what he could do for the rest of the day. He thought about practicing the guitar. He and his school friends were trying to form a band, but he just didn't seem to be mastering the guitar. After further deliberation, though, Adam supposed there would not be much point in continuing with that because he was bound to lose touch with his schoolmates. It seemed everything had gone so wrong so suddenly. It was so unfair to pay such a high price for such a stupid joke.

Perhaps, he thought, *I should give in and give a list of names to Stilson.* He knew it would make his parents happy and solve all the problems.

After finishing breakfast, he stood and noticed his bare feet felt cold on the stone floor of the cottage kitchen. Looking down, he realised his dressing gown was open and not tied. He blushed, knowing the postman must have seen him in his boxers. That thought spurred him into action. He had been walking around in a daydream, and his mother would say, 'Dreaming doesn't get the garden dug.'

He left the kitchen, showered, and got properly dressed. He had decided to go fishing for the rest of the day. He knew standing on the bank of the stream for the day in the sunny weather would help him think things through much better than moping around in the house alone. He had some maggots in a bait box in the fridge, much to his sister's disgust, so he thought he might stand a chance of catching one of those large, timid Roach fish in the nearby stream. He left a note for his parents on the kitchen table, grabbed a bottle of water and his tackle from the untidy garden shed, then set off for the stream.

For some reason, the fish were being cautious. He had a few nibbles and a couple of bobs of the fishing float, but he caught nothing large. He did catch a few tiny inexperienced fish but he released those straightaway. By three o'clock in the afternoon, he was beginning to feel hungry and thought it was time to go home. He was feeling much calmer now and was ready to face the arguments with his parents over his refusal to name the other boys involved in the prank. He had thought about giving in but soon realised there was no way could he face his friends if he got them into trouble just to save his own skin. After all, the whole thing was his idea, and he had done most of the planning. The despair of the morning had now gone, and he had decided to face his new path in life without worry.

He arrived home to find the back door open and his mother in the kitchen.

"So, how are you feeling now? I notice you didn't have time to tidy the breakfast things from the table. Did you catch anything?"

"Sorry, Mum. I wasn't awake properly this morning when I left. Did you see the letter from school?"

"Yes, I did. It was no real change from what we already know. They did say there are some unfilled places at Davison High. I really don't want you going there. There is so much more travel, and their results are not so good."

"Mom, I'm not changing my mind on this."

"We'll see what your father has to say tonight. Meanwhile, go get your lunch from the fridge and then tidy that garden shed. I need to clean the house if we are having a stranger visit us this evening."

Adam had forgotten about the guy who had phoned the night before. He grinned at the thought of his mother having to clean the house because she always kept it spotless. He grabbed his lunch from the fridge and sat to eat it. Mindful of his mother in the house, he even washed the plate afterwards.

Knowing that cleaning the shed would put him in his mother's good book, he went to the garden and got stuck into the tedious task. He built a pile of junk to be taken to the local tip and carefully organised all the tools in a logical order. He knew his parents would not understand the logic of his organisation and would be continually asking him where he had hidden the tools, but that was just the price they had to pay for his assistance. By the time he finished reorganising the garden shed, both his sister and father had arrived home.

"Adam, go have a wash and put clean clothes on. You are filthy from doing the shed. I'm not having you running around the house in dirty clothes when there is a visitor."

"Err, ok, Mum. Dad, do you want to check out the shed first?"

"No. Thanks for tidying it, but you can show on at the weekend. We have more important things to discuss this evening. We'll see what this Mr. Robertson has to say first, and then we will talk about you apologising and staying at your current school. He will be arriving in thirty minutes, but I don't see what he can do to help solve the problem."

"Ok, Dad. I'll only be five minutes."

"Please remember to use soap and water and don't leave the dirt all over the towels. I've only just changed them all. Don't forget to put your dirty clothes in the basket."

Adam climbed the stairs. He knew this was going to a tough evening, but no way was he going to give in. As he walked past Gilly's bedroom at the back of the cottage, he noticed she was at the desk working on her homework. "Hi, Troll Face. How was school today?" Troll Face was the cruel family nickname given to his sister when she was a baby. She was really a rather pretty girl, but it was a term of endearment that had stuck nevertheless.

"It was ok, I guess. So, Mr. Hero, are you going back to school? Some of the girls in class asked about you. I think you have a fan club. I know Mom is going to give you a real tough time if you don't apologise to Stilson. My class teacher even asked me if I knew who was involved in the prank."

"That's not fair. What did you tell her?"

"I said you are a dork with the brain of a hamster and couldn't remember that far back."

"Thanks for that vote of support, sis!"

"At least it got her off my back. So... are you going to give in?"

"No way."

"Even if it means going to Davison High?"

"Nope."

"Ah, well, good luck with Mom tonight. I hope there won't be too much blood on the kitchen floor afterwards."

Adam turned and went to the bathroom to shower and then changed into clean clothes. It was seven p.m. by the time Adam had finished and dried his hair. He looked out the front window to see a black Range Rover arrive outside in the lane. It had dark tinted windows, so he couldn't see inside the car. Clearly, it was a sports version, and its engine rumble sounded like the V8 petrol engine. A tall grey-haired man got out of the rear passenger door speaking to the driver as he left the car. Adam assumed it was the mysterious Mr. Robertson. He was dressed in a charcoal grey business suit and sunglasses. The man carried a black leather briefcase.

Adam rattled down the stairs to meet the man, but by the time he reached the door, his father had gone out through the front door to greet the man on the garden path. After briefly discussing the pretty roses in the garden, they turned and headed to the house. His father noticed Adam standing at the doorway. "Ah, Mr. Robertson, let me introduce you to the cause of your visit... my son Adam."

The man stretched out his right hand to Adam. As they shook hands, the man spoke. "Adam, I'm Robertson. I've heard a lot about you. I thought it was the ideal time that we met."

He spoke with a deep, unhurried voice. Adam could not place the accent. Possibly it had a hint of a Yorkshire, but it was precise like that of a radio announcer. He was a bit puzzled that a total stranger had heard so much about him. The man had startling blue eyes—so startling, in fact, that the rest of his face seemed anonymous. People meeting Robertson for the first time would surely always remember his blue eyes.

"I'm, ah, pleased to meet you, Mr. Robertson."

Gordon Cranford guided the stranger into the sitting room. It was sparkling clean with fresh flowers on the side table. Amanda Cranford showed Mr. Robertson to an armchair. He turned down the offer of a cup of tea. Adam was perched on a hard wooden chair. They all sat, not sure who should break the awkward silence.

Finally, Robertson spoke first. "I'm sure you're wondering who I am and whom I represent. I will explain and try not to take too much of your time. You are going to have some important decisions to make tonight. Those decisions will potentially affect Adam for the rest of his life. We were going to wait a little longer before making contact, but the weekend's events have given us reason to act sooner."

As he spoke, he opened the leather briefcase and extracted a thick green cardboard document folder. Adam could see his name written on a label on the front of the folder. The man opened the folder and pulled out two printed brochures. Each contained about twenty colour printed pages. He passed them to Adam's parents.

"These will help answer the questions that will arise after I leave. They also contain contact details, so you can phone us to make further arrangements as the need arises. Firstly, you should know I am the representative of a charitable foundation. It is called the Foundation of Honour, but most just refer to it as 'The Foundation'. We like to keep a low profile, but we have been around for a few hundred years. One of our purposes is to recognise exceptional young men and assist them to achieve their maximum potential during their lives. Each year, we select ten such people from each county in the UK and provide assistance. We have a large research program and contact network that helps us identify such candidates. This programme is by invitation only and ensures the young man does not have any lack of resources to achieve his full potential. It will also mean attending training sessions at least once a week, but that will not interfere with schoolwork."

"Thanks, Mr. Robertson. I think I understood most of that, but what does it really mean to me?" interrupted Adam.

The man smiled. "Yes, Adam, I remember your file said you are not afraid to speak bluntly. To explain the immediate opportunity for you, what we are prepared to provide, subject to a couple of conditions, is full funding of your attendance at Holliston's Grammar School. We will also take such measures necessary to ensure that you are offered a place at that school."

"But why me? I've just been thrown out of my current school, though I guess you already know that. Holliston's won't want someone like me."

"Adam, like I said, we already know a lot about you. We know you are stubborn— a rebel. Regardless, we also think you have a lot of potential. We know the real reason why you were asked to leave the Scout troop, and we know about that charity event you helped organise. We also know how much preparation you put into organising those photographs of your Headmaster's car in his study. It is obvious you have good leadership potential and that you are willing to stand up for your team. With some training and guidance, we know we can channel your energy to do great things to the benefit of society."

"What do I have to do in return? It's going to cost you a lot of money, and it might be wasted."

"All we ask is that you work hard, attend the training, and be honest to yourself. We have been providing this support for many years for hundreds of young men. We rarely get it wrong. We rarely have failures. If you find you don't like it, all you have to do is walk away. There is no other commitment."

"So I can stop doing the training after three months and still go to Grammar School?"

The boy noticed the man's blue eyes harden a little in expression—not in annoyance, but more like an opponent in a chess match. "Of course you can Adam, but don't expect us to continue the funding."

"So how long does this so-called training take?"

"Oh, not too long... just a day each week and three weeks in summer camp. You will enjoy it."

Adam quickly calculated the impact on his lifestyle. "A day every week? Wow. That's harsh. What type of training? Who pays for this summer camp?"

"Adam, if you want to achieve you will have to work hard. The choice is up to you. This is not like school, and we will not treat you like a child. The training is both physical and educational. It will teach you how to reach your maximum potential. As far as summer camp, we pay all costs. All you have to provide is your body."

"You mentioned conditions, Mr. Robertson?"

The man smiled again. "Good. I'm glad you caught that, though it doesn't surprise me. Firstly, you must write a full apology to Mr. Stilson. Secondly, you must attend a meeting with the principal of Holliston's at two p.m. tomorrow afternoon and convince her you are prepared to work hard and be an asset to their school. Thirdly, if there are any costs arising from your Mini car stunt, you have to personally earn the money to pay those costs—not your father."

"I don't have to name the other boys in the Mini car event?"

"No, you don't. You know the entire event was really your responsibility, so I see no reason for them to get into trouble—not even those people who you might be thinking gave you away to Mr. Stilson. Sometimes things are different from what they seem."

"Deal! When do I start?"

Adam's parents sat with mouths agog that their son had taken over the negotiations with this stranger and had arranged himself a place at the prestigious local Grammar School. Amanda Cranford realised she should perhaps intervene and bring some control to the proceedings. "There are a couple things we need to clear up. This is all rather sudden. We should really take a little longer to consider the options. With all due respect, Mr. Robertson, we know nothing about you and your organisation. We need to find out more. There is also the ultimatum from Mr. Stilson, the Headmaster of Adam's current school. That expires tomorrow morning. There is no way I can get Adam a new uniform for the new school in time."

"Don't worry, Mrs. Cranford. If you let me have the documents the school sent you today, I'll pass them over to our lawyers tonight, and they will be on to the local education authority first thing in the morning. The school will have the ultimatum extended by a week or face an expensive court session. I just need you and Mr. Cranford to sign this lawyer appointment document. You will not be charged any fees. If you call the contact numbers in the brochures, I can arrange for a car to take you to our Headquarters in London. You can also meet other parents of young men whom we have helped. New school uniforms will not be a problem, for we are used to making those arrangements."

"Thank you very much, Mr. Robertson. I guess we had best read these brochures and contact you tomorrow. Adam, what do you say to Mr. Robertson?"

"Thanks, Mr. Robertson. I'm off upstairs to write the apology to Mr. Stilson. Do I have to deliver it in person?"

"Yes, Adam, I'm afraid so... but just wait one moment before you leave us." The tall man opened his briefcase and lifted out a box. It was a computer games program Adam had seen before but could not afford. The man offered it to the boy. "As a welcome to our organisation, we like to provide a gift. It has been personalised for you. You will find a user identity code and password inside the box."

"Kewl, Mr. Robertson! Thank you very much."

Adam dashed upstairs to his bedroom to write the apology letter to Mr. Stilson. He knew it had to be a real apology, and it had to be polite. During his short conversation with Mr. Robertson, he had the feeling that while the Foundation was generous, they expected him to behave responsibly. He sat at his PC and started his word processing software. He knew it was going to be hard to write an apology to a man he hated.

In the room below, the man was continuing to speak with Adam's parents. "I'm sure you find this offer rather sudden, but let me assure you it is genuine. We will need a firm decision by the end of the week if want to go ahead with this. Details are in the brochure, but what we will do is set up a trust fund for Adam to help him through school and university. You are not allowed to directly benefit from the funding yourselves, though as you come to learn more about the Foundation, you are welcome to provide support for its activities. One more thing... we have found over the years that we can work much more effectively if we work on the basis of some secrecy. So, we would be obliged if you mention no details of this offer to anyone else. Feel free to have the paperwork checked over by your solicitor, and please do take up our offer to visit our Headquarters in London. Here is my card. You can call me on this number any time of the day if you have any worries about Adam's training."

"Mr. Robertson, did you mention university?" queried Gordon Cranford.

"Yes, I did. If Adam chooses to go to university, we will fund his way through the years. We will help all of you choose the best course."

"But why do you do this? What does your Foundation gain from it?"

"I'm sorry, but that is a question we never answer. The reason will become obvious in good time. Now, I am afraid I must leave you and go to my next meeting."

Adam saw him leave the cottage and enter the Range Rover that had waited outside. As he opened the door of the vehicle, he turned and waved to Adam. Returning the wave, the boy heard his parents calling him from downstairs to come down and talk to them. He had wanted to try out the new game on his PC, but that would have to wait. Before he left his bedroom, he saved his written apology on his PC:

Dear Mr. Stilson,

I wish to sincerely tell you that I cannot apologise enough for having been caught in the picture of your Mini in your study. Let me say we took great care to cause no damage or inconvenience to you.

I regret to say I am unwilling to name the other people involved, so I will take full responsibility for the event. I have discussed the matter with my parents, and we have decided it is best that I no longer enjoy the opportunities of attending your school. We will make alternative arrangements for my education.

I hope this will see closure of the matter.

Yours sincerely,

Adam Cranford

Adam found his parents each reading through the brochures that Mr. Robertson had left behind.

"What do you think, Mom?"

"It all seems too good to be true, but the Foundation seems real enough. If it turns out to be true, it would solve a lot of problems. Do you think you can cope with all the work at Holliston's? It will be a different exam board, and they get a lot more homework."

"Yeah. If it means getting away from Stilson, I'd do five hour's homework every night. Does it say anything more about the training Mr. Robertson was talking about?"

"It looks like you have to go to meetings on Friday evenings and Sunday mornings every week. They say you also get support for fitness training in karate or whatever is available in the area."

"I don't know how they found out about me and the Mini car so quickly. Dad, did you see the size of that file he had about me? They must have been keeping records for ages."

"I'm not sure, Adam. I've never heard of them before. I guess we can do a search on the Internet. They have got a website listed in the brochure. He did ask us not to mention this to people outside of the family. How do you feel about it?"

"I love it, Dad. It couldn't have come at a better time, could it?"

"Right. Well, you had best get that apology written. Your mother can go along when you meet the principal of Holliston's. If it all goes wrong, you won't have lost much. All I can say is that you have been very lucky."

"Ok. I'll go print the letter. I've already thought of what to say."

Adam left the room, and Gilly intercepted him from her seat on the stairs. "Ok, bro. Tell me what is happening. I always get left out from the discussions. Gimme the goss?"

"I've got six months detention at a Youth Offender's Centre."

Gilly gave a gasp of horror at the harsh treatment of her brother and then, at the last moment, caught a hint of a grin on her brother's face. Adam was desperately trying to keep a straight face. She thumped him hard on his arm. For a petite girl, she sure packed a hard punch. "Oh, you beast! You deserve a whole year in prison. Come on... tell me the truth."

Rubbing his sore upper arm, he told her what had happened and how he would be going to Holliston's school.

"You are so lucky. You do it every time, don't you? You fall in the muck pile and come up smelling of roses. That means we won't be going to the same school anymore."

"Oh, I feel sorry for the school—you going there alone without a big brother to keep you under control."

She pulled her hand back, forming a fist and ready to strike again. This time, however, Adam was ready and dodged the blow to dash upstairs. In his room, he noticed there was a text on his mobile phone. It was from Bill. "W8td 4 u but no sho??"

Adam cursed as he suddenly realised he had forgotten he'd arranged to meet Bill on the Village Square at seven p.m. that evening. He punched the speed-dial code for his friend. It was answered quickly.

"Hey, Bill. Wassup?"

"Adz! A fine mate you are leaving me hanging around on the Square waiting for you all night. What happened?"

"I gave in to Mom and Dad. I have agreed to apologise to Stilson. Then I'm going down to the Police Station to do a deal for leniency with a full list of the names of the boys involved. You are all probably going to be arrested tomorrow morning for car theft and breaking and entering. I will get off with a warning by cooperating with their enquiries."

There was a silence at the other end of the phone call for a few seconds, and then, "You liar! Come on... tell me. What really happened?"

"Ok, so I am apologising by letter to Stilson, but I'm not coming back. I'm not giving away any of the names of who was involved."

"So where are you going to go to school? Surely not Davison High? You might as well come back here."

"What, and have to get all you guys in trouble just so I can come back?"

"But Davison High is miles away, and they have got gangs there."

"No, I'm going to wear the Five Buttons," responded Adam, referring to the unusual five solid brass buttons that distinguished the front of school blazers for pupils in Holliston's Grammar School.

"No way."

"Yes way. Someone Dad knows is helping fix it up." Adam remembered he was expected to keep arrangements of the deal confidential.

"But what about the entrance exams?"

"That is all sorted apparently. I just have to go for an interview with the Head tomorrow."

"That is so cool. Adz, I don't know how you do it, but you always seem to get a good result from total chaos. At least the rest of us can breathe easy now. I bet old Stilson will be stomping around the school for weeks when he learns he won't find who did it. He is going to go crazy when he hears you are going to Holliston's and have escaped him. You'll still stay friends with me even though you are going to the posh school, won't you?"

"You bet I will. After all, we do live in the same village. You want to come over tomorrow afternoon after school? You can tell me how Stilson is reacting. He will have probably heard by the end of the day."

"Yeah, that sounds good. Just remember to call me this time if you have been called away to Buckingham Palace to meet the Queen. I don't want to turn up at an empty house."

"I don't know if I can spare the Queen the time. I'm kinda busy. Ok. See you tomorrow. I can show you the new computer game I just got today. I can't wait to try it. No homework tonight, unlike you."

"Hah. Very funny. Speak to you later."

Bill ended the call, and Adam picked up the new computer game box and started to read the description printed on outside of the box.

Chapter 4   Adam on Parade

Chalky Benson looked over the parade of forty uniformed boys standing at ease in front of him. Their ages ranged from a junior eleven years to a senior eighteen years old. As this was just a routine training session, they were dressed in their dark blue No. 2 uniforms, but even so, they were still very smart. Boot toe-caps were bulled to a deep black shine. Their trousers with neatly pressed creases showed little evidence of the twenty-minute drill session that had just taken place, though their cotton shirts were damp from sweat.

Chalky had been a Foundation Company Master for a long time, more than twenty years. He knew the names of every boy and parent without having to check records. Each boy received a birthday card from Chalky while they were in the Company and for many years afterwards. Once again, he knew all those dates by heart. He had helped guide many boys through the Foundation's training scheme. Part of that training scheme involved training each nine-boy squad in precision marching skills. It helped them work together, to learn trust between themselves. Each boy quickly learned they had to contribute the maximum to their squad if they were to avoid receiving a harsh tongue lashing from Chalky or their Squad Leader. The Company Master knew each boy would moan about how they hated the boring marching drills. However, when regional parades were due, there would be fierce competition between the boys to ensure their own squad had perfect uniform and made no mistakes in their marching routines. Any boy who let down the other members of his squad would suffer for that mistake.

While the Foundation pushed the boys hard to achieve perfection in the formalities of parade uniforms and marching, they would not permit bullying. The boys were taught to help each other and to jointly accept the limitations of any one individual in their squad. There were situations where arrangements were made to enable physically disabled boys to take an effective part in their squad.

Those boys who could not accept the ethos and responsibility would find themselves standing in front of a Council of Honour. Those who did not accept the guidance from the Council of Honour would soon leave the ranks of the Foundation.

Chalky had noticed that young Adam Cranford had quickly joined into the squad team structure over the few weeks he had been attending. To Chalky's experienced eye, it was obvious Adam was a rebel. He was sure there would be clashes from Adam with the authority of the Foundation at some point in the future. The first battle in the first week had been persuading the boy to have his mop of brown cut to a tidy short length. The longer hair was out of place with the Foundation uniform.

Soon, it would be time to give Adam his detailed training schedule. The young boy would groan under the weight of the additional work imposed, but the pressure would strengthen rather than destroy him. This strengthening would be both physical and mental. Adam would be given situations to handle that he would think were impossible to handle, but he would find a way to be successful. Chalky and Adam's Squad Leader would ensure that support would be there at the critical times so Adam would not fail. At first, Adam had been uncomfortable with having a range of uniforms to wear and that they had to be well cared for while they were in his possession. While the Foundation had seemingly limitless funds, they did not waste money, so most of the uniforms Adam possessed had been handed down by previous cadets. At this stage of life, the cadets would outgrow the uniforms much more quickly than wear and tear would destroy them. Having to wear hand-me-downs had surprised Adam.

Adam soon learned from other squad members that Chalky was like a steel fist in a velvet glove, soft on the outside but actually rock hard on the inside. Chalky chuckled when he remembered the times when Adam's Squad Leader had intervened between Adam and the Company Master to prevent stubbornness escalating into a war. The reason for Adam leaving his old school had been kept secret. That meant it took at least a whole week for the legend of Adam and the Mini car to become embedded in the squad history and folklore. After the end of the third week, Adam's Squad Leader had complained to Chalky Benson that the boy was impossible to lead. Chalky had just smiled and told the young man it was just one of the joys of leadership.

Adam's level of physical fitness had been measured on the first night of attendance at the Company Hall. It had been no surprise he was of normal fitness for a boy his age. His slim 157-cm body was the average weight for a boy of his age and height.

Adam soon discovered, to his surprise, that his level of fitness was far exceeded by the other boys in the squad. A physiotherapist skilled in athletics helped to set new targets for Adam, together with a training plan for the six months. One of the other boys was assigned to act as a fitness buddy for Adam. He was also asked to select a martial arts discipline for training. Adam learned his fitness buddy attended aikido sessions not far from Holliston's, so he chose aikido. He did not want to learn an aggressive style of martial arts like karate, so aikido was an ideal choice.

Chalky Benson decided that perhaps today would be a good time to start the mental training process for Adam. Not all the boys undertook this training so early, but the Company Master had noted in his file that Adam was quite a good chess player. They assumed Adam would prove to be well equipped to handle the first stage. He first dismissed the parade and released them to their squad rooms but signalled to Brian Harrison, Adam's Squad Leader, to wait for a moment. "Sergeant Harrison, how are things going with Cadet Cranford?"

"He seems to be settling in quite well now, Master. I think he will turn out quite well as long as he learns how to be a good team member."

"Do you think it may be time to have him shown the card pack?"

The Squad Leader smiled, knowing this apparently easy task could actually be quite difficult. It would certainly present a challenge to his difficult new team member, and it might actually cut him down to size. "Yes, Master, I think he is ready."

"Ask him to meet Instructor Bradford and to take a pack of cards with him." The Sergeant saluted and headed to his squad room.

"Cranford, you know Instructor Bradford, don't you? Take a pack of playing cards and go see him. Tell him I sent you."

Adam made an unfamiliar salute to his Squad Leader, turned, and grabbed a pack of cards from the squad games box. He soon found Instructor Bradford. The man was a lay member of the Foundation, so he wore no uniform and was dressed in casual clothes. "Instructor Bradford," said Adam, "I've been asked to bring this pack of cards. Sergeant Harrison asked me to bring them."

"It's Adam, isn't it? Adam Cranford. I'm not a uniformed member, so please call me by my Christian name. I'm Bill, ok?"

"Yes, sir... err, I mean Bill."

"Take a seat in that chair on the other side of this desk. I don't know if anyone has told you yet, but the Foundation thinks it very important all its cadets have good memory and observational skills. I will be training you in some basic techniques. The first is called the card pack test."

Bill Bradford picked up the pack and shuffled it. Then, one card at, a time he showed Adam a card face and then placed the card face down on the desk. This continued until five cards lay face down on the desktop. "Adam, starting with the lowest value card, turn them over one by one until you reach the highest value. Red are worth more than black cards."

Adam gave a startled look because he had not expected this type of test. Pausing to think a little while, he turned the cards successfully.

Bill smiled, picked up the used cards, and reshuffled the pack. This time, he laid out ten cards. He signalled to Adam to repeat the test. Adam made his first mistake at about the fifth card.

"Adam, let's try it again next week. Each week, we will increase the number of cards by five. Within three months, you should be able to manage the whole pack. One tip is to try and form visual links—like a story between each card. This will help your brain get used to remembering long sequences of articles. Try to practice a little each day in the morning when you are not tired."

"Bill, that's impossible. Nobody except magicians can do that."

"Don't worry, Adam. All cadets do this eventually, though sometimes it takes them six months. I'm sure you will do well. By the way, here's one more test for you. How many red cars are there in the park by the front door of this Hall?"

"I didn't notice."

"If you ask any of your squad when you go back, they will be able to tell you. You will soon learn to develop better observation skills."

Adam picked up the cards and returned to his squad room. The other boys were practising map reading.

Brian Harrison looked up. "Three red ones."

Adam didn't know what the Squad Leader was talking about.

"Three red cars outside the Hall."

The other boys laughed. They had all gone through the same test and knew what Adam had just been through. "So, did you get all ten cards?"

"No. just five cards. On the first try though."

"That's not bad. Most people don't even get the five the first time. You'll get the hang of it, don't worry. If you get stuck or have problems, let me know and we will help you. How are you on map reading? Come and join in."

The training session was about how to recognise land features from what was shown on the map. Brian led the session with the aid of a training CD and video projector. Adam was amazed by the quality and quantity of training facilities in each squad room. They were much better than he had seen in school. There was even a library of training CDs that the boys could borrow and take home. When he was first shown around the place, the Squad Leader had made it clear that if Adam didn't have access to a PC at home, they would provide him with a laptop and Internet access.

After another twenty minutes. the squad joined the others for a refreshment break in the main hall. Adam sought out Barry Davies. He had befriended Adam from the first week. "That memory training they have given me is going to be really tough. Is it always going to be this hard?"

Barry laughed. "The card pack is not that hard when you get into it. Some of the stuff they do is really incredible. You can show Bill Bradford a map—something like the London Underground map—for just ten minutes, and he will memorise it. All 270 stations! You can ask him which is the quickest route between any stations and how many station stops there are along the route."

"No way. He's probably memorised it before."

"No. They have special printed versions of the maps where the station names and locations have been changed. Don't worry. As we say in the Foundation 'if you have been selected, you will deliver'. It always seems terrible at first, but you get used to it. Have they told you what your special skill training will be yet?"

"No. What's that?"

"Mine is marksmanship with rifles and handgun. I go to a range for two hours a week and then have two weeks of training in the summer. It can be anything really. One of the others is learning conjuring, and another is doing climbing. I guess they will tell you soon. It normally happens in the first few months. Hey, break time is over. We have to get changed into rough clothes for games."

The team games were, as in previous weeks, fast and furious. In cold weather, they would be run inside the main hall with any breakable furniture removed; today, however, the weather was warm, so the games were out in the playing field. The Foundation provided what they called No. 4 uniforms as rough clothes. When new, they were coarse, dark blue, heavy sail canvas trousers and shirt smocks, though with frequent washes and many repairs, they became tough, soft, blue-grey clothing. The games seemed to be a combination of rugby and unarmed combat designed to carry treasure in the shape of a small ball from end of the field to another. Anyone close to the ball would be tackled and brought down on the basis that they might protect or steal it. If the back of the boy holding the ball touched the ground, he had to release the ball. It was not unusual for the boys to go home with a bruise or two, but broken bones were unusual. As the teams were well matched in strength and speed, it usually required cunning and deceitful plans to gain winning points.

This week, Adam's squad did not win. They had won in the two previous weeks, but this week, the other squads conspired and overwhelmed his squad. The final whistle blew, and they dashed back to their squad rooms to change back into their street clothes before gathering in the final assembly. There were only five minutes allowed for this clothes changing. Except on special occasions, the boys rarely wore their uniforms in the outside world. Each week, two of the boys in each squad would be expected to come in to launder and, where necessary, repair the uniforms. Keeping the parade boots shiny was an individual responsibility for each of the boys.

Chalky and the Lieutenant Master read what was called the "Final Address" to the assembly. This usually offered some guidance on how the boys were expected to develop themselves or to take their responsibilities in society. There was normally a Final Address at each meeting. Chalky reminded the boys that Weekend Night Trek was due in a couple of weeks and that there would be a kit inspection on the Friday evening for those going on the Trek. He also reminded the Squad Leaders that their submissions for the Regional Congress were due by the end of the week. Other squad announcements would be handled by email and their Internet bulletin board system. With that completed, he dismissed the Company for the night.

The boys charged out of the Hall to climb into the mini buses that would take them back to their hometowns and villages. The Foundation preferred not to have parents waiting by the Hall except on special occasions or ceremonies. They found that having the boys travel back in the buses helped to improve independence and time keeping. Most of the boys were talking about the Trek and trying to guess what awful route Chalky Benson would be setting for them. The older boys had horror stories of earlier tough Treks.

Adam was comfortable in his bus seat, and the next thing he knew, the coach driver was shaking him awake. "Come on, lad. Wakey wakey. You are home now. Don't forget your bag." As the driver used his driving mirror to watch the boy walk along the lane to his home, he chuckled to himself. The new cadets always got very tired during the first couple of months of their Foundation training nights.

Chapter 5   Action at Sea

The black sea was cold and choppy in the shadow of the island. The deep water in the channel was still showing the effects of the recent storm. The confused wave pattern threw the thirteen-metre open decked workboat around in an uncomfortable dance. This motion would have made the inexperienced crew seasick had the Captain of the *Lively Archer* not insisted that they take travel sickness pills. They were hard, cruel men, but they were used to operating on the land rather than on the waters of this choppy channel. There was no choice in the matter, however, for the freighter was due to arrive now, and they could not afford to have nosy local fishermen seeing the transfer take place. It had to be done at night, and the cargo freighter could not be seen to change its route.

The overpowered diesel engine of their workboat easily overcame the currents in the main channel, but as it smashed into each wave, the shock caused the crew members to grasp tightly on the handrails. They were cold and wet. The so-called waterproof oil skins they wore did not provide much protection from the sea spray in the open deck of the workboat. The normally brave men were intimidated by the roar of the distant breaking waves just some 150 metres away in the dark. The sea channel had underwater rock ridge formation just below the surface, which caused an overfall of boiling water as the tidal waters raced along. If their engines failed, their small boat would be dragged into the chaos and torn apart. Their Captain have taken delight in telling his crew if their boat fell into that tidal trap, there would be no escape and no rescue.

The Captain was sheltered in the warmth of his small cabin as he checked his GPS navigation system. Fergus McCrinnon didn't really need such a device, as he knew these waters, but it was worth a double check to be sure they were in the right place. To him, the sea looked normal, considering the fury of the earlier storm. He did notice some green water hurling itself over the sides of his vessel, but the automatic bilge pumps would easily deal with any leakage without any problem.

The rain and spray reduced visibility somewhat, and he could see no other vessel in the darkness. He reached across the control panel and flicked a switch a few times. The small search light on the roof of his cabin flashed a beam of white light towards where he was expecting the other vessel to be found. They had agreed on radio silence for the night. A few seconds later, a white light blinked back from the darkness. They exchanged recognition signals by means of coded light flashes. It was the vessel he had been expecting. It was, according to Lloyds Register of Shipping, a sixty-five-metre coastal freighter, but its name had been changed twice during its long journey, so it would be difficult to track in the shipping database.

The crew of the other vessel hung a red light over the side of their vessel to indicate where the workboat should come alongside. Fergus matched his speed with the other vessel and carefully pulled alongside. The crew on the deck of the workboat hurled light throwing ropes to the crew of freighter. These were used to pull heavy mooring hawsers that loosely connected the two vessels. Fergus set the boat engine and steering to pull firmly against the hawsers, leaving a small gap between the vessels. The paired vessels moved slowly up the channel against the flow of the current. Satisfied that the connection was stable, Fergus signalled by flashlight to the bridge of the other vessel to commence the transfer.

The crane arm swung over from the freighter, delivering two heavy metal cylinders slung from a heavy wire strop. The cylinders were like a small oil drums approximately fifty cm in diameter and 150 cm long. They were painted a dark green that appeared almost black under the deck lights of the workboat. The crew on the deck of the workboat guided the cylinders safely to a pre-prepared cradle wooden cradle in the hold area of the workboat. Releasing the wire lifting strop on the cylinders, they signalled to the freighter crew to take the lifting strop back. This process was repeated until thirty of the cylinders had been transferred from the larger vessel. Ten bundles each containing three heavy steel anchors followed. Finally, two loads of coils of steel wire were transferred across in a large net. As soon as the final net was unhooked, the freighter crew signalled to Fergus that they should untie their vessel. He changed the direction of the steering of the workboat to reduce the tension on the mooring lines. There was a faint splash as the freighter crew untied and dropped their end of the lines into the water. Fearing his propeller might get fouled by the line, he came out of his cabin and shouted at his crew to quickly retrieve the mooring ropes from the water. With a rumble of power, the freighter increased its propeller revolutions and pulled away into the darkness. No further signals were exchanged between the boats.

Fergus checked that his new load was secure and then turned his boat to head back to the entrance of the loch. He saw his crew sitting on the load of cylinders, chatting quietly. They had been warmed by the exercise of the loading process, and the change of direction of the heavily laden vessel meant less spray coming over the bows. Fergus smiled to himself. *If they knew what those cylinders contain, they would not be sitting on top of them.*

After forty-five minutes of steady progress, the *Lively Archer* approached the entrance of the sea loch. While most of the loch was deep, its entrance to the sea was shallow and required careful navigation. The GPS system made that fairly easy, but Fergus preferred to rely on the temporary transit lights he had set up on the hillside earlier in the day. By carefully aligning the lights on the shore, he knew when and where he had to make turns to avoid the treacherous rocks in the entrance to the loch. Now that his boat was heavily laden, it lay deeper in the water, and its hull could easily touch a rock if it wandered off channel. The tough rocks would tear open the steel hull of his boat as if it were made of tissue paper. In some places, the deep channel was only twenty-five metres wide. A moment's lack of concentration on his part in the dark could lead to disaster. The handling of the boat was complicated by the tidal waters rushing into the loch from the sea behind them. There were small buoys marking the channel, but they were of little use during the dark of night. The deck crew were unaware of the risks faced by their vessel during those few critical minutes.

Soon, however, they were through the worst. Fergus slowed the engine of the *Lively Archer* to reduce the noise in the quiet loch. The vessel slowed to half its normal cruising speed. It was unlikely anyone was around on that dark, rainy night, but there was no point in taking any chances. This part of the country rarely had any coastal smuggling activity, so it was unusual for any Coast Guard officers to be on the lookout.

As Fergus approached the jetty, he pressed a remote control, and the lights came on all along it. This was hidden from sight to anyone who might be up in the mountains. He gently nudged the vessel into place against the jetty with careful steering and switching between forward and reverse gears. The desk crew jumped out and moored the vessel to the jetty. It was a floating jetty, so they did not have to worry about the effects of tide changing the height of the water. Before they left the boat, Fergus had them cover the load with tarpaulin sheets, which they carefully tied down securely with cord. It was not a load he wanted to appear on any spy satellite photograph.

He told his crew, "Go get some sleep. We'll have a busy day ahead of us tomorrow."

Chapter 6   New Boy at School

The food in the canteen was surprisingly good. Adam had been enrolled in Holliston's School for four weeks and was having lunch with his new friend, Simon Davidson, in the school canteen. Adam had been in the habit of not eating school food, as it had been so bad at the previous school. Now, that had all changed.

"Simon, are you not going to eat that banana?"

"No, Adam, I'm full. You eat it if you want. Did you get that chemistry homework done? We have to hand it in tomorrow."

"Just about finished it, but I still have to do some more reading. You guys are so far ahead of what I was doing at my old school. I hope Miss Richardson will take that into account when she marks the homework."

"No chance. She always marks tough. You still finding it hard here?"

"Not really, except where there are some gaps in my knowledge. When I had the entrance interview with Mrs. Embleton, she said I might have some troubles like that on some of the subjects, but I should let the teachers know."

Adam didn't tell Simon that in the interview with Mrs. Embleton, she made it clear she thought Adam would not cope with the work. She also made it plain that she was not happy taking on a boy at her school when that boy had been expelled from his previous school. Her exact words were. "I hope you live up to the expectations of your powerful friends."

Simon was the only real friend Adam had made in his new school. It was not that the other boys were unfriendly, but more that they already had their own circles of friends. Most of the boys came from wealthy families and had a very different type of life from what he had experienced. He did not feel he had a lot in common with most of the other boys. There wasn't really any actual bullying in the school, but the others in class just seemed to ignore him. The Foundation had arranged that he had all of the correct uniform and sports equipment on the day he started at the school, but it was obvious his outfit was brand new right at the end of the school year. It was just another factor that showed that he was not "one of them." Many of the boys took part in activities and holidays that cost large amounts of money Adam's family could never afford.

"Do you do any kind of music, Adam?" Simon asked to bring his new friend out from the daydream.

"I play the guitar, but not too well. We are trying to form a band, but I just can't get the chords right all the time. I guess I don't put enough time into it."

"I play the piano and guitar, but that is mostly classical stuff. Mum put me through loads of music lessons, ever since I was seven. I help in the school orchestra and the school play. The orchestra is practicing for a Gilbert and Sullivan opera on Friday evening if you want to come along. I help back stage with the makeup and lights."

One of Simon's strengths was his sensitivity and empathy with other people. He had noticed Adam was lonely and was trying to get him involved in more school activities, helping him to get to meet more people.

"I'd like to come, but I'm already tied up on Friday evenings. I go to a youth club most Fridays. Do you have practice any other nights?"

His Squad Leader had suggested "youth club" as the best way to describe his activity in the Foundation. He said not to mention about the uniforms and drill or people might think it was a military cadet force and ask to join. The Foundation was definitely invitation only, and while Adam could recommend people, it was unlikely they would be invited to join.

"No. Friday tends to be the easiest because of the homework on other nights. Do you do any other games or sports?"

"I started aikido a few weeks ago, and I've always been good at chess."

"You know, we have a good chess club in the school. They are always looking for new players. They have a section on the notice board in the main hall if you want to join them. Aikido is a martial art, isn't it?"

"Yes, though it is not as aggressive or competitive as karate. It's more defensive and attitude of mind."

"Did you get much bullying at your old school?"

"There was some, but if you stood up for yourself, you would be ok. The Headmaster there was really strict on bullies."

Adam wondered how Simon would have survived at his old school and came to the conclusion that his new friend would have been a victim.

"So, why did you leave your old school so suddenly then? It must have really messed up your exam syllabus."

Adam had been advised by Mrs. Embleton at the initial interview not to mention his expulsion from his old school. Adam knew, however, that it would only be a matter of time before someone connected with his old school said something to someone at this school.

"I got expelled for bad parking," he fibbed.

At that point, the school bell rang.

"Time to go, Adam. We've got religion next, and the class is right at the other end of school in the new annex. You just have got to tell me the real story about why you got expelled."

As they walked together, Adam told his new friend about how he'd arranged for the Headmaster's Mini to be parked in his office. He made no mention of the Foundation, but he did ask his new friend not to tell anyone about why he'd left the old school. He already knew Simon loved to gossip and would only tell a few people on the condition of secrecy within the next day or so. No doubt that by the time the story got around the school, the Mini car would have changed into a

Land Rover parked on the roof of his old school. Adam was careful not to mention any names of who had really been involved just in case the news found its way back to Stilson.

Adam sat with Simon during the religion class. The way it was taught was more interesting than at his previous school, so he managed to stay awake. While Holliston's School had a heritage based on the Church of England, the teacher was happy to debate the differences with other religions such as Hinduism and Islam. Previously, Adam would have left the class wanting to argue with the teacher for being so dogmatic. He was beginning to realise that their way of teaching, though much more intense and more hard work than his previous school, also taught them how to think about what was behind issues like politics and religion. At the end of the lesson, the two boys split up and went to different classes for the rest of the afternoon.

His last class had been physical education, and he left school a little bit after having had a longer shower than he should have done. He had about fifteen minutes before his school bus left the pickup point, but he wanted to quickly call into the local music shop. It was Gilly's birthday soon, and he wanted to get her a great CD. The shortcut to the shop was a pathway through a local park.

He could see Simon ahead talking to three bigger boys in the same school year. Something looked wrong about the way Simon was standing. Adam saw one of the boys try to pull Simon's bag away. He hurried to join the group of boys. "Hi, Simon. There you are. I thought you were waiting for me at the school gates before we went to the record shop?"

The largest boy, John Nelson, spoke in a sneering voice, "Oh, Simee, were you going shopping with your new boyfriend? We are so sorry to have kept him waiting."

Simon blushed and tried to push past Nelson. The larger boy pushed back, preventing him from getting away.

"That's very rude, Simee. What will your new boyfriend think?"

Adam suddenly realised Simon was being bullied because he might be gay. Adam knew that if he didn't do something to defuse this situation, Simon might get hurt. He was sure Holliston's would clamp down on this bullying, but it was happening outside the school grounds. He thought Simon would try and avoid confrontation rather than face up to the situation. Adam grabbed Simon and tried to step around the boys. They moved to prevent their prey from leaving.

Simon said quietly, "Adam, leave it. I'll just go the other way around."

Adam knew this was turning into a fight situation. He groaned inwardly, not wanting to have got into trouble so soon at the new school, but he hated bullies, and there was no way he could leave his new friend unprotected. He turned to face John Nelson. The boy was a good ten cms taller than Adam. He dropped his school bag to one side. "John, walk away now, and I'll forget this ever happened. I hate bullies, and if you want to get at Simon, you will have to come through me first."

"So, the new boy thinks he's tough, does he? Get out of my way, Cranford."

He shoved Adam's shoulder. Adam deflected the push and stood there. He knew he'd escalated the situation to a point where John Nelson would either strike out or walk away. Nelson's body signalled the next action. He swung a hard right fist at Adam's face. Adam didn't move out of the way. He let the punch connect but swayed with it to reduce the effect of the blow. Nelson swung a left fist. Adam had guessed it was coming but swayed out of the way.

Adam stood his ground, staring at Nelson. "John, I'm warning you to walk away now before you get hurt, but as an ape, you probably can't understand plain English."

Nelson charged at Adam with a roar of anger. At the last moment, Adam moved to one side and with an ankle throw flipped the larger boy to land hard on his back on the pathway. He chose not to soften the landing, as he wanted Nelson out of action while he dealt with the other two boys. The taller boy lay gasping on the ground. Still standing, Adam turned and faced the other two. "Who is going to be next, or are you going pick up your friend?" he huffed. "Don't worry... he will be able to breathe properly in a few seconds."

They moved around Adam, avoiding him. At that moment, a school prefect came along the path, his academic gown billowing in the breeze. Adam turned to help Nelson get up from the ground, taking care to stand his foot hard on the boy's hand out of sight of the prefect.

Adam hissed in his face, "Get up, you idiot. Next time you try anything like that with me, you will need to go visit a dentist for months after." With that, Adam hauled the speechless boy to his feet.

Nelson was beginning to breathe again. The prefect recognised most of the boys and realised some kind of fight had happened. John Nelson often caused trouble, but it was unusual for him to be the one on the ground. "Ok, what is going on here then? If it is fighting, I'll have you all up before the Head tomorrow morning."

Adam spoke, "It's no fight. Nelson here was showing us a new break dance move and he got it wrong. He landed on his back, the poor guy. I just helped him up."

"You're the new boy, aren't you? What's your name? I'm Greg Wallace. What happened to your face?"

"Oh, I'm Adam Cranford. I just bashed my face on the bars in PE."

"Is that what happened, Nelson? It looks like you had better practice those dance moves more carefully."

The boy just sullenly nodded his head and moved away with his two friends.

The prefect looked at Simon and then Adam. "If there is any bullying going on, let the prefects know. We will deal with it. I would hate for you to get into trouble just for giving dancing lessons and accidentally injuring someone."

"Ok, thanks Wallace. Like I said, nothing happened."

The prefect left and disappeared along the path.

Simon picked up Adam's bag and handed it to him. "Thanks, Adam. You didn't have to get involved in that. How did you move so fast? I thought you just started aikido."

"It's no problem, Simon. The big boys were a lot tougher at my last school. You had to stand up to them or suffer all the way through school. Are you going to be ok getting home? I ought to go catch my bus before it leaves."

"Yeah, I'll be fine, thanks to you." Simon smiled and left Adam.

Adam walked back to the bus stop and found a seat on his waiting bus a couple of minutes before it left. By the time he reached home, his left cheek was sore from where Nelson had hit him. He could feel a bit of a swelling just below his eye.

His mother had met him in the garden and of course immediately saw the swelling. "I see you have been getting to know the other boys at school. Please don't try and tell me you walked into a door. Come closer and let me check it out."

"It's nothing, Mom. You don't need to fuss."

"Let me be the judge of that. From the looks of it, I don't think you will get a black eye. Seeing how that is the only mark on you, I guess the other boy will be feeling very sore tonight. I presume he was bigger than you? You are not going to get in trouble again, are you?"

"No, Mom. It's over."

"Is everything ok at the school, Adam? They do seem to be working you hard. Have you got any new friends there yet?"

"Yeah, it's fine. I'm friends with a boy called Simon. He's in my class."

"You'd best get a bag of frozen peas from the freezer. Wrap it in a tea towel and hold it against the bruise for half an hour. That will help reduce the swelling. Just let me know if you get a headache or your vision gets blurred. Check your uniform for any damage."

Adam dealt with the bruise and sat watching television with the cold compress held to his cheek.

Gilly breezed into the room. She saw the cold compress. "Show me," she said imperiously.

He lifted the bag of peas away so she could see the bruise. He knew it was better than trying to argue with his sister; she always won.

"Hmmm... not too bad. You must be getting better at it. How many were there?"

"Three of them, but I only had to take out one. He walked away, but he will feel it in the morning. I took him down quite hard."

"So, what caused it this time? Did they break your pencil?"

"No. They were bullying one of the other boys, my new friend Simon. And what do you mean *this time*? I haven't been in a fight for ages." Then Adam realised that Gilly seemed to be exceptionally cheerful. "Ok, you look like the cat that got the cream. Come on and tell me what's going on."

"I've got a date this weekend."

"With who? Will he have to bring his guide dog along as well? The poor guy. Two whole hours with Gruesome Gilly."

"Oh, he's no one you would know."

Adam could see she was dying to tell him. "Come on! It's me, your favouritist brother. I won't tell Mum. Tell me."

"It's Bill. He asked me how you are doing at Holliston's, and we got to talking. To think I used to hate him one time. He's really dreamy."

"Not my best mate Bill. Ugh. No way. That is so gross. He is too old for you. Does Mum know?"

"No, she doesn't yet, and you swore you wouldn't tell her. He's only eighteen months older than me. Don't you dare say anything to Bill either." She stormed out of the room before Adam could say anymore. She was not really angry but did like to put on a good show. One of the pictures rattled on the wall as she slammed the door.

Adam decided he had used the cold compress for long enough and returned the peas to the freezer. He went upstairs to start on his homework. When he finished, he called Bill on his mobile phone. "Hi, Bill. What's happening?"

"Not a lot. Just started doing homework. How is school going for you?"

"Ah, so you won't have time to come over tonight then if you have just started homework. School's ok, but I got into a fight after."

"A fight again? Who got in your way this time then?"

"It was just self-defence. I was stopping them from bullying a smaller boy. I don't think he'll have any more trouble."

"Them? Did you get hurt?"

"No, just one bruise. I only had to deal with one of them, and they quit. Hey, if you can't come tonight, how about going fishing Saturday morning?"

"Yeah... err, I mean no. I'm kind of tied up on Saturday morning. How about tomorrow night?"

"Yeah, that's cool. You want me to come over about sixish?"

"Ah, well, erm, I think Mum has got visitors, Adam. Can I come over to you?"

"Sure. No problemo. I'll see you tomorrow. You can see my new game. It is wicked."

Adam ended the call on the mobile. He knew Bill would never turn down a chance to go fishing. *Right*, he thought. *That definitely confirms it. Gilly was serious. Wow!* He picked up the pack of cards from his bedside table and practised memorising them. So far, he'd gotten up to remembering seven correctly but didn't seem to progress from there. Soon his brain was numb, so he left the cards and turned to his computer.

First, he signed in to the Foundation home website and clicked on the portal link. The home site gave very little information. There were hints that it was a charity and that it had a long history, but not much more. As a contact point, it gave a telephone number that could be called for further information. Adam's father Gordon had tried calling the number, but the only response was a recording asking him to leave a message after the tone. No one had called back. Adam had been shown how to get through the portal by his Squad Leader on his first night at the Company Hall. Holding down one of the function keys on his keyboard, he clicked on the eye of the dragon shown on the Foundation crest of arms.

A challenge phrase flashed up on the screen: *What is the first duty of every cadet?*

It was from the Ten Laws used to guide the Foundation cadets. He had had to learn all of them within a week of joining the Foundation.

He typed the expected response: *Always be true to thyself.*

The webpage background changed to a dark purple colour, and then Adam was asked for a user identity code and also a password. He'd been told this would trigger special secret coding of his messages. While connected, his messages would be diverted by a secure route that prevented anyone—including the Intelligence Agencies—from listening in on the conversation. Brian Harrison had told him it was 2048-bit encryption, but that made no sense to Adam. He was just happy that it worked ok.

A Foundation webpage appeared on the screen with the message:

> *Welcome, Cadet Cranford. You last connected to the system at 18:35 yesterday. Please choose your desired option from the menu:*
>
> ** Contact Central Headquarters*
>
> ** Contact local Company*
>
> ** Email and announcements*
>
> ** IM Chat*
>
> ** Calendar and diary*
>
> ** Conferencing*
>
> ** Help and support*

He selected the email option and checked for messages. There were two. The first was from Brian, his Squad Leader. He opened the message. It was addressed to the Blue Squad:

> *Hi, everyone,*
>
> *I would like to hold a short web videoconference at six p.m. on Wednes-*

day with the whole squad. I want to tell you about the plans for the Night Trek on the weekend after next. It should only take twenty minutes. Please reply and let me know if you can make it. Use Conference Number SQD4367.

Sergeant Harrison

Adam replied saying he would be online for the videoconference. He clicked on the next message. He did not immediately recognise the sender, but as it was sent via the Foundation Network, he knew it would be safe. The message opened on the screen, and Adam read it:

Hi, Adam.

I hope you are now settling down well in your new squad in your local Company and also at your new school. Mrs. Embleton tells me she is receiving good reports about you from the teachers.

You should receive a parcel at home tomorrow. It will contain your first assignment. Don't worry... it is not a lot of more boring schoolwork. You should enjoy this.

With respect,

Hermes, Council of the Elders, UK Division

P.S. You will probably not recognise my Foundation name, but a few weeks ago, you saw my arrival outside of your cottage in a black Range Rover.

Oh, wow, thought Adam, *it's Mr Robertson. Hermes? What a weird name for him.*

Now that he'd checked the messages, Adam decided it was time to fire up the computer game and chill out for a while. He closed the connection to the Foundation computers.

Chapter 7   Entering Thorn World

The new game he'd received from Mr. Robertson was really hot. It was called *Thorn World,* and it was an Internet multiplayer game. Adam thought the central servers must be really powerful, as there was never any delay in its operation. Adam's chose "BaD Totem" as his gaming alias. Part of the game was interactive fighting against other players and program generated opponents or hazards. The other part involved the construction of roads, bridges, buildings, factories, or vehicles. Some players concentrated on taking part in construction and trading, while other players were soldiers or mercenaries. People became more powerful as they led greater numbers of people or owned more property and land. Secret alliances and access to information helped build powerful forces.

BaD Totem had joined a band of roving mercenaries called Visiting Havoc. He was already making himself a reputation for winning battles, finding ways of making friends and alliances with other powerful groups. Previously, Adam had swapped the combat prize of a manor house for a magic map artefact. He had won the manor house during a battle by defeating a player called Longbow. The magic map gave no special powers other than to be able to have an overhead view of the virtual landscape around him. He did not indulge in any fighting during that evening session, but he did manage to win a contract to supply power packs to the Iqar Tribe. It had taken many messages before he succeeded, but he was able to barter coal from the Iqar mines in exchange for power packs from the region of Gandarn. The deal would make a steady profit of Thorn Dollars for BaD Totem. He planned to use some of this profit to buy equipment for the other mercenaries in his group. He did not yet lead the group, but he had already told the mercenary leader of his plan for the equipment. The mercenary leader, Bright Petal, could not understand the motive of BaD Totem but agreed to the offer anyway. It was unusual to deal with someone who was both a trader and a fighter.

BaD Totem's player was dragged away from the virtual world by a knocking on his real-world bedroom door. "Bed time for you now, young man," said his mother. "You have been on that computer for too long. It has gone past nine thirty, and you have aikido practice early in the morning before school. Now come and let me check your bruise. I'll be downstairs."

Adam quickly sent a few messages to warn his online colleagues of his departure and signed off. He knew he was losing some profit, but his mum had to be obeyed or he might suddenly lose Internet connection by being virtually grounded. He thought perhaps he should have some people working for him to maintain the trade for the Iqar contract in the virtual world when he was not online.

§

The morning came too soon for Adam. Bright sunlight was streaming into his room at six a.m. when his mother drew back the curtains. "Come on, sleepy head.

Time to get moving. Go have a shower, and I'll have breakfast waiting downstairs."

The breakfast cereal tasted like cardboard to Adam, and he really didn't know how his mother could be so cheerful so early in the morning. The thunder of the hot shower on his head had started to wake him, but he was more of a night owl than an early bird.

"Come on, Adam! We have to be on our way by six twenty if you are to reach the dojo on time. You know Sensei Black will be annoyed if you are late."

"Is my face ok? Can you see the bruise?"

"No. It has just about gone. No one will notice it. It looks like the ice pack worked last night. Come on. I'm going out to the car."

Trevor Black was a Yondan Sensei, the chief instructor of a nearby aikido club. He had studied martial arts in Japan. His assistants had laid out the training area, and he stood talking to club members while he waited for the seven-a.m. start time. He saw Adam dash into the hall with his clothes bag on one shoulder and his school bag on the other. To save time, Adam had dressed in his aikido uniform at home and would change into his school uniform after showering at the end of the session. The Sensei walked out on to the mat covered centre of the hall and signalled for the students to assemble.

Billy Leeds and Adam, both from the Foundation, were the youngest attending. They would have preferred to be with people their own age but the sessions for their age group would have clashed with the weekly Foundation meetings. Most of the people present were adults, attending this session before their day at work. Adam was in the front row of attendees. The Sensei bowed briefly to the students and started speaking, looking at each person as he spoke.

"Today, we shall work on Open Hand..." he paused, looking at Adam's face moving closer.

"Ah, young man, from the look of that bruise on your face, it seems we need to give attention to your technique. Clearly, you did not avoid a punch. Please tell us what happened? What moves did you and your opponent make?"

Adam blushed.

"Adam, do not be ashamed to share your experience with us. We can all learn from your experiences."

The boy described how he had intervened with the three bullies and then had let Nelson make the first blow so he would not get into trouble with school. He then described the ankle throw used to disable the bully.

"Ah, you were either lucky or skilled in that the first blow did not cause you real injury. It was not necessary to take that blow. As you progress in aikido, you will learn ways to anticipate and get inside your opponent's attack without aggressive moves. Aikido is about force avoiding force. The best defence is to avoid the situation by running away, but in this case, that was not possible. You should also be careful about causing your opponent to land too hard, as that may cause long-term injury. Usually, a simple display that you can easily disarm their attack is sufficient to defuse the situation. It is honourable that you showed courage to defend others."

The Sensei turned to face the whole class and spoke. "Ok. I will demonstrate the basic moves that can be used to handle such a situation. First, we move to the side of the line of attack, and I will then use a wrist lock throw to bring down the opponent. Mr. Rogers, if you would be so kind as to attack me by throwing a punch at my face."

Mr. Rogers had taken part in this type of demonstration before and eagerly charged at the Sensei, trying his hardest to land a punch on the face. The Sensei effortlessly stepped half a pace aside from the attack. As the fist passed by his head, he grabbed the arm and used the momentum of the attacker to swing him to the ground. He helped Mr. Rogers up and gave three further demonstrations of the same moves in slow motion. "We will practice these moves later, but let us return to our planned lessons."

The Sensei winked kindly at Adam, and the lesson continued. All too soon, the session was over, and Adam and Billy had to shower and change into school uniform. His mother was waiting outside in the car. Billy's father was also waiting to drive his son to school.

Adam arrived at the school on time. In the corridors and classroom, he noticed a change in the atmosphere. He was no longer being ignored by the other boys. Most looked up and said hello when he approached. Simon was at the back of the form room at his usual desk. He smiled when Adam took his seat at the front of class.

When the morning attendance roll call took place, John Nelson did not answer, but a shout came from the back of the room. "He's off sick, sir. He hurt his back... skateboarding or dancing or something."

Chapter 8   The First Assignment

It felt like it had been a long day at school by the time Adam finally got home. All through the day, he had been expecting a demand to go to the principal's office, but that call had never come. His new friend Simon seemed a bit quiet during the day, but the other boys were beginning to include him in conversation. Even one of the prefects whom he did not know said hello to him in one of the school corridors.

When he walked up the lane from his school bus drop-off, he could see his mother working in the front garden. It was a hot summer day. She was out tracking down weeds in the garden then destroying them. Adam felt hot in his five-button blazer. His mother looked up as he arrived. "You look hot and sweaty in that blazer. You will find a jug of fresh lemonade in the fridge. Can you get some ice and bring me a glass of lemonade too?" As he disappeared through the door, she called after him. "By the way, a big heavy parcel arrived for you today. It's in your bedroom."

He went up to his room to drop off his school bag and blazer. He saw the brown paper wrapped parcel resting on his bed. He then remembered the Foundation had said they would be sending one to arrive today. He wondered what might be inside, but first he had to get a cold drink for his mother. His room was sweltering hot, so he opened a window before dashing downstairs. They had a big old chest freezer in an outhouse at the back of their cottage to keep their frozen food. There were always plenty of ice cubes stored in the corner of the freezer. He noticed that icy frost had built up a thick layer on the inside of the freezer. He groaned because he knew it would be his job to defrost the whole unit. Maybe he could do that when Bill came around.

He filled a container with ice cubes and went to the kitchen. There, he filled two tall glasses with ice cubes, added some lemon slices, and then poured the cloudy pale yellow fresh lemonade over the ice. Their family had cousins living in California in the USA, and they had shared the "secret family recipe" for preparing fresh lemonade. It was one of the great treats for hot summer days in the Cranford's cottage.

Carrying the glasses, he went out to join his mother in the garden. He stretched out in the garden hammock and watched as she worked. Amanda Cranford had long since learned the dangers of allowing her son loose in the garden; he would create more damage than a plague of locusts, so she was happy for him to just sit and relax. They chatted about their day's activities.

"So, what's in the parcel, Adam? I didn't know you were expecting anything, and there is nothing on the outside to say where it came from."

"I haven't opened it yet, so I don't know."

"You must have been expecting such a large parcel. It has a typed label, so it can't be from the family."

"I guess it must be the Superman outfit and the Martian stun gun I ordered off the Internet."

His mother gave him the 'look' that told him he had five seconds to stop messing around or he would be washing dishes for a month.

"Ok. I think it is from the Foundation. They sent me an email message last night. It's some kind of assignment."

"They do keep you busy, I must say."

Then Adam remembered the freezer. "I guess you wouldn't mind if I defrost the freezer. Bill is coming around later this evening. He can help me."

"Well, that would be good. I've been meaning to mention it to you before. If Bill is coming around, you had best go and start your homework. Don't you dare open the parcel until your homework is done, otherwise it will never get finished. If Bill comes a bit early, I'm sure Gilly would be only too pleased to keep him entertained for a while." Adam gave his mother a surprised look. He'd thought Gilly wanted that kept secret. His mother smiled. "Oh, we mothers always know about our daughter's secret boyfriends, but I suppose the four or five phone calls they make each evening are a bit of a giveaway too! You had best get going on that homework."

Adam drained his glass and then went upstairs to start on the day's homework.

He had almost finished the work by the time Bill arrived through the front gate. He went downstairs to meet him at the door but was not surprised to see Gilly loitering but trying to look uninterested. His mum called out, "Hi, Bill! If you've not eaten, there's food on the table. You are welcome to join Adam for a meal."

Adam suddenly realised he was hungry, so the two of them sat at the table quickly demolishing the pile of sandwiches that was in front of them. Bill was always hungry and eating, but he never seemed to get fat.

"Bill, I need to defrost our freezer. Do you want to give me a hand? It won't take long."

The red-headed boy rolled his eyes and groaned. "Yeah, whatever. I am your slave, oh great master."

Gilly appeared through the door as if by magic. "Adam, do you want me to give you a hand too?"

It was Cranford family lore that Gilly never helped on chores. She always found some way to avoid doing them. Adam glanced at Bill and grinned. "No, it's ok, Gilly. We can cope ok... alone!"

"Don't say I never offer." Gilly stomped upstairs to her room. Adam noticed Bill's eyes following her.

"Ok, Bill, we'll go and find the boxes and blankets to store the frozen food while we get rid of the frost."

Adam found the necessary equipment, scrapers, and hot air gun and went out to the outhouse with his friend. He'd been shown by his father how to do this job and was trusted. He started the task. "Bill, can you check the expiry dates on the food? We'll chuck any old stuff."

"Won't your mom complain?"

"It will be too late then, won't it? She always tries to hoard stuff she'll never use. So, you have a date with Gilly this weekend? Going somewhere nice?"

Bill blushed. "Er, you don't mind, do you Adam?"

Adam laughed. "No. Why should I worry? I have to put up with her all the time. It will be good to have someone else sharing that job. Are you sure you don't want to go fishing with me on Saturday? It is Open Season now. She hasn't told Mum about the date, but I get the feeling Mum has already guessed."

"So the date's off then?"

"I don't think so. Gilly will regard Mum as a minor obstacle. My sister can be very stubborn."

"I see it runs in the family then."

The two boys worked hard until there was a sparkling clean freezer reloaded with food and also a pile of expired food ready for the bin. The work had taken longer than expected.

Bill looked at his watch. "I have to go now. I guess I'll see you Saturday morning."

"Yeah, thanks for your help. Good luck on Saturday. I think you are very brave."

As Bill left, Adam tidied the boxes and blankets and then went to his bedroom. At long last, he could open the parcel. Removing the outer layer of brown paper, he found a brown cardboard box. There was a booklet glued on the outside marked *Read Me first*. Ignoring the booklet, Adam opened the box. It was well packaged inside, and he had to burrow through the packaging to find all the contents. Inside the box were three large training manuals—or at least they looked like training manuals; but when he opened them, he found inside a small tool kit containing pliers, needle files, a small metal vice, and oddly shaped metal wires. There was a normal door lock, a metal cylinder type like the one on his cottage front door, along with some spare keys to fit the lock. The keys looked a bit odd in that no teeth had been cut, and they were blanks.

There was also a lock labelled *Training Lock*. It was like the normal cylinder lock but had a clear plastic body so he see the moving parts inside the lock. Inside the third fake manual, he found an envelope marked *Bump Key* and also a computer CD. The label on the CD stated *Basic Lock Picking Guide*. After he had thoroughly searched the box and manuals and found these things, he pulled the *Read Me First* booklet off the box and started to read.

The pages were headed *Confidential – Foundation Members Only*. There was a summary paragraph on the first page:

> *Dear Cadet,*

Welcome to your assignment pack. This package is the first of a set of five packages that make up this assignment. You will be sent the next part of your assignment when you can demonstrate mastery of this first part.

It has been decided that you should be taught the skills of gaining entry to secure areas. You are warned, however, that you must never use this skill for criminal purposes; if you do, we will immediately and permanently expel you from the Foundation.

You have two tasks in this part of the assignment:

1. You should make one working key that will reliably unlock the enclosed cylinder lock. You should not alter the lock, as we will check the lock with a master key.

2. You should learn how to pick the lock in less than thirty seconds using the enclosed lock pick tools.

The enclosed CD contains full instructions and diagrams. There is no time limit on this assignment, so you can progress at your own pace. The CD contains instructions on how to contact us when you are ready to demonstrate that you are ready for the next part.

If you should damage any part of this kit, just let us know, and we will provide replacement items.

You should not tell anyone other than your Squad Leader about this assignment. If your family should ask, just tell them the parcel contained training manuals.

Best wishes,

Escradon, Master – Cadet Skills Development

The rest of the booklet contained parts diagrams and codes to allow for reordering if the parts were lost or damaged.

By the time Adam was ready to sleep, he had already unlocked the lock using a lock pick and a tension bar. He had also dismantled the lock and successfully reassembled it. He had even used the Bump Key to pick open the lock. He had started using the training lock before progressing onto the real lock. He now understood how the brass pins in the lock cylinder worked to lock or unlock the device.

He thought he understood the principles of measuring the pins and marking the correct places to cut teeth on the blank key with a needle file. He decided to leave the key-cutting task to the next day when he was less tired.

He browsed the CD on his PC and found that the latter part of the assignment also dealt with combination locks, security lever locks, padlocks, vehicle locks, and making improvised lock-picking tools.

As he dozed off to sleep, he wondered why the Foundation had decided to teach him lock-picking skills. He also wondered what other skills might be taught to the cadets. Perhaps there was more to the Foundation than just marching drills, fitness, and games after all.

§

The following day at school was a normal day except that the kids had cricket practice for most of the afternoon. Adam had rarely played cricket at his previous school, so he didn't fully understand all of the rules and the silly names used for fielding positions in the games. Simon was away playing tennis and couldn't offer much cricket advice, so once again, Adam felt a bit out of touch from the other boys.

He had the correct cricket whites outfit at least, for the Foundation had taken care of that problem, but all the other boys already knew their best roles on the team. When it came to the team captains picking their teams for the afternoon match, Adam had been left out and was given the job of keeping score.

Thankfully, one of the other boys, Darren Nichols, who was not playing because of a wrist injury, was available to help Adam with keeping score and recognising the signals from the umpire. By the end of the afternoon, Adam found he was getting on well with Darren and had received an invitation to meet at the weekend for a family barbeque at Darren's home. After cricket practice, they changed back into school uniforms and left to go home.

They walked down the private road from the school to the pickup area to catch a bus to get home. They had to dodge around a smelly fuel tanker that was blocking the road while it delivered fuel to the tank for the school boilers. Darren was really friendly, chatting about the school history and the system of different Houses in the school. At the bus stop, Adam was a bit surprised to see that Darren didn't wait for a bus but was picked up by his mother, who was driving a new silver coloured Bentley Arnage.

When he arrived home at the cottage, Adam found it empty. There was note left on the kitchen table telling Adam that his mother had taken Gilly to swimming lessons. He grabbed some food and went to his room to try and cut a key for the lock from the Foundation assignment. After careful measuring and marking, he fixed the key in the vice and carefully started filing the brass key blank with a needle file from the tool kit. At last, he finished. He gave the key a quick polish with a wire brush, and finally, the big moment had arrived.

He slipped the key in the lock and gave it a turn. Nothing happened, and the key would not turn in the lock. He jiggled it a little and tried to turn the key again, but still, he had no success in getting the lock to open.

Frustrated, he turned on his PC and loaded the Foundation instructional CD. When he had first loaded the software, he had noticed a trouble-shooter, which he intended to put to good use now. Following the guidelines provided on the CD, he dismantled the lock, turning it using the lock-picking wires and took the cylinder out. He pushed his recently cut key in and checked the pin alignment.

He noticed that one of the pins dipped slightly below the surface of the lock cylinder. He realised he'd filed one of the teeth too deeply and would have to start again. He took a deep breath and calmed his annoyance. He grabbed another key blank and started again. This time, he checked and rechecked the measurements while filing the metal carefully. Twenty minutes later, he tried the new key in the lock cylinder. This time, all of the pins aligned properly. He rebuilt the lock and retried the key. It turned easily in the lock.

He practiced picking the lock and got his time for unlocking the Foundation supplied sample lock down to ten seconds. He even tried the lock on the front door of their cottage. His first attempt on the cottage door lock took fifteen seconds. As he climbed the stairs back to his bedroom, a thought occurred to him. *I ought to warn Mom and Dad about the lack of security in this place.*

Putting the lock materials and tools away, he turned to his homework. Having spent most of the afternoon in cricket, there was not too much homework. He settled in and opened his books. He heard an alarm chime from his PC speaker, and he looked at the clock on his monitor: *17:45*, it said. It would soon be time for the videoconference with the rest of his squad.

He signed into the Foundation's central computer and selected the videoconference option. He entered Conference Number SQD4367. Adam adjusted the webcam on his PC so his face could be seen on the screen. While he waited, he practised the memory game with the card pack. Soon, the video images of the other team members started to appear on his screen.

At exactly 18:00, the voice of Squad Leader Brian came across the PC speakers; his face appeared in the central panel of the conference application. "Ok, guys, everyone is here. Can I remind you all to set your microphones to mute unless you wish to speak? The subject of this call is to take you through the plans for the Night Trek. Any questions at this time?"

He waited for any responses, and when there were none, he continued. "This hike is at night in mountain country. The length of the shortest route will be about eight miles. We will be taken by coach from outside the Foundation Hall at seven p.m. and dropped off as a squad at approximately eleven p.m. at the roadside in the middle of nowhere. We will have to work out where we have been dropped and plan a cross-country hiking route. There will be no rush, as we will have four hours to reach the base camp and get some sleep. We do not have to carry sleeping kits or tents. That will all be laid out for us at base camp."

Barry Davies interrupted the call. "That's too easy, Squad Leader. All we have to do is get a GPS handheld, and we will find out where we are with no problem."

Harrison continued his briefing. "We will be taking a GPS device and one mobile phone for safety purposes. The GPS and phone will be in a sealed container and carried in my rucksack. We will not be allowed to use them except in an emergency. Each of you will carry a map and a compass. I will be asking each of you to navigate and lead the squad in the dark for part of the route. If we take a wrong turn, you will all have to walk further, so let us hope everyone does their map reading properly." He paused briefly and then went on. "At present, the weather forecast is good, so you should be in No. 3 uniform and have a bivouac cape in your rucksack. Each person should carry an LED head torch, two sets of spare batteries, four light sticks, one day's emergency rations, and a water bottle. Carry one spare shirt, two changes of underwear, and two spare pairs of socks as well." Once he was sure he still had their attention, his instructions continued. "Two of you—Hutchinson and Walters—will carry first-aid kits. Williamson will carry a fifty-metre, nine-mm climbing rope, some slings, and three screw locking kara- biners. There will be eight squads on this night hike exercise, all starting from different places. The first two squads to check in will be given driving training. The squad arriving third will have canoe training. The squad who arrives last will be given cooking duties at camp and will also have to dismantle the camp at the end of the weekend."

Williamson interrupted, "Driving training? What kind of vehicles will we get, Sergeant?"

"I'm told it will be a mixture of Land Rovers and quad bikes at an off-road training centre. I have heard rumours about a vehicle skid pan as well. You will all get a chance on each type of vehicle, so let's just make sure we do not make any mistakes or go too slowly on the hike. We are going to be the first squad back to base camp. I will not be a happy bunny if I have to watch you lot washing dishes and peeling potatoes. Do any of you have any further questions?"

"What time do we get back home?" Adam asked.

"You can tell your parents that if all goes well, we will be back at the Hall about seven p.m. on the Sunday evening. Foundation mini buses will take you home from there. Make sure you get any homework done before the Foundation meet- ing at seven p.m. next Friday. Are there no more questions?" There was a brief pause of silence, and then he said, "This conference call is now terminated."

One by one, the video images of the squad members disappeared from Adam's PC screen as they left the videoconference. Adam thought through what he had just heard. During his first night in the Foundation Hall, someone had told him he would be driving within a year, but he had not taken much notice at the time, as he knew it would be at least three years before he could legally get a driving licence. The driver training for the squads must cost the Foundation a lot of money, but cost never seemed to worry them, and best of all, they never asked his parents to contribute. He was a bit worried about the night hike and route finding. He had never done that type of night work before, though he had done a seven-mile daytime hike in the mountains with his father once before.

Adam heard his family downstairs in the cottage and went down to greet them. There would be time later in the evening to get back to a game of *Thorn World* on his PC.

Chapter 9   Phase 1 is Complete

It was a sad day. The bus company had been owned and run by the Howell family for three generations. Selwyn Howell had finally decided that with the ever increasing motor fuel costs, European legislation, and competition from national coach companies that he could no longer continue business. His grandfather, Gwillam Howell, had moved the company from South Wales to Buckinghamshire when it was obvious the mines were starting to run out of coal. Without the coal, local industry would die.

His grandfather had made a wise decision, and his coach business had prospered. Gwillam Howell had been able to buy a large field from a farmer and erect buildings back in those days when planning rules were not so tight. All the local Council had insisted on was that the site was surrounded by woodland so that the neighbours would not see the unsightly bus garage. The trees Gwillam had planted were now large and mature. In fact, it was difficult for people passing by to realise there was a bus company operating from the site.

However, today Selwyn would be handing the keys of the site to another company. The fleet of eight coaches had now been auctioned off, and their contracted business was either cancelled or sold to other bus companies. All that remained were the company offices and the large, empty garage for the buses. Selwyn was hoping to sell the land to property developers so they could build houses. All of that depended on planning decisions that could take years to complete. The local neighbours of course objected to the plans to build housing on the site.

Simon Berwyck had told Selwyn he was the Director of a new company called Doveland Support Services that provided support services for film companies. They needed a short-term rental storage building for scenery and props. Simon had thought that bus garage was ideal for those purposes. When Simon asked Selwyn what might be charged for renting the site, Selwyn had mentioned a large amount of money per month, expecting to be negotiated down. In fact, the amount was twice what a local property surveyor had previously suggested. To Selwyn's surprise, the other man immediately agreed and offered to pay six months' rent in advance. It had taken only a week for legal documentation and credit checks before the men had agreed to do business.

At twelve noon, as previously agreed, Selwyn was on site when Simon Berwyck arrived in an old Mercedes. As before, the new tenant was wearing wraparound mirrored sunglasses. Selwyn guessed this was what working in the film industry did to a man. He couldn't quite place the faint accent Berwyck spoke with, but he thought it might be South African.

As always, Berwyck wore a broad smile and proffered a handshake as he approached Selwyn. "Hi, Selwyn. So, this is it... the final day for you? What will you be doing with all the money? Retirement, perhaps?"

"Hi, Simon. It is good to see you again. Your agent has been really efficient in sorting out all the paperwork so quickly. You must owe her a large bunch of flowers. I'm not sure about retirement just yet. We still have the development opportunity here. Strange thing is, my wife recently received a fantastic three-month holiday offer on a farm in South Africa. After I settle some business here, we are both going to take a break down there, in the Karoo area. Have you ever heard of such a place?"

"It's been a long time since I've been to South Africa, though people tell me the Karoo is very peaceful."

Simon Berwyck knew a lot more about the Karoo area than he let on. It was an isolated semi-desert area that had massive farms in the centre of South Africa. He also knew about the Howell's holiday and had ensured they would be treated to a luxurious time during their stay, though it was unfortunate Selwyn would suffer a broken leg on a certain day and would require a long stint in a good South African hospital before he could return to the UK. The location of the farm was not included in mobile phone coverage, and the farm was only equipped with a landline—and even landlines were known to occasionally break down. The couple would be totally out of touch from home for at least four months.

"Selwyn, you had best show me around and then hand over the keys. I am afraid my agent can't make it today, but she has given me a full checklist. Where do you want to start?"

"Yes, Simon, let's start with the fuel tank. It has a pump and meter for refuelling the buses. It was a relief when your agent told me you wanted to continue to use it for your vans. It has a capacity of 15,000 litres and is currently half full with normal road diesel. Note that it's not the winter diesel, so you might want to think about how you handle that later in the year."

Selwyn then took his visitor to the workshop area to show him that the inspection pit in the floor was clean and freshly painted. He showed him the pump used to drain the inspection pit if it should become flooded. All of the machine tools had been removed, leaving the workshop area as an empty space.

Next to the workshop was the bus garage area. It had large metal doors that folded back on rails in the concrete floor. Selwyn unlocked the small Judas Gate built into the main doors and hopped through into the bus garage. A few seconds later, with a whirring and creaking noise, the main doors opened. The bus garage was large and high enough to hold five full-sized coaches while at the same time providing manoeuvring space when parking the coaches. The floor of the garage had been freshly painted; it glistened in a dark red. The smell of the floor paint was quite choking.

Simon looked up at the steel roof high above. He could see no damage or holes. Lighting units were suspended from the roof girders. "Yes, this all very nice and clean, Selwyn. Can I now see the offices?"

They walked to far end of the garage and opened a door to find a large, dark, windowless room. Selwyn flicked a light on. "This used to be the drivers' rest area and canteen. The toilets are through those two doors at the back."

The room contained no furniture, and like the rest of the garage, it was freshly painted, but there was new lino covering on the floor. Simon inspected the wash-room area and came back with a nod of his head, expressing his satisfaction.

The administration office was next to the drivers' room and was of similar size, though this room had a large window in the wall to let light into the room. Like the drivers' room, the walls were made from concrete blocks and painted a boring glossy magnolia colour. As before, the room was clean and smelt of paint. Two doors led off from the office, and Simon peeked through them. He remembered from the floor plan that they were storerooms.

Ok, Selwyn, everything appears to be in order. We did agree you would continue to pay business rates and utility bills through your company, didn't we? If you let us know the amount, we will pay you within the week."

Selwyn smiled and held out a large bunch of keys. "Yes, Simon, that has all been confirmed with your agent. The place is yours now. Look after it, won't you? If there are any problems, just give me or my agent a call."

As Simon reached out for the keys, Selwyn noticed for the first time that the tip of the little finger was missing from his client's hand. He'd not noticed before, but out of politeness, he made no mention of the deformity.

Simon took the bunch of keys and watched the older man leave. As soon as he heard the other car depart, he pulled out a mobile phone, pressed a key and spoke. "Ok. He has gone now. Get your vehicles moving and park them inside the garage. There will be a satellite overhead in thirty minutes, and I don't want any unnecessary appearances on their photographs."

He stepped out of the garage and spoke with the driver of the Mercedes. "Take this car to the wreckers like we planned. I want it crushed into a bale of metal by the end of today." He watched the car drive away and waited for the others.

Within ten minutes, two flatbed lorries and two vans arrived in the garage. Simon closed the garage doors, switched on the overhead lights, and then banged on the side of one of the vans. The doors burst open, and a team of six men stepped out inside the garage. Simon assembled the men and drivers in a line.

"Ok, gentlemen. I will first remind you this is confidential government work. You are not to discuss it with anyone. You will be well paid for this work. My name is Darren. If you unload the other van first, you will find tool kits, drawings, food, and drink. The restroom and toilets can be found at the end of the garage." He pointed to the old drivers' restroom and then continued, "Once you have set up your tools and food, unload the lorries. The plans are printed in some detail, but the objective is to build a large cage over there in the corner. There is also a smaller cage to be built in the corner of the large cage. The sequence of works and part numbers are clearly shown on the plan drawings, but if you have any questions, ask me straightaway. You must remember to wear your work gloves at all times."

He pointed to the corner where the lorries were parked. "Ok, now unload the lorries and lay out the materials over there. Make sure you leave space for a lorry to back out of the garage. Get to work, gentlemen."

They opened the other van and unloaded the tools, welding equipment, and food. The tools were laid out on a spare area of floor. The food and drink was moved into the restroom.

Soon, using the crane lifts built into the lorries, the load of scaffolding, steel plates, reinforcing mesh, and bars was unloaded from the lorries. Several large rolls of fine wire copper mesh were carefully lifted off and stood next to the steel plates. Next, the men marked the outline of the large cage on the floor of the garage. Scaffolding was erected around the outline. The scaffold structure stretched from the floor to roof beams of the garage.

Carefully using the plan to guide them, they laid the pre-cut steel sheets, welding them in place to form a large steel dish resting on the garage floor. The dish formed the base of the large cage. With the steel bars and reinforcing mesh, the men welded and fabricated a large cage that rested on the steel dish on the garage floor. The steel cage bars created a square grid with no gap greater than fifteen cms. The steel grid was covered by the mesh. The cage almost reached up to the roof beams, and the width of the cage was twice its height. The depth of the cage was three-quarters of the length of the garage floor. The front of the cage had a large steel mesh gate almost as high as the cage itself. Even with pre-shaped materials, the first cage had taken until midnight to construct, so Simon had let the men rest until seven the following morning.

The next task was to line the inside of the large steel cage with the copper mesh. The copper mesh covered the cage ceiling, walls, and gate. Where the copper mesh panel overlapped, they were carefully soldered together to ensure electrical contacts between the panels. Where the mesh panels met the steel floor pan of the cage, a substantial overlap of some thirty cms. was allowed, and those were then clamped to the steel and the edges finished with electrical conducting tape.

While the main cage was being lined, Simon started two of the men building the smaller steel cage. It was two and a half metres high and wide. The depth of the small cage was approximately three metres. This time, the cage also had a steel grid base. The steel grid on the small cage had no gap wider than twenty cms. Space had been left in the side of the cage for a steel door to be added at a later stage. There was no copper mesh lining.

Finally, the main cage was fully lined along the walls, ceiling, and gate with copper mesh and was properly bonded to the steel base. Simon checked that the massive gate swung easily and swung closed when released.

"Alright, guys. It's time for you all to take a coffee break. I need a bit of privacy for this next stage," he said.

Once all the men had gone into the old drivers' restroom, Simon stood outside the large cage and checked the signal strength on his mobile phone. It registered five bars on the signal meter. He moved inside the cage and checked again. This time, the mobile had only one bar of signal strength. Leaving the cage, he went to the back of the van containing equipment. He found a torch and a battery radio set and returned to the cage. He swung the heavy gate of the cage closed, slipping inside the cage before the gate closed. With the gate closed, it was dark inside the cage. He switched the torch on and checked his phone. As expected, he could get no mobile phone signal. He turned on the battery radio. There was no sound from the speaker apart from a slight hiss, even when he set it to scan all of the bands and frequencies. He walked around in the cage trying different positions and heights. Satisfied, he opened the gate of the cage. Almost instantly, the radio tuned into a local music station. He switched off the radio and returned it to the van, then returned to the large cage with some temporary lights, which he then connected to the power.

Simon went to the rest area to speak to his men. "Ok, guys, we are almost finished. I just need you to move the small cage inside the large one and weld it in place on the floor. We then need to paint the construction."

The team members stretched and filed out of the room. While the small cage was only a framework of steel bars, it was heavy and needed all of their combined strength to lift it into the main cage. With Simon providing directions, they positioned the small cage in the far corner of the main cage. Its frame was one metre away from the nearest wall of the main cage. Within five minutes, the small cage had been welded to the steel floor of the large cage.

Simon then directed the men to take drums of silvery grey paint from the equipment van. They unloaded paint-spraying equipment and full face masks. After his brief description of what they needed to do, the men set to work. Soon, the whole cage construction had been coated inside and out with thick, silver-grey electro-conductive paint. The paint clogged most of the copper mesh holes of the cage, but that did not worry Simon. After the paint had been checked, they cleaned away all the tools and painting equipment. The scaffolding poles and planks had been removed and repacked on one of the lorries. Finally, the work was complete.

He lined his team up. Walking past them, he dropped a clean set of blue cotton work overalls and a brown paper envelope in front of each man. "You have all worked well, but you have also been paid well. The envelope contains an additional bonus of £500 each. The paint you have just used will have ruined your outer clothes. Change into the new overalls and leave your old clothes on the floor. When you get home, throw away the boots you are wearing now and buy new ones. Remember, gentlemen, that this is national security work, so you are forbidden from talking about it to others. In case you are wondering what you have just built, it is a security cage for testing some special communications equipment. As soon as you are ready, please get into your vehicles, and you will be driven home."

He stood and watched as the men changed their clothes and climbed into the vehicles to leave. He kicked their discarded clothes into a pile in the corner of the garage and then switched off the lights to the building. He located the control switch and set the building alarm and closed the main gate of the garage. After locking the gates, he went to a section of empty ground at the edge of the yard and made a mobile phone call to another mobile phone—the first time the remote phone had received a call. "This is Alpha Two. The first phase of transport plan is complete. Please send someone to collect me at Location Three. Message ends." He dropped the phone to the ground.

Reaching in his jacket pocket, he pulled out a polythene bag containing a silvery powder. He ripped open the bag and poured the contents over the phone, building a small pyramid of silver powder that completely covered it. He dropped a lit match onto the powder. Immediately, a noisy, crackling, brilliant white flame started to consume the powder. Large clouds of bright white smoke were given off. He did not look at the flame, as the light it gave off was too bright. After a few minutes, the bright flame had died away, and there was no trace left of the mobile phone—just white scorch marks on the baked ground. He stood in the shadow of the trees and waited.

§

Five miles away on an unused road, there were similar scorch marks, as an anonymous white van pulled away and headed towards the old bus garage. In the centre of London, a temporarily rented office suite containing only a low-cost second-hand chair and desk was vacated following a phone call from the driver of the white van. The telephone handset had been removed. All surfaces in the room where hands might have touched had been scrubbed down and cleaned with an abrasive kitchen cleaning material.

Chapter 10 Trashing the Head's Car

When Adam woke that morning, the sky was laden with heavy rain clouds. It was dark in his bedroom, but he felt ready to go and face the world. The previous evening, he had had some success with his trading activities on the computer game *Thorn World*. Part of the profit he was generating was helping to equip the other members of Visiting Havoc. Their leader, Bright Petal, had told him their success had attracted several new members to their roving band of mercenaries. Adam had been able to recruit two non-combatant farmers to act as trading agents for him when he was not logged into the game. This reduced his profit slightly per ton of Iqar coal, but it would increase the overall amount of trade.

Bright Petal told the mercenaries that Visiting Havoc would soon be agreeing to a mercenary contract with one of the larger tribes. Visiting Havoc would also be entering battle to gain control of a command and supply base from one the largest tribes. Adam, aka BaD Totem, had played for two hours the previous evening, stopping only when his father had threatened to come and unplug the network cable.

The Foundation had arranged for the broadband network link to their home to be upgraded to a business quality optical fibre network link so Adam could reliably take part in Foundation activities such as video conferencing. One side effect of the network upgrade was that Adam saw no network delays in the game fighting sequences. It made the game particularly addictive.

"Adam, have you had your shower yet? I need to go in there," said Gilly from outside his bedroom door.

"No, not yet. I was just about to go in there. Hang on ten seconds, and I'll be there." He hurtled out of bed, grabbing a towel as he went, and disappeared into the bathroom for a shower. He was surprised Gilly had bothered to check first. If she had gone in first, he would have been delayed forever waiting for her.

After a quick shower and hurried scramble into school uniform, he was soon downstairs at the breakfast table.

"Oh, Adam, are we forgetting something?" His father pointed at his necktie.

Adam looked down at his own school tie. In the rush, he had tied it in the old way of his previous school. It was way too loose, and the ends were too short. "Dad, it's stupid they make such a fuss over the school tie. It's about the only school in the whole country that insists on us doing it in the old-fashioned way. It is soooo seventies! It doesn't make the slightest difference in the way we study."

"I know, son, but that's the way it is. You don't want to start getting demerits from the prefects. Tie it properly. If you want, I can show you again how to do it."

"No, it's ok. You don't need to show me. I'm not some kind of baby. I know how to do it."

His father watched his son intently as he struggled to get the tie knot right. Adam knew his father was doing it deliberately just to make him lose concentration. It took the boy two attempts to get it right. He deliberately ignored his dad for the rest of breakfast as a punishment.

"Adam, do you want a cooked breakfast today?"

Adam beamed up at his mother. "Yes, please, Mom. I've got loads of time before the school bus. I get fed up with the rabbit mix that you buy us."

"That so-called *rabbit mix* is their best quality muesli. It is much better for you than eggs and bacon. By the way, did you put your cricket whites in the wash basket?"

"No, I didn't need to, Mum. They are not dirty."

"So, you didn't get picked for a team again yesterday? Are things going ok for you at school?"

"No, it's alright, Mum. It's not surprising, really, because I don't know much about cricket. I guess they only want the best on the teams they pick, and they don't really know me yet. It will be better next school year. I did make a new friend yesterday though. He helped me with scoring, and he's invited me to their family barbeque at the weekend."

"Oh? What's his name?"

"Darren Nichols. He's in the same school form and House as me."

"So, have you got any details yet like time and place? Do you know how you are going to get there?"

"No. I'll ask him today. I don't know his number yet."

Adam had received and eaten his cooked English breakfast of eggs, bacon, sausage, mushrooms, and tomatoes by the time Gilly arrived in the room. She was in her school uniform but still had a towel wrapped around her damp hair. "Oh, I see the Indian Princess has deigned to grace us with her presence. What are they called... Sultana, isn't it? Part of a nutty fruit cake." Adam ducked as she tried to cuff his ear.

"Now, come on, Gillian. Get a move-on and stop messing around with your brother. By the time we get that hair of yours dry, you are going to be late for school. You are not going to miss out on breakfast today, young lady. It is the most important meal of the day."

Gilly pouted her lips for having been told she must eat breakfast. She felt it made her so fat, and she wanted to lose some weight. Adam could see another kitchen storm between his sister and his mother developing, so he made his excuses and left the table. Gilly had been getting really moody recently, and brief explosions of temper were not all that rare. Adam preferred not to get caught in the crossfire.

He had about twenty minutes to spare before he had to catch his school bus. He went to his bedroom to practice at the playing card memory game. To his own surprise, he found he could now easily remember ten random cards and was beginning to succeed with fifteen. The diversion almost caused him to lose track of time, and he had to run for his school bus. Today, the driver was patient and waited when he saw Adam running for the bus.

When his bus arrived at the school drop-off, he could see Simon chatting to another boy. He waved and wandered over to them.

"Hi, Adam. This is Nigel Roberson. Nigel, this is Adam Cranford."

The two boys smiled at other in greeting.

"Nigel works with me in the theatre group. He's in Year 10. We'd best get going, though, 'cause the bell is going to ring soon."

They walked up the school driveway towards the school. Along the route, they had to move one side to allow room for a long crocodile of Year 7 boys who were walking down the road toward them.

"They must be going on their summer day trip. I thought I saw extra coaches waiting down there," said Simon.

"So, have I missed the annual trip?"

"No, Adam. We get ours when we come back after the summer holidays. I think we are going jointly with the girls from St. Josephine's to the rebuilt Globe Theatre in London."

A large fuel tanker was blocking most of the road at the edge of the staff car park, and they had to move to one side to get past it. Adam paused and took a second look at the tanker. Its pump was running, and the driver and an assistant were attending to the controls at the side of the lorry. The driver looked up and saw Adam watching him and smiled in return.

Adam drew Simon and Nigel down the road to one side of the lorry out of view of the driver. "Simon, have you got a mobile phone with you?"

"Yes. Why?"

"Call 999 now and get the police. That guy is stealing fuel."

"What?"

"Do it now, Simon! Don't let him see you. I saw a tanker delivering here yesterday. His uniform is wrong, and the fuel hose is wrong. It is too narrow and is running inside the fuel tank coupling. He's pumping fuel out from the school tanks!" Adam turned to look at his new acquaintance. "Nigel, can you run up to the school and get help? We will need at least six big prefects or teachers to deal with them."

The older boy ran up the road past the tanker and into the main schoolyard. Meanwhile, Simon had his mobile phone out and was having to repeat information to the emergency police operator. "No, this is no joke. You have to come now! We are at Holliston's Grammar School. We are watching them now... No, I don't know the road name or post code... Yes, my name is Simon Davidson... No, we won't approach them… Yes, we will wait until the police get here."

He ended the call and looked at Adam. "They didn't believe me at first, but they are coming. I hope you are right about this, or we are going to get in so much trouble. Oh no! Watch out! Those two are getting nervous, and they saw us. I think they're going to make a run for it."

Adam had already realised and was watching the driver get into the tanker lorry. The driver's mate was hurriedly disconnecting the hose at the side of the tanker. "Simon, we've got to stop them from escaping. If they drive down this road, there are all those Year 7 kids at the bottom," Adam warned.

Adam had noticed a large old green Range Rover parked on a slope leading onto the road. He knew he had to act quickly. He bent and picked up a large pebble from the garden border at the edge of the road and ran to the Range Rover. As he approached, he threw the pebble through the driver's side window of the car. The window turned opaque as the safety glass broke. As soon as he reached the door, he punched the rest of the glass out. He could hear the tanker lorry engine revving as it began to move towards them. He leaned in through the shattered window and released the door lock. The lorry was beginning to move more quickly down the road. Adam quickly jumped into the Range Rover and released the handbrake. After a moment's pause, the large car rolled backwards across the road and crashed into a tree. It blocked the whole road. Adam dived out of the car to safety at the side of road, dragging the open-mouthed Simon as he ran. With a sudden *hiss* of the air brakes, the lorry skidded to a halt, just avoiding a collision with the side of the car blocking the road.

"Look, Simon! The others are coming."

At the top of the road, he could see Nigel, some prefects, and a couple of teachers running down the road towards them. He could also see the two fuel thieves scrambling to escape from the lorry. They jumped out of the tanker. The driver's mate ran past both Adam and Simon down the road to escape.

The driver ran at Adam with a steel crowbar in his raised right hand. "I'll stop you from ever interfering again, you nosy little do-gooder!" he roared as he rushed at Adam.

"Oh, no… not again," Adam groaned to himself. He knew if he ran to safety, Simon might not escape. He faced the man as though he was rooted to the spot in terror. At the last moment, just as the blow from the iron bar started to descend, he moved a partial step towards the man and slightly to one side so that the blow just missed him. He grasped the wrist of the man as his momentum carried him past the boy. Adam converted the motion into a body throw as he swept the man around him. The man thudded to the road surface on his back, dropping the crowbar with a clatter.

Adam continued to hold the man in a wristlock and shouted, "Simon! Quick… grab that bar and hit hard any part of him that tries to get up!"

At that point, Nigel and the prefects arrived. Four of them took over from Adam and restrained the man. It was not difficult, as the fall Adam had given him had knocked all the fight out of him. The thief was still gasping, trying to recover his breath.

"Cranford, it looks like you have been giving someone dancing lessons again, doesn't it?"

One of the teachers, Mr. Williams, said to him with a grin.

"No. I was just using force to avoid force. I would have let him go if he hadn't attacked me."

They could hear approaching police sirens in the distance.

"Right. Cranford—and you, Davidson—we will take over here for the time being. No doubt the police will want to speak with you at some point in the day. You have both done really well here today, but now you had better both go get registered. If you get a late mark, just refer them to me, ok?"

"Yes, sir. We are on our way," the boys both chimed together.

"Oh, Cranford, please straighten your school tie. It is a mess, and we can't have our boys untidy, can we?"

"Yes, sir."

As they wandered up the road to the school, the boys talked over what had just happened. "Are you some kind of ninja, Adam?" his friend asked. "When you didn't move, I thought you were going to get smacked by the bar that guy was waving. And that move you did? Wow! He must be twice your weight. How could you lift him so easily? I've never seen anyone move so fast. You actually moved towards him!"

"It's nothing special. It just comes down to concentration and training. You don't lift your opponent. You just use the momentum of their own movement and throw them off balance. Anyway, how are you? You have been quite quiet with me recently."

"It's nothing, Adam. I just thought you might not want to be friends with me after what Nelson called me the other day."

Adam finally realised what it was that had been bugging his new friend. "No, I'm not that shallow, Simon. I just take people as they are. I don't have any prejudices except against bullies."

When they arrived in their form classroom, the attendance register had already been taken. Some of the boys were trying to peer out of the windows to see why the blue lights of the police cars were flashing in the school driveway.

Their form teacher looked up sharply at Adam and Simon. "You two are late for register. That will be five demerits for each of your houses."

Adam spoke. "We are sorry, sir. We got a bit delayed on the way in. Mr. Williams says that if you speak with him, he will explain."

"Ok, boys. I will check that. Now go and sit at your desks. I have a few things that need to be covered before the assembly bell. And Mr. Cranford, kindly sort out your school tie. It's a total mess. You also have a button missing from your blazer. Please get that sorted out by the end of the week."

"Yes, sir."

As Adam went to sit down, Darren slipped Adam a white envelope and hissed, "Read it later, ok?"

Adam nodded and tucked the envelope into his inside blazer pocket.

The rest of the morning went normally, though rumours were flying around the school about the attempted theft of heating fuel. Some said it was £10,000 worth of fuel and that one of the boys had captured the thieves. The day was normal for Adam and Simon until eleven thirty when a school secretary appeared through the class door with a note for them to immediately go to the principal's office.

They bundled their books into their bags and set off along the school corridors to the principal's office. Entrance to the room was usually governed by the principal's secretary, a formidable, slim, grey-haired, middle-aged lady. Before entering the secretary's office, Adam paused to check out his school tie; he hadn't been able to get a replacement blazer button yet. He rubbed the top of his school shoes against the back of his trouser leg to give some shine to his shoes. Approaching the school principal's office did not hold good memories for Adam.

Inside the secretary's office, Simon spoke up. "Miss Nevis, we have been asked to come to Mrs. Embleton's office. We're Davidson and Cranford."

She paused her typing for a moment and peered at them over the top of her slim, rectangular spectacles and then glanced down at a document on her desk. She lifted her head and spoke.

"Hmm. Ok. Go straight in. She is waiting for you... but knock first." She pointed to a door to her side.

Adam led the way. He knocked on the door and paused. A faint "Enter" command came through the wood panels. Adam opened the door, and the two boys walked into the room.

Mrs. Embleton and two men were seated at a large, round conference table. She pointed to two vacant chairs at the table. Both boys recognised Mr. Williams, and Adam recognised the other man—Detective Inspector Norris. The boys sat in the chairs and dropped their school bags to the floor.

Mrs. Embleton spoke first. "I'm sure you boys can guess why you have been asked here. I've already spoken with Roberson, so I have a reasonably good idea as to what has happened. Detective Inspector Norris will want to interview you two and take statements about the events with the fuel tanker this morning. However, there is one matter I should deal with first. Adam, the Detective Inspector tells me you have a bit of a history with doing foolish things with Headmasters' cars. It seems like you also wish to establish the tradition at this school as well?"

Adam looked blankly at Mrs. Embleton. He hadn't made any plans to transport her car into the office. He didn't even know what it looked like. Simon giggled.

"That old green Range Rover you decided to use as a road block has served me well for the past ten years. I'm rather pleased the tanker managed to stop without destroying my car."

Adam blushed as he realised he had not only broken the window of the principal's car, but he had almost turned it into a wreck. *Thank goodness the lorry stopped,* he thought. He stammered a response, all the while wondering how on earth he could tell his parents that they needed to find him a new school. "I'm... I'm sorry, Mrs. Embleton. I... errm, didn't know it was yours. It wasn't deliberate. I just thought the tanker had to be stopped because all the Year 7's were at the end of the road. They might have been hit."

"I see. Adam, don't worry about it. I'm sure the school will not mind paying for a new window for my car. There were already dents in the back bumper anyway. I'm just relieved you did not get injured. You should not have tackled the driver. That could have been very dangerous."

"I didn't have much choice, ma'am. He attacked me. I couldn't just run away and leave Simon there. I wasn't trying to capture the man—just disarm him so he wouldn't attack us. It was self-defence, ma'am."

Detective Inspector Norris spoke up. "Adam, don't worry. We know it was self-defence. That man will be charged not only with theft, but also with Attempted Grievous Bodily Harm. Of course, his charges will have to wait until he is released from hospital. He is currently in the Casualty Department handcuffed to a bed and guarded by a police officer. You took him down very hard, but we think there are no long-term injuries."

"I didn't really have the time or strength to soften his landing. I'm glad I didn't really hurt him though."

"You should know he has previous convictions for armed robbery. We were actually searching for him. You have done the police a really great favour by stopping him. We have caught the other guy as well. He is currently being questioned at the Police Station. We suspect they were responsible for a string of similar thefts in the region. With the rocketing price of fuel, it is an increasingly common crime. The tanker they were using was also stolen. I believe there may be a reward coming from the insurance company for the recovery of the vehicle."

"If there is a reward, it's not just me. Simon and Roberson did just as much as me, and they should get equal shares."

Mrs. Embleton interrupted, "Yes, young man, I'm sure that can all be sorted out later. You are all to be commended for your brave and prompt actions. However, Adam, your alertness in spotting the thieves and then taking control of the situation deserves particular praise. I shall be writing to the parents of each of the three boys involved to record the school's thanks for your actions. You three will be commended in assembly on Monday morning in front of the whole school." She added, "There is one teacher, however, who will be having some sharp words from me. She actually told the thieves where the fuel pipes were, thinking it was for a fuel delivery. There must have been 300 people walking past the thieves this morning without realising they were stealing fuel."

"Aw, Mrs. Embleton, I don't know about Simon, but I'd prefer this was kept quiet. I really don't want the whole school to know. It would be so embarrassing. We are no heroes. We just happened to be in the wrong place at the right time." He looked at Simon, who nodded in agreement.

"If you insist, young men, we will keep this under wraps, but I shall be writing to your parents to congratulate you, no matter what you say. I'm sure the whole school will find out fairly soon anyway, however much we try to keep it quiet."

She stood and walked to the outer door of her office and held it open for the two boys and the policeman. "Now, if you two will kindly accompany the Inspector, he has a couple of men waiting in offices to take your evidence statements. I have arranged for both of you to take a late lunch in the canteen today. Just one final word to you, young Cranford, before you go..."

Simon and Norris left the room.

"The prefects have mentioned your 'dancing lessons' to me and the circumstances. I'm sure you won't need to give anymore to any of the boys, but I would be most grateful if you could avoid these 'lessons' of yours in this school in the future. You are turning out a lot better than I expected, so let's not ruin it, hmm?"

"Yes, ma'am."

Adam left the room and joined the two others in the corridor. As they walked to the offices to give statements, Norris broke the silence. "Adam, I was surprised to have to meet you again so soon. This time, though, it is under better circumstances." The man raised an enquiring glance in the direction of Simon.

"Oh, Simon knows about my school history, Inspector. He's my friend, so I told him why I left the last school."

Simon grinned in response. "I also know, Inspector, that Adam is a total nutcase."

"I can agree with you there, Simon. I'm pleased he got into this school though. It is a very good one. I just hope Mrs. Embleton's Range Rover doesn't end up on the roof."

Adam protested, "Now, would I do that, Inspector?" He tried to bat his eyes in a most innocent manner. "As if I'd get involved in that kind of thing! I also suspect you know a great deal more than you let on about how I gained a place in this school."

Norris just smiled as he opened the office door and guided the boys to his men to take their evidence statements.

After giving statements to the police and having lunch, Adam and Simon returned to their class. As was to be expected, there were questions from the other boys in the class on their return as to why they had had to go to the principal's office.

"Oh, apparently we saw the vehicle involved in the robbery, and the police wanted statements from us. We don't know too much," Adam lied. With his cleverly boring (and completely untruthful) answer, the interest in the class moved away from Adam and Simon to important things such as girlfriends and the cricket test match against India.

Adam suddenly remembered the letter from Darren. When the teacher was busy, he pulled the envelope from his blazer pocket and opened it. There was a card addressed to Adam Cranford, a formal invitation to the barbecue at Darren's home on the following Saturday. There was also a map of where Darren's house was located. Catching Darren's eye, he waved the card and gave a thumbs-up signal.

The next class for the rest of the day was design and technology. Adam was standing at a work bench ruining a perfectly good piece of wood with a chisel when he looked up and saw Greg Wallace, the prefect, approaching him.

Wallace dropped a brown paper envelope on the bench in front of Adam. "Mr. Williams thought you might need this, Cranford." Having delivered his message, the older boy turned and left the room.

Adam grabbed the envelope and tore it open. He tipped the contents onto the bench top. There were three brass blazer buttons engraved with the school crest. He picked them up and popped them in his pocket.

Simon was standing at the workbench behind him. "You must be important, what with the prefects acting as messengers for you."

"I don't suppose it will last very long, Simon. Give them another couple of days, and we'll just be their serfs again."

"I saw you got an invite to Darren's barbecue. Are you going to go? I'll be there as well. I've known him since primary school. Our families are friends."

"Yes. I'm going to go, though I have to ask my parents first. I'll need them to give me a lift to Darren's house. It will be good to have someone I know there."

"You should enjoy it. Darren's house is quite something."

"Get on with your work back there and stop chattering!" called the technology teacher, rudely interrupting their conversation.

As Adam arrived home later that afternoon, his mother's opening word were, "Adam, what have you done to your blazer? There is a button missing."

"It's no problem, Mom. I just caught it on something. Don't worry... I've got a replacement button, and I can sew it on. You know I've got loads of practice from the old school at doing blazer buttons."

"So how was your day at school today? Make anymore friends?"

"Oh, it was just a normal day, Mom. Nothing special happened. Oh... I got a proper invite from Darren for the barbecue. It's got a map and everything."

"Pass it over and let me have a look," she said. "Ah, it has an RSVP, and dress is casual. Did you respond and let Darren know you will be going?"

"I gave him a thumbs-up, but I needed to check with you and Dad first. Can one of you give me a lift over and back on Saturday?"

"Yes, of course we will. What with you and your sister, I'm just going to be a taxi service on Saturday. You had best go and call Darren now and confirm. It is only a couple of days away. Their home phone number is on the invitation."

"Oh, Mum, did I tell you I'm out with the Foundation the following weekend? We are going on Friday night and get back Sunday evening. There's a night hike involved."

"No, son, you didn't tell me. We were planning to go and visit your Auntie Joyce on Saturday, but I don't suppose you have to come with us. Do we need to get you any equipment? Will you need picking up from somewhere?"

"No, Mom. It is just like going to the usual Friday meeting, and they will get me back on Sunday evening. I'll just need spare underwear and socks, I think."

"What about your homework? If you have been out all weekend, you will be too tired to do it properly on the Sunday evening."

"I'll do it on the Friday night before I go. I doubt there will be much because it is so close to the end of term."

"Ok. Well, you'd best get changed out of uniform. Fix that button on now. It will be too much rush in the morning as you have aikido first thing... don't forget. I'm going to do a big cooked supper tonight for the whole family. I am going to give Gilly some bad news later this evening, so expect some storms. On Monday evening next week, I'm going to take her for the first appointment with the orthodontist to get her teeth straightened. She is not going to be happy about having to wear braces."

Adam remembered the discomfort and the long dental sessions he had suffered with the orthodontist. The wire braces were certainly ugly, but his parents couldn't really afford the plastic braces that were only available through private treatment. Both he and his sister had inherited slightly deformed teeth from their father. "Oh no! She will be terrible to live with until the braces come off. Can't we persuade the dentist to wire her teeth shut so she can't speak?"

"That is so tempting, Adam, but I guess we should just all get used to the idea of her in braces," his mom said with a smile.

"Ok, well, I'm off to play some computer games or something. I don't think Bill is around tonight. I think he has badminton club or something."

After calling Darren to reply to the invitation, Adam went to his bedroom to change clothes and fix his blazer. From experience at his previous school and some help from his mother, he had developed a technique of attaching the blazer buttons so they did not tear the blazer material if they were pulled off. Satisfied with the result, he went downstairs to show his mother.

"The button is upside down, Adam."

He looked at all of the buttons carefully, and sure enough, the one he'd put on was wrong. He groaned. "It won't matter, Mum. No one will notice."

She just smiled and looked at him. "Here... give it to me, and I'll do it for you."

Adam just sighed and returned to his room to fix the problem. His mother was easygoing, but things had to be done properly or she would not rest until they were fixed. A couple of minutes later, he'd fixed the blazer.

Remembering that it would be the Foundation meeting the following evening, he spent some time practising with the card pack memory game. When his brain began to protest the workload, he stopped to switch on the PC to check first for messages on the Foundation website. He then connected to *Thorn World* to join in with the activities of Visiting Havoc.

All too soon, he was called to join the family for supper and the ambush that his mum had planned for Gilly. Her prediction of storms was correct and the cottage walls rattled to crash of Gilly slamming her bedroom door. The family was clearly informed that they hated her and that she would never be seen alive in braces. Adam thought about talking with his sister about how it had not been so bad having to wear braces, but he sensibly decided to leave that to the greater skills of his mother.

Chapter 11 Site Construction

James Buchanan had been a land agent in the area for over fifteen years. He was relieved his new tenant, Salmar Enterprises, had one month earlier taken on the old research station. Most of the negotiations had taken place remotely by telephone to the temporary London offices of Salmar Enterprises.

An international investment bank had purchased most of the uninhabited land along the coastline in this part of Scotland a few years before. The old research station was part of that land. Now, they were keen to see a return on their investment, but potential clients for places such as an isolated research station were few and far between. Until Salmar Enterprises turned up, James was beginning to despair, feeling he would never be able to rent the site. The easiest way to reach the site was by boat from the sea through a narrow channel into the loch. There was also a track to the research station, but it had fallen into disrepair and until recently could only be driven by a four-wheel-drive Land Rover or similar. There was no main power to the site and no telephone connection either.

Since Salmar Enterprises had taken on the site and the premises on an initial three-year rental, they had rebuilt the track to the station with many lorry loads of crushed rock and a bulldozer. They had also replaced the old failed electricity generators with two new powerful units. Work was in progress to restore the water supply from the small loch higher up the mountain, and they had already rebuilt the sewage plant. David Prentice, Chief Executive of Salmar Enterprises, had been a tough negotiator. Before he would agree to rent the site, Prentice had forced the investment bank to reduce the first year's rent payments to cover the cost of the necessary repairs. It was part of James' job to ensure that the costs to the landlords for repairs were not excessive. For example, when David Prentice insisted in building a strong, high, double-layer wire fence around the site to keep out wandering red deer, James had to insist that the cost was an improvement and not a repair.

Salmar Enterprises was setting the site up as a fish breeding research station and had built the fence high to keep the deer out. They had made it clear that the isolated location and clean waters of the loch was just what they wanted for their research work. Whatever the research was going to be, it was clear Salmar Enterprises had plenty of money behind them, as they had paid the telecom company to install an optical fibre cable to the site from the local phone exchange for telephones and network connection. In that case, "local" had required a five-mile cable to be run through countryside on the old telephone posts.

David Prentice's builders had already repaired the jetty at the edge of the loch, making it much easier to ship in new equipment by boat rather than to bring it via the new track. In the first couple of weeks after taking the site, they had already unloaded steel cables and metal drums from their workboat and stacked them on the jetty. Those drums and cable were now safely covered with tarpaulins to protect them from the weather.

James had parked his reliable old Shogun at the edge of the site. He had come for the monthly progress meeting with David Prentice and could see him standing on the jetty wearing a bright yellow workman's jacket and construction helmet. David was talking to another man who looked familiar to James. He waved to attract the attention of his client and then walked over to the jetty.

It amused James that David always insisted on wearing wraparound sunglasses, even in the worst weather. He liked dealing with David. The man always had a smile and was charming even during hard negotiations. The way he told jokes with his faint South African accent always brightened James' day, though he never really believed the story about a lion having bitten off the tip of David's little finger.

"Hi, James. How are you doing today? I guess you know Sergeant Maclean from the local police. I've been showing him around the site and telling him about the security arrangements. We will be doing some advanced research here, and we have some nosy competitors who would love to know what we are doing, so we have to be sure to be able to keep them out until help arrives."

"Aye, James, it looks very good to me—better security than our local jail almost. You must be pleased to see the old place being done up. With all these dark mountains and deep water, the place can look pretty gloomy. There is a long history around this loch, and some bad things have happened in the past. It is good to see it will now be put to good use. David has invited me to the official opening in three weeks. From the looks of the place, I don't think the police will ever have to visit here beyond that!"

"Well, Sergeant your men in blue will be welcome anytime, just so long as they call ahead to give us time to prepare a welcome. Maybe we could find a wee dram of your local malt whisky to keep the cold out."

"David, James, I must be off. Thank you for taking the time to show me around. It looks very impressive. Once you are open, I'll be in contact with you about who will be the key holders and contact numbers for this site in case there are any emergencies. You will be getting a visit from the local fire officer to check your fire safety and give you a certificate. You know, it will be very difficult to get a fire engine up here quickly even though your track is much improved."

"Ok, Sergeant. Thank you for coming. You have a good day now."

The men watched the policeman stride away to his police van and drive away, bumping along the track.

"It's a good idea to get Sergeant Maclean on your side. He can be a miserable old guy if you upset him. Now, David, can you show me around so I can check progress on the building works and confirm they are all as agreed on the plan with the landlords? Firstly, are you planning any changes?"

"Since you were last here, we have had a visit from our financial backers. They have asked us to increase security a little. It is nothing really major—just some extra cameras—and they want us to clear the ditch that runs outside the main fence. There are a couple of small trees we want to take down. We also want to put a sand bed between the inner and outer fences so we can see if any animals or intruders have jumped the outer fence."

"That sounds ok to me. If you would confirm that in, writing I'll approve it on behalf of the landlord."

David first took James to inspect the power centre containing power generators and the fuel storage tank. One of the generators was running, but an excellent silencing system had reduced the engine noise to a quiet rumble.

"Wow! Those are big beasts. How much will they generate?"

"I believe they are 2000 KVA for each of the pair. They are bigger than we needed, but we managed to get a special deal, as they are previously used. Each one provides enough power for the whole site. If one fails, the other will start automatically. We had to do some repair work on the containing bund wall around the foot of the fuel tanks. We found cracks that would cause leaks if there was a fuel spillage. We don't want any pollution in this beautiful countryside, do we?"

"Ok, well, let me know what the extra cost was, and we can negotiate how much that will affect the rent agreement."

James looked up and saw the inner fence behind the power centre. "Just a moment... can I see electrical insulators on the fence? Is it going to be electrified?"

"No, James. Don't worry, this is not Fort Knox. We bought the fencing second-hand from another site. It used to be electrified there, but we don't need that here. Buying second-hand has saved us thousands of pounds over the cost of a new fence built to the security standards we need. Let's go and see the main buildings. There are no changes to the plans, and work is going well."

David took the land agent into the largest building, which used to serve as a storage warehouse. A hallway with double doors had been added, as had a reception area, some offices, and an airlock. The walls and ceiling had been relined, and air conditioning had been installed. A new metal framework was standing on the floor. A network of different coloured pipes ran under the framework.

"James, as it shows in the plans, we will be installing the tanks on the metal framework. They will be used for the breeding research. The air coming into this room will be filtered and temperature controlled. We have the unused area at the back of the warehouse, but we have that sealed off temporarily, as there is too much space at the moment. Do you want to see it?"

"No. This all looks good to me. Shall we go and see the other buildings?"

"We'll have a look at the basement first. We won't be using it, but we have cleaned it out and given it a quick coat of paint and renewed some power and lighting wiring. They are still working down there."

"Ok. Let's have a quick look."

The last time James had been in the basement of the building, it had been filled with rubbish and dusty rubble from the previous tenants. It was now brightly lit and clean. The workmen in protective builders' overalls were chatting in a language he didn't recognise.

"You haven't got local guys doing the work?"

"No. We asked the local contractors to quote, but they were too expensive and could not do it in the timescale. These guys are Albanians. Most don't speak English, but their boss does. They are low cost and work hard."

"Ah, I see. Well, you certainly have improved things down here. I hope we are not being charged, as this was not on the plan."

"No, James. You won't see any cost for this. The work is superficial, but it makes it look so much better, and we need the building to be clean."

David took James to see the other buildings. Next to the warehouse was a smaller building. It had been previously been sleeping accommodation for twenty military personnel. Work had been done to clean out and redecorate the rooms, and kitchen equipment had been installed for a small canteen area. A new liquid propane gas tank had been installed to provide fuel and heating. The gas tank was set some twenty metres away from the building in a brick containment tank. The signs of ground disturbance that now hid the trench where the pipes had been laid were obvious.

"That gas tank is quite large. How did you manage to get it here?"

David pointed to the workboat tied up by the jetty. "Having sea access has been pretty useful for bringing in lots of the building materials. It is a good job that it is summer and calm seas, otherwise, the work would have been behind schedule and we would be delayed even further by the October storms when they arrive."

The remaining buildings were an old two-story office block and a vehicle garage with a small workshop, neither of which had any major repair work.

"James, we don't need these buildings, but we might tidy up one or two of the offices. If there are any major works, we will contact you and let you agree to the plans first. We have left the garage alone, and it's just full old junk. When things are quieter, we may tidy that up too."

David pointed out a weed covered flat area that formed a square contained by the other buildings. "We will be resurfacing the car park, but that is about all."

"Your company is going to make quite an improvement to this site, David. I'll send the landlords a report and photographs. I'm sure that if you want to extend the rental period, they will be more than willing take the improvements into account."

"Yes, that will be good. We will start real operations soon, and if they turn out well, we will probably need the buildings for a few more years. We will need approval and a licence from the agricultural ministry before we can transfer the breeding research into the loch itself. That process is likely to take a couple of years."

"David, thank you for taking your time to show me around. I see no problem with your plans and work. Perhaps you would like to join me for lunch in the Railway Hotel in town for lunch tomorrow, say twelve thirty?"

"Yes, James, that would be good. I will see you there."

David stood and watched the land agent climb into his Shogun and drive away down the track. He didn't like the thought of being seen in a public place such as a hotel, but it couldn't be avoided. He had to be careful to act normally and avoid giving the land agent any reason to be suspicious. Soon, the Albanian workers would be returned to their own country, and the next stage of the project would commence, and he had to be sure there were no curious eyes overlooking that activity. His meeting with the local police had been very successful; he knew there would be no problems from that quarter.

While in town the next day, he planned to call the one-time phone number to make a report to his bosses. Mobile phones could not get a signal this side of the mountain, which suited David's plans ideally.

Chapter 12 At the Company Hall

His eyes were screwed tight in concentration "… ace of diamonds, four of clubs, two of hearts, seven of spades."

"Good, Adam! That is fifteen cards you can remember reliably. You almost got to twenty cards, but you got one of them wrong. That will be your target for our next meeting… twenty cards memorised in less than five minutes. Practice the trick of forming story links between the cards. It helps you develop the memory techniques."

Bill Bradford was pleased with the progress of his new pupil. He taught memory techniques to most of the Foundation cadets in the region. It was a good sign when a cadet showed such early progress. This usually meant they would develop excellent memories, given suitable training. Some of the cadets would struggle for months but would show patience passing the basic tests.

"Now, Adam, remember the test last time about the cars outside the Hall? This time I want you to tell me what the total is if you add up all of the numbers in the number plates of the cars parked outside of the Hall tonight."

Adam paused for a while to recall a mental picture of what he saw when he had arrived at the Foundation Hall. It was as if he had taken a photograph of the scene. He performed some mental calculations and answered, "1,635, I think."

"Are you sure?"

He repeated the mental calculation. "Yes, Bill, I'm sure."

"Ok. That is good. You are right. Did you specifically memorise each of the number plates?"

"No. I just kind of remembered a picture of the scene when I arrived."

"So, this time you were prepared for my question?"

"Yes. It made it a lot easier."

"Good. Next time, concentrate on people rather than cars. We will be asking you questions the week following the night hike. For the playing cards memory test, your target for next week will be twenty cards. You will find this is a lot harder than ten or fifteen cards, but don't worry. We are just helping you train your brain to use its capability to memorise things. It will take some time to reach even 50 percent of your real potential. Eventually, you will properly memorise what you see without even thinking about it. This will be important, Adam, for when we start teaching you observation and surveillance skills."

"Is it true you can memorise a map by just looking at it?"

"Well, I can remember the main things, but it takes a lot of practice to reach that level. You will find the memory techniques you learn here useful for your school stuff and exams. As part of the Foundation training, they also want to help you to excel at school, but you will still need to work hard academically and listen to your teachers. I want to introduce you to a new game. You will probably play this in your squad when there is a gap in the schedule. It is called the memory tray."

Bill lifted a cloth covered tray onto the table top. "There are fifteen items on this tray. When I take the cover off, you will have fifteen seconds to memorise them. Are you ready?"

Adam nodded, and Bill removed the cloth, exposing the objects on the tray, and started timing with his watch. After fifteen seconds, he recovered the tray.

Adam expected the man would ask him questions about the tray, but he didn't. Instead, he put his hand in his pocket and pulled out a brown paper envelope. He then pulled out a folded document, opened the document, turned it over, and passed it to Adam. "I want you to read the first three paragraphs aloud. This is one of my old credit card bills, and you will be reading the terms and conditions."

The printed text had a tiny font and was printed in a pale blue colour. Adam had to concentrate hard to focus and read the complicated text aloud. When he'd finished the task, he passed the paper back to Bill.

"Ok, Adam. How many items were there on the tray?"

Adam almost replied 'fifteen' without thinking but then paused and recalled the mental image of the tray and the objects. "There were sixteen items on the tray. Do you want me to list them, Bill?"

"No. Just tell me what was to the right of the postage stamp."

"It was a one-pound coin."

"What was the value on the postage stamp?"

"There wasn't one. It was just a first-class stamp."

"That is excellent, Adam. It seems you already have a good memory and good observational skills. It is now time for you to meet your assignment tutor to discuss your assignment. Her name is Grace Richards, and you will find her in Meeting Room No 2. I'll see you in a couple of weeks."

Adam stood and almost saluted Bill but remembered just in time that the man was a non-uniformed instructor of the Foundation. "Cheers, Bill. I'll see you."

Having done that, he rushed off to the meeting room and knocked on the door.

"Come on in."

Adam opened the door and went in the room. Sitting at the table was a slim, grey-haired Afro-Caribbean lady dressed in a smart black dress. She stood and shook hands with Adam. He was surprised at her height; she was almost 1.9 metres tall. "Please sit down, young man."

She guided him to a chair at the table. On the table were a door lock and some keys. It looked like a high-security lever lock. Next to it were some lock picks.

"You are Adam Cranford, I believe. Please call me Grace. I am employed by the Foundation to teach cadets about security. We select some of the cadets to undergo full training by the way of assignments. Your assignment is to acquire the skills of a locksmith. Have you had any problems with the assignment package that was sent to you?"

"No. I've been able to cut a key that works and can also pick the Yale type lock with no problems. I was really surprised they can be picked so easily."

"How long does it take you to pick a cylinder lock now?"

"About fifteen seconds, ma'am."

"That's good, but please call me Grace. By the way, when do you have to start your next session?"

Adam looked at his wrist; his watch was gone. He was confused, as he rarely took his watch off.

Grace opened her hand on top of the desk. "I think you will be needing this."

The boy grinned and picked up his watch from Grace's hand. "I didn't notice you do that. It must have been when you shook hands with me."

"I think you may need this later as well." Grace held out a Foundation record book.

Adam patted his back pocket. Sure enough, his own Cadet Record Book was missing. He grabbed the book and slid it back into his pocket.

"Yes, young man, I have other skills. If you do well in the locksmith assignment, I have no doubt the Foundation will ask me to train you in those too. They normally do that for the locksmiths. First, though, we should concentrate on the next type of lock, the lever lock."

"Aren't you going to check my work on the cylinder lock?"

Grace gave Adam a steady look. "Do I need to?"

"No."

"Good. I'm happy to work on the basis of trust. Just let me know when you have problems with any part of the assignment, ok?"

"Cool."

Grace then showed him the inner workings of a lever lock and some techniques for the picking of that type of lock. The lock picks she used were a different shape from the ones used for cylinder locks, but the general principles were the same. As in the assignment pack Adam had received, she had a training lock with a transparent cover. It made the process a lot more obvious.

After demonstrating the techniques, she let Adam try on the training lock. He fairly quickly got used to the technique.

"Try again... wearing this." She held out a blindfold.

Adam took it and put it on himself. She guided his hands to the tools and the training lock. "This is weird. It is more difficult because I can't see what I'm doing, but in a way, it is easier because I can visualise the inside of the lock."

"Yes, Adam, the secret is to project your mind inside the lock and forget the outside world. Don't worry about the complexity of the lock. Just visualise yourself inside the lock, lifting the individual levers."

Soon the time came to finish the session. As Adam stood to leave, she lifted a carrier bag from under the table. "This is the next part of your assignment. Have fun, young man."

Adam left the meeting room and returned to his squad room. He noticed other members of the squad returning from their own assignment training sessions.

As they entered the room, Brian, their Squad Leader, looked up from the chair where he was seated and reading a magazine. "Ah, you ladies have finally returned from your life of leisure in your assignment training. Well, I think it is time for you to get your lazy bones into some action. We are going to play Monkeys for the next twenty minutes before the final assembly."

Adam had never heard of the game. He turned and whispered to Barry, who was sitting next to him. "What's 'Monkeys', Barry?"

"Oh, you will love this, Adam, though you will feel it tomorrow morning when you wake up."

"Davies, you seem to know so much about this. Why don't you carry the rope and kit out and be the first across? Get moving," ordered the Squad Leader.

Barry went to a storage cupboard and took a couple of bundled climbing ropes, helmets, some karabiners, and a couple of harnesses. Leading the way for the rest of the squad, Barry went into the main assembly hall. At one point, a thick rope hung from the steel ceiling beam close to a wall. Across the floor, a similar thick rope hung from the ceiling.

Scarcely pausing to uncoil the climbing rope, Barry shot up the thick hanging rope hand over hand. When he reached the top, he threaded one end of the climbing rope through a large steel ring mounted on the ceiling beam. As he did this, one of the other boys, Alan Williamson, took the other end of the climbing rope and dashed across to the other side of the floor. With equal agility, he swarmed up the thick rope and threaded the climbing rope through a similar steel ring on the other end of the ceiling beam. Both boys simultaneously slid down their thick hanging rope, taking their end of the climbing rope with them. When Alan reached the ground, he quickly tied off the climbing rope in a solid eyebolt set in the wall close to the ground. Barry took his end of the climbing rope and pulled all the slack climbing rope through until there was a taut rope at ceiling height running under the steel ceiling beam. The other boys helped maintain tension as Barry tied off the rope in another steel eyebolt mounted in the wall.

The Squad Leader picked up a climbing harness and handed it to Barry. "Cranford, watch this carefully. I think you are the only boy in the squad who has not done this before. We have enough time for everyone to go across twice if we get a move-on."

Barry, already wearing a helmet, stepped into and strapped the climbing harness onto his waist. Taking the other climbing rope, he uncoiled it and tied a figure eight knot in the end. Using a karabiner, he clipped the rope onto the climbing harness. Adam's heart sunk as he began to realise what was going to happen. He had a great fear of heights, and the ceiling looked awfully high and the floor looked very hard.

Barry climbed up the thick hanging rope without pausing. When he reached the top, hanging on with one hand, he quickly clipped a karabiner onto the taut horizontal climbing rope. He then clipped the rope from his waist into the karabiner on the horizontal rope. Below him, Alan took hold of the climbing rope dangling from Barry above and wrapped it around himself in a rock-climbing belay position.

"Cranford, why do you think Davies did that?"

"To act as a safety rope in case he falls off?"

"Yeah. Now watch this."

Brian blew a whistle once. Above him, Barry stretched out further along the ceiling beam with his free hand and grasped part of the beam. Then, hanging horizontally with his back to the floor, he hooked his toes just above the beam where it joined the wall. With graceful monkey-like action, Barry climbed across the ceiling hanging under the beam. His hands and feet did not pause in the continuous motion as he made his way across. Below him, Alan held the safety rope, walking in time with Barry as he made his way across. When he reached the other side, Barry slid down the thick hanging rope and unclipped the safety rope from his climbing harness. Barry exchanged positions with Alan. Alan swarmed up the wall and across under the ceiling beam with an agility which matched Barry's monkey-like actions.

Adam watched fearfully as the rest of the squad climbed up the wall rope, across the ceiling, and down the other side. None of them were as agile as Barry and Alan, but all got there after some encouragement from the rest of the squad. His turn had come. The ceiling beam five metres above him looked impossibly high. "Sergeant Harrison, I don't think I can do this. I hate heights. I even get worried on ladders."

"Yes, you can make it, Cranford. Just do your best. I'll be holding your safety rope. Get the helmet and harness on."

Adam sighed and pulled the harness on and flipped the helmet onto his head.

Barry was there helping him and checking that the equipment was safe. "Go on, Adam. You will be ok. I was scared, too, the first time I did it."

Adam took the thick hanging rope in his hands, took a deep breath, and glanced at the rest of the squad. They were urging him on. He started to climb the rope. He was not used to this. He wondered how Barry seemed to make it look so easy. After a struggle, he reached the top of the rope. He looked out at the beam. The paint on it looked slippery. He stretched out a hand. He knew if he looked down, he would fall off and crash on the floor below. His hands were sweaty. The steel beam felt slippery. Holding his weight with his legs on the thick hanging rope and the hand on the beam, he released his other hand from the thick rope and stretched out to reach further along the beam. He made it. He clamped his hands tight and kicked his legs free from the rope and swung one up to hook it on the beam, but he couldn't do it. He tried again. This time, he almost did it, but his foot swung free again. His muscles were beginning to ache. He could feel his fingers slipping on the painted steel. He scrabbled with his legs to try and catch the vertical hanging rope, with no luck. He could hear his squad cheering below, urging him on. He was now hanging above the hard floor, supported just by his two hands. He looked down, and a surge of panic swept through him. Panicking, he swung his legs again to try and hook the beam. Suddenly, he felt his arm begin to shake, and then one hand slipped off the beam. His other hand was too tired to hold him. He fell, hurtling towards the floor. There was a collective groan from the boys below.

With a smooth, elastic jerk at his waist, he felt the climbing harness stop his fall. He was swinging horizontally face-up, about two metres below the beam. Barry Harrison yelled up, "Well done, Cranford! That was a good attempt for the first time. I'm going to lower you down now."

The climbing rope supporting him vibrated under tension as he was lowered to the ground. The hands of the boys greeted and supported Adam as he reached ground level.

Brian Harrison spoke, "Ok, let's see the rest of you go across again. Cranford can take a rest for a while."

The remainder of the squad each took their turns and repeated the monkey crawl under the ceiling beam. When they'd finished, the Squad Leader turned to Adam. "Do you want to try again?"

"No, sorry. I'm absolutely shattered, and my arms feel like lead. I'll do it next time. Is that alright, Sergeant?"

"Yes, no problem, Cranford. At least you gave it a good try. Don't worry. Everyone has problems the first time."

He signalled to Alan and Barry to tidy away the rest of the equipment and then turned to the rest of the squad. "Get your street clothes on for the final assembly. Don't forget the night hike next weekend."

As they changed out of their uniforms, Barry came alongside and smirked. "So, what did you think of that then? I hold the squad record of going across under the monkey beam five times without stopping."

Adam thumped him playfully on the upper arm. "You idiot. You could have told me you were an expert at it. I was absolutely terrified. I hate heights. I'm not going to let it beat me though. You must be really strong to do that, but you don't look as though you do a lot of training."

"If you want to practice, just let me know. If you ask Chalky and tell him why, they will let

you in the Hall outside of normal meeting times. You don't need big bulky muscles to do the monkey crawl. It is just stamina and technique. If you just hang there, your muscles get choked up with lactic acid, and you go weak or shaky. Once you get your feet up there on the beam, they take some of your weight. I've seen one guy stop halfway along under the beam and take his whole weight on his feet while hanging upside down. It was just so he could rest his arms. He carried on after that."

"Ok, deal! I'll call you if I can get the Hall."

Chapter 13 The Barbecue

The following morning when Adam woke up, he realised Barry had been absolutely right the previous night. He was really stiff in his arms, shoulders, and stomach muscles. He had to roll out of bed and make his way to the shower like a creaky old man. His muscles eased a bit under the hot shower. He remembered as he stood under the hot stream of water that it was the day of Darren's family barbecue. The invite had said *casual clothes,* so he guessed clean jeans and a white t-shirt would be fine.

It was nine a.m. before he finally arrived at the breakfast table. Just his mother and father were sitting at the table drinking coffee. He grabbed a box of cereal and sat in his usual place at the table. As he poured the cereal into his dish, he realised his mother and father were quiet and watching him intently. He waved at them. "Hi, folks. Good morning. Is there anyone home?"

His dad picked up a cream coloured envelope from the kitchen table and waved it at Adam.

"Adam, is there something you should have been telling us?"

"What?" The teen was puzzled. So far as he knew, he had done nothing wrong recently.

"It seems as though we are the last to know. Mrs. Embleton has written to us to tell us that our son is some kind of hero, and we didn't even know about it."

It suddenly dawned on Adam that his principal had said she would be writing to his parents about his part in the capture of the fuel thieves. He'd either forgotten or preferred not to tell his mother because he didn't want a big fuss about the episode. He blushed at the thought of having forgotten to tell his parents. "Oh, that. It was nothing really. I told her I didn't want a fuss."

His father read from the letter:

He acted with great courage and initiative in a dangerous situation... He prevented injury to junior children...He prevented the theft of valuable school property and aided the arrest of dangerous criminals... He refused public recognition ... We are proud to have him at our school ...

"Amanda, we have bred ourselves a Grade A, Class 1 nutcase for a son. Adam, you had better tell us the full details. We will decide if it was a case of 'nothing really'."

Adam told them the full story. His parents looked concerned when he told them about how the driver had attacked him, but Adam emphasised that he was only protecting Simon or he would have run away.

His mother came around to his side of the table and gave him a big hug. "It is good that you are a hero, but you should be much more careful in such dangerous situations. I'd hate to see you injured."

"Yes, Mom. I was just in the wrong place at the right time."

"I suppose you will need a lift to the barbecue this afternoon?" asked his father.

"Yes, please, Dad."

"Your mother has to go to town to get the weekly shopping done, but I guess I can manage to give you a lift without too much trouble. I'm not working today."

It was hot and sunny in the early afternoon when Gordon Cranford's car arrived at the front gate of the Nichols' house. It would almost be better to call the place an estate. It had previously been a farm but was now converted for residential purposes. There were two entrance gates with a long sweeping gravel drive joining the gates to the house. Set off to one side of the drive were some stables, and across the other side were a pair of double garages. A Bentley, Range Rover, and a Ferrari could be seen inside the garages. The main house was big and imposing. It looked as though it had many bedrooms. The high automatic gates were normally locked, but Gordon was able to follow in behind a delivery van.

As they arrived outside the house, a young man approached their old Ford Estate car. "Parking is just down the road about 100 metres. We have arranged parking in one of the farmer's fields. If you are delivering catering, just park temporarily by the garages when you unload and then go to the car park."

Adam's father waved the invitation card Adam had had been given at the young man.

"Oh, Sorry, sir. You are guests? If you are just dropping off, here is fine. Otherwise, give me your keys, and I'll park the car for you."

Adam jumped out of the car. "Ok, Dad, I'll call you when it is time to be picked up. Thanks for the lift!"

The parking attendant pointed Adam to the back of the main house. "The family is out back. If you just go around and make yourself known, someone will look after you."

As Adam went around the back of the house, he saw that a large white marquee tent had been erected on a large lawn. He could see a drinks bar at one end inside the marquee and tables laden with breads, salads, dips, cold meat, cheeses, and fruits. Uniformed waiters were assisting the guests. A small band of musicians was standing on a small stage assembling their equipment. In the centre of the marquee was a large wooden dance floor laid over the grass of the lawn.

Outside the marquee and to one side were two large, smoky barbecue ranges, each with a white uniformed chef at work behind them. Next to the barbecue ranges was a longer unit with a chimney spouting smoke. Inside the unit, Adam could see a large pig roasting on a spit.

Adam estimated there were at least fifty guests already milling around by the marquee. There was a more tightly grouped knot of people by the bar. From that group, a smartly dressed, middle-aged blonde lady broke away and walked over towards Adam. "Young man, I'm Mrs. Nichols. Can I help you? You seem a bit lost."

"I'm Adam Cranford. Darren invited me to the barbecue."

Adam could almost feel the scanning gaze of Darren's mother as she cast a glance over his jeans and t-shirt. He felt very scruffy compared to the smart clothes of the other people at the party. This was no ordinary family barbecue.

"Oh, I see. Yes, he did mention he was inviting a couple of extra boys from school. Well, you are most welcome I'm sure. There is plenty of food and drink, so just help yourself. Darren and the other boys are by the pool. I guess he can find you a spare bathing suit."

"Errm, excuse me, but where is the pool?"

Mrs. Nichols waved a heavily gold ringed hand in the direction of some trees behind the marquee. "Over there, my dear. Now, if you will excuse me, I have to go and look after the other guests."

She turned and walked back to the other guests, leaving Adam alone. He set off to find the swimming pool. Once he got to the other side of the marquee, he could hear the shrieks and splashing from children playing in and around the pool. It was a large twenty-five-metre concrete pool sunk down into the garden. At one end was a large open patio with white plastic garden furniture. To the side of the patio was a pool house. Younger children played in the shallow water under the watchful eye of a lifeguard dressed in a red jacket and shorts. He saw Darren and the others lounging under sun umbrellas in a corner of the patio. There was a small group of teen girls sitting and relaxing under the sun at a nearby table. They were all dressed in beach and swimwear.

On seeing Adam approaching, one of the girls nudged Darren, who looked up and called out, "Hi, Adam! You were able to come then? That's great. We'd best get you a drink and get you out of those clothes. We've got some spare suits in the pool house. Go have a look in the basket in there and grab yourself a towel. I'll get you a drink while you're changing. What do you want? A beer or lager, perhaps?"

Adam hesitated. He was not used to drinking alcohol apart from when he some-times had wine at a meal with his parents. He could see that the other boys had beers, and a beer would help him fit in better. "Err, thanks Darren. I think I'll just start with a cold lemonade, ice and some cranberry juice if you have it."

"Sure thing! It will be here when you get back," responded Darren as he picked up a telephone and dialled. When the call was answered, he ordered Adam's drinks and some extra drinks for the rest of the boys.

Adam went into the pool house and found the basket containing swimming gear. All of it was new and still wrapped in the plastic sales packaging. There was a large pile of neatly folded large soft cotton towels. On the floor was a box containing flip-flop sandals. He could see the other boys' and girls' clothes in heaps on a bench by the wall. There was nowhere obvious to get changed, so Adam selected what he needed, moved to a darker part of the pool house, and changed into swimming trunks. He left his clothes in a pile on the bench with the others. With a towel over his shoulder and flip-flops on his feet, he padded out to join the other boys.

Darren was seated at a table under a sun umbrella. Simon and a couple of girls were seated with him. There was another group of boys lazing in the sun on flat loungers closer to the pool. John Nelson was amongst them. He gave Adam a sour glance.

"Come on, Adam. Don't stand around looking like a lost soul. Grab one of the chairs and join us. The drinks will be here soon," Darren said as he leaned over and pulled a spare chair up to the table with a scraping noise across the floor tiles.

Just as Adam sat down, a waiter appeared with a large tray containing drinks, including Adam's lemonade and cranberry in a tall glass of ice surrounded by almost a dozen bottles of beer. They all glistened with condensation. Darren signalled to the waiter to serve the beers to all of the teen boys. The girls already had full drinks glasses and ice filled jugs of juice on their tables.

"You already know Simon. Meet Sally and Deepa. Sally, Deepa, this is Adam. He has recently joined us at Holliston's. Sally and Deepa go to St. Josephine's down the road from Holliston's."

Adam, having a sister like Gilly, was not at all shy around girls. He smiled at them. "Hi, everyone," he said and then sat in the chair.

He could see by the way Sally sat closely to Darren and glanced at him that she was his girlfriend. Sally was a beautiful, slim, blonde, blue-eyed girl. Her friend Deepa was clearly of Indian origin and was dark-haired and had a dark complexion. Simon was sitting between the two girls, clearly relaxed and laid back with some cool sunglasses.

"You haven't seen much sun recently, have you?" commented Darren, looking at Adam's pale body. Darren had an all-over pale tan. "I go sailing quite a lot on the weekends with Father on his boat down at Cowes, so I get plenty of sun. During the holidays, we will be sailing around the Greek Islands. I might even let Sally come along if she behaves. She might even get an all-over tan." He grunted as his girlfriend dug a knuckle into his ribs.

"He is such a pig, Adam. You really don't want to mix with his kind." Darren silenced his girlfriend by pulling her lips to his briefly.

"Are you getting away, Simon?" asked Adam.

"Probably. I think my dad is going to some research camp on Spitzbergen. He'll want me to come, so we'll probably be camping on volcanic ash and eaten alive by midges and bugs. I don't suppose I'll get much of a tan, even though it will be twenty-four-hour daylight."

"So, what does your father do then, Simon?"

"Oh he's just a research scientist—some kind of thing to do with DNA of arctic bacteria. It's really boring, Adam."

Darren jumped up from his chair. "This is all too serious. Who's going swimming? Adam, have you ever played water polo before? Come on, girls, you too. You can put bathing caps on."

"No, Darren. I haven't played water polo, but if you explain the rules, I guess I can try. I can swim ok."

Darren shouted at the other boys. "Come on, you lot! You can be the opposition in water polo. Once we've eaten, you will all be feeling too heavy to swim. I won't be able to play, though, because of my wrist, so I can be the umpire." He held up his wrist which was still enclosed in a plastic support brace.

The other boys grumbled but got up. Darren was always the life and soul of the party and was difficult to resist. Adam was standing at the edge of the pool dipping his foot to feel the temperature of the water as John Nelson brushed past to bombshell in the pool. Adam felt the little push from the bully but kept his balance. Nelson surfaced, facing Adam, looking to see if there would be a reaction from him. Darren had seen this and started moving to intervene. Adam didn't respond. He just did a standing dive from the edge of the pool and plopped into the water at the deep end with barely a splash. From the dive, he swam the length of the pool underwater using a dolphin stroke without surfacing. Reaching the other end, he turned without surfacing and swam back to the deep end where he surfaced and calmly trod water. He ignored Nelson. Darren just smiled, relieved that an argument had been avoided. He hadn't wanted to invite John Nelson, but Mr. Nelson was a senior partner in his father's Hedge Fund company, so there had been no choice in the matter when barbeque invitations were being sent out.

It was an improvised game, as there were no nets into which the youths could score goals. The lifeguard roped off the deep end of the pool to keep the younger children away. Darren declared that given the relative small size of the pool area, they had to play that the offside rule would not apply. They divided into two teams of five. Adam joined up with Simon, Sally, Deepa, and one of the other girls called Anita. Deepa and Anita were strong swimmers, while Simon and Sally could swim reasonably well. They chose Deepa as their team captain. The first team to score three goals would win. Deepa's wore swim caps and were playing against an all-boy team. John Nelson was on the opposing team and was chosen as their captain.

While the teams were getting ready, Deepa showed Adam and Simon how to do the eggbeater stroke that would give them lift in the water while staying in the same position. Adam had never tried it before, so it took a few attempts before he could angle his feet correctly to get some good lift. Adam was chosen as the goalie for his side.

The boys on the opposing team knew they would win this easily, as two of their members were on the school swimming team. They had not realised that the girls had practised in their school synchronised swimming club for a couple of years.

Darren blew the whistle, and both teams got in the pool at the side by their goals, ready to swim off against each other. Both teams had the same configuration: two on offense, two defending, and one at goal. Darren blew his whistle and dropped the ball into the water at the edge of the pool halfway between the two teams.

There was a splashing dash as the offense pairs rushed from their side of the pool to try and capture it. John's partner beat Deepa to the ball and swam, dribbling it to attack the goal Adam defended. The attacker swam too close to Sally. She struck with the speed of a praying mantis, snatching the ball and passing it to Deepa, who was ready. Pausing for a brief moment, she looked around for support, ignoring the boys rushing towards her. Then, with a casual flick of her wrist, Deepa scored a goal.

At the next start, the boys gained control of the ball again. This time, they were more cautious of Sally and got closer to the goal guarded by Adam. John faked a shot at the goal, and Adam dived in anticipation. With the way left clear, John was easily able to score a goal.

As Darren retrieved the ball, John passed by Adam and hissed, "Well, new boy, it shows you really don't know how to fit in with us, doesn't it? You were easily fooled by a simple dummy pass. I guess coming from a comprehensive school, the only sport you know is football."

Adam blushed slightly but said nothing. Like most bullies, John Nelson had tuned into the fear of his victim. Adam had feared he would not fit in with the wealthy, privileged people here. Darren and Simon seemed ok, but he wasn't sure about the others. Simon noticed the event between the two boys but hadn't heard what had been said by John. He saw the change of expression on his friend's face and worried that John was attempting to bully again. He was tempted to swim over and find out, but Darren had already restarted play after the last goal. Once again, the boys had won possession. Sally attempted to grab the ball but was blocked from reaching the opponent by John.

As they lined up to attempt another goal, they did not see Anita sneak in close. The boy launched the shot. Anita intercepted and knocked the ball to Simon. The two offense players converged on Simon, who hurriedly passed the ball to Sally. Just as she started to swim towards the other goal, John charged in and dunked her head underwater and took possession of the ball. He shot at the goal. It was deflected by Adam, who knocked the ball into open water. John rushed across and grabbed the ball and lined up another shot at goal. Adam was ready again, although one of the offense opponents was trying to obstruct him. Adam suddenly felt a painful kick to his upper leg from the opponent boy in front of him. Distracted, he missed the shot that John made, and a second goal was scored. Simon and Sally appealed to Darren, but he had not seen the foul, so he allowed the goal.

At the next start, Deepa took possession of the ball and raced towards the opposition goal. John caught her and dunked her head underwater. Once again, Darren missed the foul. John turned and raced towards the other goal, intending to score. He avoided Sally by pushing her off. No one noticed Deepa dive under the water and swim towards her own goal. John lined up another shot. Adam was defending, carefully watching John's eyes. Suddenly, John let out a roar and dropped the ball on the water. He reached down in the water with his arms, but it was too late. Deepa was swimming away. She surfaced and chucked a dark piece of clothing on the side of the pool. John was cursing and swearing as everybody realised what Deepa had done to John. Darren was laughing as he scooped up John's swimming shorts from the side and chucked them back to the embarrassed boy. This time, Darren had seen the foul, so he awarded a penalty shot to John's team. Despite Adam's best efforts, John scored the winning goal.

They all climbed out of the pool. John's team was running a victory lap around the pool while Sally was giving Darren hell for being such a poor referee, having missed all the fouls done by John's team.

At that point, Darren's mother appeared and told them they should come and grab some food, as the barbecue was ready to be served. The lifeguard made everyone get out of the water and closed the pool. The young children were herded back to their parents. The teens went to the marquee and were served food before returning with their loaded plates to their poolside tables. Darren ordered more drinks, and this time, Adam joined them with a beer. They sat relaxing, enjoying their foods and drinks, while ignoring the boasts from John's winning polo team.

"You swim well, Adam. Do you have a pool at home to practice in every day?" asked Deepa.

Adam frowned a little at the assumption that he had the same lifestyle as these other teens. "No, just swimming in the local Council pool. My mum started me on swimming lessons when I was five years old, and I was on the local club team for a while. I won some badges."

Adam thought it best to change the subject. "Hey, Darren, when will your wrist get better? Or are you going to milk it as an excuse for ages?"

"I'm going to drag it out as long as possible, mate. No, really though, the physiotherapist said I should go gentle on it about a week longer and then she will reassess it."

"What did you do to it?"

Sally burst out laughing and interrupted. "He learned he is not as good at horse riding as I am, Adam. We were going over jumps, and he fell off."

"Oh. What did your folks say?"

"Oh, they were truly sympathetic. They said I still had one good hand I could use for brushing down my horse when I got out of hospital."

Their conversation was interrupted when Adam detected a familiar smell—a strong, sweet aroma. He looked over at the other group of boys. They were smoking, and it wasn't tobacco. He knew the smell of cannabis from his previous school where some of the older boys would use it in the hidden parts of the school.

Darren groaned. "Do you guys have to do that here? Mum will go crazy if she sees you."

"Chill, man. She's not going to see anything. Hey, new boy, are you big enough to try some?" John Nelson offered a reefer in the direction of Adam.

"No, thanks. It rots your lungs and turns you schizo."

"Suit yourself."

The drugs usage killed the good mood at for the boys and girls seated around Darren's table. He stood up. He was seething at John's behaviour but knew there was not a lot he could do at the moment. "Hey, folks, let's get changed and go join the main barbecue party. It looks as though it might get a bit cloudy soon."

The group around Darren's table went to the pool house to change out of their swimming kit. The girls changed at one end of the room under their towels, and the boys at the other end.

"I'm sorry about those idiots. They get stupid at every party, and my parents still invite them," Darren explained to Adam as they got dressed.

After he'd dressed, Adam remembered he'd left his beer by the table and went to pick it up.

John stood up, swaying slightly, when Adam approached. "Isn't that a bit strong for you, little boy? Are you sure your mommy won't be cross with you?"

"Nelson, it is none of your business. You look stoned. Why don't you go somewhere and sleep it off?"

Adam turned to leave, but John grabbed his shoulder to turn him back. "Not so fast, Cranford. I'm still talking to you. It is rude to leave without saying goodbye."

Adam ignored him and released the restraining hand, then turned to walk towards the others waiting by the pool. He suddenly felt a tap on his ankle, and his foot tangled with the other. He could not avoid falling and tilted over into the pool. As he fell, he knew he should not have turned his back on John. It was no great danger, as he could swim well and it was the deep end of the pool. He just climbed out of the pool with his wet clothes sticking to him. John Nelson had rejoined his group of friends, and they were just laughing at Adam. Adam knew he could easily deal with John and his friends if necessary, but he remembered the words of his aikido Sensei, forbidding him to use the skills in revenge or in anger.

Darren was rushing over to break up what looked to be a fight developing. He knew his parents would never believe John had caused the problems.

Adam saw Darren and stopped. "Darren, I can't say too much about your choice of family friends, but I think it is about time I left this barbecue. Can I borrow a phone? I don't suppose my mobile is working right now, and I need to call my dad for a lift back."

"Adam, this is stupid. He's just being an ass. You can borrow some of my clothes. Come into the house with me and have a shower and then dry off properly."

"Darren, I've had enough. Thanks for the invite, but this is just not working out. If you can just point me to a phone, I'd like to call for a ride home. If Nelson is around me much longer, you are going to need to call an ambulance. He's not learned his lesson yet."

Darren gave a resigned shrug of his shoulders. "Look, come with me. I'll get someone to drive you home. I think Father's driver is around. He won't mind giving you a lift."

Darren led Adam away, glaring over his shoulder at John Nelson. He had to ask his father about the driver. When his father asked what had had happened, Darren explained there had been an accident at the pool and that Adam needed to go home.

As Adam was shown into the Range Rover by the driver, he overheard a comment by Darren's mother. "He didn't stay very long. He didn't seem at all comfortable with us."

Adam flushed with anger and sank back into the seat of the car as he was driven home. He hadn't heard Darren's angry response to his mother. "*Your* guest, John Nelson, was not exactly hospitable either, Mother. He pushed Adam into the pool, fully clothed. He's absolute trouble, and we should never invite him again."

Chapter 14 Night Hike

The following school week was a quiet one for Adam. Despite the best efforts of Darren and Simon to cheer him up, he felt a bit distant and removed from the other boys in his class. He'd noted there was now a total breakdown of communication between Darren and John Nelson, but it gave him no real satisfaction. He knew John was a total idiot anyway. Adam's clothes had soon been washed and dried. After some drying in an airing cupboard, his mobile phone was now working properly. He just felt there was a divide between him and the other boys from rich families. He decided the best thing to do was to get on with his schoolwork and make that a success. There were only a couple of weeks left before the summer holidays, and then he could forget about school altogether.

The end of the week came soon enough, and it was time for the Foundation Night Trek. As he bundled into the Foundation mini bus, both parents and his sister were there to see him off.

"You will be careful won't you darling?" asked his mother.

"Yes, Mum, I always am careful. Gilly, if I die on the hike, you will pass on my best wishes to Bill, won't you?"

Gilly squealed and pushed her brother onto the bus. "Go on, Porky. Be sure to call me for help when you get lost in the dark up to your knees in mud. I could do with a good laugh."

When the mini bus arrived at Foundation Hall, Adam could see the other boys milling around a couple of larger buses and loading equipment onto a four-wheel-drive lorry. He quickly found the other members of his squad.

"Hi, Adam. We've got kit inspection in five minutes in the main hall," said Barry.

They rushed in to lay out their equipment on the floor in the approved layout on top of their waterproof ponchos. Brian Harrison called his squad to order and then inspected each item of their kits and also the uniforms they were wearing. "Cranford, you need some practice at laying equipment out properly," he said. Then, he turned to someone else. "Williamson, go to the stores and swap out your compass. This one is damaged."

The Squad Leader was soon satisfied with their equipment. He demonstrated the preferred way of packing it into their rucksacks, explaining as he went along. They quickly packed their equipment into their rucksacks and stood ready.

"Pay attention, squad. The coach trip will be approximately 175 miles, and the journey will take about four hours. Make sure you go to the toilet before we set off. These coaches do not have on-board toilets. Anyone who suffers from travel sickness and does not have their travel pills, come and see me. Right, now carry on and go get on the coach. Make sure your rucksack is loaded on your coach in the place allocated by the driver. We will be unloading in the dark."

Adam found a seat next to Barry. Within ten minutes, the coaches were loaded and roll calls were taken. The lorry had already departed while they were having kit inspection.

"Have you done these night hikes before, Barry?"

"Yeah. It's not that difficult, though we usually get lost on the way. With a bit of luck, we might get there before the pubs close."

"What, they let you drink beer?"

"Not exactly, but you do get very thirsty, and there is no one keeping an eye on what we do. I always bring some money in case we need 'supplies'."

"Will we hike the distance in time?"

"Yeah. It will be dead easy, Adam. You are lucky this is not a third-weight hike."

"What's that?"

"Your pack is filled until it weighs one-third your body weight. That's like sixteen kilograms. They had us hike twenty-five kilometres with third weight last time. It's ok to start, but towards the end of the route, your pack gets so heavy that you want to lose things along the way. They are crafty, though, because they reweigh your pack at the end of the hike."

"Wow! That's like fifteen miles."

"Yeah. The Foundation may pay for lots of things and give you loads of training, but they really expect you to work hard. They say they want you to stretch your limits and achieve what you didn't think was possible."

"Like being a super monkey, you mean? I still can't believe you can go across the roof beam five times in one go. How did you get into the Foundation, Barry? Are you the nephew of some superhero?"

"As far as I know, a friend of my dad recommended me to the Foundation, and they said yes."

"So, is your dad's friend someone famous in the banks in the City of London or royalty?"

"No. He just runs a local pharmacy in a nearby town."

The boys chatted while the bus continued towards the destination. A lot of the route was boring motorway, though there was a brief stop at a motorway rest and service area along the route. Barry drifted off to sleep after a while, so Adam just watched the scenery outside the bus window. Gradually, the evening light faded until it got too dark to see much outside the bus.

Adam jerked his head suddenly and realised he must have fallen asleep too. The bus had stopped, and its interior lighting had been switched on. It was dark outside the bus.

One of the instructors walked down the aisle between the rows of seat and handed Brian a large brown envelope containing maps. "Harrison, it is time for Blue Squad to leave the comforts of this bus and go walk some of their fat off. Let me see your equipment checklist while your boys are unloading."

"Come on, squad, you heard the man! Get your lazy tails out of those seats and unload our rucksacks. We are all going on a little walk."

To the jeers of the other boys about how they would get lost and need rescuing, Brian Harrison's Blue Squad tumbled out of the bus into the darkness.

"Ok, grab your kit and line up over there for buddy inspection. Remember to put your reflective safety tabards on over your jackets. This is not a covert hike, and we may be on roads."

The boys pulled on jackets, head torches, and rucksacks, then checked each other's equipment and clothing. That was done quickly, and they followed by standing at ease in a line at the side of the road. The instructor approved the equipment list, checked the seal on the pouch held by Brian containing the GPS unit, and then left. The bus door slammed shut, the engine started, and the bus drove away, leaving the squad alone. Apart from the light of their head torches, the night seemed pitch black. They were alone with no streetlights or buildings in view. The only light came from a crescent shaped quarter moon, but even that was occasionally hidden by clouds.

Their Squad Leader briefed them. "Let's just go over that safety briefing again, guys. We stay together at all times. Always keep your buddy in sight and tell him if you are going to move away. If you get lost from the group, stay where you are, and we will come and find you. You should all be equipped with whistles, but only use them if you get into trouble. I'll be handing out safety cards in a minute. They contain contact phone numbers if you need them for assistance. Keep to the side of the road and move to safety if you hear vehicles coming."

They have told me which road we are on and roughly where we are on that road. The first thing is to work out exactly where we are, and then I'll show you the whole proposed route on the map. I suggest you keep torches turned off unless they are really needed. Your night vision will kick in soon as it is not totally dark out here. If you get an injury or blisters, let me know. The first thing I want to find is a side road on the left-hand side of this road. There should be a small bridge about 200 metres along the side road. Williamson and Walters, you two lead off in that direction and see if you can find the side road. The rest of you follow on. Bryant and Hutchinson, you two take the rear position."

Adam paired up with Barry. The whole environment seemed alien to Adam. To him, it felt as though their squad had suddenly become isolated from the rest of the world. "Hey, Barry, does Harrison ever call his squad members by their forenames? It seems daft when we are out here away from the Foundation Company."

"It's just tradition, Adam. Hey, you'll have to walk a bit faster. There is a gap opening up between us and Smithy."

The group walked quietly along the dark road for approximately fifteen minutes before Alan Williamson called out that he'd seen the side road. Signalling for the others to wait, the lead couple trotted along the side road looking for the bridge. They soon came back. "Sergeant, this is the right road. We paced out the bridge distance. It is almost exactly 200 metres. It is a foot bridge over a stream, and the stream is flowing from right to left under the bridge."

The Squad Leader gathered them around his map and showed them their location and the proposed route for the night hike. The path from the foot bridge would lead them through some fields up to an old quarry. From there, their path rose up the side of a steep hill, then on into mountains. Harrison showed them the route he expected to follow across the mountains before descending into a valley where the Foundation camp would be waiting for them. He told them that from this point forward, he would not be navigating. It was down to the leading pair to find the route. Each pair of boys would have thirty minutes of navigating in turn.

"Ok, Williamson and Walters, you have led so far, so you might as well continue navigating from here. Bryant and Hutchinson, you will take the next leg. Spend five minutes and agree between you the route you intend to take. The rest of the squad should also keep track as you go along. I'll be following along at the rear. Don't get lost and remember there is driver training at stake here, so let's not hang around waiting! The other squads will be setting off soon."

There was a brief delay as the lead pair worked out the route and got the agreement of the rest of the squad. Adam had now seen it marked out on the map and could remember most of the features of the route. They hoisted their rucksacks on their shoulders and set off in a column of two. They were not marching but just walking at a steady pace. They were all equipped with lightweight hiking boots rather than nailed parade boots. Their progress was quiet as they crossed the foot bridge and set off along the path. By now, Adam's night vision was working ok, so he could see the path dimly illuminated by the grey moonlight. Barry walked comfortably alongside him. Brian Harrison was following a few paces behind the column of boys.

Before long, the soft grass of the fields changed to a rockier pathway as it steepened up the side of the hill, leaving the farm fields and trees behind. The boots made a combination of sound from the crunch of rock fragments against sand to the squishy sound of peat and mud. It looked as though it had been raining heavily earlier in the day, as there was a lot of water in pools on the pathway. Initially, the boys stumbled against the larger rocks in the path until they became more used to walking in the dark.

Adam grumbled to Barry, "We can walk faster than this. The other squads are going to get there before us. I'm going to get Alan to speed up a bit."

"No, don't bother, Adam. This is what is called 'mountain pace'. It is a steady speed without any rushing. You will only overheat and get out of breath if you rush it. Trust us... we have done this before."

"Don't complain to me when you are standing next to me washing dishes tomorrow."

After half an hour's walking, the path levelled out for a while. The lead couple called a brief halt, and the squad rested on a pile of stones at the side of the track.

It was time for the next couple of boys to take the lead. Mickey Bryant and Alan Williamson checked the planned route with the previous leaders and then checked their compass bearing and set off. The path was level for a few hundred metres, then steepened up the hillside where it joined another track running steeply down from the hill above to the valley below. Adam was concerned about the route they had taken since the last resting place. Where they were now did not match his recollection of what he had seen on the map. With it being so dark, it was difficult to be sure.

"Barry, I think we are on the wrong pathway. This doesn't seem right. We should have taken another path back at that last rest place."

"Don't worry, Adam. They are good at map reading. Mickey rarely gets it wrong. Anyway, these are easy mountains. We can always change direction when we get to the top of this hill."

Brian Harrison spoke from behind them. "You are both right in a way, guys. Yes, we are off track, but also it should be easy to correct it when we reach the top. It will just be a bit steeper this way."

Their Squad Leader was right. The path was easy to see, but it was definitely steep as it zigzagged up the hill slope. The boys toiled up the hill. Most of the grass had gone and was replaced by rocky scree of small rock chippings and some small boulders. After ten minutes of hard slogging up the path, it suddenly levelled out for about 150 metres, and then they could see the path dimly in the distance rising up the hill slope again. They paused briefly to catch their breath and then set off again. As they started to move, low cloud swept across the hillside, obscuring the moon and the path ahead in a thick mist. Their Squad Leader called out for them to stay together and not to lose touch with each other. Walking forward, they could not see much at all. Switching a head torch on only caused a reflection against the mist, making it difficult to see anything.

They had moved forward about 100 metres when Adam heard a sound behind him and slightly to his right. "Arrgh…"

There was silence apart from the crunching of hiking boots on the gravel. He checked behind him to ask Brian Harrison if he had heard the sound. There was no sign of their Squad Leader. "Harrison, are you there? Hang on, guys. I think we lost the Squad Leader."

The cloud and mist cleared as suddenly as it had appeared. There was no sign of their Squad Leader. Adam got his whistle out and blew two short, sharp blasts. There was no response. He knew Harrison could not have gone far. "Have any of you guys seen Harrison? Is this some kind of test he is running?" asked Adam.

They all shook their heads and seemed puzzled.

"I suppose we had best backtrack and see if we can find him. How about if we spread in a line either side of the track and walk back to the steep bit, ok?"

Adam organised the rest of the squad into a line with five-metre gaps between each boy. "Ok, let's keep this in a straight line and walk back slowly until I call a halt. Look out for anything odd."

They had walked perhaps fifty metres when Billy Leeds called out, "Hang on, guys! I think I see something. It looks like a hole in the ground."

They rushed towards it, but Adam called out, "Wait! It might be old mine workings. Alan, you are carrying the rope aren't you? Get it out, and I'll tie on and investigate while you belay me."

Alan Williamson dropped his pack and removed the rope. He swiftly uncoiled the length of the rope while Barry found a safe point for Alan to attach his belay. Barry then helped Adam tie onto the end of the rope using a bowline knot around his waist.

Adam switched on his head torch and walked to the edge of the hole and looked down. "It looks deep—like an old mine shaft, I guess. I think it was covered by timber planks, and they have rotted. Wait! I can see Brian down there. He's about five metres down and has landed on some kind of ledge. Brian? Can you hear me? Wave or do something!"

Adam pulled back from the edge of the shaft and gathered the squad together. "This looks bad. Brian is on a ledge and looks unconscious or worse. The shaft looks deep, and I think if he moves, he will fall down the shaft. We are going to have to go down and attach a rope to him to stop him from falling any further and then go and get some rescue. I can't see his rucksack anywhere, so I guess it has fallen down the shaft. That means we have no GPS or mobile phone. We've got to get moving quickly to help Brian. I'll go down now if you guys can lower me."

Barry spoke up. "Don't be daft, Adam! You are terrified of heights. You will just freeze up. I've done a lot of climbing and first aid, so it's best you stay up top and organise. I'll go down the mine."

Adam untied the rope and passed it over to his friend. Barry emptied his rucksack and placed one of the squad first-aid kits inside. Alan and Barry rearranged the rope so one end was lowered down to the unconscious Brian while Barry would be lowered on the other end of the rope. They made a figure of eight with the climbing tape slings, and Barry stepped into that like a harness. Using a carabiner, he clipped it onto his end of the rope.

As the cadets took his weight on the rope, Barry descended through the hole and paused by the ledge. "He's breathing ok, and his pulse is not too bad. I can't see any bleeding. His leg looks wrong though. I think it might be broken. I'm going to tie him off. He isn't resting on a ledge. It is old timber, and it looks very rotten."

Barry retrieved a reflective plastic rescue blanket from his rucksack and wrapped it around the body of their Squad Leader. Using the end of the rope, he created an improvised harness around Brian's waist and upper legs. He then signalled for the team to pull him back up. Barry was able to climb part of the way, thus reducing the load on the team above.

100

"What do you think, Barry? Is he going to be ok there for a while?" asked Adam.

"I think we have done the best we can. I don't want to move him unless we have to. We need the proper rescue people."

"Ok. Let's get some rescue sorted out. Mickey, have you got the map handy? I think we got a bit lost after the rest place when you took over. I think we have stumbled into an old mining area."

They gathered around the map, trying to work out exactly where they were on the mountain.

Mickey sighed. "Hell, Adam, I think you are right about us getting lost. Look... you can see the track we took merges with an old mine runway that goes down the hillside. That is why it was so steep and straight. And you can see the level bit where we are now. It looks like there may be a farmhouse just down the road on the other side of the valley. We should be able to get some help there."

The squad was acting indecisively, so Adam decided to take the lead. "I'm going to split the squad into two. Four of you should go down and get help. Barry, Alan, Billy, and I will stay here and look after Brian. Don't forget to leave a few light sticks marking the way points on the path in case the moon goes in again. Mickey, do you have the map reference of this place written down?"

Mickey nodded and folded the map, stuffing it in his pocket.

The group of four turned and grabbed their rucksacks and then set off down the track. They kept their LED head torches lit so they could move more quickly.

"Barry, can you keep an eye on Brian? The rest of us should make some shelter in case it starts to rain while we are waiting. If we can make a fire, too, that would be good. There are some old mine buildings marked on the map, and we might be able to use them."

The buildings were mostly ruined and pulled down, though one corner of a brick shed remained to about head height. It was twenty metres or so off the path and facing the mine shaft Brian had fallen down. By clipping a couple of ponchos together, they were able to form a sheltering roof over the corner of the building. They piled rocks at the edge to hold the ponchos down. The sharp eyes of Billy found some old wooden fence posts from a deserted old fence. Adam and Alan tore them down and used a couple of the spare maps as kindling to start a fire near to their shelter.

Adam left Billy and Alan by the fire and went to talk to Barry. "How is he looking,?"

"He's woken up and says his leg hurts a lot. I managed to stop him moving around too much."

Adam tied on and peered over the edge of the hole as Barry belayed him from further back. He called down to the injured boy, "Hey, Brian! It looks like we'll be washing the dishes this weekend thanks to you. I've sent half the team back down to get some rescue."

"How long, Adam? My leg really hurts."

"I'm not sure. They should be at the farm now. If there are people there, I don't suppose it will take too long. Do you have a mobile phone handy?"

"No. It was in my rucksack, but I don't think you would get a signal here anyway. Is everyone else safe?"

"The four gone down to the farm should be ok. I've fixed up some shelter and a fire for us up here. I'll make sure one of us is at the top here all the time, but I'll leave you to rest now, ok?"

"Oh... Adam..."

"What's up boss?"

"Thanks for taking charge and arranging things."

"No problem."

Adam shuffled back on his stomach away from the edge of the hole, untied, and turned to Barry. "Go get Alan to relieve you for a while."

The boys kept their vigil, waiting for the rescue to arrive. After an hour, Adam went back down the path a little ways to see if he could see anything in the valley. He could see four head torches bobbing at the base of the mine runway. It was a good sign, as it meant the rest of the squad was on its way back. They must have made contact with the rescue services.

After another thirty minutes, Billy was first to hear the *thwop thwop* of a helicopter. They knew it must be the rescue. They piled the reserve wood on the fire. Adam had the team make a large H by poking their light sticks into the clearing on the level ground of the old mine area. Soon, they saw the navigation lights of the helicopter and heard the roar of its rotors. Adam could see it hovering over the headlights of the half squad on the path below. Their yellow reflective jackets glowed in the Night Sun light from the helicopter. They waved their lights in the direction of the mine area.

Adam called the other three boys over to where he was on the path. "Come on! Wave your lights in the direction of the helicopter."

The crew in the helicopter saw the lights, and the aircraft changed direction and flew up to them. It hovered over them and then lowered a crewman on the winch cable to the ground. The helicopter flew away a little higher and to one side of the mine area.

Adam ran over to the man who was now on the ground and was removing his helmet. "Hi! I am Adam, We have one boy fallen down the mine shaft. He is resting on a wooden ledge, and we suspect he has a broken leg. He is about five metres down, and we have secured him with a climbing rope. I've marked a space over there where you can land."

"I am Victor. We'll go and a have look at your friends and then decide what to do. The mountain rescue team will take about an hour to arrive, but we are expecting an ambulance will be down in the valley fairly soon. "

Adam took Victor to the top of the mine shaft. The man produced a powerful torch and looked down the shaft at Brian. "Hi, I'm Victor from the rescue helicopter. How are you doing down there?"

"My leg hurts like hell. Can you get me out now? I don't know how long this wood platform is going to support me. It is creaking a lot."

"Hang on, Brian. I need to talk to the rest of my crew. I'll be right back." The aircrew man turned to Adam. "How long has he been down there?"

"About an hour and a half, Victor."

"He's already been too long without medical attention. We'd best get him out now." Victor spoke with the helicopter pilot over his portable radio and agreed a plan of action. "Adam, we are going to strap him to a rescue stretcher and winch him out. The pilot says the ambulance and paramedics have arrived down by the farm, so they can give him some treatment and take him to the hospital. We don't think we should wait for the mountain rescue team."

Just then, Adam saw the four head torches of the remaining squad members bob into view on the path from the valley. "Ok, Victor, Wave to us if you need any assistance. By the way, can you do us one small favour?"

"Sure, what is it?"

Glancing briefly at the other three boys standing nearby, he leant forward and talked quietly in Victor's ear. The man grinned and replied. "I guess so. I'll ask the pilot."

Victor called the helicopter closer in and then signalled the boys to stand back away from the blast of the rotors. The winch cable was lowered from the Sea King. This time it had a rescue strop and a rescue stretcher attached. He clipped onto the winch cable and was lifted into the air. By hand signals, he guided the helicopter to hover over the entrance to the mine shaft. After some manoeuvring of the stretcher, he was lowered through and down in the dark of the shaft to Brian.

"Hi. I told you I'd be back. I'm going to strap you on this stretcher and hoist you into the helicopter. Do you think you are up to that?"

"Yes. Anything just get me out of here. My leg hurts."

The rescue man unclipped a face mask from an anaesthetic gas and air unit and fixed the mask onto Brian's face. "This will help to dull the pain."

Brian nodded, already feeling some of the benefit. At that signal, the man carefully eased the boy onto the stretcher. Part of Victor's weight was resting on the wooden platform as well, causing it to creak even more. He quickly strapped Brian into the stretcher. No sooner than he had done that than the wooden structure collapsed and dropped away into the darkness. The rope harness Barry had made earlier took the weight of Brian briefly before the helicopter pilot adjusted for the change in weight. Victor signalled for the winch man above to commence the winch lift back to the helicopter. As they cleared the hole, Victor produced a knife and cut through the climbing rope.

The man and the rescued boy were smoothly winched into main cabin of the Sea King, which then turned and flew away to the farm in the valley. Silence returned to the old mine site. By now, all the boys in the squad were grouped together to watch the helicopter depart.

"Wow. Well, what do we do now? I suppose we had best do the hike?" asked Trevor.

"We've got a fire going over there. At least some of it is left after the helicopter blast. Let's stop and make a brew of tea while we think about what to do next. Has anyone got any red light sticks to mark the edge of the mine?" asked Adam.

Nick rummaged in his rucksack and pulled out a couple of light sticks, which he cracked into life. He carefully approached the mine shaft entrance and marked the position. The squad brewed tea and sat drinking it and repacking their equipment. While the rope had been cut at one end, they salvaged the remainder in case they needed it again.

Adam packed his sack and looked at his watch. He called out to the others. "Hey, guys, can you find some water and put the fire out? Leave your rucksacks over by the building corner shelter. We'll be leaving soon."

They boys looked a bit puzzled at their younger team member but followed his advice anyway. They all sat down by the shelter they had built, though their ponchos had been blown away during the rescue.

Billy's sensitive hearing detected the helicopter leaving the farm site below in the valley. "Sounds like they are going. Brian will be on his way to hospital soon. Will there be someone there to look after him, like family or such?"

Mickey spoke up. "Yes. I called the Foundation contact number from the farm. They said they would get someone to the hospital and that we wouldn't need to worry about Brian. Come on, Adam. We'd best get moving, even though we are going to be washing dishes this weekend."

Adam checked the time on his watch again. "I reckon just about now, Mickey."

Shortly after Adam had said that, the roar of the helicopter blades increased, and its navigation lights appeared from behind a slope as it came towards them from the valley. It rose above them and hovered above the light stick H the boys had set up. Then it turned a full circle before gently descending to land. A door opened in the side of the Sea King, and Victor jumped out and ran over to Adam.

"The pilot says yes, at least it will save having to rescue any of you again, and it is on our way back home."

Adam grabbed his rucksack and turned to the rest of the squad. "Come on, you lot. Stop staring. Grab your bags and keep your heads down. I've organised us a lift to base camp."

There was a small stampede of boys rushing to get into the helicopter. Once inside, Adam was handed a helmet with a built-in microphone and headphone. A voice crackled through the headphones. "Welcome aboard, Adam. I'm Flight Lieutenant Terry Hewitt, the pilot. I just wanted to let you know your mate Brian is going to be fine. The medics say it looks like a simple break in his leg and it should mend ok. Right now, he is in an ambulance heading for hospital and is as high as a kite on gas and air. We should be at your base camp in about ten minutes. We have called ahead, and they are arranging a landing spot to be marked out. I must say you did a really good job organising the rescue like that."

"Thanks, Terry. It was really good of you to give us the lift. We would have been out all night otherwise."

"You have shown a lot of initiative, young man. Give me a call sometime, and we'll invite your squad to have an official visit to our base." The pilot handed Adam a business card with contact details on it.

Just as the pilot had predicted, they were over the Foundation's base camp ten minutes later. In a flat field near the camp, two rows of cars with dipped headlights marked out the landing area, and one of the instructors had set off a smoke flare to help the pilot gauge the wind direction. The helicopter swooped into land. With the engines and rotors still running, the squad members jumped out of the side door and ran over to the Foundation officers waiting for them. The squad waved as the helicopter rose and then disappeared in to the night.

The squad lined up in rank before the senior officer, stood at attention, and chanted in unison, as recently planned in the hold of the helicopter, "Blue Squad from South Bucks reporting as the first team to arrive on the night hike, sir."

"Blue Squad, you have given us an interesting night so far. We are pleased you have arrived safe and well. I'm afraid that the rules say your Squad Leader has to report your arrival. Under the circumstances, however, I will allow you to elect a temporary Squad Leader."

Without hesitation, all of the squad turned and pointed at Adam.

"Young man, it looks like you have been elected as Squad Leader. Make your report please."

Adam was dumbfounded at being elected.

"Come on, man. What is the identity of the squad? I don't have all night."

"Sorry, sir." Adam marched out in front to the officer, stood at attention and saluted. "Cadet Cranford, Acting Squad Leader, reporting the arrival of the Blue Squad South Bucks at 0105 hours, sir. One of our squad is missing but accounted for in the hospital, Sir."

"Cadet I seem to remember the rules state that anyone taking a lift to complete the hike would be disqualified from the hike unless they were injured and unable to walk."

"Yes, sir, I remember the rules clearly also. They clearly state anyone taking a lift in a vehicle would be disqualified. We did not, sir. We took a lift in an aircraft, sir."

"Hmm... I see, Cadet. I must talk to the other officers about that before a decision is made. Meanwhile, dismiss your squad and make sure they are fed. I will want to talk to you all later to get full details of the accident."

Adam saluted the officer and turned facing his squad. "Squad, Blue Squad dismiss."

They walked away from the field following the other officers and Foundation members. As they approached the gate of the camp, one of the other Sergeants called out to them. "Sergeant, if you follow me, I'll take you to your accommodation tents and show you the canteen."

Barry hissed, "Adam, he means you, dufus! A Squad Leader automatically gets the rank of Cadet Sergeant."

"Oh! I didn't know. Come on, you lot. Let's go get some food and sleep."

Chapter 15 Adam the Squad Leader

Adam groaned as he felt the hand shaking him into wakefulness. He had fallen asleep four hours earlier, thinking he would never be able to sleep on the hard soil beneath his sleeping mat. Nevertheless, his sleeping bag was warm and comfortable. He cracked his eyes open and peered up.

It was Alan Williamson, the oldest member of the squad besides Brian. "Adam, sorry mate but it's time for you to get up. The Squad Leaders always have a seven-thirty meeting with the Camp Commander every day at camp."

"Aw, gawd. I'm absolutely shattered, Alan." Alan grinned.

"It's tough being a Squad Leader. Here... I've got some tea brewed for you. Grab a shower and get dressed. I'll make sure the rest of the squad are up and dressed for morning assembly."

Adam scrubbed his eyes with his fists and sat up and grabbed the mug of tea. Sipping the tea, he smiled at Alan. "Thanks. I guess I'd best get going. What time is breakfast?"

"They are serving it now, but if you go to the Commander's meeting, I'll get Billy to save you some bacon butties for when you get back. We got you a copy of today's camp notices. You will need to read them before the meeting."

Adam finished the tea and shrugged off his sleeping bag. Grabbing a towel, he left the tent to go to the shower tent. When he got back to his tent, he found his uniform had been laid out, along with his kit, smartly arranged in the approved Foundation layout. He had time to dress and then read the camp notices before strolling down to the Commander's tent. When he arrived, he found five other Squad Leaders were already there. Two were from his own local Company: Neal Trenchard of Red Squad and Terry Fowler of Green Squad.

Neal looked up and waved Adam over to the seat next to him. "Sounds like you had an eventful night, Cranford," said Neal with a grin. "We have phoned the hospital already, and it sounds as if Harrison is going to be ok, though his leg is in plaster up to his hip. We got here a bit later, so we missed seeing the helicopter arriving at camp. A slick move that... hitching a lift in one of those."

At that point, two Foundation officers and a couple more Squad Leaders emerged through the tent doorway. The Squad Leaders quickly joined the others who had risen. The boys saluted the officers, and they returned the salute.

"Good morning, gentlemen. Please take your seats. I'd like to brief you on last night's events and the orders of the day. I trust you have all read today's camp notices?" The Camp Commander looked around the seated boys to check that all had read the notices. They nodded briefly in agreement, and he continued. "Last night's night hike exercise went well. All squads completed the exercise within the time limit. There were four minor injuries and one major injury, which seems to have been well managed. We have reports from the hospital that Squad Leader

Harrison is comfortable. We have made arrangements for his parents to visit him today. Cranford, here, was field elected by his squad to act as their Squad Leader. He is fairly new to the Foundation, so I would be grateful if you other Leaders could give him support if he needs it. Cranford, I need to spend ten minutes with you after morning assembly to start the enquiry process into last night's accident." He looked toward Adam, who nodded at him.

"Today's activities will focus on pioneering training. At this morning's assembly, you will be allocated to instructors. We have a substantial project that needs completion today ready for exercises tomorrow. Camp inspection is at 08:00 followed by assembly at 08:30. Lunch will be at 14:00, and supper will be at 19:00. campfire will commence at 20:00, and lights out is at 22:30, though given last night's activities, you may want to get the younger boys to bed earlier.

"Finally, here is the part you are all waiting for...the special training today is four-wheel-drive vehicle driver training. The two winning squads will assemble by the gates at 09:30 and will return to camp at 18:00. The two winning squads are Blue Squad from the South Bucks Region and Red Squad from the Oxfordshire Region. You should note as a matter of clarification that on all future competition hikes, the Foundation rules on disqualification will be extended to include motorised vehicles, aircraft, and vessels. In the case of last night, Blue Squad were declared winners, as it was decided that the actions of the team hitching a lift in the helicopter were opportunistic rather than planned. As you all know, one of the guiding aims of the Foundation is to train you to take advantage of opportunities." He stopped briefly to clear his throat. "Ok, gentlemen, my bit is done. Do any of you have any problems or issues?"

Neal raised his hand. "Excuse me, sir, but who came in last on the hike?"

"Ah, I forgot that. It was Blue Squad from Oxfordshire. Meeting dismissed. Please hand your squad reports to the Camp Adjutant as you leave."

The boys stood and saluted the officers. The Camp Commander returned the salute and left. Adam was a bit puzzled about the squad report but had an inspiration and looked through the documents handed to him by Alan. Sure enough, there was a document labelled *Squad Report – Blue Squad Sth. Bucks.* It was signed by Trevor Hutchinson.

As he left the tent he handed the report to the Adjutant who gave a look of surprise. "Well done, lad. We didn't expect that from your squad, seeing that Harrison is in hospital."

Adam walked back to his squad to find Billy Leeds waiting for him with two bacon sandwiches and a mug of hot coffee. He briefed them on the day's activities and that Brian Harrison was comfortable in hospital. He didn't mention they had won driver training. While he had been at the Commander's briefing, the boys in the squad had laid out their equipment ready for inspection. Promptly at 08:00, one of the instructors appeared at their tent to undertake kit inspection with Adam. There were no problems found during the inspection.

A bugle call summoned the squads right at 08:30 am for Assembly. Adam took position in front of his squad. Once again, Alan had told him what he needed to do as the Squad Leader. The assembly was a simple ceremony that commenced with the raising of the Union flag and then the Foundation flag on two central flagpoles. That was followed by squad roll call and sickness reporting. The Camp Adjutant gave them all a briefing on the camp rules and the layout of the site. Finally, one of the older Squad Leaders gave a brief reading to the assembled members from the Guiding Principles book of the Foundation.

When the assembly was dismissed, Adam turned and spoke to his squad. "Hey, guys! Thanks for helping me out so much. I really needed help. I've got to go talk with the Commandant about the accident last night. You are free now until 09:20. Meet me back here in No. 3 uniforms. It is probably going to be dirty work today."

Adam found the Camp Commandant at his desk in the Commandant's tent.

"Come on in, lad, and take a seat. This shouldn't take long, and it isn't too formal. You want some tea?"

"Umm, yes, please, sir. White with two sugars."

The Commandant signalled to his Runner to go find some tea. The Runner was a junior cadet. It was a tradition that the Camp Commandant always had a Runner available from the start of day at assembly right through to lights out.

"It's Adam, isn't it? I'm John Stannage. Feel free to call me just John when we are not in a formal situation. Tell me about last night's accident and what went wrong. I'll need a written report from you before the end of camp, but I want to hear it from you now."

Adam told John how they had missed the right path at the first rest point but that Brian Harrison was aware of that and was comfortable to correct the route later. He then told the Commandant about how the squad had stumbled into the old mine workings that had not been obvious on the map. Then he covered the realisation that their Squad Leader was missing and the search for him.

There was a brief pause when the Runner arrived with two mugs of tea. He set them on the desk and left the tent.

"So tell me, Adam, how did you know how to arrange a search line? It is not a standard part of Foundation training."

"I've just seen it in the movies, John."

"So, why did you take charge? There were older, more experienced boys there last night."

"I saw that no one was leading and thought we had to move quickly in case Brian was injured more severely. So, I just stepped in and helped the squad do what they already knew to do. It was nothing special. They did all the hard work."

"Why didn't you phone for help?"

"The only phone was in Brian's rucksack, and that was lost somewhere in the depths of the mine shaft. In hindsight, I see we should really have carried two phones or radios separately in case one got lost or damaged, but the hike rules prevented that."

"Hmm, yes, I think the Foundation may have to change those rules. So, tell me, why did you split the squad?"

"It was obvious we needed to get help for Brian as quickly as possible for his injury, and we didn't have the equipment to safely rescue him from the mine by ourselves. I knew someone had to go down to the farm in the valley for help. Four boys seemed a safe number to travel together, and that left enough people to keep an eye on Brian—and each other—until rescue arrived."

"Tell me, Adam, why did you hitch a lift in the helicopter and not just go back down to the valley to wait for the base camp to come and pick you all up?"

"I thought about continuing the hike but wasn't sure about the skills of the other boys to carry on at night. I didn't know how the base camp was equipped to come and rescue us with all of the other teams out on the hill. When I saw the Sea King, I remembered they could carry up to fifteen people, so the idea came to me then. Anyway, would you miss out on the chance to get a ride in a helicopter—particularly if it saved you slogging over mountains in the dark?"

John Stannage grinned. "I should mention that when the helicopter pilot called us last night to arrange the landing area, he said he was particularly impressed about how your squad had marked out the landing area and taken precautions to prevent Brian from falling further into the mine. He said your rescue plan was well coordinated given your limited facilities."

"It was nothing. Like I said, the squad did most of the work."

"Sergeant Cranford, you are being too modest. We are finished here for now. You'd best go to the Camp Adjutant and pick up your Sergeant stripes. As this is a temporary field promotion, you may not have them too long, but you should at least be properly dressed while you are at this camp. No doubt your Company Master will decide later what to do about your rank."

Adam stood and saluted the Commandant and then left the tent. When he reached the Camp Adjutant, he was given two armlet bands bearing the three chevron stripes of a Sergeant. Returning to his tent, he slipped the armlets up outside of the sleeves of his shirt and buttoned them under his shirt epaulettes at the shoulders. He noticed that while he had been away the rest of his kit had been tidied away. It was now getting close to 09:20, so he went and joined the rest of his squad, who were sitting waiting in the Assembly area.

They did not look very happy, but Barry looked up and saw Adam. "Ooh, look who's got his new Sergeant stripes on already."

Adam blushed and said, "Barry, do you have to go on about it?" The others just laughed at his embarrassment.

Alan spoke out, "I guess we had best go over to the canteen and get started on the washing up then."

"Why's that?" asked Adam.

"You didn't need to tell us. We've heard Blue Squad were listed as last in the hike last night and have got camp duties this weekend. We knew they wouldn't let us get away with catching a lift."

"Sorry, guys it must have slipped my mind this morning in all the excitement and getting used to the new job."

The squad stood and started walking from the assembly area towards the canteen tent. Adam stood still and let them get about twenty metres away. "Hey, guys, don't you want to go driving training today? It was Blue Squad of the Oxfordshire Division who came last in the hike—not us!"

They turned and looked at him, then charged back at him as a group. One of them yelled, "You idiot, Cranford! You knew all along, and you didn't tell us. You just let us think we had kitchen duties and latrines all weekend."

"You should just trust me, guys. Didn't I get you a ride in a helicopter last night and now driving training as well? Ok! So let's go to the main gate. The bus is waiting there to take us to the off-road driving centre."

They trotted in squad formation to the gates where the bus was waiting for them and then piled on to it. As they arrived, their Foundation instructor took their names. The bus journey was about half an hour long, taking them along narrow and winding country lanes. They arrived at what appeared to be an old hill farm, but there were notices referring to the driver training school. Before their instructor would allow them off the coach, he gave them a short safety briefing and told them the coach would be back at 16:00 in the afternoon.

Both squads piled out of the bus and saw notices guiding them to some old barns at the back of the farm. The track was covered in brown, sticky mud, but no one cared. There were six driving instructors and six muddy green Land Rovers lined up and waiting for them.

One of the instructors stepped forward and spoke to them. "Good morning, boys, and welcome to the Treffynnon Mountain Driving School. I am Charles Bryson, Chief Driving Instructor. You are here to learn about driving four-wheel-drive vehicles on hill roads and across country. Enjoy yourselves and ask plenty of questions. This can be dangerous if you don't follow the instructions you will receive from your instructor. This morning it will be instruction, and then we meet back here at 14:00 for lunch. In the afternoon, there will be a driving competition. You are mostly young cadets. Have any of you got any training and experience at driving four-wheel-drive vehicles under these conditions?"

Adam was quite surprised when most of the boys put up their hands to indicate they already had experience.

"Ok. Let's try that another way. Those boys *without* any experience, please go and stand by the first Land Rover."

Six boys, including Adam, went and stood by the first vehicle.

"The rest of you go and split yourselves up among the other vehicles. The trainee group should stay with me."

The boys split up into their teams, and one by one, the Land Rovers were started up and driven away until just one remained with the six boys and the Chief Instructor. He showed them over the vehicle, making sure they knew all of the parts of the Land Rover. He reached into the back of the vehicle and grabbed three safety helmets. He chucked one to each of the three boys and said, "Put the helmets on guys and get in the back, we are going for a drive round the course. I'll show what these vehicles are capable of doing. You other three, please wait on the bench for a moment. Someone else will be along to entertain you."

Adam and two other boys went and sat on the bench, a bit disappointed they had not gotten a place in the Land Rover. The instructor jumped into the front of the vehicle and drove off, bumping along a muddy track.

No sooner than the vehicle had disappeared out of sight than they heard someone calling them—a girl about sixteen dressed in a t-shirt and torn jeans. She had spiky gelled hair that had been dyed black with purple tips. "Don't worry, boys. You'll get your chance to go in the Land Rovers, but first you are going to have some fun with me. Let's get moving then."

She strode off out of sight round the side of the nearby barn, and the three boys ran after her. When they rounded the corner, they found a row of quad bike ATVs and some trail motorbikes. Safety helmets, goggles, and protective arm pads were piled in a heap on the ground.

"I'm Stella. I'll be your instructor for the next hour or so, and then you will swap with the guys in Charlie's Land Rover. Put on a helmet and some protective knee pads, then choose yourselves an ATV. They all have the same power. First, tell me your names."

"Adam."

"Roger."

"Matty."

The boys scrambled to get their protective kits on and then grabbed an ATV each and stood by it. Stella got on one of the remaining units, started it, and drove in front of the boys before she stopped to talk to them. "Ok, Adam, Roger, and Matty, have any of you got experience riding one of these?"

All three boys shook their heads.

"They can be great fun, but they also can be dangerous. I've been riding them since I was six and have managed to break an arm and a leg. You will be ok if you listen to what I say, ok? These are Honda TRX450R quad bikes. They can travel at over seventy MPH. It may not sound like much, but believe me, it's really scary over rough ground at that speed. The 'R' in the name stands for 'racing'. Today, we won't be going that fast. Jump on your bikes, and I'll show you the important parts. One thing to remember is that these have manual gear boxes like a motor-bike. They are not automatic, so you will have to get used to using a clutch lever and changing gear."

She showed the brakes, the throttle, the clutch lever, the gear change lever and then showed them how to start the ATV and pull away in first gear. After several failed attempts, the boys got the hang of pulling away from standing. She made sure they all knew how to stop before leading them out into a large field with a track running round its edge. The field was on a slope, so it had uphill and downhill sections as well as level track. She got them used to changing gear and stopping quickly. Gradually, they increased the speed until she was showing them how to lean their bodies into the bends as the quads cornered the field. Satisfied that the boys were beginning to get comfortable on the machines, she took them onto an ATV training track that had climbs, descents, bumps, log piles, and tra-versing tracks. She carefully took them twice around the track, showing them the correct way to deal with the obstacles before calling them to a halt in a flat part of the track.

"Ok, boys, we'll go a bit faster this time, but try not to get airborne. You need more practice before we get to that stage. Remember, these are powerful racing quads, so don't use too much sudden throttle, or you will do a wheelie. I'll lead off... then you, Matty, then Roger, then Adam. Don't race each other."

Stella took off slowly and then suddenly accelerated, and the boys followed on their quads. It felt a lot faster to them, and they had to concentrate hard to try and keep up with her. At the last hump before the flat part of the track, Adam noticed Roger's wheels were in the air after he'd crested the hump. Suddenly, Adam real-ised he'd taken off on the crest of the hump too, but he landed without a problem. Stella had stopped and was talking to Charles Bryson, who had arrived on a quad bike.

"Ok, guys, it is time for you to swap over with the other lads and go in the Land Rover. Did you enjoy it?"

"Yeah! It's wicked. It must be amazing a race speeds," piped Matty.

Stella cocked her head at Bryson. "Well, old man, do you reckon you can catch up with a girl?"

With that, she revved her engine and charged off around the track with the man in hot pursuit. It was much faster than the speed used during training, and she was literally flying metres in the air after some humps. Charles Bryson had no chance to catch her, and the gap between them increased. She waved to the boys as she sped past them and disappeared in the direction of the barn.

He pulled up alongside the boys and cut his engine. He was laughing. "I didn't stand a chance. She is a regional champion on ATVs in her part of the country. If you guys follow me, we'll go out in the Land Rover."

The four drove back and parked their ATVs. Stella was already starting the train-ing with the other boys.

The training in the Land Rover was similar, except Charles took them for a demonstration drive around a training track first. When it was their turn to drive, it took them a little while to get used to changing gear using manual gears and their foot on the clutch, but they all managed to drive around the course at least once. Each of the boys got stuck in the mud wallow part of the course and had to be rescued. It was suddenly two p.m. and time for lunch, so they sadly drove back to the barn, wishing the driving hadn't finished so soon.

Their lunch consisted of large piles of mixed sandwiches made from thickly cut fresh farmhouse bread with large mugs tea or fruit juice. While the boys were sitting, eating, and recounting tales of their near misses in the morning driving, they suddenly heard a large vehicle engine start. With squealing metal tracks, a fifty-five-ton Chieftain Mark 7 Battle Tank drove into view in front of the barn. The purple-tipped head of Stella poked out of the tank driver position at the front of the tank as she manoeuvred it past the barn and out into a nearby field.

Charles Bryson stood in front of the two assembled squads to announce the activities planned for the afternoon. "Good afternoon, gentlemen. We were very pleased with your progress this morning. We were especially pleased none of you crashed or damaged any of our vehicles. Believe me, when we have Foundation cadets turn up for training, we always expect something spectacular to happen. This afternoon will be a driving competition between Blue Squad and Red Squad. It will be a combination of endurance and teamwork. There will be an hour-long distance endurance race on the quad bikes, and the team with the greatest number of laps will win. You will have to change riders every five laps, and there will be two quad bikes per squad. There will also be driving over the obstacle course in Land Rovers to see which team can deliver the most buckets of water to the other end. It is not that simple of a course, as your drivers will be blindfolded and will have to be guided by the front seat passenger. As Blue Squad is missing one member, we will lend you one of the cooks from here to act as a Land Rover driver. Please give a round of applause to Ben."

The boys cheered and whistled as an ancient old man with a bent back creaked out from the barn and introduced himself to Adam and the Blue Squad. Red Squad laughed at Blue Squad and mimicked old doddery men shuffling along with walking sticks.

"The winning squad will be given the chance to drive the Chieftain Tank along a route. Unfortunately, the Defence Ministry will not let us have live ammunition, so you are not allowed to blast the losing side with the main gun. You will all be allowed to have paint ball guns to attack and defend the tank. This is going to get very messy and muddy, so you should all change into coveralls. You'll find plenty in the barn."

By the time the squads had put on protective clothing, Stella had returned to the barn. She took Adam to one side. "Look, don't worry about old Ben. He's Charlie's dad and is ex-Special Forces. He used to drive Jeeps all over the desert in Oman and other war zones. He taught me how to drive the tank. His creeping around is just an act."

Adam split his squad with four on the quad bikes and four on the Land Rovers and a plan to swap people every fifteen minutes. Red Squad had a similar division. The training centre had organised a Monte Carlo Rally type of start where the drivers had to run to their vehicles from a start line.

Bryson raised his hand, holding an air horn, and a loud honking blast started the races. The boys ran to their quad bike and also to grab buckets to fill with water. The Red Squad boys raced off on their quad bikes leaving the Blue Squad behind. Their quad bikes would not start.

Stella ran over and inspected the quad bikes. "Ah, it looks there is some fierce competition going on here between you and the Reds. They have loosened the power leads to your spark plugs. Never mind... it won't take a moment to fix." She quickly fixed the problem and the Blues raced off after their competition.

At the same time, the two Land Rovers charged off, laden with buckets of water. Ben drove a lot more smoothly than the lesser experienced Red Squad driver, so he got to the off-loading point later, but the Blue Squad had more water to unload.

There was fierce competition between the two squads for the next hour with many dirty tactics between the opposing teams. A long blast of the air horn marked the end of the competition and recalled the squads to the barn. They were given mugs of tea while they waited for the final scores to be calculated.

Finally, Charles strode in front of the teams with a piece of paper in his hand. "After a fiercely fought competition with lots of cheating by both teams and a few more dents in our Land Rovers, I have the results. Blue team won the water carrying race by fifteen points. Red Team won the quad bike racing by sixteen points. I hereby declare Red Squad to be the overall winners. Stella will now take them to show them how to drive the tank."

The Red Squad triumphantly marched off, following the girl to the field where the Chieftain Tank was waiting with its engine rumbling idly.

Charles turned to Blue Squad. "Now then, gentlemen, we all know Red Squad would have lost if they had not cheated at the start of the race. The competition is not over quite yet. Mixing large tanks and boys obviously presents a great danger of someone getting squashed. If you get squashed by a Chieftain, you are either dead or disabled for the rest of your life, so to prevent this from happening, we have a track the tank has to follow. At the edge of the track is a single-wire electric cattle fence, then a ditch, and then a soil ramp. Any boy not in the tank must be on the safe side of the soil ramp while the tank engine is running. Stella will be riding on the tank with a remote control. If the tank goes off course, she can use the remote control to stop it immediately. If the tank touches the electric fence, a sensor will immediately stall the tank engine."

The man bent over and opened the lid of an olive green metal box at his feet. It contained several ball-like metal objects and some metal tubes. The boys could hear the revving engine of the tank and the squealing of tracks as the other team learned how to get it moving and how to steer it. Pointing at the objects in box, Charles said, "These are going to be your advantage in the coming battle. Your objective is to stop the Red Squad from reaching the other end of the track 'alive'. Each squad will be given paint ball rifles. Your squad will have eight rifles and ammunition. The effective range of the rifle is about thirty metres. Red Squad will have four rifles and the tank. The Chieftain holds four crew members. These items are six paint grenades and ten smoke grenades. The paint grenades have a seven-second fuse, and the smoke canisters will burn for 150 seconds. There is a map of the tank field on the wall behind you. You will have green paint balls and green helmets, and your opposition will use red. Don't use the grenades or smoke inside the tank."

He gave Adam a safety instruction card. "Please make sure everyone in your squad is aware of the contents of this card. I will come back in ten minutes to collect you all. Oh... one final thing to remember. Don't accidentally shoot Stella, whatever you do. She will be armed with her own automatic paint ball assault rifle and will not hesitate to 'execute' those attacking her. As an umpire, she doesn't die if a paint ball gets her. She's basically invincible, and you, my friends, are not."

As the man disappeared, Adam turned to his squad and read the safety instructions aloud. "Has everyone got that? I don't want any accidents, but no way are we going to let Red Squad win this final bit. They started the cheating, and we didn't. Let's go and check out the map and make some plans. I already have a couple ideas. I think we have enough time to go look at the fields before it all starts anyway."

Soon, the two teams were facing each from opposite ends of the field. The track for the tank was at one side of the field and ran for about 150 metres up a slight hill towards the Blue Squad position. The Red Squad driver, impatient to start, was revving the tank engine, sending billowing black clouds of exhaust smoke into the air. The Squad Leader had taken the Commander position in the turret of the tank. The five remaining Red Squad boys were in a line at the back of the tank, ready to advance.

The blast from an air horn started the battle. With a roar from the tank engine, the tank jerked forward, heading up the hill at a walking pace. They reached roughly half the way up the field when without warning, a smoke grenade landed just in front of them billowing large clouds of orange smoke across the line of boys and the tank. The Red Squad Commander urged his squad on through the smoke. Suddenly, another smoke grenade landed ten metres front of them, creating another wall of smoke.

"Red Squad, watch to your front! They are going to try and attack us through the smoke."

The boy at the end of the line groaned as he was shot by two green paint balls in the back. Following the rules, he fell to the ground, dropping his weapon. The Red Squad boys turned to briefly see in the smoke the outlines of two Blue Squad boys. They had been hiding in ambush in the rusting wreck of an old car and had emerged when Red Squad passed by them. The Reds fired a couple of volleys at the boys behind them, but in the confusion of the dense orange smoke, they didn't score any hits. Adam led the remainder of his squad into a screaming charge down the hill. The tank Commander saw the danger and urged his team, just emerging from the second smoke wall, to be ready to defend. Stella was watching the action carefully. She saw Adam detach four of his squad to attack the driver position of the tank. Adam and Alan stayed midfield and concentrated on keeping the heads of the four opposition boys down by the use of paint ball grenades.

Stella felt the whack of a paint ball on her left leg. She looked down and saw a wet red paint stain. She had been shot by someone in the field from Red Squad. She calmly shouldered her AK47 automatic paint ball gun. Her precise targeting mowed down four members of Red Squad in the field. Feeling the sting of the paint pellets, they looked in dismay at the yellow paint splattered on their bodies.

The Blue Squad charged the tank. Six rifles targeted the driver, and two concentrated on the commander. The two boys in the tank under attack ducked down and tried to close their hatches. In the confusion, the driver caused the tank to swing slightly to the left. It charged into the electric cattle fence wire. The tank engine cut out. Blue Squad swarmed over the tank, forcing those inside to surrender just thirty metres from their objective.

Following the battle, Charles drove up on a quad bike. He inspected the coveralls and helmets of both squads. "That was a pretty decisive result. One captured tank, no dead Blues, and only two surviving Reds. In the last part of the attack, your tank commander and driver were hit. Blue Squad can have a lift back on top of the tank, and Stella will be driving. Red Squad, you have to walk."

Just before they left, Barry Davies walked over to the Red Squad member who had been the first to be shot and handed him a paint ball gun. "I think you dropped this gun when you died."

When the boys got back to the old farm, they discovered the bus waiting to take them back to the Foundation base camp. The boys quickly handed in their equipment and then got cleaned up and assembled into two squads. The two Squad Leaders, Adam and Neal Allan, went to thank Charles and his instructors for giving them a great day.

"Thank you, Mr. Bryson. Will you please thank your instructor team. We had a really great day, and we learned loads."

"As always, it was good to have Foundation cadets visit us. Your guys didn't disappoint us. I have only one regret today in that I didn't get to film Blue Squad's wipe-out of their opposition in the tank exercise! It was textbook stuff and very devious."

Neal wryly said, "Yes, sir, I quite agree. I'm sure we will be able to return the pleasure of a wipe-out to Blue Squad tomorrow during field exercises."

Both boys saluted Charles Bryson and then dismissed their squads. As Adam's squad walked over to the bus, old Ben walked out from the barn and put his arm around Adam's shoulders. "Great going today, my lad. I haven't enjoyed myself so much in months. You will go far, even if you do end up being a Rupert[1]."

Adam didn't really understand what Ben was talking about but smiled anyway and shook the old man's hand before he climbed onto the bus.

---

[1]   "Rupert" - British Army slang name for an officer..

Chapter 16 Field Exercise

The bus arrived back at camp a little later than planned. That was no great problem, as there were no scheduled activities for the Blue and Red Squads following their driver training until supper at 19:00. The other squads had been busy while they had been away. A temporary dam had been built across the river using planks and poles driven into the riverbed. The blocked river had flooded out to form a large pool before spilling over a runway at the side of the dam. A rope bridge had been constructed and suspended across the pool, leading to a campfire area. The bridge had a plank walkway just wide enough for two people side by side. A large ceremonial pyramid wood fire had been prepared ready for lighting in the centre of the campfire area. It had not been lit yet but would be shortly after supper. Some seating benches had been built around the site of the fire.

Alan pointed out a throne constructed from branches. It was sited not far from the fire and in front of the semi-circle of benches. "That's the Commandant's throne, Adam. Only he is allowed to sit in it. They build one for every campfire. It is a Foundation tradition. If possible, we always try to have a campfire meeting on the last night of camp."

On the camp side of the river, a large trampoline had been set up in the field, and some cadets were practising on it. Further out in the field, archery targets had been set out, but these were not in use at present.

Some of the boys in Adam's Blue Squad went swimming in the pool, and others went across the rope bridge to explore the woods the other side of the river. Adam didn't join them but went with Alan to see the Camp Adjutant to see if he could arrange a lift to the hospital to visit Brian Harrison. "Excuse me, sir. Is there some way we could get a lift into the hospital to visit Cadet Harrison who broke his leg last night?"

"Yes, I should think so. I have one of the instructors driving into town to pick up some supplies. He's about to leave, so you'd best get going. Wait down by the gate for a dark green panel van. Please be back in time for supper."

The two boys briefly flipped a salute to the Adjutant before rushing off to the camp gate. Just as they arrived, the large green van was driving from the back of the camp. There was already a passenger seated in the front seat.

The boys flagged it down by the gate. "Can you give us a lift into town please? The Adjutant said you are going that way and might give us a lift."

"I guess so. Hop in the back. What part of town do you want to go to? If you don't hang around too long, I could give you a lift back. I'll be about half an hour in town."

"We want to go and see our Squad Leader who broke his leg last night, so some-where near the hospital would be good. Half an hour should be fine."

They walked to the back of the van, opened the door, and jumped inside, closing the doors after themselves. They found a thick roll of old tent canvas to sit on and then banged on the side of the van to let the driver know they were ready. It was quite dark inside, but enough light beamed through holes in the van to let the boys see each other. It pulled away with a jolt and then bumped along the track towards the main road.

"Adam, do you know what is happening tomorrow in camp?"

"No. It is part of the reason I wanted to see Brian. He will probably know something rather than me having to wait for the Commandant's briefing tomorrow morning. Of course, I also want to see how boss man is doing. I want him to hear about my temporary promotion from me rather than other people. I don't want him to think I'm trying to steal his position in the Company after being there for only a few weeks."

The journey to town lasted about twenty minutes. Then, without warning, the van stopped. They heard one of the van front doors open and shut. With a creak of an un-oiled door hinge, the back door swung open and daylight flooded in to the interior. Adam and Alan jumped down from the van.

It was the passenger, who was one of the camp instructors, had opened the door for them. "This is where you two boys get to walk. We are at the hospital gates. We'll be back here in forty minutes. We won't wait around for you because the supplies are needed back in camp. If you miss us, you should either grab a taxi or give the Camp Adjutant a call. This note gives the address of the campsite. Do you have some money for a cab just in case?"

Alan replied, "Yes. I've got plenty of money with me, but we'll be back here on time anyway."

The instructor nodded to the boys and then swung into the front of the passenger seat in the van. It drove off with a beep of its horn. There were big blue and white direction signs close to the entrance of the hospital. The boys found their way to the reception desk.

When the receptionist smiled at the boys, Adam asked if they could find Brian Harrison. "He came in last night. He broke his leg on a night hike."

The receptionist tapped a few keys on her keyboard, waited for a response on the terminal screen and then looked up. "You will find him on the Lloyd Ward, third floor. The lifts are over there. You'd best get a move-on, as visiting time will be over soon. If you have a word with the Ward Sister, she might let you stay a bit longer."

They took the lift to the third floor and followed the signs to Lloyd Ward. At the nurses' station, Adam found the Ward Sister and asked where Brian could be found.

"He's over in the bed in the far corner. His parents just left. You can't stay long, as visiting hours are nearly over."

"Do you mind if we have a few extra minutes? We have hitched a lift from camp just to come and see him. He's our Squad Leader and was leading us on the night hike last night before he fell in the mine shaft and broke his leg."

"I guess ten extra minutes or so won't hurt, but make yourself scarce if the nurses need to work around there."

They found Brian lying on a bed with his broken leg in a full-length plaster cast. It was raised slightly and supported in a cradle. Brian had headphones on and was reading. Adam tickled one of the exposed toes on the plastered leg.

Brian looked up and smiled when he recognised the two visitors. "Hey, guys! How are you doing? Did you get to the camp alright last night?"

Alan spoke first. "We hitched a ride in the helicopter. Mr. Organiser here talked the crew into giving us a lift. He didn't tell us though. I was just planning how to navigate to the camp and then suddenly the helicopter lands next to us."

"So it sounds like you guys got a longer ride than I did in the helicopter. I bet all the guys in camp were astonished."

Adam wanted to change the subject away from the helicopter and his election as Squad Leader. "How is your leg? Is it still hurting?"

"Well, it aches a lot still, but they have me on some strong painkillers, so it's ok now. They say they think it is going to mend well. I saw the X-rays, and it is a simple break. I won't need any metal pins. They reckon it will take about three months to fully heal, but I'll be up and around on crutches fairly soon. So, I guess you've been washing dishes and cooking today because you didn't finish the hike?"

"Nope. Adam argued with the Camp Officers that under the rules as they were written, we had arrived legally since we technically rode in an *aircraft* and not a *vehicle*. He won, so we were marked as first home."

"I bet they weren't too keen on that—having to give in to a young cadet. Is the squad behaving well, Alan?"

"You had best ask the new Squad Leader." Alan turned and looked in the direction of Adam before he leant over and pulled the boy's arm around so Brian could see the Sergeant's stripes.

"Hey, I'm not trying to push you out, Brian. They just elected me when we got back to camp. I wasn't even asked. I have to say the squad has really been looking after me. I would have been really lost without their help."

"It isn't a problem, Adam. You really took control last night and organised things. I could have fallen down further into the mine shaft if you hadn't done that. I'll be here for a few more days yet, and my mother is arranging a bedside phone for me. I'll give Chalky Benson a call and sort things out for you to keep the job until I'm fit enough to come back. If the rest of the squad voted you in, you must be up to the task. You're not going to have any problems letting me be Squad Leader again when I'm fit, are you?"

"No way. It is really scary. I don't know anything about how the Foundation works or how to do all the ceremonies."

"Don't worry about it. I should think Alan will look after you until you get the hang of things. Just make sure you look after my squad while I'm away. So you all got the driver training today? I was looking forward to doing that myself."

"Yeah. Cranford struck again with that," Alan quickly interrupted. He explained how the Red Squad had been cheating in the quad bike race and how Adam had completely turned the tables on the Reds with a total wipe-out during the paint ball battle.

"I've met the Squad Leader of the Oxfordshire Red Squad before, and he is a real piece of work. The Camp Adjutant is his uncle, and I guess he will be none too pleased that you guys wiped out his nephew's squad during the paint ball battle. The Oxfordshire Company always rates themselves as the best during field exercises. There has been needle between the Foundation's South Bucks and Oxford companies for years now. Chalky Benson will be pleased when he hears this, if he hasn't already." Brian cracked a smile. "You are going to have to watch out in tomorrow's field exercise. The other squads will try and gang up on you with Adam being such a young leader. As you won today, your squad will be out in the woods being hunted by the others, so watch out. It gets very competitive, and they won't mind giving you all a few bruises along the way."

At this point, a nurse came over to Brian's bed. "I'm sorry, boys, but you will have to leave now. You have been here well past visiting time, and we need to get on with things."

Both boys stood up to leave, but before they left, they borrowed a pen from Brian's bedside table and signed their names on his plaster cast, leaving rude messages.

"Ok, Brian, Alan and I had best get going or we are going to miss our lift back to camp. Hope you are up and around soon. Is there anything you need us to get you?"

"No, I'm fine. My mother just visited, so I have enough books, games, and fruit to last me for a week. Catch you guys later. Don't miss your lift. Thanks for coming."

As soon as they were out of the hospital, they had to run to get back to the meeting point on time. When they arrived, there was no sign of the van. After a delay of five minutes, it appeared and stopped next to them. "Sorry we were a bit delayed guys. Jump in the back. You might have to move some stuff around a bit, but there is still plenty of space back there."

When they got back to the camp, Adam had the squad gather before supper, and he told them all about the visit at the hospital and that Brian was on the road to full recovery. "Billy, I'd like you to keep an eye on the Red Squad Leader this evening. If you can, listen in to any conversations he has with his squad or other people."

"Yeah, sure, Sergeant. I've made friends with one of their squad, so I can hang around with him this evening."

"Cool. Don't get yourself in trouble though. It would be good if the rest of Blue

Squad keeps their eyes and ears open as well. Go and mix with the other squads at the campfire tonight rather than sitting together as Blue Squad. If you all drop hints that you are not too happy about having me as the Squad Leader, that might get them talking. Tonight I want to have someone awake and on guard by our tent in case any of the other squads tries a raid. We'll have ninety-minute watch sessions. I'll do the first from ten thirty till midnight. Alan, you will relieve me, and so on. We are not going to start any trouble, but we should be prepared in case any of the other squads try some pre-emptive action. In the morning after the Commandant's meeting, I'll work out with you all how we are going to handle tomorrow's field exercise."

Supper was a mixture of barbecued meats and fish with mounds of freshly baked potatoes, hunks of fresh bread, and plenty of green salad. There were a range of salsas and dips to go with the barbecued food. Some were plain, but some were spicy and were labelled *mild* to *suicide*. Blue Squad had a competition to see the hottest sauce any one of them could eat. The Caribbean cook who helped was watching and laughing as Nick and Barry tried without success to eat a burger coated with suicide sauce.

While they were enjoying supper, Adam saw the Squad Leader of the Oxfordshire Blue Squad. They had come in last in the night hike and as a result were spending the weekend doing the cooking and mundane jobs around the campsite. He wandered over and introduced himself to Nigel Robins. They chatted for a while, and Adam discovered that two of the inexperienced boys in the Oxford Squad had developed bad blisters during the hike and hadn't been able to walk very quickly. That was the reason Oxford team had been last.

"It's bit tough on your guys having to do all the work, Nigel. It is only by luck that we were first, because of the accident we were delivered by helicopter. I feel a bit guilty, but enjoyed beating the Officers over the rules."

"Yeah, that's life though. Things go wrong sometimes, and you just have to accept the consequences. If I'd checked that they had the right socks, they would not have developed blisters on their feet. I heard Steve Davies, the Camp Adjutant, was really annoyed that you had argued about the rules of the night hike and won. He had a big row with John Stannage, the Commandant, about you being awarded first place, but had to give in the end. Did you know Neal Allan the Red Squad Leader is Steve Davies' nephew? I didn't think the Foundation allowed related people in the same local Company, but in this case, Neal moved to Oxfordshire after he became a cadet in Wales. Neal can be a real pain at times. I'm glad you brought him down a peg or two in the battle today."

"Ah, well, Nigel, life can be full of challenges, can't it? I'd best get the rest of my squad rounded up. It looks like people are getting ready for the campfire. You let me know if we can help you out on some of the camp chores. I'm sure I can talk some of my guys into it as long as we are not assigned to other stuff."

The boys parted. Nigel started chivvying his squad to tidy up the residue of the evening meal and to run the flag lowering ceremony before they were allowed to join the campfire. Adam watched as his squad crossed the rope bridge to join the other squads on the campfire bench seats.

Alan came over to him to speak before crossing over the bridge. "From what we have heard so far, I don't think we will get any raids on our tent tonight, but I think it is best that we still keep a lookout tonight."

"Good. I'm feeling quite tired after having been up most of last night on the hike. Have you got the rest of the watch rotation organised?"

"Yes, it's all done. Should we be letting Billy Leeds stay up until lights out?"

"He's looking quite wired, and I don't think he'll sleep anyway. We had best go join the campfire. It looks like things are going to start soon."

The pair crossed over the swaying rope bridge and found seats for themselves. Soon the noisy chatter from the assembled boys quietened to a silence as a bugle sounded "End of Day." The Camp Commandant crossed the rope bridge, then paused by his throne and stood waiting to complete the end-of-day ceremony. All the assembled cadets and officers stood to attention, awaiting the flag. The flag bearer was a cadet dressed in a ceremonial tabard bearing the folded flag on a silver tray. He was guarded front and back by two other cadets bearing naked ceremonial swords held upright in front of them. Behind the flag party was a cadet bearing a massive flaming torch held above his head. Having crossed the bridge, the flag bearer marched to the Commandant and presented the Foundation flag. The Commandant received the flag and saluted the cadets. He then signalled to the cadet bearing the flaming torch to light the fire. The torch bearer thrust the flaming torch into the heart of the pyramid fire, and it burst into flames. The Cadet flag party then returned to the camp to remove their ceremonial uniforms before joining the campfire.

When the boys returned over the bridge, the Commandant turned to address the assembled cadets and officers. "Gentlemen, you may be seated and relax. As you all know, we try and hold the campfire at the end of every camp. With this short camp, there has been no chance to organize any entertainment. You have all been working hard and had little time to organize any activities. 'Serve to advance' is the motto of the Foundation. I would like to take this time to recognise the contribution of Oxford Blue Squad, who have served us during this camp. While they were awarded such duty for being last in the night hike, they have still made a significant contribution to the success of this camp. Oxford Blue Squad, please stand, and I welcome the rest of you to show your appreciation in the usual way."

The seventy assembled cadets and officers burst into clapping and cheering as Oxford Blue Squad took a bow.

The Commandant resumed his speech as the applause died. "I will take this opportunity to remind you of the purpose of the Foundation. Our primary purpose is to serve others, but we are assisted in achieving this purpose through good training, caring for others, good experience, and taking advantage of opportunities as they arise. Tomorrow is another day, and it will be a challenge for you. I expect you all to sleep well tonight and then work hard to win at tomorrow's challenges. With that, I bid you all good evening and encourage you to have a drink and relax by the fire."

By this time, the fire had reached its full height and was projecting heat all around. The burning apple tree logs gave off sweet smelling smoke. Next to the throne was a pile of canned drinks—beer for the officers and soft drinks for the cadets. The Commandant stood and left the fireside, leaving the campfire site to the boys and some officers. For the next hour or so, the men and boys sat chatting and drinking by the warmth of the fire before drifting off to their tents. As the sky darkened, more flaming torches had been lit around the perimeter of the campfire area.

Adam signalled to the rest of his squad to join him on the bench seating. "Ok, Billy, did you hear anything new?"

"I heard the Adjutant talking to Neal Allan about the field exercise tomorrow. It seems the Adjutant is planning to give Red Squad an advantage over our squad. I heard him say he would transmit our GPS position to them when we arrive at our base. I don't know anything more than that, but I definitely heard them saying that."

"Was there anyone else around at the time who might have overheard what they were saying?"

"No, Adam. They were talking inside the tent alone, and I was hiding outside. I could hear them through the canvas."

"So we don't really have any proof of their plans so far? Well, I guess I'd best make sure any plans I have take that into account. You have done well, Billy. This might save us some trouble tomorrow. Meanwhile, I think we should all get a good night's sleep, though I will be taking the first watch."

The boys briefly went to the wash tent to brush their teeth before going to sleep. On arriving back at their tent, they were soon bedded down and fast asleep in their sleeping bags. Adam stayed awake outside the tent, determined to prevent any attack during the night. After ninety minutes, Adam was more than ready to climb into his sleeping bag after he had awoken Alan to take his place on guard. He felt he had only just gone to sleep when he was awoken by shaking.

It was Billy, holding a mug of tea. "Come on, sleepy Squad Leader. It is time for you to get up and take control. We will sort your kit out, and Alan says you will need these documents. You have fifteen minutes to get to the Commandant's morning conference."

Adam made it to the Commandant's meeting in time and in uniform. He'd had chance to quickly read the daily camp notices, so he was aware of the schedule for the rest of the day. The first part of the meeting was dedicated to dealing with how the camp would be packed up at the end of the day. The second half concentrated on the morning's field exercise.

After morning assembly, each squad was being sent out to different parts of the surrounding woods. They would be carrying their trophy flag with them as they went into the woods and moved around. The objective for each squad was to try and capture as many of the other squads' flags as possible. Individual squad members would carry "lives" in the form of a breakable coloured tape draped over their shoulders. Extra points would be awarded at the end of the exercise for lives taken from other cadets. The colours of the tape bands would match their squad and company colours. Once a person's "life" was taken, they could no longer take part in the activity. Officers would wear gold life tape, and umpires would wear white tape. Cadets would not be able to interfere with the movement of umpires nor take their lives.

Each team would be required to carry a GPS tracking device for safety. The central command tent would be able to track the teams using the GPS tracker signals. The teams were also required to carry a portable radio transceiver to be able to call for assistance if necessary. The recall of the teams would be signalled by a loud siren. If the cadets did not hear the siren by midday, they were to return to camp.

The Adjutant moved among the Squad Leaders, handing out large brown envelopes containing maps, copies of the rules, and the "life" tape for their squad. The trophy flags were handed to the Leaders as they left the tent to go and meet with their squads and explain the activity for the morning.

Adam bumped into Nigel Robins on the way out of the tent. He grinned at Nigel. "Say, Nigel, do you think your squad would like a break from the kitchen duties this morning? If you meet me alone just down the road from camp by the old barn in about thirty minutes, I'll explain what I have in mind."

Nigel looked quizzically at Adam for a moment. "I don't know what you are up to, Adam, but I'll play along. I'll see you in thirty."

Adam walked back to his squad. As before, Billy was waiting for Adam with a fresh mug of tea and a thick bacon sandwich. One of the other cadets had already laid Adam's kit out for inspection.

The boys were waiting to hear from Adam about the morning field exercise, so he sat them down and talked them through what he'd heard in the Commandant's briefing. "So that is what is facing us. As you have all probably heard, it is likely that at least one of the other teams might be getting some extra help that is not in the rules, so we might need to even the odds a little bit. I need you all to be ready to leave in camouflage jackets five minutes after the assembly. Don't put any camouflage paint on your faces, but do bring some with you. We are going to need it. We are going to have to move quickly on this activity if we are to succeed. Mickey, do you think you can borrow about fifty small polythene bags and three fifty-metre lengths of non-stretchy rope about eleven-mm thickness from the camp stores? You should bring them with us, hidden in the squad rucksacks."

"No problem, Adam. I think they have plenty of spare rope left over from the bridge-building exercise. It is polyester marine rope rather than stretchy nylon climbing rope. I'll go and sort that out now."

The morning assembly was soon over, and the squads were told to meet by the rope bridge to start the morning field exercise. Adam's squad was the first to cross the bridge. Officers checked that each boy was correctly showing their life tape. The squad set off at a trot along a path, following the river towards their designated site in the woodland. They had travelled about 400 metres and were out of sight of the Foundation campsite when Adam called a halt.

"Everyone down to the river! I need to build a simple bridge across the river. We need to find two strong trees close to the bank opposite each other. I then want to just have two ropes across the river—one above the other. One rope for feet, and one rope as a handrail."

Barry found some suitable trees just fifty metres further down the river. Adam assembled the squad at that place, and they unpacked the ropes.

Billy asked the obvious question. "How are we going to get the rope across the river? It looks like it is at least ten metres wide here."

Adam was already stripping off his uniform until he was just in his boxers. He picked up the ropes and looped them over his shoulder. "It would be good if one of you goes upstream a bit and one of you goes downstream on the riverbank. If I get into trouble, just pull me back into the side."

He waded out and then swam when the water got too deep but had no real problems crossing the river. On reaching the other side, he walked back up to the tree that Barry had identified. The boys fixed the ropes to the trees and tied them off securely, leaving a simple two-strand bridge crossing the river. Barry was first across. He carried Adam's clothes and boots in his rucksack.

Adam shivered from the cold as he quickly got dressed. "I have to go and meet someone. I'll be back in ten minutes or so. Can you get everyone across the river? Leave the rope bridge in place, 'cause we will need it later. Keep hidden. I don't want anyone to accidentally see us."

Adam found his way through the woods to the road. Nigel Robins was waiting by the old barn as previously agreed. "Hi, Nigel. Do you think your squad would like to take a break from camp duties and maybe go for a walk in the woods this morning? I can get my squad to take your squad's place in the canteen. All I want in return is that your guys set up a base in the place where my squad is supposed to be this morning."

"I don't think I'll have the slightest problem persuading them to do that, but we don't have any trophy flags or lives."

"No problem, but if you want to have some fun with the other squads, I have some ideas that might be good. They are bound to come hunting for Blue Squad."

Adam explained the plan to Nigel in some detail before they both set off to collect their squads. Adam went back to the riverbank to explain the plan to his squad.

"So, let's get this right, Adam. You want us to go back to camp and take over

Oxford's Blue Squad duties? We are going to have to wash dishes and peel potatoes rather than track down the other squads and take their flags?"

"Yep, that is right, Alan. The other squads are going to get unfair information about our location, so I just thought we should make things a little bit more even. We don't have to use physical strength to win this when it is easier to use some cunning. Come on, everyone. We need to get back to the barn. The Oxford Squad will be there soon."

The squads exchanged places. Adam handed over to Nigel a bag containing some support equipment. Soon, Adam was leading his squad back to camp, and Nigel was leading his squad across the improvised rope bridge and then up into the woods.

Back at camp, Adam detailed jobs for his squad. "Nick, you go and report to the Camp Commandant as his Runner. Just say the other boy got sick, and don't forget to tuck your life tape out of obvious sight. Billy and Barry, you stay with me. The rest of you report to the chef at the canteen. He won't mind who does the work, as long as he has enough boys around to do it."

The boys split up for their tasks. Adam led his two towards the utility trailer. The Foundation had these trailer units specially designed and built. Part of the trailer had a diesel-powered electricity generator. There was also a water purification plant to provide safe drinking water. The waste heat from the generator was used to provide hot water. The remainder of the trailer provided toilets and a wash-room. For safety and security, the cabin containing the generator had a locked door. Power cables ran from the utility trailer to the command tent and also to the kitchen area. At the trailer, Adam warned the other two boys to keep a lookout while he got to work. He pulled the lock-picking kit from his rucksack and then went to work on the door of the generator cabin.

He opened the lock within fifteen seconds. Once the door was open, he removed the door lock and dismantled it. Adam swapped the position of two pins within the barrel of the lock. He reassembled the lock and mounted it back in place on the door. He then found the power generator engine cut-off lever and pulled it. The muffled roar of the engine ceased. Adam quickly shut the door of the cabin and led his team away towards the command tent.

There were shouts of protest from the kitchen area and the command tent as the electricity failed. The boys ducked out of sight as the Adjutant, followed by the Commandant, strode out of the command tent towards the utility trailer with a door key in his hand to investigate the cause of the power failure. At the door of the trailer, he struggled without success to open the lock. "It seems the lock is jammed. It was ok this morning when I started the generator."

"It is an inconvenience, that is all, Steven. When the squads come back in, we will ask them if there is a locksmith cadet amongst them."

"It means we can't track the squads using their GPS transmitters. Our satellite base station needs mains power to work."

"It is not critical. We will carry on with the field exercises. The radio system is battery operated, so we still have that if we need it. Let's leave it and get back to the command tent."

At that point, Barry, prompted by Adam, approached the two men. He saluted and spoke to the Commandant. "Excuse me, sir. The cook sends his compliments and asks if you could meet him in the store tent?"

"Steven, I'll go and deal with this. You might as well go back to the command tent."

The Commandant followed the cadet back to store tent and went inside but was surprised to find it was not the cook waiting for him. Adam was standing there with a slight smile on his face. "Sir, it is my privilege to inform you that under the rules of this morning's game, you are now my captive. I will not do you the discourtesy of taking your life from you, but I will ask you to remain in this tent until you are released. You will be treated with every courtesy."

"This is outrageous! You can't go around capturing the officers of the camp. You should be across the river dealing with the other squads."

"I'm sorry, sir, but I believe the objective is to win the game. I have information that my squad may not have been treated fairly, so I have just made some adjustments to the plot. You are wearing a life tape, which implies you are part of the game, but there is nothing in the rules that says officers cannot be captured."

"Ok, young man, you have been right so far during this camp, so I will play along with your game. I should have been suspicious when my Runner suddenly changed. I presume you must have had something to do with the sudden loss of power in this camp. It would be good if you could restore the power before lunchtime. But you can start by getting me a good cup of tea and my book from my tent."

Adam nodded at Nick, who had been standing by outside of the tent. The cadet dashed off to get some tea for the Commandant. Billy came into the tent as previously arranged by Adam to take up guard duty over the Commandant. Billy's bright red hair was too easily recognisable for him to be used for other tasks around the camp. Within another couple of minutes, the Commandant's book had arrived, along with a steaming hot cup of tea. He sat down to relax for the rest of the game.

A short while later, Adam could see Barry frantically signalling from outside of the tent. He popped out to meet his friend to find out what was wrong. Adam quickly came back into the tent and addressed the Commandant. "Sir, if you would please accompany me, I believe I can show you some information you might find useful in the future."

They followed Barry to the back of the command tent. Barry signalled for them to listen carefully as to what was happening inside. They could hear the Camp Adjutant speaking over the walkie talkie. "... yes, Red Leader, I can confirm the GPS System is down. I cannot give you the precise location of Blue Squad, but here is the map reference of where they should be. Make sure they feel well and truly beaten."

Adam signalled the Commandant that they should return to the store tent. "That was precisely what I was telling you about. I had one of the cadets follow the Red Squad Leader last night, and he overheard that plan being discussed. Of course, there was nothing definite that we could present as evidence."

"I will deal with this right away, young Cranford. It is intolerable that this unfair play takes place."

"No, please don't, sir. This is a battle I can win by myself with the help of my squad. I think you will rather like the end result of this game. However, I must now get on with the rest of my plans. Cadet Billy Leeds will be around if you need any further assistance."

Barry's next visit was to the command tent to carry a message to the Camp Adjutant. "Excuse me, sir. The Commandant's compliments, would you please meet with him in the store tent?"

"Cadet, we are very shorthanded here. Are you sure the Commandant needs me now?"

"Yes, sir. He seem to think it is quite urgent. If you like, I will wait here, and if any messages come in, I will come and collect you."

The Adjutant stormed out of the command tent across to the store tent to find the Commandant reading a book and sipping a cup of tea. There was a red-haired cadet standing in front of him.

"Your Runner just told me you needed to see me urgently, sir?"

"It wasn't me, Adjutant, but maybe it was the young man behind you?"

The Adjutant turned to see Adam standing in the tent doorway behind him.

"Sir, under the rules of this game, I am now declaring you my prisoner. I will not do you the discourtesy of removing your life, provided you follow my instructions."

"That is total nonsense, boy!" The Adjutant stormed past Adam out through the tent door until he heard the Commandant's voice calling him back. He swivelled and turned to face them. The red-haired cadet was holding up a life tape. He realised immediately that in the terms of the game, he was now dead.

"Adjutant, come and join me in the tent. We have been beaten fairly and squarely under the rules of the game."

The man reluctantly walked into the tent and sat down in a spare chair.

Adam spoke to him. "Thank you, sir. I request you now stay in this tent until you have been relieved at the end of the game by one of my squad members. Cadet Leeds, here, will take care of you and provide assistance until that time. I will pop in here from time to time to see if you need anything else."

"Barry, can you go to the other end of the rope bridge by the campfire site and ask to the officer there to go to the command tent where they're shorthanded? Tell him the Commandant and the Adjutant have been unavoidably detained and that you will wait by the bridge to receive any squads that may be returning. I'm just going to have a chat with Mickey, and then I will be along to see you later."

A few minutes later, the officers sitting in the store tent heard the rumble of the generator in the utility trailer as it started up again.

Out in the woods on the other side of the river, the Oxfordshire Red Squad were approaching the location given to them by the Adjutant. The cadets were carefully camouflaged and were creeping up very quietly. The location of the supposed base was at the edge of a small clearing in the woods. Suddenly, at the other end of the clearing, they saw a boy leap up and dash in the opposite direction in the woods. They could see the flash of the blue shoulder pad of a boy from Blue Squad. Realising they had been seen, they gave up the stealthy approach and charged after him as a squad.

It was a frantic chase with the boys running as quickly as they could. Their prey led them into a small wooded gully rising steeply in the side of the hill. It was a dark place with only a single narrow track through. Their Squad Leader, Neal Allan, urged them on. "Come on, boys! We've almost got him now. He's trapped, and he won't be able to get out of the top of this gully. We need a captive so we can force him to tell us where their base is to be found."

At that precise moment, a smoke grenade landed three metres in front of them, spewing out a thick orange smoke. A second later, another smoke grenade landed behind them creating a thick wall of dense smoke encircling them. Expecting trouble, Adam had liberated two spare smoke grenades from the previous day's driving school exercise. Nigel Robins was now making good use of them. Seated in a tree high above the raiders, he chuckled as he heard the panicked response from Neal Allan to the sudden use of smoke.

"It's a trap! Red Squad, fall back to the clearing! They are not gonna catch us like that again."

As he shouted the warning, the cadet next to him swore in surprise as a polythene bag filled with gooey black river mud burst on his head. All around them, bags of black mud were falling from above and bursting on the ground and their heads. As the boys ran back down the gully, most tripped and fell on a black rope now stretched taut across the path between the trees at ankle height. A couple of confused minutes later, the cadets had all gotten back in the clearing. About half of them were mud splattered.

Neal Allan gathered his squad and decided the next actions. "We are going to have to leave them alone. Their new Squad Leader, Cranford, is much too sneaky. We have already captured two flags and lives from other squads, and it seems pointless to put those of risk. We might as well go back to our base and wait until the game finishes. Be especially alert around here for any sudden ambush."

The Oxford Red Squad carefully retraced their route to their original base position and waited for the game to finish. About half an hour later, they heard the recall siren from the base camp and set off to hand in their prizes won from the other squads. Arriving back at the campfire site, they waited as the squad in front of them handed in their flags and life tapes to a cadet checking them in at the rope bridge.

The cadet with a clipboard looked up when they approached and gave them instructions. "Drop your flags in the red bin over there and the life tapes in the blue bin. Name of squad, please? Name of Squad Leader? Ok, I count total of three flags and a twenty-seven life tapes, correct?"

Neal Allan gave him the information and then set off across the footbridge with his squad.

The receiving cadet shouted further instructions as they crossed the bridge. "All squads should wait in the assembly area to await the announcement of the results."

Behind him, Neal could see the Blue Squad from South Bucks arriving at the campfire area. He yelled back at them. "I see you guys were afraid to take us on in a proper battle, but we have won anyway by getting more flags than you!"

Adam just waved back at Neal Allan, ignoring the taunt, and then proceeded to check his team in at the checkpoint by the rope bridge. Neal Allan turned and led his squad off to the assembly area.

Soon, all of the squads were waiting for the Commandant. After a short delay, he appeared with the Adjutant next to him. The Adjutant called the assembled squads to order, and then the Commandant spoke. "Will the Squad Leaders please come forward and present the life tapes and trophy flags they have following this day's activities?"

The Squad Leaders looked puzzled at that request, and Neal Allan spoke up. "Excuse me, sir, but we have already checked them in by the foot bridge."

"Have you, Cadet Allan? I seem to remember the rules clearly state they have to be handed in here in the squad assembly."

Adam signalled, and Mickey Bryant came from behind a tent and stepped forward carrying a red bin and a blue bin filled with flags and life tapes. "Excuse me, sir. Blue Squad South Bucks reporting with seven trophy flags and sixty-two cadet life tapes and one officer's tape."

There was a roar of protest as the other Squad Leaders realised they had been duped by Adam's squad into handing over their trophies at the foot bridge.

The Commandant realised he had to act decisively. "The assembly will stand at ease. There will be a brief meeting of Squad Leaders in my command tent now."

The Commandant, followed by Squad Leaders, marched off to the command tent. Once inside, he turned and addressed the Squad Leaders. "Gentlemen, I can understand your surprise at the way in which South Bucks Blue Squad managed to hijack all of your trophies. I was, in fact, personally involved in this, as Cadet Cranford actually captured me during the game. He treated me with full courtesy as due an Officer. So far as I can see, he has not broken any rules of the game. Nowhere in the rules were you were required to hand over the trophies by the foot bridge. In fact, the rules said the game ended when you reached the assembly point. You should have been more careful and not assumed the cadets collecting the trophy flags at the foot bridge were the game officials."

Neal Allan burst out in anger. "Sir, he broke the rules in that he split his squad and did not guard his trophy flag. He must have split his squad because we had attacked them over a mile away. There is no way they could have gotten back to the foot bridge in time."

The Commandant turned to Adam and asked, "Cadet Cranford, what do you say in response?"

"Cadet Allan assumed he was attacking my Blue Squad in the woods when all they got was a coating of mud. However, as you know, all of my squad was located in and around camp. The camp cook can testify to that effect. As to my trophy flag, that was in fact installed on roof of the store tent in which you were held captive. That tent was at all times guarded by one or more of my cadets."

"Squad Leaders, you have heard both sides of the argument. From my viewpoint, what we have seen was a carefully planned campaign executed in a well timed and accurate manner. He stretched the rules and resources available to him to achieve the target, which was to win the game. He did not see the objective as inflicting physical defeat on the other squads. Unlike one other squad, he did not attempt to cheat. It has been an important lesson to you all and is quite remarkable from such an inexperienced Squad Leader. If no one has anything else to say, we had best return to the other boys."

He paused a moment, and getting no response from the Squad Leaders, he led them out back to the assembly area. When the leaders had returned to their squads, he addressed the whole assembly. "It has been a unanimously agreed that South Bucks Blue Squad are the winners of this morning's field exercise. Now, it is time for lunch and then on to this afternoon's activities."

Adam was carried on the shoulders of his cheering squad from the assembly area and then was thrown in celebration into the flooded pool under the footbridge.

Alan helped him as he squelched out from the river. "The whole squad thought we should cool you off a bit because you are way too hot as a Squad Leader. We would hate to think you might get too big headed."

Adam changed into dry clothes and then joined the rest of his squad at the canteen. As he arrived, he saw Nigel Robins serving food. Nigel looked up and gave him the thumbs-up sign.

The rest of camp was uneventful, and all too soon, Blue Squad were back on the coach heading homewards.

Chapter 17 The Turning Point

Chalky Benson had been expecting the phone call that came late on the Sunday evening after camp. It was normal practice that the Camp Commandant would call the Company Masters of the Foundation Companies whose cadets had been involved in a weekend camp.

"Hi, Chalky. I just thought I'd give you a call and let you know how your boys got on at the camp. Of course you already know about young Brian Harrison and his accident. We will hold an enquiry into the causes of the accident, and I will let you know once those findings are available. I understand from the hospital that he will be home in a couple of days. So far, it seems he will make a full recovery with no complications."

"Thanks, John. From what I have heard so far, it sounds like it was just an accident that would have been impossible to foresee. How did the rest of the camp go?"

"I will be sending you a full copy of the report, but I think we are going to have to pay some special attention to young Adam Cranford. His leadership during the weekend was quite remarkable. I believe he has only been with the Foundation for a few weeks, but when he was elected as Squad Leader by his squad, he took to it like a duck to water. It was the first time for many years that a single squad in a weekend camp has won so many of the events. He certainly stretched the rules, but his performance in the field exercise was outstanding and brilliant. He just wiped the floor with the other experienced Squad Leaders. I have never seen anything like it."

"Yes, John, I have already had a phone call from Brian Harrison, their Squad Leader, about young Adam. He thinks it would be a good idea for Adam to run the squad until his leg is fully healed."

"I'm sure he will be able to handle that role, though you might have to give him a hand with some of the ceremonies. At camp, his new squad was very supportive of him, so my guess is they will help him in the Company Hall as well. I'm sure you will have some future battles with him over the interpretation of the Foundation rules."

§

Back at home in the cottage, Adam's mother and his sister Gilly insisted he sit with them and tell them the full story of what happened over the weekend. It was the first time he had really been away from home without the family. Of course, his mother immediately spotted the Sergeant's stripes on his arm. Her first question was how Adam got those stripes. He started with the story of the night hike and how the Squad Leader had become injured. Gilly was really jealous when she heard about the helicopter ride. His mother was concerned that the hike had been so dangerous, so Adam took time to explain it had just been an accident. He even took a map out from his rucksack to show his mother the route and how they had gone wrong.

When he mentioned the driver training, Gilly's reaction was even stronger. "No way, Adam! Nobody would be daft enough to let you behind the wheel of a car. There must be laws against letting something so dangerous loose on the road."

"It was all on private land. The road laws don't apply there. Anyway, we were supervised by experienced trainers all of the time."

Adam knew his mother did not like guns, so he glossed over the battle of the paint balls and grenades. When he told her about the field exercise, she was surprised they had let him get away with cheating by collecting the flags at the foot bridge.

"No, Mum, I didn't break any rules. I just thought of a solution everybody else had ignored. Even the Camp Commandant agreed that I didn't break rules. So anyway, next week at the Foundation meeting, I will be in charge of the squad."

"You must be tired after all that, Adam. Do you have any homework that needs completing?"

"No. That has all been done, but if you don't mind, I feel like going upstairs and playing on my computer for a while."

His mother didn't object, so he went upstairs and changed out of his uniform into jeans and a t-shirt. He powered up his PC and first went to the Foundation web site. There were a couple emails waiting for him. The first was from Chalky Benson. Adam clicked on the email to open it:

> *Dear Cadet Cranford,*
>
> *I would like to be the first to offer congratulations to your temporary election as Squad Leader of Blue Squad. There are a couple of points I need to discuss with you, so I would be grateful if you would give me a call on the video conference link. I will be available online from eight p.m. to ten p.m. this Sunday evening.*
>
> *Master Benson*

He closed the email and clicked on the next. It was from Nigel Robins, Squad Leader of the Oxfordshire Blue Squad:

> *Hi, Adam.*
>
> *Thanks for giving our squad a break this weekend. We have been dying to get one-up on Neal Allan's squad for ages. Being able to cover them with mud bombs was excellent. They have all been a pain in the neck, but they are not so big headed now that you have thoroughly beaten them at the weekend camp. Do keep in touch, and I hope I might get to see you at summer camp.*
>
> *Yours,*
>
> *Nigel, Blue Squad, Oxfordshire Company*

Adam replied briefly saying he had enjoyed the weekend camp and looked forward to meeting Nigel in the future.

He left the Foundation web site and loaded the *Thorn World* game. There were a couple of messages waiting for him there as well. The first message was from one of his traders to tell Adam they had a lot of new customers who wanted supplies of cyber energy packs. The trader also complained he was quite busy and that Adam really needed more people to handle the volume of business. Adam responded, offering the trader an increased share of profits and also mentioning he would be recruiting more staff. The second message was from Bright Petal asking him to make contact when he next signed on. Bright Petal hinted that the Visiting Havoc cyber mercenaries were facing some serious problems. He checked Bright Petal's online status. There was no sign of the cyber mercenary leader, so he decided to come back later.

Looking at the clock on his PC, he noted it would be some time before Chalky Benson would be available. To fill the time, he got out the components of the lock-picking training and settled down to rehearse the actions of picking high-security lever locks. After several failed attempts, he finally succeeded in picking the demonstration lock that had been provided by the Foundation. He had to cheat a little bit by looking through the clear plastic cover on a demonstration lock. However, he was quite pleased that he was now getting the feel of using the lock-picking tools on these complicated locks.

It was starting to get dark again outside his bedroom window, so Adam looked at his clock and decided it was time to try again to contact the Master. Once again, he logged on to the Foundation web site and entered the cadet portal. Looking up Chalky Benson's details, he could see the man was now online. Clicking on the voice icon next to Chalky's picture, Adam made contact using the Foundation's Voice Over Internet Protocol software. The sound of a ringing telephone bell came through the speaker on Adam's computer while he was waiting for a response. The Master accepted the call.

"Good evening, Cadet. Thank you for calling me. I hope you're feeling well after a busy weekend?"

"Yes, Master. I've got to say I had rather more excitement than I had been expecting. I thought it would just be a simple hike. Do you happen to know when Brian Harrison will be returning home?"

"Yes. I believe he will be collected from hospital tomorrow and will reach his home sometime in the afternoon. He will be in a wheelchair for a while and then migrate on to crutches. The Camp Commandant told me something of what happened during the weekend, but I will want to spend some time with you discussing what happened. However, that can wait until I receive the report from the Camp Commandant. It is probably best we spend some time next Friday evening at the next Foundation Company meeting discussing the details."

"In your email message, Master, you mentioned you wanted to talk to me about a couple of things."

"Yes, there are a couple of things. Firstly, I want to tell you I am happy for you to continue to be the temporary Squad Leader for Blue Squad. When Brian Harrison is fit, you will revert to being a plain cadet, however, your performance will be noted on your records, and when the next opportunity arises we will be looking at you for promotion. Are you happy with that arrangement?"

"Yes, that's fine. It would be unfair on Brian to lose out just because of an accidental injury. I also think I have a lot to learn before I could do the job properly. The other guys in the squad gave me a lot of help in camp. I could not have managed without them."

"Well done, Cadet. You have clearly already learned an important lesson. The squad works as a team, and each person supports each other regardless of their rank or position. I am sure Brian Harrison would have no problems advising you if you need help while you are temporarily leading the squad. So, now, let me get to the second point I wanted to discuss with you. As you are already aware, the Foundation takes great care to train its cadets in skills and fitness and many other ways to prepare them to be good citizens in future life.

"I am about to send you some files concerning a young man we shall call Ali. He lives in the village not far from you, and I want you to get in contact with him. He is the son of a political asylum refugee family that came to this country about a year ago. There are full details in the file I will send to you, but you should be aware that a couple of years ago, Ali was injured when he stepped on a land mine in a field near his farm. He has lost one foot and was blinded by the explosion. He is twelve years old and is having trouble making new friends in this country. At present, his spoken English is not too good, and his family has a difficult time getting him to come out of the house."

"Excuse me, but that sounds like something social workers should be handling,"

"Yes, Cadet, you are absolutely right. There are already social workers assigned to support the family, but they are having real problems in getting through to Ali. He is even having some psychiatric support, but it has been decided that contact with somebody closer to his own age will help a lot."

"So what exactly does the Foundation want me to do?"

"It is really quite simple. We just want you to give him hope. It will probably take many visits over a long period of time. I am sure you will have to be very patient with him because he is very angry with the world. Anyway, read the files and let me know if you are willing to accept this assignment. You do not have to do so, but we feel it will give you a good exposure to some of the realities of life in the rest of the world. I should just remind you that at no time should you mention the Foundation is involved in this activity. You may use the resources of the Foundation to help, but any such activities have to be kept confidential."

"It looks like the files have arrived on my PC now, Master. I'll have a look at them later tonight and let you know what I decide."

"I'll look forward to your call, Cadet Sergeant Cranford." The Master terminated the call to Adam's PC.

Adam looked at the time and realised he had time to rejoin *Thorn World* before needing to go to sleep this evening. He loaded the game and logged in to the remote server. There was still no sign of Bright Petal in the virtual world, so he contacted his virtual traders to find out how business was going. It was indeed going well, and there was a large backlog of orders. His team had also made a substantial profit on their trades of the power packs. It seemed many of the game players found it much more convenient to buy power packs from BaD Totem rather than having to hunt for them or to win them from other players. He tried contacting some of the other cyber mercenaries, but none of them seemed to be online. He left a brief message for Bright Petal and then signed off from his computer.

He was now feeling quite tired, so he brushed his teeth and popped downstairs to say good night to the rest of his family. Soon, temporary Squad Leader Adam Cranford was in bed fast asleep.

Chapter 18 The Second Assignment

Adam woke early in the morning and had time to read through Ali's files on his PC. It was indeed a sad story. Ali's family had owned a farm in Pakistan near the border with Afghanistan.

When Ali was nine years old, he picked up and dropped something he thought was a toy. It was a land mine, and it had exploded when it hit the ground. Ali was severely injured. Fortunately for him, his older brother had been a soldier, so he knew what to do to stop the blood flow from his injured leg. He was rushed to the hospital on the back of an old truck. Ali survived but lost a foot and was blinded in both eyes. Not long after that, his father had decided their family had to leave the area and find a safer country to live in. After a troubled journey, Ali's family reached England, and through a family friend, they were able to find housing in the same village as Adam. Ali's father had since been able to find some work, but his young son was not coping so well. There were family photographs of Ali playing cricket in his backyard when he was younger and uninjured. His eyes were sparkling, and he had a cheerful smile in those earlier years. The more recent photographs of him were not so cheerful.

Adam decided he would do what he could to give Ali some hope. He would let the Master know he was prepared to accept the assignment. As he dressed for school, he realised how lucky he was with the lifestyle the Cranford family had in their comfortable cottage.

When he went down to breakfast, he found Gilly and his mother at the kitchen table eating breakfast. "Hi, Troll Face. How did your date go with poor Billy over the weekend? Did he survive, or did he run away raving mad at the end of it all?"

Gilly pouted. "It is none of your business. You're so jealous just because you don't have any girlfriends. Bill is a sweet guy, much nicer than you are. So, have you recovered from your weekend of running around waving sticks and wearing makeup in the woods?"

"Actually, Gilly, I feel quite good. I'm not at all stiff like I thought I'd be, and I slept very well last night. I'm looking forward to school today. There are now just a couple weeks left before the main school holiday starts, so the pace of work has become a lot easier. Mum, do you think I could have a bacon sandwich this morning? I am actually quite hungry. If you're too busy, I'll just have cereal."

"Nothing is too much for my 'hero' son. You have your cereal, and by the time you've finished, a bacon sandwich will be ready. Do you have all your books ready for school yet? Have you put all your dirty clothes in the wash basket?"

"Yeah, it's all done. I already got it done last night in case I woke up late."

The family finished their breakfast. Both children managed to catch their school buses and get to school on time. For both of them, their day in school was fairly normal. No one at Adam's school knew about the activities that had taken place in the Welsh mountains over the weekend. Adam was dying to tell Simon about the driver training, but knew he could not really talk about the Foundation's activities. He was a Foundation cadet, and he had to obey the Code of Conduct.

Adam called Billy at home one evening after school. "Hi, Billy. How are you doing? Do you fancy going out for a game of cricket tonight? I thought we could just go for a knock-up just down the road."

"Yes, sure. I didn't know you are that interested in cricket. Have you got a bat and some cricket stumps?"

"No. I thought we might use yours, though I have got a couple of old cricket balls here. Do you still have your stuff from when you played in the junior Cricket Club?"

"Yes. I've still got that. I'll get a couple of the other boys to come along. Is that ok? If you come over now, I will have the kit ready by the time you get here."

"Yep. I am on my way now. If you can get some other boys to play, that would be great, but it's no great problem if you can't."

Adam told his mum he was just popping out to play cricket with Billy and that he would be back before dark. He met up with Billy and two other old friends and led them to where he wanted to try playing cricket, an area of level grass next to a row of houses.

Adam planted one set of stumps in the ground and waited for Billy to bowl at him. Billy was a fast bowler, but he knew Adam was not too good at cricket, so his first few balls were very easy. Adam was batting surprisingly well, as he had learnt some good tips from the cricket play at school. He accurately batted the cricket ball in the direction of the other two boys in the first two attempts. Each time, one of the boys managed to catch the ball.

Billy could see that Adam was better at batting than he had previously thought. "You have improved a lot. It must be that posh new school of yours. How about me giving you some tougher bowls to try and beat?"

This was the moment Adam had been waiting for. He swung his bat hard as Billy's fast ball hurtled towards him. There was a sudden crack of red leather against willow wood as Adam's bat whacked the ball into the distance. It sailed well over the heads of the two boys trying to catch him and towards the houses at the edge of the grassy strip of land. There was a tinkle of breaking glass as the cricket ball crashed through one of the bedroom windows of a house. The other three boys looked a little stunned at Adam's bad luck and wondered if they should start running.

Adam smiled and calmed them. "Look, guys, don't worry. That was my fault. I will go and deal with it. You can hang around if you want to. I won't be very long."

Adam tucked the cricket bat under his arm and walked to meet the angry man who had emerged from the back of the house. "I'm very sorry, sir. I guess I accidentally hit my ball through your bedroom window. I will pay for any repairs. If you will let me, I want to make sure the window is given a temporary repair now. Then I will have somebody come to replace the glass within a couple of days."

"I cannot say it is nice to meet you under the circumstances. You should have been more careful with your batting. You scared my family and made a mess in the bedroom. Cleaning up the mess and making a repair is the very least you can do to put things right. We always seem to have problems in this country."

"If you have a dustpan and brush, I'll come up to the bedroom now and tidy up the broken glass, or if you want to wait half an hour, I will come back with some repair materials, and we can then tidy up the mess."

"Hmm, you sound as though you are serious, young man. Tell me your name and address, and I will expect to see you back in thirty minutes. If you don't turn up, I will come around and see your parents and make them pay for your damage."

Adam truthfully gave the man his parents' details and returned to his friends. He told them he had to go home to get some repair materials for the window. They packed their equipment and went home while Adam returned back to his own home to see his father.

"Hi, Dad. I had a bit of an accident with a window when we were playing cricket. Do you still have that sheet of thin polycarbonate plastic? I want to do a temporary repair. Then tomorrow, I will arrange a proper repair with a glazier."

"Yes, I do. I think it is in the roof of the garden shed, unless you have managed to tidy that away too. But who is going to pay for the glazier?"

"Dad, don't worry about it. I am arranging this through the Foundation. It was not exactly an accident."

"Ah, I see. My mystery son is up to his tricks again? In that case, you will also need some strong plastic adhesive tape and some good scissors. If you wait two minutes, I will find a roll of the tape for you."

Adam arrived back at the man's house with ten minutes to spare. He knocked on the door. After a short delay, the angry man opened the door for him. He was much calmer now, and pleasantly surprised that Adam had returned. "Ah, I see you have kept your promise, young man. Follow me up to the bedroom."

Adam followed the man up the stairs to the bedroom where the broken window was. When they arrived, he found that the broken glass had already been cleared up. There was just a gaping hole in the window itself. With the help of the man, he cut the plastic sheet to the right size, and they then taped it to cover the hole.

With that work done, the man turned to Adam and shook his hand. The man had a strong handshake, and the skin on his hands felt rough. "Ah, it is good to find young men in this country who keep their promises. Do you know when the proper repair can be done to the window? If the landlord comes around, I might have to tell him when it will be fixed."

"I will try and make arrangements tomorrow, sir. I will try and let you know in the evening when a man can come to fix the glass."

"Ah, that is good. I must admit I was very angry at first when you broke the window, but you have been very good and have faced up to your responsibilities. I like to see that character in a young man. You must come downstairs and have a cup of tea with my family before you go."

The man led Adam downstairs to the front room of the house, where he signalled that Adam should sit and wait for the family. The man left the room and spoke to his wife in a foreign language. Adam could hear the clatter in the kitchen of a kettle being put on the stove and cups and saucers being assembled. After a few minutes, the man led his family into the room. Shortly after, the mother arrived in the room bearing the tray of cups, a sugar bowl, saucers, and a large brown teapot. She set the tray down on the table and passed around cups of tea as her husband introduced the family. She put some dishes on the table containing flat bread, salt, and pistachio nuts.

The man first introduced his wife and then gestured to the boy before introducing his daughters. "… and this is my youngest son, Ali."

The boy sitting in front of Adam was about twelve years old and had one foot missing. "Hi, Ali. My name is Adam Cranford. I hear you like cricket," Adam said to him.

The boy turned his sightless eyes towards Adam, and for a brief instant, the sadness left his face as a faint smile briefly appeared. He held out a battered red cricket ball for Adam.

The summer holidays gave Adam a chance to discover more about Ali. The great obstacles in the younger boy's life had caused him to create himself a mental shell, a barrier to protect himself from any other dangerous experiences. For Adam, what had started as a task from the Foundation became a personal challenge to break open that shell. He knew there would be no magic bullet to solve this problem. He tried to spend some time each day with Ali. Whenever he could, Adam would take the boy out from the cocoon of his bedroom. It might be a walk in the village or the local countryside. Ali would walk with the assistance of a crutch, listening as Adam described what was around them. Adam learned that Ali had begun to rely greatly on his senses of hearing, touch, and smell. It was not an easy task to describe the countryside to someone whose spoken English was limited and whose blindness had prevented them from seeing it. In many ways, Adam was learning as well in the process of teaching Ali.

When the weather was poor, Adam would invite Ali back to the Cranford cottage to experience the Cranford family lifestyle. One game they would play was that Adam would be blindfolded and Ali would try and guide Adam. To Adam, it was a revelation. In the absence of sight, he relied heavily on his other senses, and this is how things were for Ali all the time.

The friends were sitting chatting in Adam's bedroom early one evening when Ali asked a difficult question. "Adam, how does your computer work and what does it do? We do not have one."

The question stunned Adam. Initially, he wasn't sure how to answer it. He had just assumed everyone knew what computers provided and also had some idea of how they worked. "Well, uh, I use it to write letters to other people. You know how words are written down in lots of characters? On a computer, you press the keys on the keyboard, and the characters appear on the screen as you form the words."

"A screen is like a television?"

"Yes. It displays pictures, but when you are typing a letter, it shows a picture of the piece of paper and the words you have typed on the keys."

"I don't understand? The keys are like keys to a door?"

Adam guided Ali's hands to the keyboard of his desk PC and let him feel the key tops. "I don't know why they are called keys, but that is their name. They are really more like buttons, each one representing a letter, number, or type of punctuation or symbol. Perhaps it is like the keys on a piano."

"Show me, Adam, so I can see this."

Adam knew Ali could not actually see the screen, but he took some time to teach Ali the layout of the computer keyboard, and as the characters appeared on the screen, he read them out to his friend. After some exploration, Ali typed A-L-I, and Adam read it out aloud to his friend. Ali beamed a happy smile, but he still had questions. "The keys are truly in a strange order. It seems all mixed up. Why is it Q-W-E-R-T-Y-U-I-O-P on the top line?"

"I don't know, Ali. That is just the way it is. I have just gotten used to that being normal."

"So why is being able to make words appear on the screen so useful, Adam?"

"The great thing about computers is that you can store the documents that you type. They have a memory that can store millions of pages of information. You can retrieve any of those pages and even print them too."

"We have books printed in Braille at the school I go to. Can your computer print in Braille?"

"No, but I think you can buy printers that will do that. I can write letters on here and send them to other people who have computers. It's called email. When they get the email, they can read it and send a reply."

"I have heard of email, but I've never understood it. How does the email travel between the computers?"

Adam gave a brief explanation, as best as he understood it, of how the Internet works. Ali seemed to be content with his explanation.

"Adam, you told me you play games on the computer. How can you do that?"

"The computer can show moving pictures of monsters and soldiers, and you pretend fight with them."

"Pretend fight? Do you punch the computer?"

Adam laughed. "No. You pretend you are a warrior and that you can control the body movements of the game character with a joystick."

"A joystick? A stick that brings you joy?"

Adam laughed again and lifted the joystick from his desk and placed it in Ali's hands. "The name comes from the stick in air planes used to control flight. You push forward to move forward and pull back to move backwards... or side to side to move sideward."

"Oh, ok. I think I understand. Can I play a game on your computer?"

"No, I am sorry, Ali, but for it to work, you would have to be able to see the soldiers or monsters on the PC screen. I could try describing them to you, but the whole process would be too slow."

The expression on the young boy's face turned to sadness. He sat quietly, saying nothing more. Adam tried to cheer him up, but he knew Ali wanted to be alone for a while, so eventually he helped the young boy on his way home. During that brief walk home, Ali was not responding as usual to Adam's description of what was happening around them.

Adam was disturbed by the incident and talked to his mother about it when he got home.

"Adam, as you can guess, being blind does bring its own set of problems, and the person has to learn how to adjust to a sighted world. There are just some things they cannot do, and no one likes to hear that. I'm off work tomorrow. What would you say to us visiting the RNIB Resource Centre in London? You can see the tools they have to help blind and partially sighted. I was planning to take Gilly to see a film at a 3-D theatre in the afternoon. You could invite Ali to come along too."

"That sounds good to me."

The trip up to town the following day excited Ali. During the journey, the Cranfords took turns in describing the sights, and he had even more questions. Ali was intrigued at the helpful devices in the Resource Centre, particularly when the staff helped him try them out. Adam bought a pack of Braille playing cards. Soon, it was time for them to leave for the 3D theatre.

As they left the Centre, Ali made a telling comment. "One day, Insha'a Allah, we will be able to afford some of those things."

Adam and Ali were sitting together in the 3-D cinema theatre watching *Bugs*! Adam was describing the action while at the same time soaking up the surrounding sounds that were synchronised with the film. For a moment, he closed his eyes to try and experience what it felt like for Ali. He was surprised at how directional the sound effects were from the loudspeakers around him. The train journey back was livened up by Adam teaching Ali and Gilly how to play poker with the new playing cards.

By the end of the day, Adam had started to formulate a plan of how he could try and help Ali. When he returned home, he went to his bedroom and logged on to his computer. He signed into the *Thorn World* program and looked for the help facility on the main menu of the program. Buried deep among many menu options, he found the details of the people who had written the original software program. After some further Googling on the Internet, he managed to track down the email address for the Chief Programmer of *Thorn World*. Adam wrote:

Dear Cody,

I really rate your game Thorn World and enjoy playing it. Do you mind if I phone you and talk to you about my ideas on how we could extend the game so disabled people could also get enjoyment from it?

Yours,

Adam Cranford

England, UK

He clicked the send button to despatch the email on its way. He knew Cody must get thousands of emails, so it was unlikely he would get a quick response, if any at all. There was nothing for him to do apart from waiting for a response. His mother called from downstairs to tell Adam that the evening meal was ready and that he should come down and join them.

Gilly was in an unusually good mood that evening. She had enjoyed the day, and to top it all, she had received a phone call from Billy inviting her out for a date at the cinema the following day. The chat around the family dining table was lively. Much of it was about how Ali had reacted to all the new things they had come across in London.

"Mom, it was really good of you to invite Ali along with us. He really enjoyed it. He told me on the way back he wished he could get hold of some of the things we saw in the Resource Centre. However, I get the feeling his family cannot afford those types of things."

"Maybe I should meet with his father and suggest that I help him find his way around the Social Services to see if they can provide some extra support for Ali."

"You can try, but Mr. Uddin is a very proud man. He is not the type of person to accept charity willingly. It is sad, because that means Ali may not get all of the tools and assistance he needs to overcome his disabilities and get on with his life."

"I know, Adam, but you can't solve all of life's problems."

"I know, but it doesn't mean that I can't try to help Ali. One day, I'll make enough money so I can help people like him."

It was Adam's turn that evening to do the washing up. In the Cranford household, it was decided there would be no automatic dishwasher when there were two perfectly healthy children who could perform that role. To Adam's annoyance, Gilly had managed to escape from her task of drying up the dishes. His mother stayed and helped him tidy the kitchen. It was another half hour before Adam returned to his bedroom and could play on his computer.

When Adam looked at his email, he was somewhat shocked to find a response from Cody Marantz. He eagerly clicked on the message to open it.

Hi, Adam.

Thanks for writing to me. I was intrigued to read your email and would like to talk to you further about your ideas. I am travelling in Europe at the moment, but I will be at the Tower Hotel in London in two days. How about we meet for lunch at twelve thirty p.m., and you can explain your ideas?

Please drop me a line to let me know if you can make it.

Regards,

Cody

Adam's feet barely touched the stairs as he ran down them to find his mother or father. "Mum! Dad! I need to go back to London in two days!"

Two days later, Adam was standing in reception lobby of the Tower Hotel at twelve twenty p.m. He had spoken to the receptionist on arrival, saying he was there to meet Cody Marantz.

The lift doors opened, and a tall, middle-aged man with sandy hair and blue eyes came out and looked around. He walked over to the reception desk and spoke to the receptionist. "I'm looking for a guy called Adam Cranford. Somebody rang up and said he is waiting for me down here."

The receptionist gestured towards Adam, and Cody strode across towards Adam, extending his hand for a handshake. "Hi, Adam. I am Cody Marantz, and I'm really pleased to see you. You are way younger than I expected, but that ain't no problem."

Adam shook his hand and smiled. "You are taller than I expected."

Cody just laughed at the swift response from Adam. "I can see we are going to get on just fine. Let's go eat. For England, they do some real good steaks in this hotel. I hope you are hungry. Are your folks around?"

"No. My mom is not the slightest bit interested in computers and has gone to be a tourist at the Tower of London around the corner. She's going to pick me up in about an hour from the reception here."

When they entered the restaurant, they were shown to a table. Adam waited until the food been ordered and then started to describe his ideas about how *Thorn World* could be modified to help blind people play.

"That is quite a remarkable idea, Adam. How did you come to think of it?"

"Oh, I was at a cinema listening to the sound effects with my eyes closed. We had taken my blind friend to a 3-D cinema for his first time."

"You will be pleased to know my company has been trying a similar technique to the one you have described. We are thinking of it as a new feature to the game.

It is not quite the same as you have described it, but with a few modifications, we should be able to do something quite quickly. Would you like to help your blind friend act as a tester for the new product? We would really appreciate some feedback as to how usable the product would be for playing."

"That sounds cool. Will it need any special equipment?"

"You will need a fast PC, but I will have my company ship you the special sound-card that is needed for the trial version of the software."

"What can I do in return for this?"

"Nothing other than you give us your feedback on any faults or problems. It will be good publicity for the company for us to be seen to be helping the disabled."

"Ok. Deal."

Adam's mother was waiting for Adam by the time he and Cody finished their meal. "Hi, Mr. Marantz. Thank you for taking the time to meet with my son. I hope it all went well."

"Yes, ma'am. He has some great ideas, and we got on like a house on fire. I am afraid I have to leave now. I have yet another meeting to get to on the other side of town."

When Adam returned to Chalfont, he phoned Chalky Benson to discuss what he needed for his project with Ali Uddin. "...so you see, I need to get hold of a battered-looking old PC for Ali, but the PC must have a powerful new heart hidden inside with the latest fast processor. I also need to get an Internet connection to his house like the one the Foundation provided for me. Is there some way the Foundation could pay for that if I promise to pay back within a year? There is no way Ali's family can pay for it. I could just say it is a loan of an old PC."

"We do have a local member who enjoys building PCs, Cadet Cranford. I will ask him to contact you. We will loan you the money for this, but how do you think you can pay us back? How will you persuade Mr. Uddin to allow the Internet link into his house?"

"Don't worry about that, Master. If the plan works out, Ali will earn the money for me. He won't know he is paying me back. I'll think of something on that. Can I let you know later when the link should be installed?"

Two weeks later, a courier delivered a parcel shipped from the USA for Adam. It contained a sound card component, some weird-looking gloves with wiring attached, a USB memory card, and some stereo headphones. There was a note inside from Cody Marantz:

Hi, Adam.

We have managed to do some great work on your idea. The memory card contains the latest version of our program for Thorn World. It seems to be working well, but you might find the occasional program bug. The memory card also contains instructions on how to fit the sound card in

Ali's PC and help to set up the new features in the software.

The gloves are a special interface device to replace the joystick for the player. You had not talked about these, but we at Thorn World thought they may help your friend.

Please keep in touch as to how your testing goes.

Kind regards,

Cody Marantz

Adam called the Foundation member who had built the PC for Ali and asked if he would not mind visiting their cottage and helping to install the new sound card. By the following morning, a whole new setup was working. He had not previously told Ali about what was happening, so he went to Ali's house and asked him if he wanted to try out a new PC game. Ali was intrigued and was soon sitting in front of the PC in Adam's bedroom.

"Here it is, Ali. The computer company has asked me to test this new games software. It is designed to let you play the game without having to look at the screen. Each creature or soldier in the game is given a slightly different type of sound. For example, a dwarf might have the sound of the bell, and a soldier might have the sound of a car horn. When you put the headphones on, the sound of the other players will appear to move around you, depending on the position of where those players are in relation to you. So you will be able to hear the others players around you and also have an idea of how close they are to you."

"That sounds very complicated, Adam."

"Yes, it is a bit difficult to explain, but you will soon get the hang of it when you try it out. Here... put the headphones on and listen to the sound. I will position a dragon creature to your left and in front of you. I will then make it walk around you."

The younger boy put the headphones on and waited to see what happened. Using a joystick and watching the screen, Adam made a dragon creature walk around Ali's position in the virtual world. A bright smile lit the boy's face as he followed the sound of the creature moving around him.

"Now, listen to a dragon and a dwarf walking around you at the same time."

"Yes, Adam, it is easy to follow them."

"Put on this special glove." Adam helped Ali put on the special interface glove provided by the Thorn World Company. "This time when the dragon moves around, you try pointing at it. Tell me what you hear."

Adam watched the action on the screen. Each time the younger boy pointed at the dragon, it moved away. When Ali used his hand to summon the dragon, it moved closer.

"This is good, Adam! I can make the sound of it go away or come closer to me.

When it is close, something inside the glove puts pressure on my fingers. It is like touching a real thing."

"Ok. Now tell me, what is around you now?"

"There are three dragons. Two are behind me and one is in front."

"The new sound is a bird. Where is it?" Ali pointed upwards and to the left to where the imaginary bird flew above him.

They practiced with the new version of the game for another hour until Adam called a halt. "I have tried it myself, Ali, and I found it quite tiring to play for too long. I found that when there were lots of creatures, it was difficult to keep track of them all."

"It is not like that for me, Adam. I have no problem following and recognising their sounds. It is almost like being able to see again. You must describe to me what each creature looks like on the screen."

Gilly came to the bedroom and gave Adam a stern look.

"I have to stop now for a while. I promised Gilly I would go swimming with her and Billy today. You can come back this afternoon. I will show you the hand gestures used to control the creatures in the game."

Over the next few days, Ali became skilled at using the features of the game. He also started to make use of the keyboard to type simple messages. Adam had shown him how to use the text-to-voice reading software, but Ali could not use that quite so easily.

"Ali, it is now time for you to go for a walk in *Thorn World*, a virtual world on the Internet. When we meet new things, we can give them new sounds. I will be on my new computer, and you can stay on this old one."

"Ok, Adam. Don't be so slow. I want to get moving. You sighted people are so slow!"

Shortly after they entered *Thorn World*, they were approached by a white wizard. A message appeared on Adam's screen:

> *"Hi Adam. I am Cody in the real world. I am glad to see that Ali is here too."*
>
> *"Yes, he is enjoying it and it getting quite good."*
>
> *"How is our new sound interface working out?"*
>
> *"Ali likes it and has no problems. I find it confusing when there are too many players closer to me."*
>
> *"Ok. That is what we expected. I have to go now."*

Cody's wizard avatar disappeared from the screen.

"Adam, who was that?"

"Ali, I'm sorry I did not introduce you, but that was the person who invented this game. I have met him before."

"He is a very clever man, I think, Adam."

"Yes, and he is a very special person and kind too."

"Let's go offline now and practice a game fighting between the two of us."

"I stand no chance against you, Adam."

Ali was correct. Adam could easily defeat him because the younger boy was not used to manipulating the weapons and the fight moves. What Adam did notice, however, was that Ali's reactions were lightning fast and that with his all-around "sound vision," it was impossible to creep up undetected behind Ali. His friend's skills grew quickly as they practiced.

Before long, Adam had introduced Ali as a new player called the "Dark Sheikh" to the Visiting Havoc band of mercenaries. He had explained to Bright Petal that Dark Sheikh's first language was not English and he might be slow in responding to typed messages. BaD Totem's new apprentice was soon taking part in the mercenary raids and also helping in BaD Totem's trading activities.

Adam persuaded Ali's father to allow the loaned "old" computer in their home. At the same time, an Internet link was installed. Mr. Uddin had no objection to the £5 monthly fee. He had noticed a considerable improvement in his son's cheerfulness as he made contact with more people on the Internet. As Ali had explained to Adam, "It is like being able to see a new world." The two boys now accessed *Thorn World* from PCs based in each of their own homes.

Adam was online chatting with one of his coal traders when Bright Petal sent an urgent message to BaD Totem:

> *"Hi, BT. I have just heard that the High Lord of Thran is jealous of our success. He is launching a mass attack of about 250 players against the Visiting Havoc mercenaries. They have more cannons than a Death Star. They want to take our Thorn World lives and claim our buildings and treasures. I can only get about thirty-five players online."*

> *"So why not just log off and avoid them, BP?"*

> *"We would lose our Mercenaries Lodge and all our treasures, including your profits from trading. It would be like starting from new for all of us."*

> *"I'll just get Dark Sheikh to log on, and then I'll come back to you, BP. Do you know where the enemy forces are located in Thorn World?"*

> *"No, BT, I don't. I have just had a report from one of my spies in Thran, but no real details. The attack on our lodge will start in about an hour."*

After contacting Ali, Adam used his Magic Map artefact to obtain a bird's eye view on his computer screen of the terrain surrounding the Mercenary's Lodge. He knew the layout of the local area well enough, but he needed the Magic Map to show him the location of the enemy forces. The lodge was at the top of a steep hill looking down over a valley to the north. Behind the hill to the south were high mountain ranges. On the eastern slopes was a deep steep sided gully which contained a fast stream rushing down to meet the river. The river ran from west to east at the foot of the hill. The other side of the river was a heavily wooded valley side. The main roadway pushed through those woods, running parallel to the river.

The route to the Lodge was along a narrow road that wound its way halfway up the northern slopes of the hill before swooping round to approach the Lodge from the west side of the hill. The narrow road crossed the river on a narrow bridge before joining the main roadway hidden amongst the woods. The road to the Lodge that snaked up the side of the hill was completely overlooked by defensive positions at the top of the hill. The hillside beneath the Lodge had been cut bare of trees and was just exposed grassland. It was a site well chosen as easy to defend and difficult to attack. The troops of the enemy were congregating in the opposite wooded slopes of the valley, preparing for the attack.

BaD Totem discussed the situation with Dark Sheikh. They both had a couple of ideas about what could be done.

> *"Bright Petal, the enemy troops are hiding in the woods across the river. Your fear about the numbers of attackers is correct. I have a plan that will make this particular walnut easier to crack."*

Adam explained the plan. Bright Petal was unhappy at the thought of sacrificing the Lodge. It had taken a year of game play to earn enough to buy the lands and to build the Lodge. Many treasures and artefacts would have to be left behind. In the end, Bright Petal agreed and led most of the protesting mercenaries away in the mountains after some defensive works had been done. There were only five mercenaries plus Dark Sheikh and BaD Totem remaining behind to defend the Lodge on the hill.

As soon as Bright Petal's refugees were out of sight, BaD Totem ran down the hill and across the bridge. The other players could see his avatar was carrying a white flag. The remaining defenders of the Lodge fired rifles at him but did not succeed in stopping him from deserting.

Once BaD Totem reached the wooded area, enemy soldiers challenged him with raised swords and rifles. BaD Totem was not armed.

> *"Take me to your commanding officer. I want to make a deal. You have got us massively outnumbered."*

> *"Ok, but the slightest trick, and you are history."*

BaD Totem was marched to the Commander's tent under guard. The avatar of the Commander sent a message to Adam's screen.

> *"Why are you deserting them? I guess you must be some kind of spy."*

> *"No, I am just a trader really. If you try and storm the hill, lots of your*

troopers will lose their lives and be no good to you. I've got 50,000 Thorn Dollars hidden in the basement of the Lodge that I'm prepared to give you if you let me live. Also I'm offering to show you the secret route into the Lodge."

"I was wrong about you. You are not a spy. You are just a cowardly, sneaky traitor."

"I'm not bothered by what you call me. Visiting Havoc has lost this time. I just want to be a survivor. In any case, I will probably make more profit working with the Thranians."

"You can show us this secret route. I have a lot of troopers who don't want to hang around for ages, so if it saves their lives and saves me time, I'll try it. What is your nickname?"

"I'm BaD Totem."

"Well BaD Totem, you can tell us about this secret way when you lead us up there. You will be at the sharp end. Any tricks, and you will lose all your lives."

"That is unfair. They will shoot me as soon as they see me."

"That will be no great loss. I hate traitors."

The Thranian Commander had BaD Totem show him the secret route. He decided to split his forces, leaving 100 troops to take part a frontal assault. The team following the secret route would also number 100 souls. A reserve of fifty would remain in the woods.

The frontal assault century charged across the bridge under the fire of machine guns from the defenders on the top of the hill. There were quite substantial casualties. The century, guided by BaD Totem, crossed the river in portable boats that had been brought for that purpose. The place where they crossed was to the east of the stream gully and out of sight of the defenders on the hill.

BaD Totem led them up the stream bed jumping from boulder to boulder. The steep sides of the gully kept the 100 attackers out of sight of the defenders above. The steep gully taxed the energy levels of the attacking soldiers, who, unlike BaD Totem, carried heavy weapons.   As they struggled up the stream bed, the other group of men engaged in the frontal assault were making slow progress under machine gunfire along the road towards the top of the hill. The defenders did not notice the reserve of fifty men crossing the river in boats to the west of the hill. The attackers in the stream gully and the attackers to the west would outflank the defenders from both sides.

The head of the column guided by BaD Totem had just reached the top of the gully when the avatar of Dark Sheikh leapt out from behind a large boulder. The two Thranians close to and guarding BaD Totem were instantly cut down by the flailing sword of Dark Sheikh. The two friends dived behind a large boulder as rifle shots came from the attackers below. BaD Totem triggered the detonator for explosives hidden behind camouflaged barrels of fuel mounted along the length of the gully. The explosives blew the fuel into a fine white fog, but this fog was immediately transformed into a massive fireball that exploded down the gully. Around the globe, 100 Internet game players suddenly lost their virtual lives without realising how it had been done.

At the sudden sound of the explosion, the five Visiting Havoc defenders left their positions and quickly moved to a rendezvous point 1,000 metres away in the mountains. The sound of the massive explosion and the ceasing of defensive fire caused the attackers to pause until urged on by their commanding officer. They met no more defensive fire but were cautious in their approach. By the time they reached the Lodge, they realised the Visiting Havoc mercenaries had fled rather than lose their virtual lives.

The computer game software had dictated that BaD Totem and Dark Sheikh had been stunned by the fuel explosion even behind the shelter of the boulder. It was thirty seconds before their energy levels were restored enough for them to move. Just as they started to stand to move to the rendezvous point, two Thranian troopers sent by the Commander to investigate the situation came across the two boys running towards the mountains. Dark Sheikh sensed the sound of the troopers raising their rifles and instantly swerved behind BaD Totem to protect him from their fire. When BaD Totem reached the safety of the rendezvous point, he found that Dark Sheikh was no longer in the game.

The six surviving mercenaries of the battle left the rendezvous point to join their comrades who had left earlier. Back at the Lodge, the victorious Thranians were annoyed that the attack had cost so many lives but started to search the building for the treasure, weapons, and artefacts they could now rightfully claim. The commander was summoned by his trusted lieutenant to witness, in the basement of the building, the opening of the safe containing the 50,000 Thorn Dollars of the treacherous BaD Totem. As the door swung open, they could see it was empty. It was the opening of the safe door that triggered the detonation of the explosives placed around the building. The building collapsed on the most of the remaining Thranian troops. There were perhaps forty left alive, though mostly injured, at the site of the Lodge.

BaD Totem and his companions were a relatively safe distance away when he received the message from Bright Petal.

> *"Hi, BaD Totem. You were right. The Lord of Thran's Hall was poorly defended with most of his supporters away attacking the Lodge. Your idea of bribing our informant with 50,000 Dollars to sneak us in to the Hall through a secret tunnel was brilliant. We totally routed them, and we are now the masters of Thran and the Hall. You will be very rich with your share of the booty."*

"Hey BP, those ideas were mostly Dark Sheikh's, but he lost his life protecting mine, so it will be another twenty-four hours before he is allowed to rejoin the game. He will be pleased to hear about the booty when he comes back."

Adam knew Ali would be a bit disappointed that he was "killed" before the end of the game. He also knew Ali would be grinning from ear to ear that he had taken part in a successful battle using the sound based visualisation system on the PC.

Adam phoned Ali to let him know the outcome of the battle and to thank him for the sacrifice of his *Thorn World* life.

"It was nothing, Adam. Troops have to protect their Commander. I can soon rebuild that cyber life now that you have shown me the way. It is partial repayment for what you have done for my real life."

"Ali, that's nothing special—just friendship. When you get back to *Thorn World*, you should hook up with Bright Petal. There was a lot of booty from their raid, and they want to give you a share."

§

While this conversation took place, there was another telephone call initiated from a Call Centre located in Oregon on the west coast of the USA. The operator was located in a darkened room shared with five other personnel. Like them, she had a bank of eight PC screens mounted in two rows of four on her desk. "You wanted a progress call whenever Cranford was involved in any significant actions in *Thorn World*? We have just had an alert, and I have watched the replay. It was an incredible strategy, and they succeeded against massive odds. I'll send you a copy of the replay."

"Thank you."

And with that, the phone call finished with no further discussion.

Chapter 19 Foundation Summer Camp

Everything about the place was hard and functional. The mattress on the bunk bed was hard, the chair at the desk was hard and uncomfortable, and even the towels provided for showers were hard and rough.

When the summer camp had been described during the Foundation Company meeting, it had seemed a very adventurous, but this was one strange camp. The first obvious thing Adam had noticed was that there were no tents. Their accommodation was located in some old Army barracks at the edge of a desolate moorland. There seemed to be little improvement from when the place was first constructed in the 1940s. The food in the canteen was good. The showers were good and effective with plenty of hot water. The bedding was clean, but the other furniture was bare and hard. There were no curtains on the windows. There was a full-height olive green metal cabinet in the corner to hold Adam's Foundation uniform, boots, clothes, and belongings. It was battered and clearly well used, but at least the door locked.

There was a desk in the corner of the room, but it was old and made of plain pine wood. Under the desk was a circular metal waste paper bin, it too was painted a dark olive green. The desk had a modern PC on it, but the printer was along the corridor, shared between several rooms. The PC had a decent flat-panel screen and suitable Internet connection. A bare wooden shelf was mounted on the wall above the desk. Below the shelf, Adam's personal camp timetable was taped on the wall. The walls of the room were painted with a faded glossy Magnolia colour. The door to the room was painted the same colour as the walls. On the back of the door was an *In Case of Emergency* notice printed on plastic laminated paper.

Adam had arrived at the camp three days earlier. On arrival, the squads were split up with the explanation that training would be done on an individual basis rather than as a squad. He could still meet with other members of his squad, but with a busy schedule and 400 boys at the camp, it didn't often happen. Their first briefing was on the rules and procedures for the camp. It was obvious right then this was going to be no relaxation camp. All the boys would be woken at six o'clock in the morning by the bugle.

By six thirty a.m., they were expected to be showered, dressed in sports gear, and have their rooms tidied. That was followed by physical training every day until seven thirty a.m. By eight thirty a.m., they were expected to have completed breakfast and be dressed in the uniform for the day. At ten thirty p.m., lights out was rigidly enforced by the electricity being switched off to the accommodation blocks. Social activities were allowed in the evenings, but there was a heavy load of homework that had to be done before the following day. The days were planned to be filled with classroom sessions, adventure training, disaster planning, and instruction in the Foundation ceremonies. While it was hard work, it was also fun at the same time. The main complaint from the boys was that they were busy all the time and there was little chance for any real rest.

Each cadet was assigned a mentor. Each boy was expected to spend at least twenty minutes a day discussing with their mentor as to how training had gone. The junior boys like Adam were given a senior cadet as a mentor. The senior cadets were assigned Foundation officers as mentors.

The previous day's activities for Adam were canoe training in the morning. It took place in a training pool in the nearest town. Most of the morning was spent learning how to manoeuvre the canoes. Training was also given on how to do the support and self-rescue strokes such as the Slap Stroke and Eskimo Roll. In the afternoon, there was a river trip so they could practice and use what they had learned in the morning.

Adam's planned activity for the next day was a visit to one of the Regional Headquarters of the Foundation. These buildings were manned on a twenty-four-hour basis by a volunteer skeleton staff but were built to provide facilities for a much larger staff when something important was happening. Adam had never been to such a place before, so he was looking forward to this visit. He and eleven other cadets were instructed to wait by the canteen for a minibus. It arrived at exactly eight thirty a.m., followed by a car containing three Foundation officers. It was quite long trip to the Regional Headquarters, taking almost an hour for them to arrive at its location. When they arrived, none of the boys recognised the Headquarters for what it was.

Adam was chatting with the cadet next to him in the minibus when they pulled into a supermarket underground car park. "It looks like we are stopping off for some supplies for the camp. I wonder when we will get to the Headquarters building."

The other cadet pointed to one of the officers who had gotten out of the car that had been following the minibus. The officer motioned to the boys to get off the minibus and led them to a steel door at the far end of the car park. In the wall to the side of the steel door, they could see a small black plastic block with a small red LED glowing. The officer looked around to make sure no strangers were watching and then waved his hand near the plastic block. There was a heavy metallic *clunk* as the door unlocked and swung open slightly. He heaved the door open and waved the boys through. In front of them was a metal staircase leading down a concrete shaft. As soon as the boys were on the staircase, he pulled the door closed and the lock sealed with another *clunk*.

"Cadets, if you would just turn and look beside the door, you will see a large red button. That is an emergency door release should you need to get out of here in a hurry. Never use the button to let any unauthorised people into the Regional Headquarters."

The metal staircase was poorly lit by fluorescent lights. The stairs led down four flights before the cadets encountered another metal door set into a bare concrete wall. Adam noticed above the dark lens of a CCTV camera that looked down on the cadets assembled outside of the door. The door-locking system was slightly different from previous door; in addition to the plastic block, there was also an iris scanning device. The Foundation officer stood in front of the scanner to allow his eye to be scanned and then waved his hand by the plastic block. The boys could hear the sound of heavy metal bolts being withdrawn by whirring electric motors, and then the heavy door swung open. As Adam passed through the doorway, he realised it was heavily reinforced and lined with steel. The door itself was made of heavy steel and was approximately twenty cms. thick. He could see the thick, circular steel bolts that had been unlocked to release the door. After the boys had passed through the doorway, the officer led them along a corridor to a meeting room.

Inside the room, other Foundation officers in full formal uniform were waiting to meet them. One of the officers in full Master's regalia stood in front of them and addressed them. "Cadets, welcome to Regional Headquarters. I am the Regional Commander, and you should address me as 'Master'. The purpose of this morning's visit is for you to understand the facilities and purpose of Regional Headquarters. As you may have guessed, this is a secret installation. For reasons of safety and security, we do not publicise it to the general public. What you see here today should not be discussed outside of the Foundation. Please feel free to ask questions at any time, even if you think they might be foolish. We will be happy to answer them. I will now hand you over to Captain Rogers, who will start the briefing process."

"Cadets, please pick up your name badge from the table and take a seat. One matter of safety that you should note is that each badge contains a small LED torch that can provide light in the unlikely event that we lose power down here."

The boys, somewhat overawed by their surroundings, quietly collected their badges and then shuffled their chairs into place around the large meeting table. Captain Rogers waited patiently as they settled down. Adam had a look at his name badge before pinning it on his tunic jacket. It was thick, heavy plastic, and his name was engraved on the surface. He found the small button that operated the torch.

"As some of you may have gathered, this establishment has been constructed under the supermarket and supermarket car park. We are standing approximately twenty five metres underground. There are several secret entrances and exits to this building. You will need a prior authorisation before you will be allowed access to any Regional Headquarters. Those name badges will give you temporary access though any door we have given permission for. The building is watertight and has powerful pumps to deal with any potential flooding. It also has its own standby power supply and filtered air. It is very similar to a nuclear shelter bunker, but that is not its purpose. This building does not appear on any official records, and few people know of its existence. When the supermarket was being built, the project management team and most of the construction staff were members of the Foundation."

Using a video projector, the Captain displayed a plan of the building on the wall screen. The cadets could see there were three floors to the building.

"In its full operational status, the centre can provide accommodation for 250 people. It is equipped with enough food, water, and fuel to last for six months. We have four 500,000-litre capacity water reservoirs below this Headquarters building. There is a regional command and communication control centre, which you will see shortly. We have private fault-resistant, high-capacity data network links to other Regional Headquarters in this and other countries. There are several meeting rooms similar to this one and also a large theatre that can hold up to 500 people. As you can see, each meeting room is equipped with full video projectors and videoconference facilities. When activated, we can hold many simultaneous videoconferences with different parts of the world. There is a small computer room with PC servers, which are replicated by central computers in the National HQ. We even have a small surgical room here where doctors can deal with injuries."

The Captain displayed a new image from the projector and explained, "In a secure location not far from here, we have an underground garage with vehicles equipped to assist in any disaster situation. We have sufficient tents, medical supplies, mobile toilet, water purification, and field kitchen equipment to provide emergency accommodation for up to 20,000 people in this region alone. We even have some mobile banks to ensure people have access to money."

A young cadet sitting in front of Adam asked the first question. "Why do we need all of these meeting rooms and disaster rescue equipment? Isn't it the job of the Army to do that type of thing?"

The Master spoke in response. "As cadets of the Foundation, you will be aware of the guiding principles that govern our actions. One of those principles is that we help other people. To do that, we must be prepared. Otherwise, in the event of a major emergency, it is very difficult to get suitable equipment organised at short notice. The government of this country used to have a civil defence organisation which could have done that, but some years ago, they decided to save money by closing down that organisation. The Army is not really equipped or trained to handle such activities. The Foundation decided at that time that we would have an alternative ready in the event that a major disaster takes place. We have sufficient funds to easily provide such facilities. This is just one of the ways the Foundation will meet its traditional obligations to the people of this country."

Adam spoke up. "One thing I don't understand is why this place has to be secret."

"That is a good question, Cadet, and it is one often asked by people new to the site. As you know, the Foundation works on the basis of keeping its activities low-key and out of public sight. We have found over many years that if we do not do this, the politicians in power at the time will, for short-term purposes, try to interfere with our activities. They might try taxing our funds or imposing unnecessary rules on our activities. At the very least, they would use it as an excuse to neglect their responsibility to the public. There are also those who might, for criminal or other antisocial purposes, want to gain control of the facilities here.

For example, we securely hold a cash stockpile here for our mobile banks. If there was a major disaster, it is highly likely the government bodies would not be able to fully control law and order. So, we keep it a secret. What we do is not illegal, but we just choose not to make people aware of the facilities. The security of the building helps us control who gains access."

"But Master, there have been disasters such as flooding in parts of the country, but I've never seen Foundation vehicles or people in Foundation uniform providing assistance. Why do you need all the communication equipment? Aren't the normal phones good enough?"

The Master peered at Adam's name badge. "Cadet Cranford, you make good points. We are saving these facilities for a major disaster. However, when there are smaller disasters, there is often a Foundation officer and a team on site providing some assistance. They will not be dressed in the Foundation uniform, but even so, we'll continue to provide assistance. As to the phone systems, we want our communications to be under our own control. The public phone system is highly controlled and spied on by the government. It is difficult to maintain our privacy if we use that system. In the event of a major emergency, it is quite likely the government will seize control of the public telephone systems. In that case, we might be denied access if we didn't have our own private system. We do have cloaked links to the public telephone system. For example, if you wanted to call our number here, you might think you were calling a small restaurant in Paris."

The Foundation officers asked the cadets if there were any further questions and then guided them into the next large room—a dormitory lined with bunk beds. They looked old with steel frames, but the mattresses were clean and in place, ready for activation of the HQ. There were cupboards full of blankets, sheets, and pillows vacuum sealed in plastic bags. There were three rooms like that, each with forty bunks, enough room for 240 people to sleep. The officer explained that this allowed for three shifts to take place on a twenty-four-hour basis. Each shift slept in a different room so that people getting up would not disturb those who were asleep. Other rooms were available to accommodate people not on active duty.

Attached to the dormitories were shower blocks and toilets. Doors from the dormitory rooms led into a large canteen area that already had tables and chairs laid out next to a large kitchen. In the corner of the canteen was a small library area holding DVDs and books. The kitchens were fully equipped with freezer rooms, cold rooms, food mixers, cookers, ovens, dishwashers, and food preparation tables. Cadets were told that the extractor fans from the kitchen area actually vented into the exhaust of a bakery above them. Adam noticed that doors to all of the rooms he had seen were heavy and steel. It looked as though they could be remotely closed in the event of an emergency.

The next part of the visit was the command and control centre. There was a large wall of flat-panel TV screens arranged in an arc in front of two rows of desks. Each desk was equipped with two PCs, four screens, and two telephone headsets. Behind each desk was a comfortable looking swivel office chair. One of the desks was occupied by a system operator.

Captain Rogers signalled to the boys to take a seat behind the desks in the swivel chairs. He spoke to them all. "I would now like to demonstrate to you the features of this command and control centre. You do not have to remember everything, but try to get a good feel for how it works. Once again, if you have any questions, please do not hesitate to ask."

The Captain signalled to the operator to commence the demonstration. The operator first demonstrated connecting to the other eight regional centres in the country. In each case, he was able to display a videoconference call on one of the screens in front of him. He also showed how he was able to control equipment in one of the remote regional centres. He explained that if necessary, it was possible to fully operate the equipment remotely if there were no skilled operators available at the remote site.

The operator then demonstrated the call out of one of the emergency vehicles from the nearby garage. In that case, the vehicle displayed on the screen looked like a bread delivery van. He showed the process of tracking the vehicle on a moving map on one of the display screens. All areas of the Regional Headquarters were covered by security cameras that recorded twenty-four hours a day. The operator was able to pull up and display the view from any camera without moving from his chair. He also showed how he was able to control the air conditioning, alarms, and security doors for each room from his command console.

Captain Rogers stood up and addressed the cadets again. "I would now like you all to watch a video on the screen on the desk in front of you which demonstrates the callout process if we need to get the emergency staff into this building."

Again, he nodded to the operator, who tapped a few keys on his keyboard, and then a video started playing on each screen at each desk. Sound came out from the speakers at the side of the desk. The film used actors to show how when an emergency call came in, a decision would be made to activate the regional command centre. It then showed how the rest of the team would be called in and emergency vehicles prepared ready for action. In the film, cadets were involved in getting the stores ready for distribution to the emergency site. When the film finished, the Captain asked one of the cadets to give him a hand with a trolley load of manuals. Each cadet was given a heavy manual of instructions on how to take part in the management of an incident.

Captain Rogers lifted a device from the desk in front of him. It had an oval handle and two rubber suction cups inline. He slammed it down onto a floor tile by his right foot. The suction cups firmly gripped the sixty-square-cm. floor tile as he lifted it out of place. "For those of you who have never been in a technology room before, have a quick look under the floor and tell me what you see."

They crowded around and looked under the floor. Adam could see a gap of about sixty cms. between the floor tile and the concrete floor below. Cables of many different colours were neatly carried in long metal baskets. He spoke out. "Captain,

I suppose that helps keep all the cables tidy?"

"Right you are, Cranford. We have about ten cables per desk position. So, with sixteen desks, video cables, and the screens, it is around 300 cables to keep tidy. The raised floor allows easy access for repairs. It also allows space to pump cooling air under the floor to the computer equipment at the desks. He dropped the tile back in position.

"Your next task is to spend a couple of hours reading through the manuals. We will then serve lunch. You will be staying here overnight, and at some time during the night, you will be taking part in an exercise that will simulate a major incident. We will expect you to play your part in these activities. Do not worry if you get things wrong... after all, it is only a training exercise. Later this afternoon you will have the opportunity to explore the Regional Headquarters by yourselves. There is a games area and a gymnasium should you wish to take part in some type of game or physical exercise. I understand there are three Squad Leaders amongst you. Please step forward, and we will divide you all into the three shifts."

Adam and two other boys stepped forward. Captain Rogers looked surprised when he saw that Adam was one of the three boys. He briefly looked at a document held on his clipboard and then smiled. He quickly allocated the rest of the cadets to the three Squad Leaders. "For the purposes of this exercise, we will be running four-hour shifts overnight. Cadet Cranford. your shift will run from eight p.m. to midnight. Cadet Wallace, your shift is from midnight through to four o'clock, and Cadet Dennis, your shift is from four a.m. through to eight a.m. At that point, Cadet Cranford will take over. There will be two Foundation officers on site overnight should you need assistance. Now, please take your shift teams, find somewhere to sit in one of the meeting rooms, and start reading through the instruction manuals. You should find them easy to read, but if you do have a problem, dial Extension 16 on one of the phones, and someone will help you."

Adam led his shift team away and found a meeting room and then introduced himself to the other boys. "I'm Adam Cranford, and I am a temporary Squad Leader of Blue Squad in the South Bucks Company."

The other boys spoke in turn.

"I am Dave Smith."

"Trevor Howells."

"Harry MacPherson from Red Squad in the Edinburgh Company. You seem young. How come you are already a Squad Leader?"

"Oh, it is only temporary, Harry. In a couple months, I'll probably go back to being a bog standard cadet. Our Squad Leader had a bit of an accident on a night hike."

"Hang on... what was it I was told? Blue Squad from Bucks? Surely you're not the guy who captured the entire camp in a weekend field exercise down in Wales a couple weeks ago?"

Adam blushed at his newfound fame. "Yeah, I guess it was me. I didn't realise rumours spread so quickly in the Foundation. It didn't seem like anything special at the time."

"And if I remember correctly, you also managed to arrive by helicopter at the site?"

"That was nothing special either. I just hitched a lift from the rescue helicopter after he'd had taken our injured Squad Leader to the ambulance. I just thought it was the safest thing to do rather than us wandering over the mountains at night without a GPS or any sort of phone."

"We all heard about it about a week before summer camp. If the Edinburgh Company knows, you can bet your bottom dollar most of the other Companies in the UK know about that camp. I guess you know the camp Adjutant was expelled from the Foundation following the camp?"

"No. I'd not heard that. He got caught cheating in the field exercise by the Camp Commandant. I didn't think it was terribly serious, though, because he was just trying to help his nephew."

"Adam, if you haven't realised it already, I think you'll find the Foundation very unforgiving of anyone who does not act honourably. From what I've heard, there was a meeting of the Council of Elders where they discussed the issue."

"I hadn't realised it had gone that far. I suppose we'd best sit down and read through this boring manual. We had better know what to do if there is an incident on our shift."

Once he started reading the instruction manual, Adam realised it was, in fact, well written and easy to read. It explained how to contact senior members in the event of an incident and how to call people into the centre when they were needed. It gave some details of the powerful computer systems that could be used to broadcast messages to the Foundation members. A large part of the manual explained what resources were available for use in the event of an incident.

Not long after they had completing reading the manual, there was an announcement over intercom speakers mounted in the ceiling. "This is an announcement for the cadets. Your lunch is ready. Please come to the canteen and tuck in."

"Right, guys. Let's go get some food. I'm sure we can leave the manuals here and collect them later." They left their manuals and trooped into the canteen.

The main course was spaghetti Bolognese followed by a fresh fruit salad with a choice of ice cream. As the food was being served, the cook spoke with Adam and asked if his shift team could help tidy up the kitchen and get the food ready for the evening meal. The other cadets in his shift were all experienced cadets, so there were no grumbles at being asked to help out. The work didn't take long, and the cadets were soon free to explore the Headquarters buildings.

Adam returned to the command centre and found the operator sitting there reading a book. He approached the man and spoke. "Hi. I am Adam. Do you mind showing me the security control process again? Having read the instruction manual, I would like to see it in operation again please."

"Sure, no problem. You can call me James."

The operator typed in his user ID and password and then activated the security control programs. A menu displaying several options flashed up on the screen. "So, Adam what is it you want to see? There are a lot of features here, most of which you would find boring."

"What I couldn't work out from the training manual is how the people that get called in are given access to the Regional Headquarters buildings. They are all locked outside, but the security badges are inside."

"It is quite simple really, Adam. When someone is called into the centre, their authorisation is automatically loaded into the security system. Any Foundation member assigned to this Regional Headquarters has an identification device. All they have to do is approach one of the secret doors and wave the device in front of the security reader. Did you notice that when the Foundation officer approached the security door in the supermarket car park, he waved his hand by the identity reader?"

"Yes I did, James, but he wasn't holding any kind of a badge in his hand."

The shift operator held out his right hand towards Adam and spread his fingers. His fingers were bare except for a gold signet ring on his right little finger. "You must be fairly new to the Foundation. Have you not seen a graduation ring before?

"When you graduate from being a cadet to being a member, you will be given a graduation ring. It contains an identity device that can be read by the access control readers in any Foundation building. Each device is unique and assigned only to one person. When we arranged access to the Regional Headquarters for the officer who brought you over here today, we would have programmed in his security ID into our system. If he tries after tomorrow, he will not be able to gain access through our security doors. In fact, he would get a phone call later that day to ask why he attempted to enter the building. We do that to protect ourselves from people who may have stolen a graduation ring."

"So what happens if somebody forgets to wear their ring when they get called in for an emergency event?"

"While we have procedures for that, they normally require someone leaving the Regional Headquarters and meeting them outside. It rarely happens."

"Ok, thanks. I understand that now. Now that you mention it, I had noticed the officers wear rings on their little fingers. I'm going to explore round this Head-quarters building for a while. Are you sure it's ok for us to go anywhere we want?"

"Yes! Explore wherever you want. We expect cadets will want to explore around the centre. It is, after all, quite an unusual place. You will only be able to get through the doors we have allowed, so there should be no problem. If you do get stuck in a room somewhere, just look for a phone and dial Extension 00 and your call will be routed through to me here. I'm sure you have probably guessed that your badges act as tracking devices, so we can always tell where you are."

Adam left the command centre and explored around the building. Only a few of the doors remained locked when he tried them. The doors that remained locked usually had some kind of safety warning notice on the outside. Some of the rooms he visited were storerooms containing many boxes of canned food. In one room, he found a row after row of hand torches connected to charging bases. In another room were coiled ropes, ready for use, tarpaulins, plastic buckets, spades and shovels, and yellow protective clothing. He even found the surgical centre. It had a couple of beds and a lot of medical equipment neatly tidied away in cupboards. One heavy steel door that did not open was marked *Armoury*. That door was additionally secured with a heavy security padlock.

After Adam had explored the full extent of the building, he returned to the games area. He found some of the cadets playing pool on the two tables that were available. He was not sure of the rules to the game. so he just stood watching.

"Don't just stand there, Adam. Join in. We are not playing seriously... just knocking around a bit." Trevor handed him a cue stick.

"You are going to have to tell me the rules, Trevor. I've not really played pool much before."

"It is not too difficult to pick up."

Trevor quickly explained the scoring method and rules for the game. Then he suggested the next shot Adam should take. Adam was not very good or accurate, but he was enjoying it. They played several games before an intercom speaker in the ceiling announced that they should assemble in the main theatre room. Adam had scored the lowest in all the matches, but he was beginning to understand the game and how to get positions to snooker the other players.

They found the Master waiting for them in the theatre auditorium. He signalled to them to sit comfortably in the two front rows of chairs. "Tonight's exercise has been planned to give you an introduction to the skills of coordinating other people during a crisis. All you will have to do when the call comes in is to contact the first level of the response team. They will then take control and manage the situation, but you will have the opportunity to watch what they do and ask questions as the exercise progresses. There is sufficient information in the instruction manuals we gave you today for you to play your part in this exercise. Please note that you will be getting real people out of bed to take part in the exercise, so make sure you only wake the people who are absolutely necessary. You should particularly watch out for the large amount of information that will start flowing in once people are deployed. It will all get very confusing unless somebody controls it," he warned.

"The first shift of cadets should be ready and waiting in the command centre at eight p.m. this evening. Most of the time will be spent just waiting, so I strongly suggest you borrow a book from the library and have something to read. There will be a shift operator present, and if you talk to him nicely, you might be able to persuade him to turn on the cable TV."

Captain Rogers stood and asked the cadets if there were any further questions. They all shook their heads, indicating there were no questions. "At six o'clock, you will find some food in the canteen. Please help yourself but tidy up afterwards. The lights-out time for any non-operational shift is ten thirty p.m. Breakfast will be served at seven thirty a.m. tomorrow morning. Please be showered and dressed in uniform by eight thirty a.m. That is all for the time being."

The cadets spent the rest of the time reading, playing pool, and exercising in the gymnasium. At eight p.m., Adam assembled his team in the command centre. James, the system operator that Adam had met, was no longer there. It was a new person.

"Hi. I am Adam Cranford. We are here to take part in tonight's exercise."

"Yes, the boss mentioned there might be some cadets floating around in here tonight. I guess your role is to start the activation process when the alert message comes in. Don't worry. It is all pretty straightforward, and I'm sure you will find it all very easy. If it goes horribly wrong, I'll step in and give you a hand."

The cadets had to wait over three boring hours before the alert call came in. A loud bell chimed three times, and one of the screens in front of them lit up. The words *Incident Escalation* flashed repeatedly on the screen in large red letters. Adam was ready. He quickly turned to the correct page in the instruction manual and started to follow the procedure. "Trevor, ring Headquarters on the red hotline phone and find out the nature of the alert. Harry, can you start noting actions on the whiteboard behind us? David, can you find the escalation lists? According to this, they should be on the shelves over there."

The cadets jumped into action, and Trevor reported back from the phone. "There is a report of a vandal attack on the site of our summer camp. We are to assemble a team of twenty observers to attend and photograph the vandals. It has been reported there is some damage to accommodation, and we should also provide temporary sleeping quarters for 400 people."

Adam started to direct his team. "David, have you got those lists ready yet? We need to alert the transport manager and the quartermaster to get trucks and some tents. I think we also need to alert the on-call Commandant so we can get people woken up to go and act as observers. Also, we need to alert the duty operations team to come and manage the events. Harry, can you note those actions on the whiteboard and cross them off when they have taken place?"

David found the correct contact numbers, and together with Trevor, he picked up the phones and started calling people. Within a few minutes, the phones were ringing with incoming calls, and the screens in front of them were beginning to list who was available and when they would arrive at their designated posts. The cadets were busy with recording details of the whole action plan that had swung into motion.

One of the first calls they received was from the on-call Commandant, who asked to speak to the Squad Leader in charge. "Hi. This is Barry Devon, the on-call

Commandant for tonight. I will be in the command centre in about ten minutes. Can you just confirm whether the alert mentioned if it was just a test or whether we should really get people out of their beds?"

"This is Sergeant Adam Cranford, shift leader. There was nothing on the message, sir, to indicate it is just a test. I believe this is an exercise, but so far no information given indicates otherwise."

"Ok. Well, we had best continue until we hear to the contrary. Do you have the location where the activity is taking place?"

"Yes, sir. We were given a map reference, and we have already notified the transport manager of the location."

By the time the Commandant arrived, it was almost time for Adam's shift team to hand over to the next shift. He sent Trevor to make sure the other team had woken up. Adam then showed the Commandant the notes on the whiteboard and the list of people who had been called for the event.

"That all seems to be under control. Well done, young man. Meanwhile, I should just call Headquarters and check on the status of this alert." He picked up a phone and made a call to the Headquarters controller. After a couple of minutes, he put the phone down and turned to Adam. "It is as I thought—a test event—but they do want people to go on site and get us to time how long it takes everybody to get there and commence operations. Some people are going to get a sleepless night tonight."

"Thank you, sir. It is about time for my shift to end. Do you want us to stay around and help out?"

"No. As soon as the other shift arrives, you four can go to bed. I will take command here."

As the other cadet shift arrived, Adam briefly told the Squad Leader what had happened and then led his team off to the dormitory. They quickly jumped into their bunk beds and fell asleep.

It was the total silence that woke Adam. It was pitch black in the room and deathly silent. During the day, they had become accustomed to the whispering sound of the air conditioning, but now there was nothing. Adam looked at the luminous dial of his watch. It was two a.m. He tried to click on the bunk light above him, but it didn't work. The other boys were still asleep. Something didn't seem right, so Adam slipped out of his bunk bed and quietly went about, feeling his way in the dark to the washroom. His blindfolded practice sessions with Ali gave him confidence in the total darkness. The lights didn't work there or in the corridor. He realised the power must have gone to the building. He felt his way back to his bunk and slipped on his uniform. Using the LED torch built into the badge, he made his way to the command centre. It was deserted, and the lights were out, although some of the PCs were still running.

Adam remembered the storeroom that had a load of standby torches. He headed out along the corridor and downstairs towards the room. When he reached the storeroom, he noticed the door was already unlocked. He suddenly realised that all of the doors he had passed through were unlocked. The magnetic locks had been designed to fail open in the event of a total power failure. He popped into the storeroom and collected six large torches. He returned to his dormitory with the torches and woke up the rest of his team.

"Something is wrong. The power is gone to the building. All the doors are unlocked, and nobody else is around. Dave, can you go check the other dormitory and see if the cadets are asleep there? Trevor, you wait here and when people arrive keep them here in this dormitory. Harry, can you come with me? I want to go and have a look around to find out what is happening."

Adam and Harry quickly searched the building room by room. They found no locked doors and no signs of people until they reached the lowest floor. They were about to descend the staircase to the lowest floor when Adam heard a strange scraping sound coming from further down. He turned and held his hand up to stop Harry. He whispered, "Wait here. There is something not quite right. I'm going to creep downstairs and pop my head around the corner to see what is happening. If anything happens, get back to the dormitory and try to escape from the building."

Adam tiptoed downstairs as carefully as possible and then silently popped his head around the corner of the corridor. He saw two men trying to saw their way through the padlock shackle on the armoury door. He heard them talking.

"Ron said all the doors in the building would be unlocked. We have been in here far too long already. It is taking ages to try and cut through this lock."

"Dave, stop moaning and concentrate on the sawing. What we have come for is behind that door."

"It is a high-security padlock. It will need at least twenty more minutes, even if the saw doesn't break again. Why can't we just have the power on and let me drill it off?"

"You know the power has to be off or all the doors will lock up!"

Adam realised these men were trying to break into the armoury. He didn't know what was inside there, but it must have been important. He pulled his head back and crept back up the stairs to the waiting Harry. He signalled that they should return back up the stairs quietly. He guided them back to the command centre.

"Harry, there are two guys down there. They are trying to break into a secure room. I don't know where the Foundation members have gone, but I think we should do something to stop them."

"What, do you mean call the police?"

"No. Don't forget this building doesn't exist in official records. It is supposed to be a secret place. It would take the police ages to find it, and by then, those robbers may have escaped."

Adam moved to the system operator console. It was still running, and the screen was powered, probably by some kind of battery backup to keep it running when the main power had failed. He pressed the enter key on the keyboard. The message *Keyboard locked... Enter your user ID and password* flashed up on the screen. Thinking hard, Adam recalled exactly what it was that system operator James had entered earlier in the afternoon. He could even remember which keystrokes were used for the password. He tried the combination of keystrokes that he remembered. A screen with many different icons appeared. Using a mouse, he clicked on the icon marked *Building Management*. A screen changed again showing many choices. He selected the *Power Management* option and clicked the mouse again. The screen changed to show a power diagram.

"Come here, Harry. What do you make of this diagram?"

The two cadets studied a power diagram on the screen. It looks like there was a good supply into the building, but there was a red box on the screen surrounding something called *Master Circuit Breakers.*

"Adam, click on the *Master Circuit Breakers* box and see what happens."

He clicked on the box as Harry had suggested. Another window opened on the screen, and they could see that three switches were marked in red and showed the symbol of being open. Adam clicked on one of the switches, but nothing happened.

"Try right clicking on it."

Adam tried again, this time pressing down the right-hand mouse button as he clicked on one of the switches. The symbol changed from red to orange, and some ceiling lights flickered on in the command centre. The switch symbol changed from orange to green. He repeated it with the other two switch symbols. All of the lights flickered on in the command centre. The murmur of air conditioning started again. The boys heard a *click* as the doors to the command centre locked and their magnetic locks recharged with power. Adam hurriedly changed the screen back to the main menu. He selected the *Access Control* option and another window popped up. One option was marked *Emergency Lock Down*. He clicked on that. After a few seconds, the response came back... *Building locked down. All zones locked.*

"That should give us breathing space to decide what to do next. Can you get on the phone and see if you can contact any of the other Regional Headquarters for some advice? Meanwhile, I will try and find if anyone else is in the building."

After a few false trials, Adam discovered how to use the access control system. On one of the options, he found a map of the building displayed on the screen. It was headed *Personnel Location*. Using the mouse, he scrolled from room to room on the plan. In their dormitory, he saw six beacon symbols on the screen located closely together. He clicked on them to discover it was the other cadets. On the lowest floor in a storeroom opposite the armoury, he found ten people marked on the plan. Checking through the list, he realised it was four cadets and six Foundation officers. In the corridor outside the armoury were two symbols marked as *Unidentified*. "Harry, I think I've found everyone," Adam said. "How did you get on with the phones?"

"I couldn't get through. I think the phone system is down."

Adam showed Harry the position of the various people located on the computer system. "I think we have to work out a way of getting the two crooks away from the people locked in the storage room. If I can work out how to control the door locks from here, I think we will give them what looks like an escape route. See if you can sign on as a system operator on that PC over there." Adam wrote down the user ID and password on a slip of paper and passed it over to Harry, who logged onto the system and was soon browsing through features. "Harry, look through and see if you can find the controls for the video camera system and also the intercom. We need to be able to speak to these people."

Both boys spent a few minutes working on the computer system until they had found what they wanted. Harry worked out how to switch the displays between the different cameras located around the building. He also determined how to direct voice messages to individual speakers in different rooms. Adam, meanwhile, had worked out how to remotely control the locks on all the doors in the building.

"Harry, the first thing we need to do is to try it out on the boys in the dormitory. If you can switch on the cameras and speaker in that room, we will get them moved to somewhere safer. Tell them to come up to the command centre."

Harry clicked a few entries on the screen with the mouse and then leaned forward and spoke into a microphone that extended from the desk on a flexible steel swan-necked tube. Adam and Harry could see the cadets displayed on one of the screens in front of them.

"Hi, guys. This is Harry. Adam and I are safe in the command centre. It looks like this Headquarters building has been taken over by other people. We have got control now, so you should be safe. We will unlock the doors for you so you can come to the command centre. Wave at the camera if you've heard the message."

The cadets waved at the camera and started moving towards the door of the dormitory. Adam had unlocked all of the doors along the route. They monitored the cadets' progress as they made their way to the command centre. Adam locked each door behind the cadets as they passed through. Soon, there were eight cadets in the command centre. Adam got them to sit down and then briefed them on what he planned to do.

Harry displayed the view from the camera in the corridor where the two crooks were trapped. They were trying to find a way out, having realised that when the lights had come back on, they were in danger of being discovered. Adam remotely unlocked the door leading to the stairwell. At a sign from Adam, Harry turned on the intercom speaker to the corridor.

Adam passed a note to the oldest cadet with the deepest voice and signalled to him to read from the note into the microphone. "Emergency Alert. This is National

Headquarters. There has been a security breach in this building. The police are in the process of searching the building. Please stay where you are and you will be rescued. You are in no danger. Please stay calm."

With that announcement, the two intruders became even more frantic in their attempts to escape. They rapidly retried all the doors in the corridor. They found that the door to the stairs would now open, and they rushed through up the stairs to try and escape. As they rushed through the doors, Adam silently locked the doors behind them. When they reached the floor above, they ran along the corridor, trying each door to see if it would open. At that point, to increase their confusion, Adam switched off the lights in the corridor, leaving them in total darkness. He then triggered the fire alarm system to sound the sirens in the corridor where the men were trapped. Adam released the door lock on a storeroom at the end of the corridor. From the screen in the command centre, the cadets could see the beam of light as the door gaped open. They saw the two men rush into the room. Adam locked the door, finally trapping the two men in the storeroom.

While Adam stayed in the command centre, Harry led the cadets down to the lowest floor, where they rescued the Foundation officers and cadets who had been locked in by the intruders. When everyone else was out of the command centre, Adam changed the password for the system operator to a combination that only he knew. As had been previously agreed with Adam, Harry led all the rescued people to the theatre. Adam reset the access control system so all of the badges and identity rings worked correctly. Before joining the others in the theatre, he logged out of the control system. When he arrived, he was greeted by the Commandant.

"Cadet Cranford, I hear you were the person responsible for our rescue. We are most grateful for your prompt and effective actions. When the training exercise was taking place, someone let unauthorised people into the building. They captured us at gunpoint and locked us in the storeroom on the bottom level. I need to get back to the command centre so I can contact National Headquarters and let them know what has happened. If the others wait here, I would be grateful if you can accompany me back to the command centre."

When they arrived back in the command centre, they found the system operator trying to log onto the control system without success. He looked up when he saw the Commandant and a cadet come into the room. "I was only trying to... uh... log back into the system. It looks like we have had a power outage, like the password file has become corrupted."

The Commandant spoke. "We have had a security breach. The only person I am allowing to log onto the system at present is Cadet Cranford here. I would be grateful if you can give me some assistance in getting the phone system working again."

The man paled and looked panicked briefly before he spoke. "You will just need to reboot the phone server, and it will restore the phones automatically. This sometimes happens after a power outage."

"Take Adam, here, into the equipment room and show him the phone server. Then show him how to reboot it."

The operator led Adam into a nearby room full of computer equipment. He showed him a metal cabinet mounted on the wall. The operator opened a panel door on the equipment cabinet. "Just press the red button on the front of the server inside the cabinet," he said.

Adam pressed the button, and then they returned to the command centre. The operator spoke to the Commandant on their return. "The phones should be working in a few minutes. Do you think I could have the password to get onto the system? I have a lot of work to do."

"No, not yet. As there has been a security breach, I first want to seek advice from the National Headquarters. Once they agree to that, I will let you get back onto the system. Now, if you don't mind waiting in the theatre, Cadet Cranford and I have a little work to do while we're waiting for the phones to come back."

They waited while the man left the room, and then Adam turned to speak to the Commandant. "I think the operator is involved in this break-in, sir. It is obviously very difficult to get inside this building without help. He didn't look very happy when you told him the password had been changed."

"I think you are right, Cadet. I will keep him away from the command centre until I can get a replacement person to come in. I first need to speak to the National Headquarters and get some people down here to help out. I'm still not sure why people would try and break into the armoury. It is just a Foundation tradition that every Headquarters building has a secure room marked *Armoury*. We no longer keep weapons in the Headquarters buildings."

"What do you want to do about the two intruders that I have trapped in the storeroom? Are you going to call the police?"

"That is a problem, Cadet Cranford. I do not really want to reveal the existence of this building to the police."

"I have an idea, sir, that may help. When I was browsing through the plans of Headquarters, I noticed that one of the emergency exits from this building comes out in the toilets of the supermarket above. How about we let those two guys escape into the supermarket? I think it would be an unpleasant surprise for them if they found the police waiting for people who had broken into the supermarket."

"You seem to be a devious young man. I like that plan."

They waited five minutes and tried the phone system again. It was now working. While the Commandant was talking on the phone to Headquarters, Adam got busy on the computer system. A few minutes later, the intruders locked in the storeroom noticed a slip of paper pushed under the door. It read:

> *Everything has gone wrong. I have arranged your escape. When the lights go out briefly, leave this room and follow the route in this diagram. I will meet you later.*

The note contained a sketch map of the route to the emergency exit. It was not signed. A few minutes later, the lights flickered in the storeroom and then came back on. They tried the door. It was unlocked. They rushed out of the room and found all of the doors marked on the map were unlocked. Finally, they opened the door that led onto a spiral metal staircase that rose upwards to the surface. As they mounted the stairs, they heard the door shut behind them. They climbed up the spiral stairs to find another doorway. It was unlocked. They had managed to escape from the Foundation building. When they passed through the doorway, they found that the room was unlit, but as they started moving in the room, the lights automatically flickered on. It was a gentleman's toilet room. They cautiously opened the door to leave. It was then that they noticed the blue flashing lights coming into the windows from outside the supermarket. They retreated back into the toilets but could find no way to escape. The secret door had re-locked behind them.

In the command centre thirty meters below, the Commandant was speaking to Adam. "They are going to have an interesting time tonight explaining to the police how they became trapped in the supermarket toilets overnight. It is going to be a couple of hours before the people arrive here from National Headquarters, so I suggest you take your team of cadets and go get some sleep. I will meet you for breakfast later in the morning."

Adam and his team were now feeling quite tired and were fast asleep within minutes of climbing back into their bunks.

Chapter 20 Stare into the Eye of the Dragon

The seat in the minibus was surprisingly comfortable at that time in the morning. Adam had woken early to make sure he was ready for its arrival. By the time it had arrived at the Cranfords' cottage, it had picked up most of Blue Squad already.

When the announcement was made at the Foundation meeting, it had been a total surprise. Even Chalky Benson had been surprised to have made such an announcement, but sure enough, it had been confirmed in writing that Adam's squad was expected to visit Foundation National Headquarters to witness Adam's induction as a full member of the Foundation. Normally, a boy remained as a cadet in the Foundation until at least the age of sixteen before going through an induction ceremony at his local Company Headquarters. Sometimes a cadet would reach the age of twenty-one before becoming a full member. All the boys were dressed in normal street clothes, but their No. 1 cadet dress uniforms were hung carefully on a rail mounted above the back seat of the minibus. Below their uniforms, the toecaps of their boots glistened with a mirror-like shine.

The last pickup stop of the minibus was at Brian Harrison's house. Alan Williamson jumped down from the bus and helped Brian onto the bus. "Hey, look guys!" he said. "I've found a wounded old veteran at the roadside. Do you think we should take pity on him and let him have a ride to London?"

"I'll be healed soon, Cadet Williamson, and I'll be back. You won't find me as soft as *Acting* Squad Leader Cranford. You will all be doing drills until your legs fall off."

His leg was still in plaster, but he was quite mobile on crutches. He had been insistent that he would attend Adam's induction ceremony. He sat at the front of the minibus with his plastered leg sticking out in the aisle.

The minibus arrived in the City of London at about eight a.m. The frantic rush hour was in full flow with thousands of people scurrying along the pavements to be at their desks in time for work. The minibus had stopped outside of an office tower block in a small parking bay at the side of the street. As the minibus arrived, two men in smart office suits came out to greet them. One of them had a wheelchair ready to assist Brian Harrison.

The other climbed into the minibus and addressed the cadets. "Good morning, boys. Welcome to the Foundation National Headquarters in London. When you go into the entrance lobby of the building, please go into the room immediately to the left of the reception desk. Please remember to pick up all of your equipment before leaving the bus, as it is not allowed to be parked here for any length of time."

After Brian Harrison had been assisted out of the minibus and wheeled into the building, the cadets picked up their uniforms and boots and then joined him inside the building. There was a man dressed in Foundation uniform waiting for them inside the room. "Good morning, cadets. I am Lieutenant Bill Smith. Can you please pick up your identity badges from the table? On the table at the other end of the room, you will find some bacon rolls, croissants, cheese, fruit, and cold meats. Feel free to tuck into the food for breakfast, as it is going to be a long morning for you. There are also tea and coffee. In fifteen minutes, I will lead you to the main part of the Headquarters. You will have the opportunity to change into your uniforms when you get there. Please make yourselves comfortable."

Adam was nervous and didn't really feel like eating. No one had told him what the induction ceremony would involve. He hated to think he might make some mistake and get it all wrong. He had even asked Chalky Benson, their local Company Commandant, what would happen during the ceremony. All Chalky said was, "Trust yourself, and you will be fine."

Barry could see that Adam looked nervous and he came over to chat with him. "Are you feeling ok, Adam? You are looking a bit nervous, which is quite unlike you—unless, of course, you are dangling more than three metres off the ground."

"Yeah, I'm alright. I just wish they would get on with it. I don't know what I'm supposed to do, but I guess someone will tell me before long."

Just as Adam said that, part of the wooden panels forming the wall to the office room swung back, opening into a corridor. The Foundation officer had returned to the room. "It is time to move on to the next stage," he said. "If you cadets would kindly pick up your uniforms and follow me, I will take you to a place where you can get changed into your uniforms. Sergeant Harrison, you had best come in the wheelchair, as there may be a lot of standing and waiting."

Lieutenant Smith wheeled Brian Harrison's wheelchair, leading them along the corridor. There were no furnishings in the corridor, just concrete walls painted with a thick, glossy magnolia coloured paint. The lighting was dim, and the sound of the boys' shoes echoed around the walls as they walked quickly. As they approached the heavy wooden door at the end of the corridor, it swung open, revealing a lift lobby. There were no signs of lift call buttons. The Foundation officer lifted and held his right hand close to the dragon motif at the side of one of the lift doors. The lift doors opened, and the cadets filed in. After thirty seconds, the lift stopped descending, and the doors opened again. They opened out into a large, well-furnished, brightly lit reception area.

The Lieutenant nodded to the receptionist and then led the cadets down another corridor. He stopped at a heavy wooden door. "Cadet Cranford, you stay with me. The rest of you can get changed into your uniforms in here. Someone will be along in a few minutes to instruct you as to your role in this induction ceremony."

Mickey Bryant took over the wheelchair, and the cadets disappeared into the room.

Lieutenant Smith led Adam further into the building complex. They passed through a doorway into an older part of the building. The walls were now bare stone. Overhead, the ceiling of the corridor was made of arched brickwork. At the end of this corridor was a heavy ancient wooden door reinforced with black iron straps loaded with large black square nail studs. The door handle was a heavy large black iron ring. Lieutenant Smith pulled a large old key from his pocket and unlocked the door. Grasping the heavy iron ring, he lifted the latch of the door and pushed. The door creaked open to reveal a small yellow brick windowless room with a table in the centre. There were black iron candelabras mounted on the walls, holding thick yellowish candles that dripped wax onto the floor below. The room was unheated and felt quite cool. The table was old and looked as though it had been rescued from some ancient monastery many years ago. There was a candlestick at each end of the table each with a thick, metre-high candle that lit the table with a flickering flame. Laying across the table surface was a simple white cotton thobe. A wicker clothes basket stood beside the table.

Lieutenant Smith pointed at the garment on the table. "I will leave you for a few minutes. Please change into the thobe, your first ceremonial uniform. Put your clothes and shoes into the basket. We will get them back to you later." With that, he left the room, giving Adam the privacy to change.

The thin cotton thobe, something like a tunic, slipped over Adam's head and buttoned at his neck. The sleeves ended above his elbows, and the hem of the thobe rested just below his knees. His bare feet felt cold on the stonework floor. He stood waiting in the dimly lit room for what seemed to be an eternity. He shivered in the cool of the room. Then, without warning, the heavy wooden door creaked open behind him.

An elderly man dressed in heavy ceremonial robes entered the room. In a poor light of the room, Adam didn't recognise him until he spoke. It was Hermes (Mr. Robertson), the man who had first introduced Adam to the Foundation. "Adam, when I first met you at your cottage earlier this year, I had no idea you would progress so fast. It has been my task over the past few years to keep an eye on your progress. You have pleasantly surprised us all, and we are delighted to offer you the chance of induction into the Foundation. It is my task now to prepare you for this ancient ceremony. You will be taking an Oath of Service to the Foundation. You can at any time now or in the future revoke this oath, but should you do so, you will lose all privilege and contact with the Foundation. Your local Company Commandant has already told you the guiding rules of the Foundation. When you make the oath of acceptance, you are agreeing to live by these rules. You must make the oath freely and without coercion. Do you understand what I'm saying?"

"Yes, Hermes, I do, but what happens if I say no? Nobody has asked me if I want to be inducted into the Foundation."

Robertson looked surprised at the question. "I don't think I remember anyone ever refusing the opportunity of induction, particularly at the National Headquarters. However, if you do not feel ready just yet, there is nothing to stop you from saying no now and returning to your Company. I think the Foundation would be more surprised than upset if you make that choice. Are you saying you don't want to go through with this?"

"No, that's not what I'm saying. I do want to go ahead. I was just surprised nobody had actually asked me if I wanted to do it, but I guess now that you have asked that question there is no problem, is there?"

"I must first explain the ceremony to you. It is based on an ancient ceremony handed down over the years by our predecessors. There are three parts. The first is called 'The Ordeal'. It is supposed to represent the many challenges you will face in future life. You have to face the Ordeal alone. You'll find it easy to come through the Ordeal unscathed, provided you have trust in the beliefs of the Foundation. If you falter during the Ordeal, you will be given a path that takes you outside of the Foundation, and you will soon find yourself out on the street with your parents. You will be ok as long as you think before making decisions. My only advice to you is to keep to the right path."

"My parents? They are here?"

"Yes, Adam. Of course they are here! Did you really think they would miss out on this? They are waiting for you, but they will not be allowed to see the actual ceremony. After you survive the Ordeal, the next part of the ceremony is called 'The Cloaking'. This is when you take the Oath of Service in front of your own peers. It is a time when you will discover whether you can trust them. Following the Oath of Service, you will be awarded your Foundation ring. From the time you first wear your ring, you will be a full member of the Foundation. Even so, given your age, you will continue training with your local company as part of your squad until you reach the age of eighteen."

"So, basically what you're saying is, this induction is nothing special? I will continue as normal cadet? Will there be no additional duties for me?"

"We have found over the years in the Foundation that younger members are most comfortable working amongst people of their own age group. After induction to full membership, you are normally assigned a rank. That rank is normally no less than any rank you have already achieved within the cadets. Early induction is a mark of great honour. It only comes about if you have been recommended by your local Company Commander. As to additional duties, we will have to wait and see."

"I'm freezing wearing just this thin cotton thing. When will the ceremony start? Hang on... you said there were three parts to the ceremony? Is the Cloaking the final part?"

"Ah, it is good to see you are still paying attention to the detail. I have not mentioned the third part just yet. Not everyone goes through the third part of the induction. During your brief time with the Foundation, you have done many remarkable things and shown great strength of character. The third part is a special award from the Council of Elders. I will say no more of this part for the present. Just realise it is a mark of respect. Few of the 15,000 members of the Foundation get to meet the Elders. Finally, I would like you to read and learn this list of traditional responses you should make during the ceremony. It is not essential that you get them all right, but it is a nice touch and shows respect for the traditions of the Foundation."

Hermes handed Adam a card containing the list of standard questions and traditional answers for the ceremony. Adam looked a bit bewildered at the request. "I have to learn these now? There's a whole page of them. Couldn't I have been given them earlier?"

Hermes just smiled, as if he had all the faith in the world in Adam Cranford's memory skills. "I'm just going to go out for ten minutes to check that everything is ready. The ceremony will start on my return." With a swirl of his cloak that caused the candles to flicker, he exited the room, leaving Adam to learn the responses for the ceremony.

Adam was now suffering from chronic shivering. It was really cold in the room. He just wanted the ceremony to begin. He read the ceremony responses by the light of candles and was warming his hands against the candle flame.

Suddenly, and without warning, Hermes returned. This time, he was carrying a large wooden black staff trimmed with silver bands. At the top of the staff was a small conical silver cup mounted upside down on a hook. Hermes walked around the room, progressively extinguishing the candles that lit the room by using the snuffer on the end of the staff. As he walked he chanted. "I call on the spirits of our ancestors to guide this young man as he descends into the darkness of the Ordeal. Guide him and protect him from the dangers and temptations that will face him in the future."

As Hermes extinguished the final candle, he banged the staff on the stone floor three times. The loud crashing *bang* of the final blow echoed in the total darkness of the room. Adam could no longer see Hermes, but he could hear the final instruction: "Go and find your destiny."

A loud scraping noise of heavy stone grating against stone echoed into the room. In the darkness, Adam could see the outline of the stone doorway opening. The ancient hinges squealed as a large force pushed the door open. It was dimly lit beyond the doorway. Adam had to bend down a little to pass through the doorway. He found a narrow corridor lit by an occasional candle flame, giving scarcely enough light to illuminate his pathway. The walls of the corridor were cold, damp rock. As he stepped through the doorway, it slowly closed with the same grating sound behind him. He looked behind him; Hermes had not followed. There was no handle on the door. The only way to go was along the corridor.

As he walked along the corridor, he found that the walls narrowed. At one point, they were so close together that he had to turn sideways to get through. After the narrow point, the walls began to widen. Adam looked up and could see nothing apart from darkness. He could hear the occasional drip of cold water falling from above. The path for his feet was now getting narrower, pulling away from the opposite wall, leaving an apparently bottomless drop on the right-hand side below the gap. The corridor had turned into two facing rock walls with an ever thinning ledge on the left-hand side that Adam had to walk along in the almost dark. The air was getting increasingly cold. The rock wall next to Adam was damp with running water. After another five metres along the ledge, Adam found it was only wide enough for his feet. The dark gap beside him had widened. If he slipped now, he would fall. He could hear water landing far below him. Adam's fear of heights suddenly kicked in, and he felt slightly dizzy. To make things worse, as he gradually edged along the path with his back pressed hard against the damp rock wall, his bare feet suddenly encountered absolute cold on the thin ledge. A layer of ice had formed on the surface, making it very slippery and dangerous. He knew if he tried to step on that part of the path, he would surely fall.

As he reached that part and hesitated, he heard a whisper of a voice from the darkness. "It is too difficult and dangerous. You will fall. Go back and knock on the door. It is safe behind you."

Adam felt really spooked and cried out, "Who is that? I can't see anyone. This is really stupid."

There was no response from the darkness. All Adam could hear was the steady drip of cold water. In his desperation, Adam suddenly recalled one of the guiding rules of the Foundation: "Have trust in the protection of the Foundation."

He remembered that this Ordeal was just a test and that the Foundation would not knowingly expose him to danger. He calmed a little and thought about what do. He then remembered what Hermes had said before he left the room: "Keep to the right path."

Keeping his back and left hand pressed against the cold rock behind him, he stretched out his right hand in the dark and found nothing. He tried again, leaning forward over the gap a little. This time, his fingers scraped against rock. He could not see anything, but he could feel it. The rock was dry. He leaned further forward and was able to press his hand against the solid rock. Keeping one foot on the ledge and using his right hand pressed against the right hand wall, he stretched out his right foot and felt around in the darkness. About fifteen cms. down, he felt rock beneath his right foot. It felt solid and dry. With his heart pounding, he stepped across the gap onto a solid ledge. He had found the right path.

He followed the path around a bend and up an ancient spiral stone staircase. At the top, he was confronted by three narrow doorways where the corridor widened. The lighting had improved. They were made from old wood, dark with age. They were mounted in carved arched stonework frames. In each door at head height was a small window, each heavily barred with a metal lattice grille. The first door had a bizarrely modern green and white *Exit* sign. Peering through the grille, Adam could see an office corridor leading to another door about ten metres away. The second door had a carved wooden sign labelled *Dining*. Adam could see a room containing a table laden with food. He could even smell baking cakes through the grille. The third door on the right was labelled *Library*. Adam peered through the grille and could see a poorly lit room. There was a small reading desk with a heavy book laying open on top. The only light was from a single candlestick. He could see no exit from the room.

Adam wondered which room he should enter. He saw a key hanging from a hook by one of the door arches. He picked it up. There was a label tied to the eye of the key. Using the light from the doors, he managed to read to read the label. It said, *This key can open all doors but can be used once only. Do not delay once you have touched me.*

Adam heard a grating rumble above his head. He looked up but could not see anything. He muttered to himself as he tried to decide what to do. "I don't know what that noise is, but I bet it isn't good news."

The obvious choice was the door marked *Exit*, but it seemed too easy. The door marked *Dining* looked good, but it was probably just a distraction. The rumbling overhead was getting closer. He assumed the answer would be in the Foundation's guiding rules. He quickly thought them through. He remembered, *Use the guiding light of knowledge.*

"That must be it! The book and the candle."

The rumbling continued. Adam felt something touch his head, pressing down. He tried to feel above him, but his hand met solid rock. Adam realised the ceiling was pressing down on him. He fumbled to put the key in the lock of the third door. The weight was forcing him to bend down, and the key wouldn't turn. The weight of the ceiling pressed him to his knees. In desperation, he tried turning the key both ways in the lock. It worked when he turned it clockwise. He pushed the door hard, and it started to move on rusty iron hinges. By the time there was enough space in the doorway to get through, Adam had to crawl on his hands and knees. As soon as his weight rested on the floor tiles in the room, the rumbling stopped. He looked behind him. There was only a fifty-cm. gap between the floor and the block of stone that had been crushing down on him. Experimentally, Adam lifted his weight off the floor and onto the door. The rumbling started immediately as the block descended further. He stood on the floor, and the rumbling stopped. It would not be possible to return the way he had come.

He looked around the room to find a way out. There was nothing obvious. Three of the walls were solid stone. The only door was behind him. In front of him to the side of the table were old wooden shelves containing books, as though the room was a small library. Adam could see in the dim candlelight an hourglass resting on the tabletop. Sand was running through the neck of the hourglass. He guessed he had to leave the room before the sand ran out. He quickly looked around the room for handles or levers that might release a hidden doorway, but he found nothing. The old books on the shelves looked were written by hand with a quill pen in a language Adam did not recognise. He sat on the corner of the table, trying to think what to do next. He couldn't leave the room because there were no other exits.

He idly looked at the old tome on the table in front of him. It looked like a massive visitor's registry book. Beside the book was a silver ink stand and a quill pen. People had written their names and a date in silver ink, one on each line. Adam could see that they had also written their Foundation ranks; most were cadets. Quickly flicking through the book, Adam could see that the names, signatures, and dates extended back over 300 years. He began to realise these were the names of the people who had undertaken the Ordeal before him. He turned back to the page that was open when he arrived. The last name had been signed three months earlier. *Whilst I am here, I might as well sign the guestbook to prove it,* Adam thought to himself. He picked up the quill pen, dipped it in the ink, and with a few scratching noises signed his name and date of the entry. For his rank he wrote *Acting Sergeant.*

He put the quill pen back on the ink stand and set to investigating the room again before the sand ran out in the hourglass. As he stood up from the table, there was a rustle and a creak above him. There was a sudden clatter and bang, then a creak of hinges as a trapdoor fell open and something fell from the ceiling above. He dodged it as it landed noisily on the stone floor. It was a rope ladder leading up through a hole in the ceiling. Adam grabbed the ladder and started climbing. The rough wooden rungs hurt his bare feet. He didn't see any point in staying where he was, and the next challenge may lead to the way out. He climbed up into a darkened room above. From the sound echoing around him, it seemed to be a very large room. He stepped off the ladder onto what felt like a wooden floor. As he let go of the rope ladder, it was whisked away upwards and out of sight. The trapdoor swung closed, leaving him once again in total darkness.

"Hello? Is there anybody here?" asked Adam. There was no reply.

Then suddenly, from each corner of the room, military marching snare drums started to beat with a steady rhythm in the darkness. A powerful spotlight clicked on from above and focused its bright beam on Adam, who was standing on the floor alone. A loud challenge was called out from the darkness. "Who stands before the Foundation of Honour? State your purpose!"

Adam remembered the responses he had read earlier. "I am Adam Cranford. I have come to pledge my Oath to serve the Foundation of Honour."

As Adam had read earlier, there was no response until he had repeated the pledge two more times in a loud voice.

"Do you solemnly swear to keep faithful to the Oath despite temptation or fear?"

"Aye, that I do."

"Do you swear before all those assembled here to keep and honour the rules of the Foundation of Honour?"

"Aye, that I do."

The intensity of the drumming reduced, and the loud voice called out again, "Who recognises Adam Cranford and proposes him to the Foundation?"

A voice Adam recognised called back in response. "I, Company Master Benson, propose Adam Cranford and call on all here assembled to accept him into our ranks."

"Adam Cranford, you have been proposed for acceptance into the Foundation. Are you ready to stand the trial of acceptance by a jury of your peers?"

"Aye, that I am."

"Adam Cranford, are you prepared to accept the penalty for falsehood, disrespect, or greed?"

"Aye, that I am."

The drumming fell totally silent.

"I call on the Jury to judge him."

The room resounded to the crashing sound from the nailed boots of a squad of men coming to attention and then marching to surround Adam. There were swishing sounds from the men surrounding Adam. They were still in darkness, though, and he could not see their faces.

"Commence the judgement."

Adam jumped as the tips of six gleaming swords appeared out of the darkness and rested on his shoulders, pointing at his bare neck. He could feel the cold metal through the thin cotton thobe.

"I call on the Jury to judge Adam Cranford. If any member has any doubt, they must now strike off his head."

Adam felt two of the swords lift from his shoulders briefly and then return with their sharp tips against his neck. He stood perfectly still.

A single drum began to beat a slow march rhythm in the darkness. The sword tips lifted from his shoulders. The men surrounding him slowly marched around him. As they did so, they meshed their sword blades to form a razor-sharp ring of steel around Adam's neck.

"Is he guilty of greed?"

There was a brief pause. Then six voices chanted as one in response, "Nay," and two of the swords were removed from the circle of steel with a scraping sound.

"Is he guilty of disrespect?"

"Often, but we forgive him, for he is young and foolish." Two more swords were removed.

"Is he guilty of falsehood?"

"Never." The final two swords were removed.

"Adam Cranford, you have been judged by a jury of your peers and found fit to join the Foundation."

The main lights in the hall were suddenly turned on. Adam blinked in the brightness. He saw that the men surrounding him were six cadets of his own squad. They were all dressed in their No. 1 uniforms and caps. They all held long ceremonial swords in their right hands, upright and parallel to their chests in the carry position. They were all grinning broadly. In the background were approximately fifty Foundation officers dressed in uniform.

The officer leading the ceremony called out again, "Bring forward the Foundation ring for this man."

Billy Leeds marched forward bearing a large red velvet cushion edged with gold braid. Nestled in the centre of the cushion was a small brown leather box. He stood by the long table at the head of the room. "Who bears the cloak for this man?"

Hermes, dressed in Master uniform, smartly marched forward bearing a golden tray. A heavy scarlet cloak with gold trim was resting on top. Hermes marched and stood beside Billy Leeds.

Blue Squad formed up either side of Adam and escorted him to the long table. By the time they arrived, the ceremonial officer was standing and waiting for them. He saluted Adam, then turned and picked the leather box from the cushion and opened it. It contained a simple gold ring. He took Adam's right hand and slipped the ring on his little finger. The officer then turned to the tray and removed the heavy cloak and draped it over Adam shoulders. He then turned Adam to face the assembled officers and spoke. "Adam Cranford is now a full member of the Foundation."

The audience burst into applause, and Blue Squad surrounded Adam, thumping him on his back in congratulations. Adam could see Brian Harrison swinging his legs over towards him using his crutches. Adam walked out to meet him.

"Cranford, it looks like you've beaten me yet again. I suppose you will be impossible to control in the squad when I get back."

"No. I have just been lucky, and I think I have a lot to learn from you."

Adam saw Chalky Benson approaching.

"I offer my congratulations on your acceptance to the Foundation, but I'm afraid we must delay celebrations for a little while longer. I need to smuggle you off with Hermes for a short while."

Adam turned to face the squad and shrugged his shoulders. "Hey, guys, I'm afraid I have to disappear for a while. I'll meet up with you as soon as I can."

Chalky Benson led Adam off to a side room. Hermes was standing beside the statue of a crouching dragon. "Here we are, Hermes. I've rescued him from his squad so you can have that chat with him. I'll leave you two to it."

The man left the room, switching off the lights as he left. There was just one spotlight focused on the head of the dragon statue.

"Adam, kneel here beside the head of the dragon. Follow what I am doing and press the oval shape of your signet ring against the nostril of the dragon. When her eyes light up, move your left eye close to hers and look into the red light. I will be doing the same thing on the other side of the dragon head."

"How do you know it is a she dragon then, Hermes?"

"Oh, I don't. It was the way I was taught fifty years ago when I first looked the dragon in the eye. Back then, we each had our own keys that had to fit in the two lock holes you can see on the throat down there. Now it is all computerised, and I don't understand how it really works, but this is an essential step in activating your signet ring. Your ring has to be in place the same time as mine, and I'm told the dragon records the pattern of your eye. Hush now and kneel by the dragon's head and let it read your mind."

Saying that, the old man knelt awkwardly by the carved dragon's head. He pulled back his hood and held his golden signet ring against the right nostril of the beast. He signalled to Adam to do the same at the other side of the head. As soon as Adam held his ring in place, the remaining lights in the room blinked out, leaving Adam in darkness once again.

"Adam, as we grant you the power of this ring, do you solemnly swear to uphold the rules of the Foundation and never use it for bad purpose?"

"Aye, I so swear."

A deep red light glowed around the rim of the dragon's eye. He leaned forward and stared into the eye of the beast. There was a sudden bright flash of green light in his eye and a grating rumble of stone against stone. He felt the dragon's head move away from his face. The room was pitch black and cold, though Adam could still see the after image of the flash in his left eye. His eyes were attracted to a tiny red light in front of him. He moved his hand to try and touch it, then realised it was his own signet ring that was glowing. It had the red star insignia of a Captain of the Foundation. He gasped as he realised he had been given immediate promotion at the time of induction.

[Figure 1 – The pattern on Adam's Foundation ring]

"Hermes, there is something wrong. They must have given me the wrong ring. Hermes? Hermes, are you there?"

There was no reply from the old man. When Adam stretched out his arm in the dark, he could find no one there. Where the dragon had been was a dark, empty space.

A strong, deep voice boomed out from the darkness, and a bright spot light shone on Adam's face. "Captain Cranford, there has been no mistake. The Council of Elders of the Foundation has been watching your progress carefully ever since we first made contact with you. You have shown great leadership, integrity, respect for others, and courage. We know you will not fail us in the future. Magister Hermes has served his role in your initial training and has left this room now. Do not worry, for you will see him again before long. Sit quietly for a moment and meditate on your success. Sadly, you cannot tell anyone outside the Foundation of your acceptance and success in promotion. Only your parents may know, and you must swear them to secrecy. You should know this is a great honour for you. Very few cadets are promoted in the first year of acceptance. You will not meet us now, but later, when you do meet one of us, you will know us by the gold medallion of light. Look on it now and learn the pattern."

The spotlight on his face faded. In front of him in the dark, Adam could see a golden glowing circle containing three golden triangle shapes.

"When the light returns to this room, stand up and leave by the door in front of you. You will know what to do."

The boy heard the gentle sounds of people pushing back chairs and leaving the room. In the darkness, he could see no one, but from the sound, it must have been a group of adults. Slowly, the lights above crept from a dim glow to brightness. Where before there had been a smooth, stone wall with a carved dragon head, there was now an open room with a large oak table in the centre. The walls of the room were lined with dark oak panelling. The ceiling above was undecorated white plaster in the form of arches. On the table in front of him, he saw a plain cream table cloth. There were seven ancient-looking, high-backed, ornately carved wooden chairs at the other side of the table. At each place was a simple gold goblet.

On the far side of the room was an arched doorway with a heavy dark wooden door that was swung slightly open on strong black iron hinges. He crossed over to the doorway, pausing to peer into one of the goblets to find it half full of dark red aromatic wine. The stone floor felt cold under his bare feet.

He reached the door and pulled on a heavy, black, cold iron ring to open it further. The room beyond was dark, but he stepped into it. As he entered, lights flickered into life and lit the room. In front of him in the centre of this new room was another table. He stepped forward. He heard a heavy *clunk* as the door behind him swung closed and the *clack* of a heavy bolt locking the door from the other side. On the floor next to the table was a large open wicker basket. A full-length mirror stood between the basket and the table. Laying on the table was a black Foundation Officer's uniform, a shirt, socks, underwear, and a pair of shiny black boots. Apart from that, the room was empty.

Propped against the clothes was a note written in the hand of Hermes:

Well done, my boy. You did not disappoint me, and you well deserve this new uniform. You will find it fits you perfectly. Dump your ceremony cloak in the basket and put on the uniform, then go and meet your parents. We will not meet again for a few months, but we will again in the future. Do not fear! We will be looking after you. The Council has set some tasks for you, but you will be told about these soon enough.

Adam was surprised to feel the prickle of a tear in his eyes. He had not thought he would miss the mysterious man whom he knew as Hermes. He wiped away the tear with the sleeve of his cloak, then slipped the thobe over his head and dropped the thin cotton garment and the heavy cloak into the waiting basket. In the cold room, he could feel goose pimples rise on his arms as he quickly grabbed some underwear and pulled it on. The shirt was cold white cotton but silky smooth; it had been pressed and starched. The buttons were small silver studs which Adam's fingers found difficult to pull through the button holes. The black trousers of the Officer's uniform felt prickly against his legs. It was a full ceremonial uniform, and the trouser legs had a stiff silver braided ribbon running along the outer seams. Hermes was absolutely right—the clothes fit him perfectly. The socks were comfortable, and the shiny leather shoes were soft and flexible, clinging to his feet perfectly like gloves.

Adam picked up the tunic jacket and looked at it. The outer cloth was heavy soot black woollen French serge, but the inside of the jacket was lined with scarlet silk. There were two button-down breast pockets and two button-down hip pockets. The buttons were real silver engraved with the dragon motif of the Foundation. The front of the jacket had eight small silver buttons, and the button holes were lined with silver thread. The jacket had a small upright collar with no lapels. The edge of the collar was lined with four rows of tiny silver glass beads. On the collar at both sides of the front of the neck was a small red star stud that denoted the rank of the holder as a Captain. The jacket had black shoulder epaulettes outlined in silver thread braid and tiny silvered glass beads in four rows.

He slipped on the jacket and started to button it up before he remembered he should be wearing a black necktie. He was glad his schoolmates could not see him actually putting a tie on in a fashion that even the Headmistress would have approved. After a couple of attempts, he got the length of the tie ends right. He slipped his arms in the jacket and shrugged it on. It matched his fit body perfectly. He struggled with the jacket buttons but eventually fully buttoned the jacket right up to his chin. Pausing to look in the mirror, he popped the black uniform cap on his head and adjusted it to the proper level.

There was a door at the other side of the room. It looked like a normal office door but had no window built into it. Now that Adam was ready in his new uniform, he decided to go and explore.

As Adam entered the room, his eyes blinking in the bright light, he saw a snowy-haired old man sitting at a desk writing in a large book. The man was in a formal black Foundation Sergeant uniform. He had many honour flashes on his breast pocket lapel. The man stood, snapped off a quick salute, and then gestured with a sweep of his arm to a chair in front of the desk. Adam was a little shocked that the old man had saluted him, but he returned the salute before sitting down.

"Ah, Captain Cranford, please take a seat. I have a couple things to explain to you before you go and meet your parents. They are expecting to meet you in about thirty minutes. They do not know of your promotion or of the great honour that has been given to you. My name is Bates. I am the Sergeant Quartermaster of the Foundation, and I am responsible for the transport, supplies, and funding of the Foundation activities. Please feel free to address me as 'Bates' or 'Sergeant Bates'. Everyone around here does—to my face at least—though I dare say there are many nicknames for me as you will discover before too long."

"Errm, Bates… Sergeant Bates, what do you mean by a great honour? I haven't done anything special to earn a great honour."

"Well, young sir, I must say the Foundation Council of Elders never gives out too much detail as to why they make their decisions, but you are the first Foundation cadet to be given immediate promotion to the rank of Captain in over 100 years. Never before in the long history of the Foundation has anyone under the age of twenty-one been made a Captain. The Council met and discussed your case for over an hour. These gentlemen are very important people in the outside world. It seems that in the short time you have been with us, you have made some important friends and some enemies too.

"Your rank of Captain gives you a lot of power within the organisation, which is why we are sitting here now, so that I can explain some of this to you. Like before, though, you will be expected to study and fully understand your authority and also your responsibilities.

"Firstly, let's explain the signet ring on your right little finger. It is made of gold, but as you may have guessed, it has some hidden features. It obtains its power from the heat of your body. If you stop wearing the ring for more than two weeks, it will need a couple of hours on your finger to recharge. It also recognises your body DNA and will only show its special features when you alone are wearing it. When you hold it close to the ring or locket of another Foundation member, it will glow briefly showing your rank. Here… touch your ring against mine."

Adam stretched his arm out to meet the hand of the old man. He briefly saw a red glow of a star on the surface of his ring and three blue bars of a Sergeant insignia on the signet ring of the Quartermaster. Then, something occurred to him. "Hang on, Bates… you said locket? Guys don't wear lockets."

"Yes, Captain Cranford, we also have a sister organisation we call the Guild. Few members of our Foundation below Officer or Master rank know that little nugget of information. We do not meet directly with them except at special Foundation Council meetings. That you realised so quickly is a measure of one of the reasons why you now wear the red star.

"Your ring is a token of your identity for those few occasions when you need to prove your identity and authority to other members and facilities of the Foundation. Look after it carefully, but you should know they are almost impossible to damage. They actually cost over £1,000 each to manufacture, and each one has its own unique code. When you next log on to your Foundation computer, try holding your ring against the dragon symbol and see what happens, but make sure you are alone when you do that."

The man picked up a cream coloured envelope from his desktop and passed it over to Adam. "You may like to open this now."

Adam briefly struggled with the sealed envelope and then looked inside. He tilted the envelope, and the contents popped out onto his hand. It was a small, black, plastic card. He had seen this type of thing before. His name was embossed on the front in small gold letters. "You are giving me a credit card? I don't have a bank account, and I don't earn enough to pay for one of these."

"Sir, you may recall that I said you have a lot of new power within the Foundation. One of those privileges is that you have been granted a Foundation Officer's credit card. There is no spending limit on this card. You could go out now and buy a new 747 airliner if you so wished."

"No spending limit?"

"Yes, sir, no spending limit, though you might find some shops asking you to prove your identity for unusual purchases. You also have a bank account in a Swiss private bank to back up the card. There are, however, some Foundation conditions we expect you to follow. Firstly, while you are at school, you may spend up to ten pounds each week as you please. You may also use the card to buy school books and uniforms. Outside of that, you should only use the card for Foundation business and never for your own personal gain. When you have spent money using the card, it is expected that you send me an email within thirty days explaining the expenditure you have made."

"No limit? What if I cheat and steal millions from the Foundation account?"

"Captain Cranford, I'll say this only once. We trust you. However, if you forget to send me the expenses email, you might just find out how I earned some of the nicknames they give me around here," said the old man with a twinkle in his eye. "On that note, the Foundation will understand if you celebrate your promotion by treating your parents to a meal at the Dorchester Hotel. In fact, I have already booked a table for you and your parents this afternoon. Just charge it to the card."

"But will they really take a credit card from a thirteen-year-old boy? I don't suppose you would want me to be in uniform at the hotel, would you?"

"I don't think there will be any problems there, particularly as the waiter who serves you will be a member of the Foundation. Just let him see your ring, and you will get the best possible service. First, however, we should talk about your Officer training. While you have been promoted, there are many things you should be doing and know about to perform your role properly. I will be sending you a training DVD that you can run at home on your PC. It contains a self-paced training course that should take you through most of the important issues. You will, however, need to spend a few weekends here at the National Headquarters going through some training. We will provide transport from your home to this building when the training is taking place.

"The Council of Elders requested I show you around the building now that you have been promoted. I will show you how to use some of the facilities, but you will also learn some from the training DVD. Before we set off, we will need to register the fingerprint of your little finger—the one that bears your Foundation ring. If you would like to poke your finger in this hole..."

Sergeant Bates pointed to a black box standing on his desk. On the front, there was a hole about three cms. in diameter. Adam poked his finger in the hole. After a short delay, the plastic bezel surrounding the hole glowed green. "If you would repeat that one more time, sir?"

Adam obliged and popped his finger in the hole a second time.

"Good. You are now registered. If you would like to follow me, we will start the royal tour."

The Sergeant escorted Adam along a corridor to the doors of a lift. There was no call button on or around the lift door. On the metal frame of the lift door was the motif of a dragon head similar to the one Adam had seen earlier that day. Sergeant Bates signalled to Adam to hold his new signet ring against the dragon head. As soon as Adam did that, the lift doors opened, revealing an empty lift car. Bates led Adam into the lift and pressed the button to descend down four levels from where they had met. The lift moved swiftly to its destination, and the doors silently slid open, revealing yet another corridor.

Adam recalled that the Regional Headquarters where he had rescued the Commandant looked similar to this corridor. "I've seen this type of thing before at the Western Regional Headquarters."

"Yes, sir, they are all built on the same basic plan. It is just that the National Headquarters is larger and has more ceremonial rooms. I saw on your record that you have been to a similar place before, but there are some features here which are quite different. As you no doubt are aware, your signet ring will act as an identity badge and will give you access to many rooms in this building. As a Captain, there are very few restrictions on which rooms you can enter. The room we are about to enter is slightly different. Could you kindly hold your ring to the dragon motif on the doorway for a brief moment?"

Adam touched his ring to the dragon motif outside the door and pulled his hand away, and nothing happened. Sergeant Bates then touched his ring to the motif, and the door lock released with a slight *click*.

"Some doors in this place need two separate authorised Officers to present their identity within ten seconds of each other before the door will unlock. This particular door also has a time lock and only opened because I scheduled the activity with the central security office."

As Adam opened the door, he realised it was extremely heavy and made with thick steel, but it swung easily outwards towards him on massive steel hinges. What he had thought was a room inside was dimly lit. Just inside the door was a small steel grating platform with safety handrails. There was no floor beneath the platform. Looking down, Adam could only see darkness. When he looked up, all he could see was darkness. He could not see walls to the side of him. Opposite the platform approximately two metres away was a smooth, metallic wall with no sign of any openings. He could hear the occasional drip of water landing in water hidden in the darkness some distance below. Otherwise, there was just silence.

"Captain Cranford, if you would please step forward onto the platform with me, we will go into the main vault."

Once they had stepped onto the steel grating, the door behind them swung closed and locked itself. They were standing there in almost total darkness and silence. After a short pause, a small light above their heads lit and illuminated the opposite wall. There was a faint whirring sound, and then Adam could see a metal foot-bridge pushing out with them from the opposite wall. It was about a metre wide but had no handrails. Once the footbridge had locked in place under them, the Sergeant stepped forward onto the footbridge and walked across to the opposite wall. Adam saw him place his ring against a small circle marked on the wall. There was a faint *hiss* and *clunk* and then suddenly another metal door swung open in the metallic wall at the other end of the footbridge. Sergeant Bates signalled to Adam to cross over to join him. They both stepped through into the room behind the secret door. Once they were inside, Sergeant Bates pressed another button on the wall behind them, and the secret door swung closed. As soon as the door had closed, the lights switched on in the room, providing a bright light.

"We just need to register who has entered this room. Please pop your little finger in the reader here." Bates led the way by inserting his Foundation ring finger in the reader, and Adam followed suit after the Sergeant had moved away.

In front of them was a heavy, circular bank vault door about three metres in diameter. From the top pocket of his uniform tunic, Sergeant Bates produced a key. It was like no other key Adam had seen before—a short, metal rod with irregular grooves cut in the surface. The grooves were pitted with small holes, apparently arranged at random. He put this key in a hole at the front of the vault door and then dialled a code on a combination lock. He then spun a hand wheel, and the massive locking bolts began to retract.

He turned to Adam and spoke, "You are very privileged to be in this room. It is at the direct request of the Council of Elders, a mark of their trust in you. This vault contains the first reserve of the funds of the Foundation. They wanted you to be aware that we have almost infinite funds that have been collected over many years should you need to call on them. I might add that this is only part of their funds. Now, if you would kindly follow me inside."

Sergeant Bates swung open the vault door and stepped inside. In front of him was yet another cage door made with thick steel bars. He produced another key, then unlocked the gate and swung it open. Inside, he found a light switch and lit up the vault. The room was about the size of the lounge in Adam's cottage. In one corner was a large security safe. Against the wall was some strong metal racking. There were several rows of gold bars stacked on the racking. Also on the racking were approximately twenty canvas bags filled with some objects.

"Captain, have a look inside the canvas bags. You might find it quite interesting."

Adam opened the neck of one the bags and looked inside. They were filled with small gold coins.

"They are gold sovereigns. Each bag holds approximately 2,500 coins, and at today's gold price, each bag is worth approximately £480,000. There are approximately twenty tons of gold bars on the shelves, and they are worth something like £500 million. Feel free to pick up one of the bars."

Adam stepped forward and attempted to pick up one of the gold bars using one hand. He did not succeed. He used both hands and was able to pick up the bar. For its size, which was about the same as his shoe, it was surprisingly heavy and slippery.

"They weigh about thirteen kilograms each. They are called London Good Delivery Bars. It is a standard size banks use to trade between themselves when they are dealing in gold. We bought this lot when the Bank of England decided to sell off some of the UK reserve at a very low price. It is now worth about two and half times what we paid for it."

"Why all this gold? Are you not afraid of being robbed, Sergeant Bates?"

"Over the years, the Foundation has learned not to fully trust the banking system, there is always some risk the banks will make stupid mistakes and lose their money. We have found gold a fairly secure method of keeping our money. We test each gold bar to make sure it is not fraudulently filled with tungsten which is a metal the same weight as gold. The security on this vault is rather better than the Bank of England. When the vault is locked, this room is entirely surrounded by five metres of steel-fibre-reinforced ultra-high-performance concrete. There are also some rather aggressive active defence systems."

"But surely keeping all of your funds in one place is a bit risky?"

"You don't understand. This is only a small fraction of our wealth. We have a lot invested in property and companies around the globe. We just like to have some ready cash like this on hand in case we need to raise money quickly. I must remind you of the great privilege you have been granted, having been allowed to see this money and gold. You must not discuss it with anyone else apart from me or the Council of Elders. I presume there is some purpose in you having seen this, but they have not told me what it is just yet. Well, now that you have seen this, we have done what I was asked to do, so you'd best go and meet with your parents."

He guided Adam out from the vault and swung the door closed. He moved over to a telephone mounted on the wall and dialled a phone extension number. "This is Sergeant Bates. The visit to the vault is now complete, and we are in the process of leaving. Please set the time lock on the vault door."

They left the vault area, and the Sergeant led the way ahead to show Adam the rest of the Headquarters complex. As they walked, Adam was doing some swift mental arithmetic. "The size of that vault must be massive and really heavy. How on earth did the Foundation get so much reinforced concrete poured without officials noticing?"

The Sergeant stopped a moment to explain. "The space occupied by the vault is approximately 12,000 cubic metres, and it weighs in the region of 30,000 tons. On the official plans, it is shown as a counterweight for the tall building above. The engineer designing the building made a 'mistake' by making it much too large during construction. Both the engineer and the buildings official happened to be Foundation members, and the Foundation quietly paid for the cost of the 'mistake', so no one bothered to investigate too closely. We had to have it shown on the official plans in case they try and build an underground railway near it. We are actually deeper than most underground railway lines."

As the Sergeant continued the tour around the underground maze, he stopped at several steel doorways. "There are several routes by which we can escape or gain access to this Headquarters complex. The doors I have shown you are the entrances to some of the routes. Few people are told about these routes, but we can, if we wish, visit or leave Headquarters without anybody detecting where it is located."

The rest of the building was very similar to the Regional Headquarters Adam had visited previously. There were many storerooms, power generation rooms, and other building services. They even came across a door marked *Armoury*.

"I believe you are familiar with this type of room from your previous adventures?"

"I was told no weapons are stored in the rooms—that it was just a hangover from the past."

"We'll open this door, and you can have a look inside. I have warned the central security team we might be going in there."

Sergeant Bates produced a different key and unlocked the heavy padlock from the door. Then he pressed his Foundation signet ring against the dragon motif on the doorway. A small amber LED lit up by the eye of the dragon. He signalled to Adam to do the same. Shortly after Adam's ring touched the door frame, the LED changed from amber to green. There was a faint whirring as electric motors pulled back heavy bolts within the door. The Sergeant swung the door open, revealing an inner door made with heavy steel bars a step away from them. He unlocked it and swung that open as well and then said, "Come in and have a look around."

As Adam stepped into the room, fluorescent lights flickered on. This room was indeed an armoury. There were several rows of assault rifles held neatly chained metal frames. In the corner of the room was a tall metal safe in the combination dial. Within wire cages mounted on the wall, Adam could see dozens of Army-style handguns and assault rifles. Short wooden boxes were stacked on the floor with military stencils on the outside.

"Sergeant Bates, it looks like there are enough weapons here to start a small war! I thought the Foundation armouries did not contain weapons? This cannot be legal."

"This stock of weapons is maintained purely for defensive purposes. There is a great deal of gold in the vault. It is not inconceivable that some ruthless people would try and steal the gold. Past experience has taught the Foundation that it cannot always rely on the authorities to provide protection. We stock these weapons as a last resort and never expect to have to use them. In any case, we would only release them to Foundation members who have been weapons trained by the military forces."

"So why did someone trying to rob the armoury in the Regional Headquarters where I was? They must have known there were no weapons in there."

"We do not tell many people about the armouries. Even fewer people know they are mostly empty rooms. Even the Foundation, for all its care and attention in selecting people, has some members whose morals and ethics are not the same as the others. Some members are less patient with the Council of Elders and want to take much more aggressive action to cure the wrongs of this world."

Sergeant Bates led Adam from the armoury and locked the doors behind him. He turned to Adam and said, "It is time, sir, that we finish this tour and that you go meet your comrades and your parents. They will be wondering what has happened to you. If you need to have a more detailed tour of this establishment, just send me an email, and I will arrange it."

They walked to the lift door and ascended to the main part of the building where the others were waiting. As they parted, they exchanged salutes. When Adam entered the canteen, the squad was seated around a table drinking tea and coffee. As was the tradition of the Foundation when an Officer in full uniform entered the room, they all rose from their chairs and stood to attention.

It was, in fact, Mickey Bryant who first realised the Officer was Adam Cranford, their very own Acting Squad Leader. "Hang on, lads! Napoleon Bonaparte has turned up. I don't believe it. They have stolen our Adam and replaced him with an officer clone."

Adam blushed as the squad unceremoniously came from the attention position and crowded around him, inspecting his new uniform. "It was a total surprise to me. I thought they had made some kind of stupid mistake, but I was actually in front of the Council of Elders. They confirmed the promotion in person."

Brian Harrison leaned forward on his crutches and touched the red star on Adam's collar. "They made you a Captain? That has never happened before! Even Chalky Benson doesn't know about this. I asked him at the end of the ceremony."

"I don't think it makes any real difference, Brian. I just go back and join the rest of the squad once you are fully healed. It is more an honorary position until I am eighteen years old. It certainly doesn't make me more important. I just met an old Sergeant who proved to me that it is the Sergeants who really run the Foundation."

"Oh, you didn't meet the infamous Sergeant Bates, did you? He is an absolute terror, and everybody is afraid of him. He has been around forever."

"He seemed like a nice guy to me, Brian. It was probably because I'm just a newbie. Anyway, why didn't you guys tell me about the cloaking ceremony? You guys scared me to death when you held the swords at my neck!"

Alan Williamson spoke up. "We didn't know anything about it until they separated us from you this morning. They gave us some quick training so we could do it safely. Those were real swords and very sharp, as you can see from Nick's finger"

Nick Walters held up his left index finger. It had a small, tidy bandage wrapped around it.

"You should have seen the look of horror on your face when it came to that bit about chopping your head off if we thought you'd been bad—particularly that time when I lifted the sword and put it back on your shoulder," said Alan.

"It was you, was it? I am so going to get you for that. I don't know when, and I don't know how, but I will. That was so evil! I was really cold from the Ordeal, and the whole thing was so disorientating."

Alan just laughed at Adam.

"You have done really well for the South Bucks Company, Adam, and we are all really proud of you, but don't worry... I'm sure we will get back to normal soon enough. I seem to remember you haven't finished the monkey climb just yet."

Brian Harrison interrupted the conversation. "Captain Cranford, you appear to be neglecting your parents. They have been waiting for you for ages. You'd best go and see them now. Just go down the corridor and take the third door on the right. You can catch up with us all later and tell us all about the Ordeal."

Adam walked down the corridor, tapped on the door, opened it, and walked in the room. His parents were sitting in comfortable chairs, reading books and waiting anxiously for their son.

His mother looked up and immediately recognised him. "Adam, you've got a new uniform. You look so smart! You must be a full member now, right?"

"Yes, Mum. I've now joined the Foundation as a member. They have been so pleased with me that they have promoted me immediately to the rank of Captain. I was told this is the first time that has happened in the history of the Foundation."

The news shocked his parents. They both stepped forward and embraced him in a hug. His father was slapping him on the back.

"Dad, please stop hitting me before you break one of my ribs. This promotion has to remain secret within the Foundation, although I am allowed to tell you about it. I've arranged a celebration meal this afternoon, and when we get there, I will tell you all about the ceremony."

Chapter 21 The Holidays are Over

Gordon Cranford yawned and rubbed his tired face. It had been a long drive, and his back ached. "Wow, it is a real relief to finally get back here, Amanda. The traffic jams on the motorway were terrible. Every year we say we are going to avoid them, but we never do."

The Cranford's trusty old estate car had just pulled up outside of their cottage following a two- week camping holiday on the coast of Devon. It had been a family tradition for several years now, but both parents were beginning to realise that maybe this was the last year this type of holiday would happen. Adam and Gilly were still asleep in the back of the car, surrounded by the debris of the camping holiday. It had been a long, eventful school summer holiday with Adam's Foundation summer camp and his sudden promotion within the Foundation. In a couple of days, the children would be returning to school.

Amanda Cranford leaned back in her seat and shook the tanned bare knee of her son. "Come on, Adam, wake up. We are back home now. Can you run down to the supermarket and get some fresh milk? I think it should still be open. We will unpack the car while you are away."

Adam enjoyed the opportunity to stretch his legs as he trotted down the lane from his cottage. He looked back at his father's car, smiling to himself at the heavily laden roof rack. There were two surfboards tied on top. He had spent much of the two weeks in the sea relearning the fundamentals of surfing. It had been a good holiday, and he had earned a wicked tan. He wondered whether this would be the year he would succeed in persuading his father to get rid of their old wreck and maybe get a new car. The current one was so uncool.

By the time Adam had returned to the cottage, all the holiday gear was stowed away. His rucksack was waiting at the foot of the stairs for him to take up. He could hear Gilly in the shower, and his mother was laying plates ready for an evening meal. He wandered into the kitchen to drop off the milk he had purchased.

His mother looked up at him. "Young man, you certainly have grown over the summer holidays. We had best check your school clothes to make sure you have not grown out of them. Tomorrow we'll go over to the school uniform shop for both you and Gilly. When she is out of the shower, you had best pop in, because you're a bit hot and sticky after that long trip. I'll have some tea ready when you get down."

"Aw, Mom, do we really have to spend the day shopping? I'm sure the uniform is just fine. It's only a couple months old."

"We'll check it in the morning. At the very least, you need a haircut before going back to school. Now go upstairs and winkle Gilly out of the shower or she will be there all evening."

Grabbing his rucksack, Adam ran up the stairs and banged on the bathroom door.

"Come on, Troll Face! There are other people who need to use the shower."

As Adam had anticipated, there was a shriek of protest from his sister, so he decided to leave it for a few more minutes before coming back. He went into his own bedroom and looked around. It seemed like he had hardly been in the room at all during the summer holidays apart from when he'd been working with Ali. The Foundation summer camp had been hard work, but he had enjoyed it. The family summer camp had been much more relaxing but somewhat spoiled by Gilly, who was always moaning that she could not contact Billy. He unpacked his rucksack and dumped his dirty clothes in the laundry basket along the corridor. As he went past the bathroom door, he knocked on it again.

Gilly responded with a shriek. "Oh, go away, Adam! I've almost finished. I'll be out in two minutes."

Adam returned to his bedroom and briefly tidied it while he waited. He could not resist running his hand over the black cloth of his Foundation Officer's uniform. He gave a little smile as he fingered the red star insignia of a Captain. He retrieved his Foundation ring from the safe place where he had hidden it while he was on holiday. He slipped it on his finger, but there was no immediate reaction. He had expected a brief red flash indicating that it recognised him. Adam then remembered the ring would need a period of a couple of hours to recharge fully after having not been on his hand.

"Come on, then, Porky. It is time for your shower."

"Porky" was the cruel nickname given by Gilly to Adam when he was younger and had gained some fat. It was no longer true, but she still used it when she was trying to tease him. He knew well enough not to react to the jibe.

Adam showered and then went downstairs to join the family meal. His mother had been able to conjure up a good meal from almost nothing in the refrigerator. As he sat down, his mother noticed that the signet ring had reappeared on his right hand.

Once they had started eating, his father spoke to him. "Did you enjoy the holiday, Adam?"

"Yes. It was really great. Thanks, Dad. I was getting really good at holding a wave in the surf by the end of the holiday. Are we going to go somewhere more exciting next year? Staying in just one place does get a bit boring."

"We will have to see what we can afford next year, but maybe we can find another location for our holiday. I presume you will be going on summer camp with the Foundation as well again next year?"

"Almost certainly, Dad, but we get a choice of three different dates, so I can arrange Foundation summer camp around any plans you might make for our holidays."

"Don't I get some say on where we go for holidays?" asked Gilly.

"Of course you will, dear, but that is a long time away, so don't worry about it now. I need you to check your school uniform and come shopping with Adam and me tomorrow."

"Adam, do you have any activities planned with the Foundation or with your school over the next term? Our father and I need to sort out our diaries."

"I have a couple of training weekends with the Foundation. The next major thing is a day trip to London with the school to go and visit Shakespeare's Globe Theatre. I don't know the timing of the training weekends, but I will log onto the computer and let you know later tonight."

Their mother looked at her watch. "Hmm, it has just gone past eight p.m. You two have had a very long day. It is probably good idea if you go up and rest in your bedrooms. We will have an early start tomorrow to make sure I can get around all the shops in time before I have to go to work in the afternoon. Unless, of course, either of you would like to stay here and help with the washing up?"

Both children decided it was a good idea for them to go and rest in their bedrooms. Gilly had her own television in her bedroom, and Adam wanted to log onto the computer to find out what had been happening while he'd been away. Shortly afterwards, they were both in their own respective bedrooms.

Adam found his digital camera from the pocket of his rucksack and loaded the holiday photographs onto his PC. He planned to call his mother upstairs later so they could together select the best photographs and upload them via the Internet to a photo processing company. He wished he could use his Foundation credit card to pay for that, but he remembered the stern warnings given by Sergeant Bates.

He pressed his signet ring against the dragon motif on his keyboard. The system automatically connected to the Foundation computer system, pausing briefly to wait for Adam to enter a password. He first checked his personal email, then switched back to the Foundation system. After he had deleted the SPAM email, there were still remaining about sixty emails from friends and from the Foundation.

It took him an hour or so to work through the emails before he was able to log on to his now-favourite computer game, *Thorn World*. There were some messages from the other mercenaries in Visiting Havoc and also some from the managers of Adam's virtual business. Combined with the loot he had gained from the big battle and the profits from his business, Adam had accumulated a substantial number of Thorn dollar credits. He wondered if there was some way he might set up a virtual bank in *Thorn World*. There was clearly money to be made in trading Thorn dollars for real money. He decided to send an email to Sergeant Bates to see if there was somebody who could help provide advice. While it was not strictly Foundation business, he could use the profits to provide further help for Ali. Switching to his Foundation email system, he started to type:

> *Dear Sergeant Bates,*
>
> *I know you must be a very busy person, but I would be grateful if you*

could find some time to give me a hand with a project I'm running. I need to talk to somebody about setting up a virtual bank in a cyber world game I regularly play. The game is called Thorn World, and I suspect it has some connection with the Foundation, as it was given to me by Hermes. I will use the profits from this game to help do some assignments given to me by the Foundation.

Kind regards,

Capt. Adam Cranford

He clicked send to despatch the message and then switched back to *Thorn World*. Bright Petal was online, so he sent a hello message.

Bright Petal: Hi, bad totem. How goes it? Not seen u 4 a while.

BaD Totem: Yes. I've been on hols. 4 2 wks. Got a gr8 tan. Have my managers looked after you?

Bright Petal: Yeah, they were fine. Missd U in the battles though, but Dark Sheikh has been around.

BaD Totem: Battles? How is that? Thought we had a serious reputation now after the Big Battle.

Bright Petal: No... there still some sharks circling. We may have beaten a big army, but they had lots of friends.

BaD Totem: Is much happnin rite now?

Bright Petal: No. I think they r all on hols 2

BaD Totem: KK. CU L8rs

Adam was now feeling tired, so he switched off his computer and went to brush his teeth before going to bed. He was soon asleep.

§

The following day, the Cranford children checked their school uniforms. Gilly needed a full outfit, and Adam had grown out of his school trousers. It appeared his legs had grown a bit during the holidays. He also needed some new school shoes, as his existing pair were rather worn down at the heel. When they arrived at the uniform shop, they found it was packed with other children and parents.

"Mum, you look after Gilly, and I'll sort out my uniform. I know what I need to get."

"Ok, Adam. Just come and find me when you are ready."

Adam eventually attracted the attention of a shop assistant, who helped him choose some school trousers, a pair of rugby boots, and a pair of shoes. The assistant checked the measurements of Adam's feet just to be sure he had the right shoes. "How do you want to pay for this, young man? Are your parents around?"

she asked.

Adam reached in his pocket and pulled out his Foundation credit card. The assistant checked the black card, turning it over to check the details. She handed the card back. "Yes, sir. I'm sure this will be fine. In total, that will be £115.12"

She wrapped the goods and put them into a carrier bag as she entered the amount on the cash register. "Please swipe your card."

Adam put the card into the reader just like he had seen his parents do on many previous occasions. The message *Please wait...* appeared on the LCD screen on the card reader. It soon changed to *Enter PIN code*.

Adam tapped in the PIN he had memorised for his card. The message on the LCD screen flashed *PIN code accepted*.

The lady sales assistant smiled and completed the transaction. When the receipt had printed, she handed it to Adam along with the bag containing his new clothes and shoes. "Don't forget your card, sir."

Adam smiled and left, bag in hand, to find his mother. She was still battling with Gilly over the size of uniform that was suitable. Adam held up the bag for his mother to see. "All done, Mum."

She looked a bit surprised.

Adam just held up his right hand and pointed to the ring on his little finger. "I have some new privileges now, Mum. Being able to pay for school uniforms is one of those."

She looked bemused for a moment and then shrugged her shoulders and turned back to dealing with her daughter. After a while, all the necessary items were purchased, packaged, and paid for. The next stop was at the local post office. There had been some attempted deliveries while they had been on holiday. Adam and Gilly waited in the car while their mother went inside. She came back carrying three parcels. When she had got back into the car, she turned and dropped one small parcel on Adam's lap. "From the postmark, I would say the Foundation has sent you something new."

"Open it up, bro. I bet they sent you some boot polish so you can get your boots really shiny."

The ritual of shining Adam's parade boots ready for the Foundation meetings was something Gilly always tried to tease Adam about at home. She didn't see the point of wasting half an hour just to get shiny boots.

"Don't be nosy, Gilly. It is none of your business. I'll open it when I get home."

"We're going food shopping next, Adam. If you want, you can wait in the car and open the parcel. Gilly and I will do the shopping together."

Adam stayed in the car while his mother and sister visited the supermarket. When he opened the package, he was surprised to find what looked to be an asthma inhaler. There was a note attached from the Foundation Quartermaster's team in

London:

> *Dear Captain Cranford,*
>
> *Please find enclosed your personal survival pack. Our records show you had mild asthma when you were younger. This inhaler contains ten doses of genuine Albuterol, but it is not intended be used for medical purposes. This is purely a disguise for the true purpose of the unit. Please access the Foundation Knowledgebase on the central computer for full details on how to use the unit and its contents.*
>
> *In summary, it has the following features:*
>
> *Basic lock pick and tension bar/screwdriver/cutting edge*
>
> *Button-sized magnetic compass, watch, and LED torch*
>
> *Pure silver Nano powder*
>
> *Potassium Permanganate crystals*
>
> *Micro flint and coated magnesium shavings for fire lighting*
>
> *30 cms. Nano diamond-coated carbon fibre wire for cutting*
>
> *Please study the instructions before attempting to disassemble the unit. It is impossible to reassemble it without guidance. This is personal equipment and should not be shown to other people. You are advised to carry it at all times.*
>
> *Yours sincerely,*
>
> *Office of the Quartermaster, National Headquarters*

Adam repackaged the parcel, intending to have a close look at the "inhaler" when he got home and could read the instructions via his computer.

When the Cranford family returned home and Gilly had gone upstairs with her new clothes, Amanda Cranford turned to her son and asked, "Now, young son, tell me how you actually paid for the school uniform. Did your father give you some money?"

Adam passed her his Foundation credit card. She turned it over in her hand. The issuing bank name was that of an exclusive private bank in Switzerland. She could see her son's name embossed on the front of the card. "So, when do we have to pay back for this, Adam?"

"You don't, Mum. Remember what Mr. Robertson said when he visited us? The Foundation will pay for my uniforms and Holliston's school. All I have to do is just send an expenses claim to the Foundation by email. They will settle the bill for the credit card."

"I'm not sure I'm too keen on this—them letting you have a credit card and spending whatever you want."

"No, Mum, don't worry. I can only use this on Foundation business. That includes school uniforms for me. They trust me not to break the rules. Are you trying to tell me you do not trust me with a credit card?"

"Of course that's not what I'm saying, Adam. Of course I trust you. It was just a surprise really. If it was your sister Gilly, I'd be worried. Do all the cadets get these cards?"

"No, Mum. I think it is just the Officers. As a Captain, I fall into that category."

Adam was dying to tell his mother he actually had no spending limit on the card, but he had been sworn to secrecy on that particular bit of information. Even his parents could not be told. As soon as he was able, he went to his bedroom to learn about the features of his Foundation inhaler. He felt uncomfortable about keeping secrets from his mother, but he supposed there were good reasons for maintaining the secrecy.

As all school children know, the last two days of the summer holiday passes extremely quickly. So, sooner than Adam and Gilly had wished, they found themselves early in the morning standing at the school bus stop waiting for the buses to arrive. They were both soon captured in the routine schoolwork and school activities.

Gilly was doing well in the arts at school. She really enjoyed drama and music and was doing very well in English. Adam, on the other hand, much preferred the scientific subjects and also mathematics. When the detailed plans for the school trip to the Globe Theatre were announced, Adam was not very interested, but he thought he should go on the trip anyway. There were to be fifteen boys from Holliston's and fifteen girls from St. Josephine's school travelling on a single coach down to London. The boys had to be at the main school bus stop by eight a.m. on Tuesday morning. It was planned that the coach would pick up the girls shortly afterwards. While they were there, they would be watching a Shakespeare play performed in period costume.

Adam was pleased Simon Davidson and Darren Nichols were going along on the trip but disappointed that his class enemy John Nelson would also be coming. The trip had almost been cancelled the day before the trip due to a fire at the bus company where three coaches had been destroyed. Fortunately, the school's temporary English Master Alan Howard had been able to persuade an alternative bus company to provide a coach at short notice.

Gilly had been quite indignant at having to get up early so the Cranford family could wave goodbye to Adam when he climbed onto the coach. To Adam's great relief, his mother was not too intrusive as the rest of the boys climbed onto the coach. There was the usual rush to try and get the back seat of the coach. Adam and Simon were seated together a few rows from the back. There were a few *clunks* and *bangs* under their feet as the coach driver and one of the teachers loaded the pre-packed lunches into a luggage storage area. Then, after a *hiss* of the air brakes, the coach set off to pick up the girls from St. Josephine's.

As the girls climbed noisily onto the coach, chatting and giggling, Adam was surprised to recognise two of them—the pretty Indian girl Deepa Gohil and Sally Busby, who had been at Darren's barbecue. Deepa was talking to one of her friends and did not notice Adam, but she and Sally waved to Darren before sitting down in the front half of the coach. Shortly before the coach departed, one of the teachers stood in the aisle of the coach and made the usual round of announcements about the organisation of the trip. Nobody took too much notice, but they did respond to the roll call that took place before the coach departed.

After negotiating its way around the town, the coach set off along the old London Road towards its eventual destination of the Globe Theatre. There was some banter between the pupils as they got settled into the trip. Mobile phones had been permitted, so some of the children were soon engrossed in phone calls and sending text messages to their friends. Darren was exchanging text messages with Sally, who was sat five rows in front.

A few miles down the road, Adam could see some of the girls at the front of the coach had suddenly stopped talking on their mobile phones and were looking at their handsets. It seemed they had suddenly gone into a dead zone where no wireless signals could be received. This part of the road was located in a deep, small valley with large trees at either side. The phone users patiently waited for the signal to resume. Then, without warning, the coach driver suddenly braked, throwing some people who were not strapped into their seatbelts off their seats. A large, dark blue van had overtaken the coach and suddenly cut in front. The blue van had come to a sudden halt, blocking the road. The coach driver beeped his horn in frustration at the bad driving. Suddenly, the back doors of the van burst open, and men dressed in dark blue coverall boiler suits and full-face ski masks jumped out, carrying sub-machine guns. Adam looked behind the coach, but that way was blocked by another blue van.

Two of the men pointed their sub-machine guns directly at the driver and forced him to open the door of the school coach. Two more of the men quickly jumped into the coach and stood at the front of the aisle. One of them issued a command to the people on the coach in a loud but calm voice. "Stay calm! Do nothing, and you will all be ok. I am the leader, and we are terrorists. You are being taken hostage and will not be harmed so long as you follow our instructions. One of my men will come amongst you and collect your mobile phones. Do not try and call for help. Your mobile phones will not work anyway."

Alan Howard, the teacher, jumped up as the man with the bag collecting the mobile phones came close. He bravely tried to wrestle the man's gun away. He succeeded and used a karate chop to knock the man down onto one of the coach seats. He swung the sub-machine gun towards the leader of the terrorists, and two rapid shots rang out. The terrorist leader stood for a moment and then walked forward as Alan Howard fell to the floor of the bus, clutching two bullet wounds in his chest.

The terrorist leader looked around and said in a loud voice, "Are there anymore heroes who want to die? No more heroics! We don't want to hurt any of you. Just obey our orders."

The leader signalled to two of his men to remove the body of Alan Howard. There was a shocked silence on the bus as the two men dragged the body along the floor and threw it into the back of their blue van. The terrorist who had been attacked by Alan Howard got up and resumed the collection of mobile phones from the teachers and pupils. Nobody hesitated to hand over their mobile phones. By that time, the coach driver had been handcuffed using heavy plastic ties. He was taken outside the coach and forced into one of the luggage compartments underneath.

The leader of the terrorists stood at the front of the coach and issued another command. "We are now going to drive you to another place. Do not attempt to escape or signal to other road users. If you do, you and the person next to you will be shot."

Two terrorists remained standing on the coach. A third got into the driver's position and started the engine. The blue van in front of the coach pulled away, and the coach followed. As they came around the next bend in the road, there was a queue of traffic in the opposite direction, held up by temporary traffic lights at what appeared to be roadwork. The passengers on the coach were numb with fear and made no attempt to signal to the other vehicles. A few minutes later, the coach pulled off the main road onto a smaller secondary road. One mile later, they pulled off the road into a gateway and of what appeared to be a disused coach garage.

A man jumped out of the leading blue van and ran over to the garage. He unlocked the small doorway and ducked inside. Shortly afterwards, the main garage doors started to slide open. They drove the coach inside the garage. Inside was a large silver-grey tunnel or shelter built on the floor. The terrorist who opened the garage doors moved over to the tunnel and swung open a massive door. The terrorist driving the coach then drove the coach into the tunnel and turned off the engine. Once the coach had stopped, the terrorists closed the door of the tunnel, completely enclosing the coach.

As the leader of the terrorists stood up at the front of the coach, fluorescent lights were switched on inside the tunnel. The first command he issued was quite simple. "Stay in your seats. Do nothing and keep quiet."

Adam sat quietly with Simon at the back of the coach. He looked around to see if there was anything he could do. He knew there was little point because these men were well armed and well organised. Still, he wondered why school children would have been taken hostage by terrorists. As he looked at the wall of the tunnel, he realised it was, in fact, a steel cage covered by some type of material or mesh.

Simon quietly whispered to Adam. "Because Darren's parents are so rich, they are afraid of kidnapping, so a security company had some special shoes made for Darren. They contain a tracking device, and he has probably switched it on already. It will be monitored by satellite, and an alert will be raised automatically. The police will know where we are and that something has gone wrong."

Simon carefully looked in the direction of Darren and pointed at his shoe. Darren looked puzzled for a moment and then gave a look of realisation before he fiddled with his shoe. He returned a brief smile to Simon and made a thumbs-up signal.

"I think he got it working, Adam. The police will now know we have been kidnapped and where we are."

"I'm not so sure, Simon. These people seem really well organised. Did you notice they had jammed all of our mobile phones before they stopped the coach? That type of mobile phone jamming needs specialist military equipment, and this tunnel they drove us into looks a bit odd. I think the walls are made from metal mesh. If I'm right, I think it will stop any radio signal from escaping, even to satellites. So far as the authorities know, we are still on our way to London. Nobody else saw the kidnapping because the terrorists stopped the traffic using those fake roadwork crews."

One of the terrorists came onto the coach carrying a small radio like device. It had a short aerial projecting from it. Using sweeping motions, he inspected the length of the coach until he came to where Darren was sitting. He paused and then tipped the tip of the aerial downwards. He pointed at Darren's feet and, using the beckoning finger signal, demanded that Darren remove his shoes. Darren shrugged his shoulders, removed his shoes, and passed them over. The terrorist left the coach with the shoes and then returned to recheck the whole coach for any radio signals. Satisfied, he left the coach.

A few minutes later, the terrorist leader came back into the coach and issued new commands. "We are now going to move you to another vehicle. The girls will get off first, followed by the boys. The teachers and other school staff will remain seated in this coach. When you get off the coach, follow the instructions you are given without question and don't try anything silly."

He pointed to the first girl and then towards the exit. She got up and left. A minute later, he pointed to the next girl, and she got up and left the coach. He repeated this process for each school child on the coach. When Adam's turn came, he got up and left the coach. When he left the silver-grey tunnel, he was directed by one of the terrorists to a large tent that had been erected inside of the garage.

Inside the tent, he was met by a terrorist bearing a machine gun. "Strip off all your clothes and walk through the detector archway, then put on one of those orange coverall boiler suits. Put all your clothes and shoes in that tub over there. Put your watch in this bin. If you have to keep anything, show it to me before you go through the detector archway. Move!"

Adam was embarrassed at stripping in front of the man but did not want to argue with somebody holding a machine gun. He removed his Foundation inhaler from his blazer pocket and also removed his Foundation ring from his little finger. He showed them to the terrorist waiting by the detector archway. The man briefly inspected the inhaler and then placed it and Adam's ring in a tray the other side of the detector as the boy undressed. Throwing away his cherished five-button school blazer made him very sad. The man signalled to Adam to walk through the detector and then made him do a 360-degree turn before letting Adam get dressed in the boiler suit. Adam picked up the inhaler and his ring. The terrorist had not noticed that Adam had made use of the skills taught him by the Foundation Instructor Grace Richards. He had palmed his Foundation credit card like a magician.

Once he had dressed in the boiler suit, he was directed out through another door of the tent. He joined the other pupils standing barefoot, also dressed in orange boiler suits waiting beside a large container lorry that had driven into the garage. They all looked subdued and scared. Some of them were crying. At the other end of the garage, Adam could see one of the terrorists pressure washing the dark blue colour from the vans to reveal a white colour under the blue paint.

When the final pupil had passed through the strip search, the terrorist leader gathered them altogether. "I am sorry about that last bit of unpleasantness, but we had to be sure there were no further tracking devices in your clothing or on your bodies. When you get to your destination, you will be given clean clothes and suitable underwear. Now, unfortunately, you have a long lorry journey ahead of you. For the duration of the journey, you will be locked in individual cubicles within the lorry. As you get onto the lorry, one of my men will give you travel sickness pills. I strongly suggest you take them. If you need to use the toilet during the trip, wave your hand outside the cubicle door, and one of the guards will lead you to the portable toilet we have installed in the lorry. Now, let's get you into your cubicles."

One by one, the terrified children were led into the lorry and locked into their individual cubicles. Inside each cubicle was a padded office chair. The cubicles had just enough space to allow each child to either stand or sit down. The cubicles themselves were made from heavy steel mesh with a cage door and were fixed along the interior long sides of the shipping container.

The terrorist leader climbed into the shipping container once all the children were locked in place. "We are now about to set off on a journey. It will be at least twelve hours long. You must all remain silent during the journey. Anyone who makes too much noise will be gagged and tied if necessary."

He jumped down from the lorry, and the doors of the shipping container were closed and bolted. Adam felt the vibration and noise as the lorry diesel engine was started. There was some jolting as the lorry found its way to the main road system and started its long journey.

As the lorry disappeared out of sight, the terrorist leader switched on a disposable mobile phone that had never been used before and made a report. "This is Alpha 3. Phase 3 complete." He then switched off the phone, removed the SIM card, and then chucked the phone in the tub containing the discarded watches. He turned to one of his men and issued a command. "Take someone in the van and take that tub full of clothes and the bin containing watches to the shredding company. When you have done that, take the van to the scrap yard and have it crushed into a cube. If you then go to assembly point Delta, you will be picked up as previously agreed."

He watched as the clothing was loaded to be taken for shredding and the van driven away. He returned to the cage accompanied by two of his men bearing sub-machineguns. Moving inside the cage, he directed the remaining teachers to leave the coach. "Get out of the coach. My men will guide you where to go. We are going to lock you in a cage temporarily. Once that is done, we will be leaving the garage. We do not intend you to come to any harm. When we're a suitable distance away, we will alert the authorities and tell them where to find you. As I said earlier, this is a hostage situation, and we will be demanding a ransom for the release of the children. They have been removed to another place. I will not waste my breath by telling you not to involve the police, but I will tell you we will make every effort to keep the children safe while negotiations are ongoing."

As the teachers left the coach, they were directed into the smaller cage that had been built within the tunnel. The cage door was locked. The terrorists removed the disorientated coach driver from the luggage compartment. His plastic tie handcuffs were removed, and he was dumped in the cage with the teachers. After re-locking the small cage, the terrorists then left the main cage, making sure the gate had been securely chained shut.

Once outside the cage, the terrorist leader pulled off his ski mask, exposing his face. His men did likewise. "Good. Now we just need to deal with the mobile phones and the bus registration plates. Can you take the car and deal with them as we have planned before?" He pointed to one of his men who nodded in agreement. He picked up the metal case containing the mobile phones of the school children and teachers. The terrorist loaded the phones into the back of the car and drove off.

"The rest of you can help tidy up and dump stuff in the van before we leave. Meanwhile, I have a few surprises to set in motion for when these people get rescued. Remember to keep your gloves on."

The men dismantled the large tent, and using the high-pressure water jets, they scrupulously cleaned the floor inside the garage outside of the main cage. While they were doing that, their leader climbed to the top of the cage and connected pre-installed wiring to a control box. Having completed that task, he returned to the ground and hung the key to the padlock on a purpose-built hook outside of the cage gate. He carefully inspected the garage for any clues that may have been left behind. Satisfied there was nothing, he signalled his men, and they climbed into the van and drove off to a prearranged rendezvous point. He closed the main door of the garage and switched off the lights, leaving the place in darkness. A car was waiting for him outside. He settled in the back seat and was driven away.

When the car was five miles away from the bus garage, the driver made a short mobile phone call to another phone located in Birmingham. "Package collected undamaged."

The teachers and driver locked in the cage in the bus garage waited until there was no more noise from the terrorists and then attempted to escape from the cage. It was very dark in there, and they had to feel their way around to look for an escape route. It was no use; the door and bars of the small cage were secure. They were still terribly shocked at the shooting of Alan Howard but knew they had to do something to raise the alarm. Miss Dunmore lamented, "If only we had a mobile phone to call for help."

The coach driver slapped his head in frustration and then felt in his pockets. "I'm stupid. They forgot to take my mobile phone. I've had it all along." He pulled it out of his pocket and felt for the dial buttons. There was no reaction, and it was then he realised that during the bumpy ride in the luggage compartment, the battery must have been jolted turning off his mobile phone. He held down the power button for three long seconds before a tune burst out from the phone. In the silence of the bus garage, it seemed so loud. All the people in the cage held their breath, hoping there were no terrorists around that might have heard the sound. The driver dialled 999 on his mobile phone. He waited but only heard the tone that indicated the call had failed. He looked at the signal strength meter, and there were no bars showing. "They are either jamming the signal still or this cage is stopping it. We should get five bars in this part of the country."

§

One hour later in the vehicle park of a motorway service station, an average-height, non-descript man attached the stolen registration plates to the front and rear of a parked tourist coach using powerful double-sided adhesive tape. Using powerful magnets, four of the kidnapped children's mobile phones were fastened to the underside of randomly selected parked cars.

§

Three hours later, a brief phone call was made from an Autoroute service station in France to the secretary's office at Holliston's school. "Hello. This is Holliston's School secretary's office."

"Do you have a pen and paper handy?"

"Yes. Who is this?"

"Don't ask questions. Write down this number."

"I beg your pardon?"

The woman with the French accent continued speaking and gave a six-digit number and then asked, "Have you got that number?"

"Yes, but what is all this about?"

"We have kidnapped your school trip children. Send the police there."

"Is this some kind of sick joke? Send the police where?"

The phone call had ceased, and there was only a dial tone.

The school secretary put the phone down thinking it was a prank. She had a nagging doubt and contacted the staff room to see if any school trips were running. She would normally know such things but had just recently come back from sickness. The food poisoning had been sudden and very debilitating. The doctor was not sure of the cause but had told her to rest and to stay away from work for a few days.

§

Shortly after the phone call to the school, an average-looking man walked past parked cars waiting to travel on the Euro-tunnel train across to France. By the time he had left, five more mobile phones were secured under randomly selected cars with powerful magnets. As he left the ferry town on the final part of his mission, he stopped in a wooded roadside pull-in and extracted Darren Nichols' shoes from a magnetically shielded box and threw them into the woodland.

A control room in Seattle in the USA immediately received an alert signal that one of their English clients had activated their emergency tracking signal. They guessed it was probably a false alarm, but they immediately phoned their counterparts in London, giving the location of the tracker beacon.

Chapter 22 Isolated

Their farmer host was indeed a happy man. It had been a few months since rain had fallen on the land of the farm in the South African semi-desert area of the Great Karoo. Instead of the diamond-bright stars that usually hung over the farm at night, the sky had gradually become heavily cloud covered with dark, humid storm clouds. Just after dark, a stunning firestorm of lightning strikes was unleashed from the heavy clouds. The storm seemed to hover over the cauldron of the valley where the farm was located. Ripples of lightning crashed repeatedly and deafeningly into the tips of the Ironstone cliffs high above their valley. Torrents of heavy rain lashed the ground, causing the streams to fill and swell as the drought was broken at long last.

In the morning, the velvet humidity of the previous afternoon had gone. The atmosphere of the morning was bright and clear. Selwyn Howell and his wife had breakfasted with the farmer. They had so enjoyed the peaceful life in this valley away from the pressures of towns and cities. Selwyn's rental of the bus garage had produced a good income and required no supervision from South Africa. The farmer had received an early-morning phone call from one of his friends suggesting it was the ideal time for the English couple to visit the Valley of Desolation. It was only about a half hour away, and the clear skies washed free of their dust by the heavy rain would give spectacular views.

The Howells had heard of this place. In this remote part of South Africa, not many foreign tourists arrived to visit the eerie beauty of the spectacular views. It seemed a great opportunity, so they readily agreed when the farmer suggested it as a day trip. The farmer was skilled in running the guest houses he had built alongside the farm to supplement his income. He had built up many contacts in the locality. When his guests had agreed to the trip, he called his friend and asked him to arrange transport. A Japanese SUV and driver turned up at the farm at nine o'clock in the morning. After a short delay, the Howells were comfortably seated in the car and on the way to see one of the areas of great natural beauty.

The day was already beginning to heat up under the strong sun as they arrived at the entrance gate to the Camdeboo National Park, the place where they would encounter The Valley of Desolation. The driver paid the entrance fee, and they then set off to drive up the narrow winding road that led up the mountain top, which formed one side of The Valley of Desolation. In places, the road ran along the edge of a cliff that dropped away many metres below the wheels of their sturdy car. The narrow road snaked around the side of the mountain, gradually gaining height.

After about fifteen minutes, they reached the small car park that gave access to the viewpoints overlooking The Valley of Desolation. The car park was deserted. There was a short walk of maybe half a mile before they could reach the best viewpoints. The driver told them the way to go, and the Howells set off by themselves in the mid-morning heat. The paths were easy to follow. After a steady walk, they reached the first viewpoint, right on the edge of the cliff with only a knee-high barrier wall stopping people from walking over. Looking over the edge, they could see the dark rock face drop eighty vertical meters before reaching the valley floor. Selwyn wanted to get some great photographs of the tumbled rocks in the cleft of The Valley of Desolation. His wife decided to go further along the path to the next viewpoint.

She did not hear the cry of surprise from her husband when a man darted out from the nearby bushes and without warning or hesitation pushed her husband over the cliff. He fell screaming in terror. The terrible sound was cut short when he landed on the rocks at the base of the cliff.

The isolated location of The Valley of Desolation meant it was some hours before a rescue team could be gathered to go to the foot of cliffs. By the time they reached Selwyn, he was unconscious due to the pain of his broken legs and severe dehydration in the heat. The rescuers were not sure whether he would live or die. They managed to arrange a military helicopter to fly him to the nearby hospital. It would be a couple of months before the Howells would leave that part of South Africa. Their farmer host was horrified at the events and allowed Selwyn's wife to stay at the farm free of charge while her husband recovered. There was no reason to return to England until Selwyn recuperated. In the isolation of the farm, communication with England was difficult, but that did not matter to Thelma, whose only concern was her husband's recovery.

Chapter 23 The Police are Called

Mrs. Embleton had immediately called the police when the worried school secretary had visited her in the study. While the phone call had probably been a hoax, the news that the school party had travelled on a different organisation's coach was concerning. The company which usually provided such transport had arranged that all of their coaches were fitted with GPS tracking, and their drivers were subject to thorough background and police checks. The school principal was well aware that the parents of some of her pupils were extremely wealthy and important people and that their sons were potential targets for kidnapping. After hurried enquiries, it seemed there was only person who had clear details of the planning. The bus company had been employed at the last moment for the trip to London by temporary English Master Alan Howard, and he was on the coach. The Health and Safety Risk Assessment forms were correctly filed by the teacher, but they didn't cover the kidnapping situation. It was a bad sign that none of the teaching staff on the school trip were answering calls to their mobile phones. There was no way of knowing where the coach was located on its trip.

The Duty Officer at the local Police Station made the important decision to treat Mrs. Embleton's call as a real kidnapping situation and immediately assigned four police officers, including Detective Inspector Norris, to act as a team to start action to trace the potentially missing school coach. His next action was to call the Chief Constable directly and warn him of the situation. After many phone calls to the local bus companies, the police managed to track down which company had supplied the coach for the school trip. They tried calling the mobile phone of the coach driver, but there was no response. On hearing that news, the Chief Constable for the local police authority decided to treat this as a major incident. More police officers were called in off the street, and a Major Incident Room was set up. Police cars and a police helicopter were sent to search the area close to the six-digit map reference that had been read over the telephone to the school secretary by the caller from France. The Chief Constable also called senior police officers in London to ask them to check their surveillance cameras to see if the coach had entered London.

Detective Inspector Norris was in the incident room when the phone call came in. There was visible relief on the phone officer's face as she relayed the message. "The coach has arrived in London. It arrived at eleven a.m. It passed some security cameras on the North Circular Road. At about midday, it was recorded on the A12 Road near the London Docklands."

Norris spoke to the Duty Officer. "Something is wrong here. The coach was too late in arriving, and it shouldn't be right out by the A12. The Globe Theatre is in the centre of London, close to the City of London. Can you ask them to email us immediately with the photographs of the coach taken by the surveillance cameras? I think it is about time we got in contact with the parents to let them know we are following up a possible incident."

"No, not yet. We don't want to raise unnecessary alarm. What I will do, however, is to get the London police to track down that coach. Meanwhile, we should have the results of the local search within a few minutes."

A few moments later, a radio message came in from one of the police officers assigned to the school secretary's office at Holliston's School. The operator wrote down the message and passed it to the Duty Officer, who read it out aloud. "The school secretary has received a request from a security firm to confirm the location of one of their pupils, Darren Nichols, because a tracking device implanted in his shoe has been activated close to Dover. Darren Nichols is one of the pupils who is on the school trip. The security firm has contacted the police in Dover and asked them to investigate at the site. Norris, can you get on the phone to the border police and ask them if that coach has gone through Dover Harbour or Eurotunnel? Tell them to stop the coach and hold it if it does arrive."

The Duty Officer turned to one of the phone operators and requested she contact the school immediately. "Please call the school and get the contact details for the parents of all the pupils on that school coach. Ask the school to ensure that any enquiries from the parents are directed to this incident room. Let them know we will be contacting all of the parents as quickly as possible. Please see if you can get the school to discreetly ask the other pupils if they know the mobile phone numbers of their friends who might have been on the coach. Emphasise that no word of the potential kidnapping should leak out."

The Duty Officer turned to the detective who was controlling the local search for the area given by the kidnapper's map reference. "Any progress on the search?"

"No. So far, it has drawn a blank. There is no sign of the coach. The helicopter has completed a sweep of an area of about five square miles."

"Are there any buildings in the vicinity big enough to hide the coach?"

"Yes. I have already thought of that, and cars have been sent to investigate those buildings. The most obvious place is an old bus garage for Howell's Coaches. Our records show the owner has recently disposed of eight coaches. The helicopter has flown over the site, but there are no buses in view. There is a patrol car already on its way to the garage. We are also trying to locate the owner of the business, but he does not answer his telephone."

"Tell the officers in the patrol car to approach the garage with caution. If this is a hostage situation, the people involved may be armed. Meanwhile, see if you can get an armed support vehicle to attend the site."

§

The patrol car going to the garage turned off its sirens for the last mile of approach. They parked in such a way that their car blocked the entrance to the bus garage site. One of the officers got out and carefully approached the garage door. The whole site seemed to be deserted. He circled around the building, trying to look in through windows and checking any doorways to see if they were unlocked. The windows had been obscured with white emulsion paint on the inside, so he could see nothing. Eventually, he returned to the main garage door and tried the small built-in door. It was unlocked. He cautiously pushed it open and then poked his head around to see if he could see anything. The interior of the garage was in darkness, apart from the weak light that filtered in through the painted windows. He stood cautiously by the door and shouted, "Hello? This is the police. Is there anybody in here?"

There was no response.

He tried again, louder this time.

This time, there was a muffled shout of response. "Help! We are in here."

The police officer radioed back to his headquarters to tell them he was going into the building. He cautiously walked inside. The building was empty apart from a large silver-grey construction in the middle of the floor. He could see a large gate at the front of the construction. He approached it and tried to open the gate. It was chained and locked with a padlock. He noticed to the side that there was a hook holding a key ring. He lifted the key ring and tried the keys in the padlock. After a little searching, he found the right key and undid the padlock. He rattled the chain free from where it had been wrapped around a steel frame of the large cage and swung the gate open. As he opened the gate, a note fluttered down to the floor in front of him. He picked it up and read it:

Congratulations! You have two minutes to rescue the prisoners from the small cage.

Inside the cage, he could see the coach they were seeking. Beside the coach was a small metal cage containing people. He radioed back to his headquarters. "This is PC102. I am inside the Howell's garage and have found the coach and some people. Send backup immediately."

On seeing the police constable in the gateway of the cage, the teachers started crying and shouting. The police officer remembered the note giving limited time and dashed over to the cage. He found a locked steel door. He dashed back to the padlock and retrieved the key ring. Returning to the small cage, he quickly opened the steel door and released the people trapped inside. Suddenly from above him he saw and felt a liquid pouring and splashing down on the coach and on the inner cage. He immediately recognised the smell; it was diesel fuel.

"Quickly! Everybody outside now. Don't wait for anything... just go! Move away from the building. Is there anybody else trapped in the building?"

"No. It is just us."

Pushing the teachers by the shoulders, he urged them all outside the building. As he reached the main doorway to the garage, there was a small explosion behind him. He instinctively looked back and saw a large fire developing in and around the large cage. A pool of blazing liquid was spreading across the floor towards him.

Black smoke was rapidly filling the garage. He turned to chase away the teachers, who were standing open mouthed, looking at the rapidly developing inferno. As he ran, he keyed his radio microphone to send a message to the headquarters. "This is PC102 at the Howell's garage. You had best send some fire appliances and ambulances. We have a major fire here now."

When the teachers were at a safe distance, he stopped them and asked, "Where are the children?"

One of the teachers replied, tears streaming down her face, "They've all been kidnapped. There were armed terrorists. They shot and killed Alan Howard, one of the teachers."

By this time, the policeman's partner had left the car and joined them. She was checking that they were all uninjured and trying to calm them down.

PC102 made another report to his headquarters. "This is PC102 confirming this is a kidnapping situation. There is no sign of the children. Armed terrorists are involved but have left the site. We have rescued the teachers. We need a lot of people here to deal with the situation."

§

On hearing of terrorist involvement, the Duty Officer in the incident room knew the whole kidnapping situation, as bad as it was, had escalated into something of national importance. He lifted a phone handset and called the Chief Constable. "Excuse me, sir. You wanted to be kept abreast of developments. It is suddenly a whole lot worse. I will come up and see you now if you are free, sir."

Just before he left the incident room, one of the constables operating the telephones waved to the Duty Officer to attract his attention. "Excuse me, sir, but I've got one of the mobile phone companies on the line at the moment. They have been able to track one of the mobile phones of the students. It appears to be heading north on the M1 motorway. They are currently trying to get a better fix on its position."

"Get on the phone to the traffic control room for that area and ask them to have the motorway blocked north of the current location of the mobile phone signal. Tell them it is a matter of national importance and that any questions should be passed to our Chief Constable. Let me know as soon as possible if you hear from the phone company with a more accurate position fix on that mobile phone."

The Duty Officer left to meet with the Chief Constable.

In the control room, the reports came in from different parts of the country where the mobile phone companies had been able to track down the phone signals from the pupils' mobile phones. They even had one reported in France, heading towards Paris.

Detective Inspector Norris picked up the telephone and called the Chief Constable's office. "Excuse me, sir. I am sorry to disturb you, but I think you should come to the Incident Room as a matter of urgency. I know the officer commanding this incident is on his way to you, but I will try and intercept him and get him to come back here."

Shortly afterwards, four senior police officers and Detective Inspector Norris were gathered in a meeting room, listening to a briefing on the situation.

"... and so far as we know, four mobile phone signals have been picked up and are being tracked in the UK. There are also two reported detections in France. We have had the initial reports about the emergency transponder built into the shoes of one of the pupils. It appears that just his shoes were thrown in the hedge down in Kent near the Dover ferry port. It may be that the kidnapped pupils are being separately transported to different destinations, or it may be that the terrorists are deliberately transporting the mobile phones to increase confusion. From what we have heard so far, these people are very well organised.

"We have contacted most of the parents of the children involved, but as of yet, no ransom demands have been received. Most of the parents are extremely wealthy and influential people. I'm sure that before long, there will be substantial pressure on the Chief Constable and the Home Office to make progress in this case. The serious crimes team is on its way from Scotland Yard, and the Home Secretary has been informed. We will be holding a press conference in approximately one hour at our conference centre.

"It is doubtful if we will get any useful information from the school coach involved in the kidnap. The bus garage and coach burned to the ground by the time that the Fire Brigade arrived on site. The coach itself was contained within what appears to have been a Faraday cage designed to prevent any radio tracking signals. This took place in relatively isolated countryside, so there will be no video footage.

"One of the teachers on the trip was apparently shot and killed when he tried to tackle one of the kidnappers. We are currently trying to find details of his next of kin so they can be informed. We are waiting for the Fire Brigade to finish on site, but so far, there is no trace of the body of Alan Howard."

The Chief Constable spoke to the assembled officers. "So, to sum this up, we have no clue as to the identity of the terrorists or which organisation is involved? We do not know their motives? We have no clues as to the whereabouts of the children?"

"That's correct, sir."

"Have we had any success contacting Mr. Howell, the owner of the garage?"

"No, sir, and we have tried many approaches. The best information we have from their neighbours is that the Howells went on a retirement holiday to South Africa. At present, we have no better information than that."

"Keep everybody working hard on this. Use whatever resources you need to do the job. When the serious crimes team arrives, please be prepared to give them a full briefing and access to all information. I do not need to remind you that what we do in the first few hours will be critical to solving this case and rescuing the children unharmed. From what we know so far, they were kidnapped about three hours before anybody made contact with the school. We have already lost a lot of time."

§

Approximately fifty miles away, a coach driver groaned as his coach load of recently embarked Japanese tourists was signalled by armed police to pull over to the side of the motorway. His passengers were going to be delayed on their visit to an ancient castle for a mediaeval meal in the Kent countryside. He did not know his coach was the one bearing the registration plates stolen from the coach in the Howell's bus garage.

Chapter 24 Taken Hostage

About the same time as those police discussions were ongoing, the lorry carrying the kidnapped school children was on a motorway not far from the northern town of Preston. They were all in shocked, sullen silence. Travelling in the enclosed shipping container with no way of seeing outside had caused some of them to suffer travel sickness.

Simon was sitting in a cage next to Adam's. They whispered quietly to each other. "Adam, I feel terrible. How much longer is this trip going to take? Why would they want to kidnap us? We are just normal school kids."

"I don't know, Simon. Their leader told us the trip will take about twelve hours. I haven't got my watch, so I can't tell how long we have been travelling, but it feels like maybe six hours. I know my family couldn't afford much of a ransom if that's what's going to happen. They seem to have gone to a lot of trouble just to kidnap us. The bus garage must have taken ages to set up. Even this lorry with its special cages must have taken a lot of work."

"Do you think we are going to be ok? They didn't hesitate to kill Mr. Howard. Do you think they are going to kill us?"

"Don't say that type of thing, Simon. Just look at all the organisation and effort they put into capturing us. We haven't done anything to harm them, so why would they do that to us? There must be some reason why they need us. Look on the bright side... it is much more exciting than tromping around an old Shakespearean theatre!"

"Are you going to try and escape? If we all did it at the same time, just two guys wouldn't be able to control us. Maybe Darren's tracking signal got out."

"That would be daft, Simon. They've got machine guns, and we are locked in these cages. We don't know what they have following this lorry. They may have a van load of armed men behind us. And as for Darren's tracking signal, that was hundreds of miles away. If it had worked, there would be police all over us by now."

"This is going to destroy my parents, Adam. Our family is a bit like yours. I don't see how my parents could afford any large ransom. It's ok for people like Darren 'cause his dad is loaded with money. My dad is just a scientist researching bugs to help deal with global warming. Maybe it's just Darren and people like him they want and we just got caught up in it."

"I just don't know, Simon. We really don't have enough information to work out what is happening here. I guess the best we can do is listen and watch carefully to find out what information we can gather. I'm going to try and make friends with the guards to see if I can find out any information."

"I don't think sucking up to the guards is going to do much good. They are our enemy, and we should do everything we can to make life difficult for them."

"No, Simon, we shouldn't do anything to antagonise the guards. If we make life easy for them, they will think we are compliant and won't be so on their guard. That might just give us a real advantage just when we most need it. They are just hired thugs. Our real enemies are the people who planned all this."

One of the terrorists had heard the two boys whispering. He came alongside the cage and kicked the bars. "Shut up, you two. The leader said keep quiet on the trip. If you talk too much, you will be gagged."

"I'm sorry, sir. My name is Adam, and I know you are only doing your job. All we were talking about was trying to work out how long it will be before we get there. These cages are really uncomfortable. Is there any chance we can have a stop to stretch our legs?"

"We will get there when we get there. Being uncomfortable won't kill you. Now shut up and keep quiet."

"I'm sorry, sir. I'll keep quiet."

The lorry journey continued for hours. There was one brief stop, when they could hear the lorry driver swapping places with another. The other stop was in a garage, where the lorry was refuelled. During that stop, the guards were patrolling the cages, making sure nobody shouted or screamed. After the refuelling stop, the guards distributed bottles of water and packets of sandwiches among the captive school children. After the food, one of the guards visited each captive and gave them each a pair of trainer shoes. Eventually, after hours of cramped boredom and loneliness, they felt the lorry pull off the motorway and major roads onto smaller roads.

"Adam, we must be getting close now. I think we're getting onto country roads," whispered Simon to his friend.

But Simon was mistaken. The narrow winding roads continued for at least four more hours. At times, they could hear the lorry labouring up steep hills, and they felt the jerks created by the lorry brakes being applied to stop it from going down the hills too fast. Most of the children had fallen asleep despite the uncomfortable conditions by the time the lorry bumped along the final track of an unmade road. It rattled over cattle grids and across two creaking wooden bridges before coming to a halt. There was a loud *hiss* as the air brakes were finally applied, and then suddenly the engine of the lorry was halted. The bolts were shot on the door of the shipping container. Cold night air rushed in as the container door was swung open. Adam could hear a wooden ramp being fixed at the back of the lorry. One by one, the cages were opened and the school child inside was grabbed and led away from the lorry.

Men were waiting outside the lorry to deal with the children. All of them wore full-length face masks. The children were all led into a large room on the ground floor of a building. As they approached the room, the heavy wooden double doors automatically swung open. Adam looked up and saw a motion sensor device controlling the doors. The room was lit by fluorescent lights and was bare of furnishings except for a pile of blankets and large gymnastic mats stacked in the corner. A portable toilet cabin stood next to the mats. In the other corner of the room, he could see an old wooden desk with some writing pads and pencils on the desktop. To Adam, it looked like a disused computer room, though there was no computer equipment installed in the room. There were no windows in the room, and there were large air-conditioning vents in the ceiling. As they walked across the floor, he could feel the floor tiles rocking slightly under his feet. The room had a raised floor that would have been be used in the past to supply cooled air to the computer equipment.

When all the captured pupils had been transferred to the room, the terrorist leader entered the room and stood in the middle to make an announcement. Like the other terrorists, his face was masked. "You have reached the end of your journey. This room and one other like it will be your home for the next week or two. Look after it and keep it tidy. If any of you need to use the toilet facilities, there is one in the corner over there. You will be served some food soon, but first I have to leave you alone for a while."

He turned to leave the room. As he approached the door, he put a walkie talkie to his mouth and issued an instruction. "This is Alpha 3. Please open the door to the accommodation room. Have everyone meet me in the dining room for a briefing in ten minutes."

Adam watched carefully as the man left the room. There had been a guard outside of the door. Alpha 3 spoke to the guard. "Lock the corridor exits and join me in the office upstairs."

Adam knew it was time to act. He had read somewhere that in kidnapping situations, it became much more difficult to escape after the first few hours of captivity. Ignoring the other captives, he walked up to the desk at the end of the room and picked up a writing pad. He approached the double doors and looked up. He could see where the motion sensor had been removed from inside the room. There was no other door-release mechanism. He removed half the pages from the writing pad and knelt by the bottom of the doors. In a single movement and without hesitation, he quickly slipped the remainder of the writing pad through the gap at the bottom of the doors and gave the pad a hard push. It slid halfway across the corridor outside the doors. The movement of the writing pad triggered the motion sensing door control, and the doors swung open. He stepped through the doorway and away from motion sensor. The other captives looked on in shocked amazement as Adam disappeared from sight and the doors swung shut again. They had not seen his trick with the writing pad.

Once in the corridor, Adam picked up the writing pad from the floor and set off to explore. The corridor was bare except for some fire extinguishers at each end of the corridor. He was relieved to note there were no CCTV cameras in the corridor. He tried the doors at each end of the corridor, and as he had expected, they were locked. He carefully opened one set of doors in the corridor and found a large room laid out as a canteen. He successively worked along the rooms in the corridor finding nothing of interest until he came to the room next to the one where the captives were held. When he opened the door, he found it was another disused computer technology room.

He entered the room. It looked as though this room had held a lot of cabling. Against the far wall, he could see a duct running from ceiling to the floor. He tried the door on the duct, but it wouldn't open. He noticed the floor tile next to the duct rocked under his feet. He looked around and found a scrap of sheet metal. Using that, he levered up the floor tile. With the floor tile out of the way, Adam could see an open duct leading down to the basement. He swiftly removed the LED button torch from his inhaler and peered down the duct. It looked big enough for him to climb down. There was a metal cable ladder fixed against the wall inside the duct, and he used it to climb down into the darkness.

Soon, his foot met a floor. He wriggled out from the cable duct and found himself in a dark room. Using the light of the button torch, he looked around. It looked as though the room had once contained electric power and air-conditioning equipment, but apart from some odd pieces of machinery, now the room was largely empty. He saw a light switch on the wall and tried it, but it didn't work. He tried to open the door from the room, but it appeared to be locked. Further along the walls from the cable duct was another large duct rising up from the room. It seemed to be an air-conditioning duct that would carry treated air through the rest of the building. A hatch cover had been removed and was resting against the wall next to the duct. Adam peered inside. It was bigger than the cabling duct and appeared to go higher than the ground floor.

He knew if he was to escape, he had to explore all possibilities. He climbed into the air-conditioning duct. It was mostly smooth and slippery, but by pushing his knees and arms against one side and his back against the other, he was able to climb up the air-conditioning duct. After some struggle, he arrived at an intersection in the duct, branching off to the left and the right and also rising above him. There was still enough space for him to crawl and wriggle along the horizontal duct. He could see some light ahead. He carefully wriggled along the duct towards the light.

When he got closer, he realised the light was coming through an air-conditioning vent cover. He wriggled up to the cover and looked out onto a canteen area. There were five rows of benches and tables. He was just about to wriggle further along the duct when he heard the room door open. The terrorist leader led in a group of men dressed in dark uniforms. They had removed their face masks. Adam thought about trying to escape back down the air ducting, but he realised the noise of him moving might attract the attention of the terrorists, so he wisely stayed where he was.

Alpha 3 motioned to the men to sit while he gave them a briefing. "Ok, gentlemen, our guests have been settled into their rooms. I've gathered you all here to remind you why we are here and about the rules that we will all have to follow. I'm only going through this once, so pay attention. I do not expect to have to repeat myself. If you have questions, ask them during this briefing. I will not tolerate any of you breaking the rules.

"We are all in this venture together. Nobody quits halfway through and walks away. We will all make a great deal of money at the end of this kidnapping—so much money that you will never have to work again. If it goes wrong, the penalties will be severe, and at best, you will spend the rest of your lives in prison. However, this venture is not going to go wrong. We have made very careful plans over several months in great secrecy. We have a secure base here, and nobody outside knows we are here.

"Firstly, the children are the most important part of this project. There are thirty of them, and they are being held for ransom. They will be released together once the ransom has been paid. For security reasons, our ransom negotiators do not know our location. They will send us a signal when the money has been transferred. Make sure the kids are kept safe and do not escape. Each one is valuable, some much more so than others. Make sure they stay healthy. We must be kind but strict with them, and if they break any of the rules, they will be punished. I will decide on any punishments. If one of them breaks the rules, the rest will be punished as well. Do not make friends with them and make sure they obey the rules without hesitation. Do not trust them at all and avoid being alone with them.

"Do not take any weapons into their areas unless I tell you to. We do not want any unfortunate accidents. They will lie, cheat, and try to escape if given the slightest chance. They are all very intelligent kids. Do not discuss business or operations in front of them. Do not mention your real names to any of them. Teach them only your rank and assigned identity number. Always wear your full face mask when dealing with them. If they don't know your face, they cannot describe you to the authorities afterwards. Do not discuss any news of the outside world with them. They will be allowed no communication with the outside world.

"You must learn all of their names and also be alert for any sickness in any of the kids. If any gets sick or injured, you must tell me straightaway. You need to make sure they all stay clean and comfortable. The kids will be fed twice a day. Their food will be set out in this dining area before they arrive. You will escort them from their accommodation room to the canteen area. After thirty minutes, you will escort them back to the accommodation room, having counted that the entire cutlery has been returned. You will check that each one is eating properly every day. If there are any who don't eat properly, tell me straightaway. They are going to have to get used to eating some basic food—not the fancy choices they have in their posh homes.

"There will be a head count every day when the kids are moved from one room to another at their shower time. They will be given clean clothes every day. You will check that they do not try to hide any unauthorised items in their clothes when they dress after the shower. After moving them from their accommodation room, you will perform a thorough search of the empty room to make sure they have hidden nothing. Their discarded clothes will be loaded into a trolley and taken for washing."

Alpha 3 held up a metallic looking ring which had a diameter of approximately eighteen cms. with a small, grey, plastic pod built into it. "The kids will all be fitted with these electronic tracking collars around their necks, and they will be electronically locked. Do not attempt to remove the collar, as it contains an explosive charge that will not only detonate and neutralise the kid, but also remove your hand in the process. If the kid attempts to move more than 100 metres from this site, the collar will start beeping. They then have thirty seconds to return within range, or the device will detonate. If, for any reason, you need to remove the collar, let me know and I will enter a control code at a central computer to release the locking device by wireless signal."

Alpha 3 gestured towards a PC on a desk in the corner of the room. "The collars are waterproof, so they can be worn continually, including in the showers. If you see any of the kids trying to remove the collar, stop them so we don't have any accidental losses."

"When you move the kids from one area of the building to another, make sure only one door is unlocked at a time. Move the kids through and then lock the door behind you before opening any other doors. When you reach the destination room, recount the kids and report the movement by your wireless comm. unit as having been completed. If there is a fire alert, activate the water sprinklers and leave the building. Do not attempt to evacuate the kids. The water will keep them safe from any fire, though they may be wet and cold afterwards.

"Any questions about the kids? No? Ok. I'll tell you about the site and then talk about the work patterns."

Alpha 3 then moved to stand by a large map on the wall highlighting parts with a laser pointer. "As you can all see, this is a map of the base and the surrounding area. This block shows this building where we are currently standing. We call it the office building, and I will tell you more about it in a moment. The building to the north is your accommodation block. You will all get to know the accommodation block without any further help from me. The long block to the right is the garage building. You are to keep vehicles in there out of sight and the garage doors closed. We don't want any visitors or nosy locals to realise we have more vehicles than would be expected for a salmon-breeding research centre.

"The smaller building to the right of the garages is the power room. It houses two standby generators, each with sufficient capacity to power the whole base in the event that we should we lose mains electricity. The fuel tanks contain enough fuel for four weeks worth of continuous operation of the generators. The other small buildings are storage rooms, a workshop, and a water and sewage treatment facility.

"The large square building to the east behind the garages is the research block. It is out of bounds to everyone unless I have given specific permission for a person to enter the building. Don't even think about being nosy and trying to find out what happens in there. If anyone asks, just call it a research building and say you do not know what happens there. The story fed to the local people is that this place is a fish-breeding research station owned by a large global corporation. There are some people working in the research block. It is unlikely you will meet them, but if you do, you should check their security pass, but do not engage in any conversation with them.

"The large open area between the buildings is the car parking area, but in normal operations, I want to see no more than one of our vehicles being parked there. To the west of the parking area is a vehicle ramp leading to the small jetty in the loch. The outer security fences run down into the water for some ten metres from the shore. The inner security fence runs parallel to the edge of the water along the shore. You can see the gate that controls access to the jetty."

Alpha 3 pointed at the water marked on the map. "The shore of the loch is very steep, and you quickly gain depth. If you go ten metres out, there is an underwater cliff which drops over thirty metres to deeper water. The mouth of the loch has been interdiction mined at the sea entrance with remotely controlled mines. This means we can activate the mines from this base when we need to close the entrance to ships and boats. The approaches to this base are monitored by an underwater sonar system sensitive enough to pick up any boat or even an underwater diver. No boat should be allowed to approach or tie up at the jetty unless I have given permission.

"The approach road is monitored by detector wires buried under the surface near the farm gate at the end of the track. We will post a twenty-four-hour lookout overlooking the road and the valley. The lookout post is camouflaged and is equipped with night vision equipment. We have anti-intruder radar, but we will normally keep it switched off apart from two test sessions every day because the radar might attract attention from the military jets that sometimes fly over on training flights. There are three remote controlled anti-tank mines buried under the approach road. These can be controlled from this base or the lookout post. It is four kilometres from the base to the nearest public road. We are five kilometres, as the crow flies, from the nearest village.

"The base is surrounded by two layers of chain link wire fences. The fences are fitted with optical fibre sensors that will detect the vibrations of anyone trying to climb the fence, cut the fence, or lift the fence. The inner fence is electrified at 20,000 volts to stop anyone from trying to climb over. Between the two fences is a set of infrared detectors that form an invisible beam wall from the ground to two metres high. This monitors the entire perimeter of the base. Anyone passing through the beam will set off the alarm. A further sensor wire is buried two metres from the inside of the inner fence. If anyone approaches the inner wire fence, that will trigger an alarm from the buried proximity sensor wire. The outer fence is built using toughened cut-resistant steel mesh and is three metres high, including coils of razor wire at the top.

"Along the length of the fence are sets of motion-detecting CCTV cameras which monitor the gap between the two fences. Anything bigger than a cat moving in the area will raise an alert here at central control. It works day and night. The inner fence has floodlights that can light up the fence area if central control detects someone in that area.

"Outside of the perimeter fence is a metre-deep, three-metre-wide ditch that prevents any attempt to ram through the fence by a vehicle. Where the track to the outside world meets the fence, there is a collapsible bridge just before a gatehouse. There are hidden anti-ram bollards to protect the outer gate. These can be activated from the gatehouse in less than a second. The inner gate is interlocked with the outer gate and cannot be opened if the other gate is open. All external doors and gates of this base are equipped with sensors to detect the opening of the door or gate. Only authorised security passes can temporarily override the alarm detection on the gates and door, and only authorised vehicles can be allowed in and out of the base. There will be a list held in the office for the number plates of the authorised vehicles."

He held up something about the size of a large beach pebble. It was painted brown. "If you look carefully, you may see some of these scattered in the outer perimeter land. These are called 'Smart Rocks'. They will detect the motion of anything larger than a cat within ten metres. The pebbles automatically wirelessly network in the form of a mesh and pass messages between themselves and back to a central controlling computer here. If any of the Smart Rocks are moved or destroyed, the others automatically mend the gap in the mesh network. The mesh is able to pinpoint the intruder's position to an accuracy of one metre. They are like guard dogs that never sleep.

"Now, to deal with the patrol duties, we shall expect you to undertake twenty-four hours a day. Firstly, on the lookout post, there will be one person on a three-hour shift. His role is to warn control of any people approaching or leaving the base. He will be expected to report in every thirty minutes by the telephone link installed in the lookout post. It takes fifteen minutes to reach the lookout post at a normal walking pace. You can see the path here on the map.

"The gatehouse will be manned continuously during the day from 07:00 to 21:00. This will be done in three-hour shifts. While manning the gatehouse, you will wear civilian clothes. The fence will be patrolled during hours of darkness by two men on a continuous basis. The route will be one complete circuit of the inner fence and jetty area. Next, on the route will be a complete patrol of the outer fence. After the outer fence patrol, the men will check all external doors of buildings to make sure they are properly secured. During the patrol, you will be expected to report in every fifteen minutes.

"The interior of the buildings will be patrolled at least once every four hours on a random basis. This will be performed on a continual twenty-four-hour basis. During daylight hours, outside the buildings, you will wear civilian clothes and no face mask. During the hours of darkness, you will wear dark camouflage. During daylight patrols, you wear concealed weapons, but during the hours of darkness, the weapons do not need to be hidden. Weapons and ammunition should be stored the armoury in the accommodation block when not in use. Two men will be based in the control centre on a three-hour shift basis for twenty-four hours a day. Their task will be to control the CCTV system, monitor the intruder alerts, and keep track of the foot patrols.

"You already know your teams and your leaders. I'll leave it to you to sort out your patrols, sleep periods, and meal breaks. Leaders will perform kit inspection once a day at the start of each shift and report to me twice a day with situation reports. You are expected to undertake at least two hours of daily fitness training. No alcohol is permitted on the site except for that served with your meals.

"There are to be no phone calls or emails to the outside world unless you have checked with me first. All phone calls will be recorded, and I will listen to them. You should all note that mobile cell phones will not work due to the remote location of this site."

Alpha 3 looked around at the assembled men. "Are there any questions, gentlemen?"

"Yeah. When do we get our money?" asked a large dark-haired man.

"You were told this when you signed on. Payment will be at the end of project. If all goes well, that will be less than two weeks from now. For those who perform well, there will be extra bonus money. If anyone gets killed, their share will be sent to their family or dependents if their exit was in support of the project. If we lose any of the kids, the money goes down. Does anyone need that translated? If the project fails, nobody will be paid.

"Now, I'll tell you about this building. This base used to be a research centre for the military. On the ground floor are three large rooms joined by one corridor. The one we are in now was a meeting room. We will be using it as a canteen area for the kids. Food will be cooked in the accommodation block and brought here for the kids. The other two rooms on the ground floor were computer and equipment rooms are where the kids will be housed. Showers and toilets are across the corridor. There are no windows on the ground floor. The walls and outer doors of this building are reinforced. This building will be our strong point if needed.

"There are stairs at each end of the corridor that lead to the first floor where there are old offices. The control room is in one of those offices. The control room windows overlook the main gate and the car park square. During the patrols, you will check each of the offices. In the basement are just disused storage rooms, and the entrance to the basement will be kept locked. The entrance doors to this building are locked electronically and can only be opened if you have the correct pass card.

"Ok, that's everything for the time being. Any last questions? Written standing orders and orders of the day will be posted in the accommodation block. If there are no further questions, Tango Squad, you have the first duty roster, go and check the kids. They will be fed in two hours, and I'll brief them after the meal. The rest of you get settled in to your quarters. Meeting dismissed."

Adam saw Alpha 3 turn and remove the map from the wall, rolling it as he strode out of the room. Adam knew he had to get back to the others before the guards came to check them. Using the sound of the men standing to mask his own noise, he wriggled back along the air duct to the main air shaft. His feet scrambled to gain a footing and avoid falling down to the basement. He couldn't see where he was going because his head and shoulders were still in the horizontal duct. Suddenly, his whole body slipped out of the horizontal air duct, bashing his chin as he went down. Adam instantly reacted and spread-eagled his feet and arms across the ducting, pushing as hard as he could against the sides. With a squealing, screeching noise, he stopped his fall as his feet gained friction against the metal side of the shaft. His muscles were giving him agony in protest at the sudden strain. He released a little pressure and then slid down a few more feet before stopping himself. He repeated this a few more times before he reached the base of the air shaft. The inspection hatch was still open, and he hurriedly dived out of the air shaft into the equipment room.

He had dropped the LED torch button during his fall in the shaft, so the basement room was in total darkness as he hurried across, trying to find the cable shaft, feeling his way as he went. There was a sudden agonising pain in his upper leg when he walked into something hard and metallic in the dark. He bit his lip to avoid crying out from the pain. He wiped tears from his eyes as he fumbled for the cable shaft. Knowing he couldn't delay too long, he paused a moment to try and work out where he was in the room. His training with Ali had helped give him confidence. Moving cautiously, he felt a wall at his fingertips. Feeling the way with his other hand, he came to the hatchway door of the cabling shaft.

Hurrying, he quickly stepped into the cabling shaft, cracking his head on the frame of the hatch door. Now there was agonising pain just above his eye as well. He felt his head and found the silky feel of blood from a cut. Not waiting any longer, he quickly started to climb inside the cable shaft up the cable ladder. He made his way to the faint glimmer of light from the room above. He soon came to the hole in the shaft wall where cables had once fed though from under the raised floor. He wriggled through the hole and wormed his way under the raised floor towards the hole left by the floor tile he had moved earlier.

As he started to wriggle out from the hole in the floor, he heard men's voices in the next room. "Ok, you lot, let's have you lined up against the wall. It is time to do a head count and then take you to meet the leader."

Oh, no, I'm screwed! Thought Adam. *Now they will find me gone, and all hell will break loose.*

Chapter 25 First Resistance

The guards had started to count the hostages before Adam was able to return to the room.

"… twenty-eight, twenty-nine… hang on. One of them is missing! Go get Alpha 3 and bring him here. I'll stand guard outside of the room. You lot go and sit facing against the wall over there. Move!"

Adam heard the sound of the automatic doors opening and one of the men running along the corridor. He ducked back under the raised floor, pulling the tile back into place on the floor. In the half light under the floor, he looked around for another escape route. Over in the far corner under the floor he saw the dark outline of a narrow slot in the wall. He wriggled forward to the slot. It looked as though it was a gap where pipes or cables had been run at one time. By turning his head sideward and breathing out, he was just able to squeeze through the slot. He came out under another raised floor. The gap was still only thirty cms. between the floor and the concrete slab. He realised he was under the floor of the room containing the rest of the children.

He remembered that in the far corner of the room was a pile of mattresses. He wriggled over to the corner and counted out two tiles distance from the wall. He gently pushed up against the underside of the floor tile above him. With a tiny *creak*, it began to move upwards. He raised one edge a couple of inches and peeked out. He could see all the other kids facing the wall. He looked around and could see no other men in the room. Gritting his teeth, he silently lifted the ten-kilogram tile and slid it onto the floor, leaving a sixty-cm. square hole that he wriggled through back out into the room. He carefully slid the heavy tile back into place. It made a slight *clunk* as it bedded back in place. He looked over at the other children. No one had moved. Adam silently crawled into the gap between the pile of mattresses and the wall and lay down.

No sooner had he lain down than the doors to the room opened, and Alpha 3 strode in, flanked by two other men. Each was dressed in a dark uniform with a helmet and a full face mask. Alpha 3 held a clipboard containing a list of names. "Ok, you lot. This is a roll call. Answer your name and stand facing the wall after it has been called."

The man called the names of the children one by one. The children stood facing the wall after their name had been called. "…Adam Cranford! Adam Cranford? Ok, does anyone know where he has gone to? Come on… speak up."

There was total silence.

Alpha 3 moved and stood behind the school children. "Ok, I understand you might want to protect him, but it is most unadvisable. Someone must know where he is. Speak up, or you will all suffer."

He pulled a short stick from the equipment belt around his waist. Holding the stick close to the ear of Adamson, he pressed a button on the handle of the stick. There was a sharp crackling noise as a bright spark appeared at the end of the stick close to Adamson's ear. "There are 20,000 volts here, and it is very painful. Speak now and tell me where he went, or you will all feel the pain from my little stick."

There was no response.

There was another sharp crackling noise. Adamson screamed loudly and fell to the floor, writhing in agony. The stick moved to the next child and gently pressed against the leg. At that point, Adam wiped the blood from his head and stood up from behind the pile of mattresses.

"Hey, can't a boy sleep around here? I'm totally whacked out. What's all the noise about?"

Alpha 3 whirled round. "Where the hell have you been hiding? Why were you hiding from us?"

"No, I wasn't hiding. I've just taken the chance to get some sleep. I've been on the go for ages now. Why didn't you guys wake me if you needed me? I was just laying down there to get some shade from the lights."

Alpha 3 turned his head to look at the guard. "Why didn't you check this room properly before you came rushing to get me? Anyway, take them all into the eating area. I'm going tell them the rules and add something to their fashion outfits. I'll be down in five minutes." He turned and went to the door and radioed for the door to be unlocked. As the door hissed open, he left the room.

Guard 12 turned and faced them. "Ok, you lot, when I tell you, form a line two abreast. Then go out of the door, turn left, and go to the next room. The doors will open, and you are to go in and sit quietly on the floor." He went and stood by the door and then pointed at the two nearest children. "You two, form the head of the queue."

The other children formed a queue behind them. Adam joined at the end of the queue with Simon. Guard 12 radioed for the door to be opened, and Guard 14 left the room, beckoning the children to follow him as he left. "Ok, you lot, move... NOW!"

"Adam, you fool, why did you come back after you managed to escape?" hissed Simon.

"I wanted to find out what is going on and look around the building. These guys mean business, and I don't think we can easily escape. Anyway, you saw what he did to Adamson. I couldn't leave you all behind."

"But you could have gone for help or something."

"Hey, you two! Stop whispering. I told you to be quiet," barked the second guard following behind them.

The group filed into the room and sat on the floor and waited silently. The doors hissed shut, and the two guards took up position either side of the doorway. The guards stood in the at-ease stance with their hands behind their backs, watching the children. Their face masks made them look like some kind of androids waiting for the next command. After what seemed like hours of waiting, the doors swung open with a *hiss,* and Alpha 3 strode in, followed by two more guards. They carried a large crate between them. The men went to the far end of the room and dropped the box on a table. They sprung the latches on the crate and lifted the lid.

Alpha 3 faced the hostages and spoke. "It is time to tell you what is going to happen and why you are here. I know you are all tired and scared, so I will get this over as quickly as possible. First, know you will not be harmed if you follow our rules. If you break the rules, you can expect to be punished. If you keep breaking the rules, you will all be punished. You are all here as hostages. We will be asking your rich parents to pay a ransom before you are released. If they pay, you will be released safely and unharmed. Do not expect to be rescued, as we have been planning this carefully for a long time. The police do not have the faintest idea where you are right now, and we have left no clues. We expect this whole thing to last no longer than two weeks.

"You are safe in this building. Do not attempt to escape from the building or from the room you are in. Outside are electrified fences with lethal voltages. Do not touch them. You must follow the orders of the guards without question. The guards will wear full face masks for your own safety. If you don't know what they look like, it will be less dangerous for you when this is all over.

"You must keep yourselves clean and healthy. If you get sick, tell us right away. You will be given clean clothes every day. You will change into those clean clothes immediately after your shower. Your used clothes will be taken away and washed. If you want to carry something over to your clean clothes such as jewellery or inhalers, you must show it to the guards. If they take something from you, it will be returned when you are released.

"You will be fed twice a day, at nine a.m. and once six p.m. You will be given thirty minutes to eat and tidy up after the meal. You will not get a choice of foods. Eat what you are given. Do not attempt to store any food.

"'Lights out will be at ten thirty p.m., and you will be woken at seven a.m. every day. You must be showered and dressed by eight a.m. You can get drinking water from the coolers located in each room. You have already seen the portable toilet cabin in the corner of the room.

"The guards have been told not to have conversations with you. If you need something, ask them to pass a message to me. I am called 'Alpha 3.' The silver band on my shoulder identifies me as the leader. A plain guard has no markings other than his number on his shoulder. A red band and number indicates a Squad Leader. Do not ask any of us personal questions like 'What is your name?'

"There are no radios, televisions, or phones at this location. Do not bother asking for them. As a privilege, you will be allowed books, notepaper, and pens. If you are not well behaved, this privilege shall be withdrawn. If you are all well behaved, you will be allowed to watch one film a day as a group in the canteen. Are there any questions on these basic rules?"

Alpha 3 turned his head to scan the faces of the children. No questions were raised. He moved a wooden chair close to the table and sat on another chair on the other side of the table. One of the guards moved to stand next to the crate they had brought into the room.

"Ok. I'm going to call out your names one by one. When you hear your name, come and sit in that chair. While you are waiting to be called, sit quietly and do not talk."

The leader looked at his list and called first name. One of the boys stood, walked to the chair by the table, and sat down. The guard reached into the crate and pulled out a metallic ring. Adam recognised the ring as the tracking device Alpha 3 had shown all of the guards earlier. The guard read from the pod in the ring and called out a number to the other guard, who was now sitting at a PC located on the table. The man keyed in the number to the PC. There was a single *beep*, and the ring unlocked. The guard fully opened the ring, which was hinged at one point. He leaned forward and snapped the ring shut like a collar around the neck of the boy seated by him. As the ring beeped again, the guard looked up at the PC operator, who nodded in confirmation that a signal had been received.

Alpha 3 looked up from the notes on his desk and started talking to the boy. After a few minutes, the boy was guided out of the room by another guard. The process was repeated until it was Adam's turn to go to the seat. He sat in the hard chair and soon felt the cold metal of the tracking collar snap around his neck.

Alpha 3 spoke to him. "We have just fitted a tracking collar to your neck. Do not attempt to remove it, as that would make it explode. If you move too far from the base station in this building, it will start beeping. Once it starts beeping, you will have only thirty seconds to get back in range, or the explosive charge in the collar will go off. Do you understand me?"

"Yes, sir."

"Do you have any questions about the rules I just told you all?"

"No, sir."

"Do you have any sickness, allergy, or medicine I should know about?"

"Only this inhaler in case I get asthma." Adam held up his special inhaler.

Alpha 3 took it and briefly pressed the button. A misty puff of Adam's Albuterol sprayed out. He examined the casing and handed it back to Adam. "It doesn't look like a standard unit."

"Nah, it was a gift from my crazy aunt."

"Do you need any refills?"

"No. I don't use it a lot nowadays, but when I do need it, I got to use it straighta-way."

Alpha 3 read out some details from his clipboard. Adam recognised it as his home phone number, parents' names, and his home address. "Those details right?"

"Yes, sir."

"How did you get that cut on your face? It looks pretty new to me."

"I got bashed when the truck was bouncing along the track just before here."

"Is that the only damage?"

"Yes, sir."

"You got a headache or feeling dizzy?"

"No, sir."

"Ok. I'm done with you for the moment. Tomorrow morning, you will be recording a message for your parents to let them know you are ok."

He signalled to a guard, who led Adam away to the next room where they had been before. As soon as he entered the room, the guard tapped him on the shoulder. "You see that pile of gym mats? Go and spread them out along the wall with the narrow end facing that wall. That's where you all get to sleep later tonight."

The guard signalled to two of the other boys. "Come over here and give him a hand."

The captive boys and girls got to sleep late that night. The lights in the room were promptly switched off at ten thirty p.m. by the terrorists. The children were exhausted but restless from the horrors of the day. They were unaware they were now the subject of a national police hunt and their pictures had appeared on the national TV evening news. Six unsuspecting motorists had had their cars stopped by armed police. The police were not surprised when they found a mobile phone attached by a magnet under each car. Other police detectives were on a flight to South Africa to try and track down Mr. Howell.

The boys bedded down at one end of the room, and the girls at the other. Adam and Simon had the dubious pleasure of being the nearest to the portable toilet cabin. Simon had been astonished when Adam had volunteered to do that. "Adam, are you crazy? It's going to smell terrible soon, and we get to hear people going to the toilet all night."

"Simon, trust me, ok? There is a reason I'm doing this. Try and get some sleep now. We've got work to do later tonight."

It was well after midnight when Adam roused Simon by shaking his shoulder. Adam held his hand over Simon's mouth to stop him from speaking. When Simon was awake and calm, Adam led him through the darkness to the double doors of the room. He repeated the trick with a notepad, and the doors swung open with a faint *hiss*. Adam led him out into the corridor. It was empty, but the lights were switched on.

"Adam, if they catch us, we are going to get into real trouble."

"Don't worry, Simon. With us all wearing these neck collars, they are going to be much more relaxed. It is impossible for us to escape while we are wearing them. I want to explore this building some more."

Adam led Simon to the locked door at the far end of the corridor. He then took the lock-picking tools he had earlier removed from his inhaler and set to work on the door lock. Simon looked puzzled at first and then suddenly realised what Adam was trying to do. About one minute later, Adam had succeeded in unlocking the door. He beckoned to his friend and then stepped through the doorway. Once through, he spent a little time to re-lock the door. "It is a bit tedious re-locking the door," he said, "but if they do a security patrol, there would be problems if they found that door unlocked."

They had entered into the stairwell. There were stairs going down to the basement and stairs leading up to the first floor. The stairwell was lit, so Adam and Simon had no trouble finding their way down. There was a brief delay while he worked on the lock. The corridor in the basement was not lit, but when Adam tried a light switch, most of the lights flickered on. He quickly walked along the corridor to find the room he had been in earlier. He tried the door. It was still locked, but the lock resisted Adam's picks for only one minute. "These lock picks are not very good. Otherwise, I wouldn't be so slow at opening these locks."

"How do you know how to do this? Are you some kind of burglar?"

"Oh, it is just a hobby I have. It proves useful sometimes, though I don't use it to earn pocket money. Here... hold the door open for a while. I need the light from the corridor."

Adam went in the room and found the ventilation shaft where he had been before. He climbed in and searched around at the base of the shaft. There was odd rubbish in there, but eventually Adam was able to find the LED torch he had dropped. He left the room and then led Simon along the corridor to the stairwell. This time, he did not re-lock the door to the basement corridor door, but he did remember to switch off the light.

"I doubt if the security patrol will come down here. It doesn't look as though they use this area. Even if they do, they will probably think someone forgot to lock the corridor ages ago."

Adam then led them up the stairs to the first floor. The corridor was not locked. "Simon, we must be quiet as we go along this corridor. If this door is unlocked, it must mean somebody is up here. Stay close to me and don't say anything."

Adam and Simon carefully explored each of the rooms on the floor in turn. All of them were unused except the one at the end of the corridor, which he knew to be the office. He guessed somebody would be keeping watch in the office, so he left that room alone. Carefully tucking below the window of the office door, he opened the door at that end of the corridor and found what he was looking for. At the top of that stairwell was an iron ladder leading up to a trapdoor towards the roof of the building. "Keep watch on the office door. If you think somebody is coming, just hiss at me."

Adam climbed up the metal ladder and set to work on the padlock that was locking the trapdoor to the roof. He was not so experienced at picking padlocks and did not have all the tools he needed, but after about five minutes, he was able to release the lock. He slipped the padlock into his pocket and started to lift the trapdoor. Just then, he heard someone enter the staircase below on the ground floor. He hissed at Simon. "Quick! Climb the ladder up to me."

Simon froze when he heard footsteps coming up the stairs.

"Now, Simon. NOW!" urged Adam.

Simon suddenly dashed for the metal ladder and climbed upwards. Adam had pushed open the trapdoor and climbed through. He helped his friend up through the trapdoor hole and closed it quietly just as he saw the heads of two of the terrorists appear up the stairway. The two boys held their breath and waited silently. The men did not look upwards and passed through the doorway into the corridor.

Using the light of his LED torch, Adam had a look around the room they had just entered. It contained a large water tank. There was also a door to the roof. He tried the door handle it was locked. He looked at the lock and realised it was just a thumb bolt that could be unlocked with a simple twist of his wrist. He cautiously opened the door and stepped out onto the flat roof of the building. Simon followed him.

Outside, it was a moonlit night. The stars were very bright, and the sky was clear of cloud. Adam and Simon carefully surveyed the landscape around the building. Adam, with the benefit of having overheard the briefing by Alpha 3, could recognise most of the features surrounding him. He realised they were probably somewhere in Scotland because of the long journey time and the fact that the water had been called a loch by the terrorist leader. He pointed out the various features of the site to Simon.

Adam's next action was to carefully check the sides of the building to see if there was some way down. He could see a metal drainpipe at each corner of the building. The pipe was recessed into brickwork to prevent people from climbing up or down the pipe. They spent some time on the roof memorising features of the site before returning to the first-floor corridor stairwell. Adam returned the padlock to the roof hatch but did not lock it. Carefully creeping past the office door, the boys made their way back to the ground floor, where Adam unlocked and then re-locked the door to the corridor. They quietly entered through the double doors of their room and lay down on their mats to try and get some sleep for what was left of the night.

Just before they went back to sleep, Adam cautioned Simon. "Don't tell anyone about what we did just now. We must keep that type of information under control or somebody will try something stupid."

Chapter 26 First Escape

Adam awoke to the sound of crashing and banging. It was seven in the morning, and one of their guards had entered the room where they all slept and was banging with a wooden baton against the door to awaken all of the captive teenagers. "It's seven a.m.!" he shouted. "Time for you all to get up. The boys are first to have the showers. I will be back for the girls in fifteen minutes. I want all of the boys out in the corridor NOW."

The boys assembled in the corridor and were led by another guard to the shower room. Inside the room, they found towels and clean clothes, just as they were promised by Alpha 3.

"Strip off your dirty boiler suits and throw them in the bin over here. You have ten minutes to get showered and dried. Make sure you wash your hair. There is shower gel and shampoo in the showers. You will find toothpaste and disposable brushes over by the sinks. If you want to transfer any items from the old boiler suit to your new one, come and show me those items."

The boys quickly showered, dried, and redressed. They were then led by the guard into the canteen. "Sit down and wait quietly for the girls. When they arrive, you should serve them with food and then have your own breakfast."

The selection of breakfast food was limited. It started with porridge, followed by scrambled eggs and bacon, toast, and fresh fruit. The only drink provided was water in metal jugs.

Adam sat next to Darren and Simon on one of the benches next to the tables. Keeping an eye on the guards, they quietly talked amongst each other.

"Adam, where did you get to yesterday when you left the room?"

"I was just looking around to see if I can find anything useful. I didn't find all that much, but every little bit will help, I'm sure. I think we need to see what happens today before trying to make any plans."

"Some of the other boys were talking about trying to grab the guard when he comes through the door."

"That's stupid, Darren. What are they going to do once they grab him? With these things around our necks, we can't escape. There will be other guards outside who are probably armed. We don't even know where we are in the country."

"I thought you were some kind of hero, Adam, but you seem to be giving in to these people. Some of us have gotten together and decided we will form a committee to plan an escape. There's going to be a vote when we are all alone together later today."

"Darren, I just know it is stupid to antagonise them when we don't have a proper plan. Just remember that if we attempt an escape, everybody has to get away—and that's thirty people. If it is only a partial success, it could be very dangerous for the people left behind. I get the feeling these guys can be very ruthless. I mean, they attached detonators to our necks and shot our English teacher, remember? We just need to be careful and smart, that's all."

When they had finished eating, the guard instructed them to wait quietly until everybody was ready. He then stood in front of them and issued further instructions. "The girls will follow me into the corridor. The boys will tidy up the breakfast dishes. I will be back for you shortly. There will be no talking while you are waiting."

Under the watchful eye of the remaining guard, the boys scraped uneaten food from the dishes into large dustbins. They stacked the dirty plates onto a trolley and then counted cutlery onto the trolley as well. The guard checked that the area was properly clean and then turned to the boys and said, "I need two volunteers to empty the bins."

There was silence at first, as none of the boys wanted to be seen helping the enemy. Adam broke the silence by volunteering himself and Simon. "We'll do it. I could do with getting some fresh air anyway." Adam seemed blissfully unaware of Simon's angry stare at him.

"You two boys wait behind when the others leave then." Shortly afterwards, the other guard reappeared and led the boys back to their humble accommodations.

Simon and Adam were told to take a trolley each and follow the guard. They were led across the parking area to the back of the accommodation block. There, they had to tip the waste food from the bins into a large dumpster. The smell arising from rotting food in the dumpster was awful.

They quickly slammed the lid shut, and Adam turned to the guard. "Aww, that is terrible. It's enough to make you puke. Don't they ever empty it?"

"Don't you worry, It will be done tomorrow, but you won't see it because you will be just about to wake up from your beauty sleep." The guard moved away, callously laughing at the boy's discomfort.

"Adam, why in the hell did you get us involved in this? We are only helping the terrorists by doing this."

Adam looked at the guard to make sure he was not listening and then spoke to his friend, "Simon, trust me on this. By volunteering for these dirty jobs, we are accomplishing a lot—gaining their trust and getting to see more of the site where we are being held captive. That may be essential later. If you think about it, there must be about sixty people on this site now. That must mean supplies are delivered from the outside world by lorry or van every day or so. That may be a method of escape."

The guard led them to the kitchen door and told them to leave the trolleys. Once the trolleys were in their correct position, he led them back to the office building where the school children were being held captive. The two boys were allowed to wash their hands in the shower room before being returned to the rest of the captives.

Adam noticed that some of the school children were giving him and Simon angry glares. They had all been moved to the second computer room—the one Adam had visited the previous evening. He knew the reason for the move was so that the terrorists could search the room where children had slept the night before. They all sat around on the floor waiting for something to happen.

While they were waiting, Deepa came over to chat with Adam. "Hi, Adam. This is very different from where we met last time. I don't suppose either of us could have guessed this would happen. Where did you really get to last night?"

Adam grabbed Deepa's elbow and guided her away from the rest of the people so they could talk in privacy. "What do you mean, 'last night', Deepa?"

"I saw you unlock the doors to the room after we first arrived. You disappeared for about half an hour before coming back. Last night, I saw you and Simon disappear again for about an hour. I know the rumours about you and him are not true, but there must have been a reason why you managed to get out but decided to come back."

"I was just looking around trying to get information. It may be essential if we get a chance to escape."

Deepa looked intently in Adam's eyes for a moment and then took his right hand and turned it to look at the ring on his little finger. "That is a strange-looking ring. I think I have seen something like that before."

Before Adam could react, she lifted his right hand and moved it to just below her throat where a pretty silver locket hung. Two jewels embedded in the lid of the locket lit up with a green glow. At the same time, the red star glowed on Adam's ring. She released his hand in shock. "You're from the Foundation of Honour! We had heard there was a brother organisation to the Guild, but we never thought we would meet any of you. In the Guild, the red star symbol means you are a senior Officer. Is it true?"

Adam paused before responding. He knew his membership of the Foundation should be kept secret, particularly his Officer grade, but these were unusual times. "Yes, I am a member of the Foundation, and I hold the rank of Captain."

"I thought there was something different about you. You seem so determined and organised. You are very young to be a Captain. You must have done some really serious stuff to gain that level of promotion. Why don't you take command here? This group needs a leader. They are even talking of electing somebody to take control, and that's never going to work."

"No, I think it is best that the terrorists do not understand my background. Becoming the leader would draw attention to me. When the time is right, I will take command, but not yet. I get the feeling this is more than just a simple kidnapping. We need to find out more before we decide what to do. In the Foundation, we are given specialist training to develop skills. My skill is picking locks. Do you have one?"

"Yes. Mine is computer technology. I have been trained to work as a hacker, though I don't think that will do us any good here where I have no access to computers. By the way, we are not alone. There is another sister of the Guild with us."

"Another? Who is it?"

"I will have to speak with her to see if she is willing to reveal herself. I'm sure the Foundation has similar rules to our Guild of keeping quiet about what we do."

"Deepa, I will probably do some things over the next couple of days that appear to be stupid. Please just trust me and do not give up hope. If your Guild sister will help us, that will be great. I'm going to need people I know I can trust."

Before they could talk any further, the doors to the room opened, and Alpha 3 marched in, accompanied by two guards. "It is time for you to earn the food I have so generously provided. You are each going to make a little video recording that we will send to your parents to prove you are safe and alive. You will be called one by one to make the recording. Meanwhile, I need a couple of volunteers to empty the portable toilet next door."

Everyone remained silent, avoiding the gaze of Alpha 3. Then, without any warning, John Nelson stepped forward from the group of boys. "I'll do it, and I'm sure Adam Cranford here will help. He seems to like sleeping next to the toilets anyway, so I'm sure he's already used to the smell."

Adam caught a hint of a shrug from Simon. He turned and nodded in agreement to Alpha 3. The terrorist leader noticed the tension between Nelson and Cranford but chose to ignore it. It suited his purposes to have disagreement between the captives. Controlling thirty people would become much more difficult if they all had a common purpose. "You two go with the guard. The rest of you remain here."

The guards led the two boys into the room where they had slept and showed them how to remove the waste bucket from the portable toilet cabin. He gave them both cleaning materials and rubber gloves and made them clean out the inside of the toilet cabin. Once that was done, he led them out of the building. The two boys carried the heavy, smelly toilet bucket between themselves.

John Nelson whispered to Adam as they walked. "Keep your hands off Deepa. She's not your class of person. We've noticed you have been brown-nosing with the guards. It isn't going to do you any good. If you want to get on with the rest of us, you had better show that you are prepared to help. I've heard you had a look around the building. You had better provide help when we plan the escape, otherwise you might find that the guards and your fancy judo moves are not going to protect you."

"Get stuffed, Nelson. I'll talk to whomever I want when I want to, and I will decide whether it is worthwhile helping you with your crazy escape plans. These are serious terrorists, and you shouldn't underestimate them."

The guard led them to the manhole cover for the septic tank and lifted the cover.

It was close to the vehicle garage. Adam was able to get a good look at the layout of the garage.

"Tip the bucket in here and don't spill any, or you will have to clear it up by hand. When it has been emptied, clean out the bucket with that hose."

Adam and John carefully tipped the foul contents into the septic tank. Adam then took the empty bucket and rinsed it out with the hose. He accidentally on purpose dropped the hose afterwards in such a way that John was soaked with cold water from the waist down. "Oh, sorry about that, Nelson. It was a pure accident."

"You two stop messing with the hose and get back with the bucket to your sleeping area."

Adam carried the clean bucket back, taking care to keep out of range of John Nelson's feet that were trying to trip him. As he entered the sleeping room, he tripped on the bucket and fell hard against the guard. Recovering his balance, he went to the toilet cabin and reinstalled the bucket. They were then led back to the second room, where the others were waiting. Over half of them had recorded the video message to their parents. Many of them had returned in tears at the reminder that they were being held captive.

When Adam's turn came about, he was led through into the canteen. He was told to sit on an office chair in front of a video camera. The video camera was connected by cables to a laptop computer. Behind the chair was a large green screen descending from a roll of material out of sight of the camera. Adam's face was brightly lit from high on the left side by a spotlight.

Alpha 3 sat at a desk behind the camera. When Adam arrived, Alpha 3 looked up to confirm who had arrived. He searched down a printed list on the desktop and then with a whiteboard marker pen wrote a figure on a large notice that he had before him. He then stood and held the notice behind the camera so Adam could read it. "Cranford, read this notice aloud and look at the camera. There will be a practice run first, followed by the real filming. Hold this newspaper below your chin so the camera can see it when you are reading."

Adam took the newspaper, which was published that morning, and held it to his chest then read the notice aloud. "Hello, Mum and Dad. I am being held for ransom. I am not allowed to tell you where I am, but I am being well treated. Please pay the ransom, which is set at £50,000. That is all I am allowed to say."

After the rehearsal, Adam read the notice without any hesitation to the camera that was recording the video. Alpha 3 signalled to Adam to return to the other captives. Before leaving, Adam hesitated and said, "Look, if I tell you a secret, can you make sure I'm protected?"

Adam moved close to the desk so the others would not hear what was being said. Alpha 3 looked at him as though making a decision and then replied, "I guess that depends on what the secret is and what you need protecting from, but I think we can provide some protection. After all, you are a valuable hostage, and I cannot have you coming to any damage."

"I think you guys don't want to really hurt us, but if we break your rules, you wouldn't be so nice."

"You have got that right, young man."

"It's just that some of the others are planning an escape. I don't know all the details, but I can tell you when I do know that stuff. We would have to find a secret way that I can tell you without the others knowing, or I might get hurt by them."

"When you do know, write down the details on a note and slip it under the door to your room. If you sign it 'Mole', I will know the message has come from you."

"Will you punish me if I'm actually involved in the escape?"

"Not if you tell me beforehand and make sure none of my men get hurt. Now, go back and join the others."

The guard departed after escorting Adam back to the second computer room. Adam found a pad of writing paper and started to write down from memory the list of names and figures he had seen on Alpha 3's desk.

As he wrote the list, he saw Deepa coming over to talk to him. She saw what he was writing and smiled. "I have already done that, Adam. I thought you might find the information useful. The total ransom is £25 million. I'm afraid you come at the bottom of the list. The terrorists apparently think I'm worth £500,000."

"So the Guild gives you memory training as well?"

"Yes, they do. I thought it was stupid at first, but since then, I've always found it very useful. It looks like Darren is their most valuable hostage. By the way, the other Guild sister has agreed to make herself known to you. She will come over in a while."

"That's cool. That will make this particular walnut easier to crack. Do you know when the others are planning to hold the vote to set up their escape planning committee?"

Deepa looked shocked and then thoughtfully stared at Adam before she carefully pronounced, "They have more cannons than a Death Star."

Adam looked equally surprised, and then a look of recognition came to his face. "You are Bright Petal? The leader of Visiting Havoc?"

For the first time in twenty-four hours, Deepa's face broke into a broad grin. "Yes, BaD Totem. I should have recognised your style. I think I'm already beginning to feel sorry for Alpha 3. He really doesn't recognise that he caught a monster from the deep when he took you off the bus."

"We are not safe and home yet. These are real terrorists with real guns. Anything could go wrong. Their security is very well planned. The first thing I have to deal with is this escape committee that the other guys want to set up. How do the other girls feel about it?"

"They are mostly for taking part. They don't know about you, so I don't think they will take too much notice of you if you argue against the committee. I'd best go now. Johnny is giving you some ugly looks. To think I used to date him once! I'll bring my copy of the list over later. It will be interesting to see what you got wrong."

Adam sat by himself, completing the process of writing out the ransom list. He totalled the figures and came to £25 million. He'd noticed Simon had not come over to join him, and he was not surprised. In this stressful environment, the captives were bound to fall into groups that demanded loyalty of each other. The others would be more comfortable in their existing social groups.

As he sat thinking, he vaguely noticed Sally walking past to get a drink from the water fountain. On the way back she paused by him. "So, how is the Toilet Attendant feeling? It was really awful of John to volunteer you for that work."

Adam then noticed the gold locket dangling from Sally's hand. It had three emeralds embedded in a line in the lid. He lifted his right hand towards the locket. When his ring approached the locket, the emeralds glowed in response to the red star.

"It looks like Deepa wasn't dreaming then. I'll come and talk to you later, Adam, when people are not watching."

Adam went and sat with the others. It seemed a long time before everyone had completed their ransom video, and it felt like it was way past lunch time. No one had a watch, so it was difficult to tell the time. Adam had his button watch built into the inhaler, but he didn't want to use that in front of other people. It was boring waiting and doing nothing.

Without warning, the doors to the room swung open. A guard walked in and dropped a large box on the floor. "The boss says you have all been cooperative this morning, so he is letting you have some midday food. Don't get used to it. In future, it will be only two meals a day. So tomorrow, make sure you all eat your breakfast. When you have finished, put the rubbish in these bags."

He dropped some polysacks on the floor, turned, and walked out through the doors that had been kept open by the other guard. No one moved at first, and then suddenly everyone dashed over to the box and tore it open. Adam immediately recognised them as MREs, Meals Ready to Eat, the typical food packs used by soldiers. Conversation broke out among the teenagers as they sat investigating the packs and choosing the food they wanted to eat. There was a certain amount of bartering as they swapped items between each other.

Most people had eaten their fill when Darren stood up in front of everyone. "I have been talking with the other guys. We all think we have to do something. We can't just wait around until the police find us. We either need to escape all together or at least get someone away so they can fetch help. If we are going to do this, we all need to pull together. I am proposing that we elect a leader who can form a committee to consider suggestions for escaping. You will each get one vote. What I want you to do is write the name of the person you want as a leader on the slips of paper I'm going to hand out now. No one has to vote, but I think we should do something."

One of the boys selected by Darren moved amongst everyone, handing out slips of paper and pencils. After another five minutes, Darren had one of the girls collect up all of the slips. A boy and a girl were selected to perform the count of the votes. Darren turned out to be the clear winner with fifteen votes. Adam came fourth in the vote with three votes cast for him.

Darren selected four people to join him on the committee. Neither Adam nor Simon was selected. John Nelson sneered at Adam as he moved to join Darren's committee. "Now we'll see some real action, Cranford. At least we are not scared like you."

Darren intervened. "John, cut it out. Everyone is entitled to their own opinion. Adam just thinks the risks are too high. You know from school that Adam can be very brave when he needs to be. Adam, if you come up with some ideas, please let us know. We need all the ideas we can get."

Adam left the committee alone to continue their planning. He lay quietly alone on the floor, thinking through the whole situation. He was worried his parents might try and pay the ransom, and they surely didn't have that kind of money to spare. He was also trying to work out what seemed to be wrong with this situation. *All this effort for only £25 million?* It just didn't seem right. Maybe it was just dedicated terrorists trying to raise funds, but the way that Alpha 3 had spoken to the guards at the briefing, it was as though they were hired mercenaries. He knew he had to get more information. He was wondering what was in the secret building where nobody was allowed to go.

His thoughts were interrupted by Sally arriving and sitting next to him. "Deepa seems very impressed with you, Adam. She says she can't wait for the action to start. Have you got some kind of mega plan already? Are commandos already flying in on helicopters?"

"No, nothing like that. I've got a few ideas, but I need a lot more information before deciding what to do. This idea of escaping could screw everything up. This place is really well defended, better than most prisons. We might be able to get a couple of people out, but that would leave most of us behind. If the police or the Army raid this place, the terrorists could easily kill us before any help got through."

"Oh, so we are not going home tomorrow then? I suppose we'd best wait for our parents to cough up the ransom money."

"I guess so, but I'm sure we can make the terrorists' lives uncomfortable while we are waiting. Has the Guild taught you any specialist skills?"

"Yes, but they won't help very much here. My dad owns a large construction company. We lived in Iraq and other countries before coming back to England. He used to let me press the plunger when they were using explosives to quarry rocks for road construction. I also used to watch when they were setting them up, so I know quite a lot about explosives. The Guild has given me some special training, but there are no explosives around here for me to play with, so I won't be much help."

"Does Darren know?"

"No. He's nice, but he thinks I'm just a dippy blonde girl with rich parents."

"Have you got any other skills like martial arts?"

"We all do self-defence training, but I really love rock climbing, though I don't think it will help a lot in here. I think my love of climbing comes from all the time I spent clambering around the rocks and boulders in the old quarries. I go climbing most weekends nowadays." She held up her right hand and showed Adam the small scars on her fingers and the back of her hand. "I get those from jamming my hands into the cracks of rock face overhangs. It drives my mum mad. She thinks I should spend all my time in a beauty spa rather than up some cold, wet mountains."

"I can think of one thing already where you might be able to help out, but I need some more time yet."

"Adam, Deepa has had an idea about how to get hold of a computer, but she will need some tools to make it work."

"Oh? What's her idea? I think I might be able to get some tools tonight if she lets me know what she needs."

"She says the plasma screen in the canteen will have quite a powerful computer built into it. If she can spend some time in there, she might be able to extract the computer. She says it is not perfect, but it would be a start. Oh, and there is one other thing. Can we do something about Simon? He really likes you but can't understand why you are helping the terrorists. Can I tell him about the Foundation? He's feeling really down about the whole thing."

"No. I'm sorry, but that has to remain secret unless it becomes a matter of life or death. He will just have to learn to trust me. What I have to do here to protect us all comes above plain friendship. I'll go talk with him and see if I can get him to understand."

Darren came over and interrupted them. "Hi. What are you two scheming? Come on, Adam, I know you must have some ideas about how we could escape from here. We haven't come up with any sensible ideas ourselves."

"I can get people out of this building, but that would not be much good because it looks as though the whole site is surrounded by an electric wire fence. Getting past the fence undetected is going to be the difficult part. I think I know a way how to get a couple of people off the site, but it is very risky and still leaves everybody else behind."

"Why don't you come and tell us what you think? At least then everybody will have the chance to make their own minds up on the risk."

"Ok, Darren. I will do that for you, but I'm not happy about it."

Adam and Darren walked over to the other group who formed the escape committee. Adam sat down amongst them and started to talk. "Darren has persuaded me to tell you how to get a couple of people to escape. I have already told Darren I think it is too risky. You will have to make your own minds up whether you want to try my ideas, but don't blame me if it all goes terribly wrong. If you are going to do this, you will have to do it early tomorrow morning. There is a rubbish lorry coming to collect the rubbish early tomorrow morning. I would guess that is some time between six thirty and seven a.m. I think that if we are lucky, we should be able to get two people to hide in the rubbish truck as it leaves the site. At present, the guards seem fairly relaxed and probably won't check the lorry as it goes out because that might alert the local Council workers. I can wake you at six o'clock tomorrow morning and let you out of this room."

John Nelson raised a question. "Adam, you know the outer doors to this building are locked using a swipe card. How are you going to get past that?"

Adam reached into his pocket and pulled out a plastic card. "Do you mean a card like this, Nelson? I think it must have accidentally fallen out of the guard's pocket when I bumped into him this morning."

"You stole it, Adam? What happens when he finds it missing?"

"Let's just say I have more need of the card than he does. I don't think he will report it missing to Alpha 3 straightaway because their boss seems to be very strict. Anyway, if he does, all they will do is disable the card. If they do that, we haven't lost much."

"So how do we get onto the rubbish truck when it arrives?"

"I don't know at the moment. I haven't seen it. You will just have to improvise and sneak on when nobody is looking, but be careful to get on AFTER they have used the rubbish compactor, or you will get crushed."

"How will you know it is time to wake up? None of us have watches to tell the time."

"I can always wake up on time just by telling myself when that should be, as though I have some kind of internal clock. So, there is the plan. It is full of holes, and I don't think you should go because the risk of getting caught is too high."

John Nelson lifted the tracking ring encircling his neck and asked another question. "You have forgotten about these tracking rings. They said the rings will explode and kill us if we leave the vicinity of this building."

"Ah, yes. I had forgotten that small item. We know the rings are safe out in the yard because we have been out when we emptied the toilet bucket and when we delivered the food waste to the bins. I suspect we would have to be outside of this base before the rings become a problem."

"But we can't remove the rings without them exploding, so how are we going to get away?"

"John, this is where some risk comes into it. I think I know how to remove these rings without causing the explosive to go off. We will need some heat insulating material and one of those carbon dioxide fire extinguishers out in the corridor. I have seen this trick done with metal padlocks. If you spray the metal with the white smoke from the CO_2 extinguisher, it cools it down really quickly. The metal becomes brittle, and you can shatter it by just tapping it with a hammer. I think the trigger mechanism for the tracking rings is in the plastic box. If we shatter the ring opposite the plastic box, I think we will be able to remove the ring without causing it to explode."

"But you are not sure? And why do you need the heat insulating material?"

"The heat insulation material is to protect your neck and shoulder from getting a freeze burn when we let off the CO_2 extinguisher. And don't worry, John, if the tracking ring explodes when you try and shatter it, I will say sorry to you afterwards. It is just a risk you are going to have to take if you want to escape before we can work something else out."

Darren interrupted the dialogue and thanked Adam. "Adam, thank you for giving us your ideas. We will talk about them and let you know if we are going to follow up. If we choose to try this escape, are you going to come with us?"

"No, I won't, Darren. I will help you get out of the building but that is as far as I'm going. I still think we need to remain here, and if you have any sense, you will heed my advice."

Following the committee meeting, the rest of the day dragged on. It was boring, and there was nothing to do. The evening meal was a greasy Irish stew followed by canned fruit. As promised, the terrorists allowed the captives to stay on in the canteen and to watch a DVD film.

After the film, Darren approached him. "Adam, we are going to try your plan. Even if the two people who escape can only get to the nearest town or village, they can at least raise the alarm and get the police to come rescue the rest of us. Can you wake John and me at six a.m. tomorrow morning?"

"Ok, Darren, I will... if you are really sure about this. I am a bit tired right now, so I am going to try and get some sleep."

When the children got back to the room where they were going to sleep, it was obvious the room had been thoroughly searched. Adam guessed that the guard who he had stolen the card from would be very carefully checking them tomorrow morning at shower time.

Adam slept for a few hours and then rose and woke Simon. "Simon, come quietly. We have got some work to do."

Adam unlocked the door to the room, checking that the coast was clear before he left with Simon in tow. He walked along the corridor, unlocked the door at the end of the corridor, and led Simon into the lobby. Before leaving, he re-locked the corridor door and then, using the stolen card key, he left the building. Crouching in the shadows, he checked to see if any guards were on patrol. When he was satisfied it was safe, he and Simon ran over to the workshop next to the garage. Once they were there, Adam set to work on the padlock of the workshop door.

"Simon, keep a lookout for any guards. If you see anybody, just hiss in my direction."

The padlock was quite stiff from age, but eventually Adam was able to overcome its barriers. He carefully opened the door and stepped inside, signalling Simon to follow him. Using the LED torch, he quickly checked out the room around him. Much of the equipment looked old and was covered in dust. There was a tool board on the wall that had a mixture of screwdrivers, spanners, hammers, pliers, saws, and other metalworking implements. There were also a couple of toolboxes standing on the floor. Adam rummaged through the toolboxes and around benches until he found what he was looking for on that visit. He looked around and found an oily rag, which he used to wrap around the tools he had claimed. He gave the bundle to Simon to carry for him.

Looking around further, he found four large cans of windscreen de-icing spray. He went over to the vehicles housed inside the main garage building and lifted the bonnets of the vehicles in turn. In each vehicle, he carefully positioned a spray can of the de-icing spray. As quietly as possible, he closed the bonnets of the vehicles. Leaving the vehicle garage, he returned to the workshop door and put the padlock back in place but did not re-lock it. He used a small piece of wood wedged in the hasp to make it appear to casual inspection as though the padlock was locked.

"Adam, can we go back now? I don't want to get caught out here."

"We have got just one more place to visit before we go back, and then you can sleep all night."

Adam led the way over to the doors of the secret building. He looked around for a lock keyhole but could find nothing. Then he noticed a card reader mounted on the wall. He did not try to use the card in his pocket because he knew the guards were not allowed in that building. Scouting around the building, he tried to look in through windows but could see nothing. He was frustrated, but he knew he could do nothing more this night. The pair returned to their sleeping quarters. Before entering the room, Adam had Simon pick up one of the CO_2 fire extinguishers and bring it from the corridor. Once Simon had settled down, Adam extracted a hammer from the bundle of tools and then hid the remainder under one of the floor tiles of the raised floor. He settled down for a few more hours' sleep.

Adam woke up at five thirty in the morning and retrieved the writing pad he'd stored nearby. He quietly tore a strip of paper from the pad and wrote a brief message on it in pencil.

They are going to escape in the morning in the rubbish lorry. John is the ring leader.

Mole

[Figure 2 - Adam's note]

He folded the strip of paper and then slipped it under the door into the corridor. At six a.m., he woke Darren and John to let them know it was time to go. John woke a couple more of the boys to help.

"Ok, Adam, it is time for you to show us the trick of cracking these neck rings open."

"It is simple. Just wrap a double layer of the blanket underneath the ring to act as an insulator. Make sure there is no exposed flesh. Then, spray the ring with CO_2 by the hinge for about ten seconds and tap the ring with this hammer with it resting against the edge of the desk. It should crack. Be careful you don't have any bare skin exposed, or you'll get a serious cold burn—maybe even frostbite."

John Nelson turned to the other two boys and said, "Right. Have you got that, boys? Now grab him."

Suddenly, Adam was grabbed from behind by the two other boys. His arms were pinioned to his side as a blanket was pulled through the ring on his neck and spread to cover his shoulders and his neck.

"It looks like you are going to be the guinea pig for this experiment, Cranford. Don't worry. I will apologise if your head gets blown off."

Adam was held firmly by the others and could not struggle. The blanket was pulled through his neck ring.

There was a sudden roar from the nozzle of the fire extinguisher. The sudden noise woke all of the other children. After a few seconds, Adam was pivoted so the ring rested on the desktop. There was a sharp *crack* as the hammer hit the ring. He then felt the opened ring being pulled roughly from his neck.

"It seems like your theory was right, Cranford."

Adam fumed at the risk they had taken with his life but chose not to react at that time. The other two neck rings were swiftly removed by the same process. Adam grabbed the three broken tracking rings and carried them. Saying no more, he opened the doors to their sleeping quarters, looked outside in the corridor, and beckoned the other two boys to follow. They were amazed to see how quickly Adam was able to pick the lock on the door of the corridor. They escaped from the building using swipe card. Adam checked for any patrolling guards and then guided the other two boys to the area where the food waste bins were stored. He showed them a good place to hide where they could wait for the rubbish lorry to turn up. Before leaving, he threw the broken neck rings into the food waste bin.

"It is up to you to now. Despite the stupid trick you pulled on me with the neck ring, I wish you both good luck. I have taken some precautions to fix their vehicles if they try and follow you."

Adam returned to the office building. After opening the door with the swipe card, he turned and threw the card like a frisbee into the main parking area. He unlocked the corridor door lock, passed through, and re-locked it before he returned to their sleeping room. On the way, he noticed his note had now disappeared from the corridor. When he returned to the room people crowded around him and asked whether this escape would be successful.

"I don't know. It is up to them now. They might not even be able to get onto the rubbish lorry. We are just going to have to wait and see. We should all get back to our sleeping positions and pretend we are asleep. Otherwise, the guards might begin to suspect something has happened."

Adam had found some new status in the group because of his part in the escape plan. All the children took his advice and settled back down as though they were asleep. He hid the hammer with the other tools under the floor.

At six forty-five, the rubbish lorry arrived for its fortnightly collection of rubbish. A guard at the gatehouse allowed them in and pointed out where the bins were stored for the collection. The refuse collectors had been there before, so they already knew the way. They reversed to the storage area and swiftly hoisted the bins to dump the accumulated rubbish within the lorry. When the men unhooked the bins and returned to the front of the lorry, the two boys broke from hiding and ran to the back of the lorry. As this visit was early in the collection route, there was not too much rubbish in the lorry and no need to compact the load. As the lorry drove off, the two boys climbed inside the back of it and sat ducked down beside the loose rubbish.

The terrorist guards did not even bother to check the lorry. It drove off bumping along the poorly made road. The vehicle had gone not much more than 200 meters when the presents that Adam had left in the rubbish exploded showering the two boys with rotten food and waste. It was a small explosion, and the driver of the vehicle did not hear it above the noise of the lorry bumping along the track.

Inside the office building, the terrorist guards were awakening the captives for their showers. As the two guards counted the boys walking out of their room, they realised there were two people missing. They quickly ordered all of the boys back into the sleeping quarters and performed a recount; still, there were definitely two boys missing. The guards radioed the control room to raise an alert.

A few minutes later, Alpha 3 came into the room in a huff. He held a piece of folded notepaper in his hand. "Does anyone know where Darren Nichols and John Nelson have gone?"

There was a defiant silence from the remaining captives.

"If you know where they are, you had better tell me now. All of your lives could be at risk if they have escaped."

The defiant silence continued.

"In that case, I am locking you all down today. There will be no showers, no clean clothes, and no breakfast."

Instructing a guard to remain outside the door, he angrily turned and stormed out of the room. He ran up to the control room and shouted in anger at the Squad Leader, whose guards had been on duty. "Why wasn't I brought this note earlier? It is obvious it was a warning that an escape was being planned. You had best send some men in Land Rovers to go and see if they can intercept the rubbish lorry. If the boys are on the lorry, bring them back and make some excuse to the driver about this being a training exercise."

The Squad Leader grabbed four men and rushed over to the garage. They hurriedly jumped into two Land Rovers and drove off in pursuit of the rubbish truck.

By now, Darren and John had cleaned the rubbish from their faces and were looking out from the back of the rubbish lorry. They had escaped. They had tried attracting the attention of the lorry driver with no success. As the lorry paused to turn onto the road from the track, the two boys could see the Land Rovers in pursuit. At Darren's urging, they both jumped out from the rubbish lorry and hid beside the track. The Land Rovers roared past out onto the public road in pursuit of the rubbish truck. The path of the road was visible for some miles as it swept round the side of the mountain. In the distance, Darren could see one of the Land Rovers had suddenly stopped with smoke pouring out from under its bonnet. Two hundred metres further along, the second Land Rover ground to a halt with smoke pouring out from under its bonnet. Both vehicles were on fire. They saw the men jump out with fire extinguishers to put out the flames. The rubbish truck disappeared into the distance. Darren and John cheered, knowing they had escaped. All they needed to do now was to walk to the nearest village and raise the alarm. They didn't know what Adam had done to fix the Land Rovers or how he had done it, but it had worked and effectively prevented any further pursuit.

Alpha 3 raged in anger when he heard the radio report from the pursuit vehicles that they were damaged and had to break off the pursuit. "You stupid imbeciles! How can you let school children escape from a locked room in a locked building surrounded by double wire fences? If it happens again, you will lose your bonus payments. It is a good job I have taken extra precautions. Bring me the boy Adam Cranford. I see from the tracker system that his tracking ring has stopped working too."

Chapter 27 Retribution and Exploration

Out in the Scottish countryside, the two boys had found a road sign pointing to a village or town that was five miles in the distance. They started walking towards it, having agreed that if a car came towards them, they would try and stop it, but if the car came from behind, they would hide in case it was the terrorists. They had walked approximately two miles when they saw a white van driving towards them. They realised it was a police vehicle, so they stood on the road waving to flag it down.

The policeman stopped and wound down his window. "You two young men seem rather anxious. What can I do to help you?"

"We have been kidnapped and held at the base a few miles up the road. You need to call for backup. They are armed terrorists and were holding us hostage for a ransom."

"You must be the boys everybody is searching for. I am afraid the radio doesn't work out here, so I'd best drive you back into town, and we will get this all sorted out. You are rather filthy, so you'd best jump into the back of the van."

The boys eagerly jumped into the van, and the policeman locked the doors before driving off.

Alpha 3 looked up as Adam entered the office. "Your note was rather late. The two boys have gotten away from the site. What happened?"

"Oh, they didn't tell me the timing of the escape until early this morning."

"So how did you get the ring off your neck without it exploding?"

"John Nelson used me as the guinea pig. He froze the metal with CO_2 from an extinguisher and then cracked it."

"I see. I'm sorry, but I'm going to have to fit a new neck ring on you anyway. How did they get out of the building?"

"I'm not sure. I saw them slide a book under the doors to the room, and then the doors opened, but they left me behind."

Alpha 3 opened a black case beside him and pulled out a spare neck ring. He checked its serial number and then logged on to his computer and started the tracker system. He clicked the new ring shut around Adam's neck and then set the status to active using his computer. At that point, the telephone rang across the room. Alpha 3 rose to answer the call. Adam overheard part of the conversation.

"So you say there is a police van coming along the track? Is there just one vehicle? In that case, let the vehicle through unharmed. Call the gatehouse and let them know the vehicle is expected."

While Alpha 3's attention had been diverted, Adam had leaned across the laptop and changed the status of his neck ring from active to disarmed. He closed the detail page on the screen, hoping Alpha 3 would not notice.

"Young Master Cranford, you may go. I am grateful for your cooperation and will not forget it. If you come across anymore important news, make sure you tell me straightaway. Meanwhile, I must go downstairs and receive some guests."

Alpha 3 handed Adam over to the guard outside the door and told him to take the boy back to the sleeping quarters. Using the video monitoring cameras, he watched the police van arrived at the gatehouse. He left the office to go out to meet the driver of the police van. "Yes, Officer, can I help you? I am the manager of this establishment."

"I have two items of lost property in the back of the van. I believe the price we agreed in your phone call was £25,000 each item?"

"Yes, that is correct. It is a good job I arranged for Sergeant MacLean to go away on a training course for the next couple of weeks and have you as a temporary substitute."

The policeman handed over the key to the van doors.

Alpha 3 signalled to one of the guards to open the back of the van. The two boys inside the back of the van were absolutely shocked when they realised the policeman had brought them back to the site. They were grabbed roughly and pulled out from the van before being led back into the office building. The police van drove away.

Darren and John were dragged back into the sleeping accommodations, followed by Alpha 3. This time, the terrorist was carrying a handgun. He stood in front of all of the captive children and addressed them. "I told you all that if you behaved and followed the rules, you would be safe. It appears you have not taken me seriously. It is time I demonstrate how serious I am."

He nodded to the guard to take the two boys out of the room. He followed, and the door swung shut behind him. A few minutes later, two pistol shots rang out above them in the building, and then there was silence. There was a shocked silence as the captive children realised what had just happened upstairs. They all stood around, not knowing what to do next. Sally burst into tears and lay sobbing on the floor. The rest of that day took a very long time to pass.

§

After they had returned from their evening meal, the children were still deeply shocked by the events of the day. Few were talking, and some were crying out of despair. Sally would speak to no one and just sat staring at the wall. The door of the room opened, and Darren staggered into the room. The door closed behind him. He walked painfully, and his head hung, just looking at the floor. He was wearing a clean new orange boiler suit, but his face was bruised.

Sally screamed and rushed over to him. "Darling, are you ok? I thought you were dead."

As she hugged him, he responded dully. "I might as well be dead. They've got ways of punishing you that I can't bear to talk about. I'm never going to try and escape again. I hope you didn't hear my screams. It was terrible. Has John come back yet?"

Adam was standing next to him and helped Sally carefully lower him to the ground to rest on some gym mats. He lay on his side, clearly in discomfort.

"They kept asking me again and again about how we got out of the building. I just told them the door wasn't locked. I didn't give you away, Adam. Where's John?"

"I'm afraid he hasn't come back yet, Darren. How did you get captured? Did they catch up with the rubbish lorry?"

"It was the police! We got away and flagged down a police van on the public road. He just brought us back to the terrorists. I can't believe the police would do that. You managed to blow up two of their Land Rovers though. I think they were really shocked about that."

Sally carefully examined her boyfriend. She had received extensive first-aid training from the Guild. "Adam, can you disappear for a moment? I just need some privacy to ask Darren some questions about what they did to him."

Adam moved out of earshot and watched as Sally quietly asked questions. He could not hear watch was said, but he could see the anger building in her face. She made Darren as comfortable as possible and covered him with a blanket. She came over to speak with Adam and signalled Deepa to join them. Sally's face was set in a hard expression, her blue eyes sparked with anger. "Adam, these people are terrible. We must destroy them. They have done unspeakable things to Darren. I don't think there are any serious injuries, but I'll keep an eye on him to see if his condition gets worse. I think he will be in pain for a few days. Do you think you can get hold of some painkillers for him? I'll try and get him to sleep, but he feels he is responsible for what has happened to John. He heard the gunshots too."

Adam clicked the tracking ring open and removed it from his neck. The two girls gasped, expecting an explosion. "No, don't worry. I managed to disarm it just after Alpha 3 fitted it on me. I suspect they will be using the tracking feature a lot more now. I will leave it here with you, Deepa, so they think I am in the room if they check their system. I need to go and re-explore the building. I need more information. The news that the local police may be involved complicates things enormously. Sally, I will need you to come outside the building with me tonight. Deepa, can you tell me what you need to take over their computers and network? I don't think we can get the plasma screen tonight. I've managed to get the tools you wanted, but I think there will be a guard in the corridor tonight, so I can't get to the canteen."

"I will need a laptop computer equipped with wireless networking and its power supply. If you can manage it, I would also like a cable connection to their network."

"I think I can get you the computer by tomorrow. How long will you need to break in to their systems?"

"It depends on what security system they have, but it should only be about an hour's work. I don't know what applications they might have, but it shouldn't take too long to find my way around."

"Do you want any particular colour of laptop case?" Adam asked with just a hint of a smile.

Deepa looked puzzled by the question and then saw Adam's smile. She did not respond.

"So, sisters of the Guild, cheer up. The terrorists may not know it yet, but they have just had war declared on them by us three. I'm going to sneak off on my own. I'll be back in about an hour. Can you distract the others so they do not see me leave? I'll be going out behind the toilet cabin."

Sally walked to the other end of the room and clapped her hands once to attract the attention of everyone. "Can I have your attention please? I just want to tell you about Darren..."

Chapter 28 Project Silver Rain

Nobody noticed when Adam lifted a floor tile behind the toilet cabinet and disappeared from sight. He wriggled over to the cable duct and descended to the basement. He spent some time searching every room in the basement until he found what he had suspected might be there.

In the corner room, he found traces of old pipe work rising up the wall. At the top, he saw a hole in the wall, covered with a sheet of plywood. He found an old wooden packaging pallet and stood it on its side against the wall. By standing on the pallet, he was able to peer into the hole. It revealed an old brick-lined pipe duct leading off to the other buildings. It was square in section and big enough to allow him to crawl along. He thought this was probably a relic from the time when the buildings were originally heated with steam using pipes from a central boiler. There were signs of recent cabling running through the tunnel. He knew he didn't have the time to explore now, so he backed out and carefully wedged the plywood board back into place. He wanted to focus on his primary objective, which was to gather more information.

He returned to the room with the air-conditioning duct and started to climb up the duct. This time, he carried on past the ground-floor level until he reached the top of the vertical duct. He could see a light ahead along the horizontal duct. Adam guessed it was the light from the terrorists' office. He carefully crept forward. The ducting was quite narrow, but he still had enough space to wriggle forward. When he reached the air vent for the office, he paused to listen. He could hear Alpha 3's voice talking to someone else in the room.

"... yes, I quite agree. We were lucky today. If those boys had escaped, it would've thrown this whole scheme into doubt. Strangely enough, the Nelson boy was not the ringleader. He started talking pretty quickly under pain, but he is out of the picture now. The other boy, Nichols, was much tougher, and he didn't really tell us anything. It seems that the boy Cranford was behind it all, despite what he told us. He was the one who unlocked the doors and came up with the idea for the escape. It is strange because Cranford was the one acting as the informant. It is almost as if he wanted the escape to fail. I will leave him where he is for the time being, but he will be watched much more closely. There is now a full-time guard in the ground-floor corridor, and the doors of those rooms will be locked with chains and padlocks."

"Cranford is new to the school. But even in the short time he has been there, he has already been a hero at least once. That lad has a spark of life in him. You do need to watch him carefully." Adam had heard that voice from somewhere before. He knew the speaker but just couldn't place a name or face to the voice. "Alpha 3, you seem to have the situation under control again. How is the hostage project coming along?"

"It is on track. The parents will receive the ransom notes tomorrow morning.

They will be given two weeks to raise the money, and then we can move on to the final phase of Project Silver Rain. Then these brats from the school can serve their purpose in destiny. It is essential that we get Davidson up here to deal with the production problem. We know he will not be able to afford to pay the ransom for his son. As we anticipated, we really need his knowledge for this final bit. Alpha 4, are you sure the virus will actually work as projected?"

"Yes. The initial tests have proven that it makes young girls sterile, unable to have children in later life. The initial symptoms are just like the common cold, but it leaves very few antibodies behind after the infection. It is as infectious as the common cold but almost impossible to trace unless you capture the actual virus itself. It will be three or four years before the effects are really seen. By that time, the virus will be widespread and will have infected most children around the world."

"Is this really necessary just to combat population growth? There must be other ways. If this goes wrong, we could eventually wipe out the human population of the world."

"You know that if we let the human population continue to grow, we will destroy the world anyway. This way, we will bring it back to manageable levels. We are already working on a cure and have made good progress. We will be able to make an absolute fortune by selling the cure when it is available."

"Is there no danger of the virus spreading to other animals? If that happens, we could destroy the world ecological system."

"Alpha 3, we have already discussed this. You know the design of the virus is tailored to human DNA. It cannot spread further. There are no victims in this method of control. We will not kill anyone. It will apply equally to all nations. We will be saving future millions of people from the agony of starvation. It just means there will be less children in the world. Anyway, enough of this discussion. We have talked over these topics before for many years. Tell me how the interesting by-product of this is coming along?"

"You mean the methyl nitrate? Yes, that will make a useful second-level cover story. I will leak the story to the foot soldiers here that we are making methyl nitrate as an explosive that we will sell to the terrorists around the world. Your scientists projected that this might happen. We are currently making a couple of litres every day. It is really quite unstable, but we are keeping the bottles at the correct temperature, so there should be no problem."

"Are you sure this base is safe from discovery? Our clients will be most upset if they suddenly lose their investment. The money they are putting towards this is slowing down their missile program."

"Yes. I received a phone call from my contact at New Scotland Yard. The police have no idea where the children are located. In any event, if people get too close to this building, even with a helicopter, it is wired with enough explosives to completely vaporise it. Just make sure you are not in it if we have to destroy it."

"I must be off. I have a long drive ahead of me before I get back to the city. Please keep me in touch with any future incidents or events. I will come back to visit you next week."

As Alpha 3's visitor moved to open the door, Adam caught sight of his face through the air-conditioning vent. It was none other than their recently deceased English teacher, Alan Howard. *The terrorists must have faked the shooting in the coach!*

"Before you go, Alpha 4, why don't you come and have a look at the laboratory? It will only take ten minutes. I know Dr. Gwon is dying to see you. She is missing her home country and would like to see a familiar face."

"Yes, that would be a good idea."

Adam waited until he heard the two men leave the room. So far as he could see, the office was now empty. He wriggled backwards as quickly as possible towards the vertical shaft. This time, he took care not to fall down the deep shaft. When he reached the bottom, he jumped out and exited the basement room. He ran up the stairs to the first floor. He was relieved to find the corridor doorway was unlocked. Running as quietly as possible, he made his way to the terrorists' office. He cautiously opened the door. The room was still empty. He quickly looked around to see if there was anything of interest. The first thing he saw was a folded Ordnance Survey map. He had a look and noted it covered part of the west coast of Scotland. Without hesitating, he tucked the map in his pocket. Looking around further, he saw the objective of his visit.

Alpha 3 had left his laptop computer open and running on a desk. Adam took his inhaler out of his pocket and carefully disassembled it to retrieve the Nano-powdered silver dust. He tapped a small amount of the powder onto a sheet of paper that had been folded to provide a V shape. Carefully picking up the paper, he moved to the fan intake of the laptop, and with a strong puff of breath, he blew the silver dust inside laptop computer. There was no immediate reaction, but after thirty seconds of delay, the display on the computer changed to a plain blue with white writing indicating a hardware error on the PC. He checked the desk drawers and found a first-aid kit, from which he took a packet of paracetamol tablets. Satisfied with his first visit to the office, Adam got up and left the room, making sure there were no traces of his visit. He returned to the basement as quickly as he could and then wriggled up the wiring duct to return to the raised floor under the ground-floor sleeping area. He wriggled back to his point of entry and cautiously lifted a floor tile by pushing upwards. He slid it to one side on the floor and popped his head out. Nobody was looking in his direction. He paused to remove the map from his pocket and then slipped back into the room. He replaced the floor tile as quietly as he could. He moved to his sleeping position and sat next to Simon.

"Hi, Adam. Did you find anything new on your travels? There isn't really much point to it, is there? We might as well wait for the ransom to be paid for the police to rescue us. You were right when you said trying to escape is stupid."

"I know you are feeling down, but that doesn't mean we should give in to them.

The more information and tools we can get, the better chance we stand of dealing with the terrorists. I have some plans, but it will take a few days before we can move on them. Until then, the more we appear to cooperate with the terrorists, the greater will be our chances of success. I need to pop over and talk to Deepa for a while. I'll come back and see you soon."

Adam walked over to Deepa and smiled. "I'd best have my tracking ring back on my neck in case they come in to check. I have just disabled their tracking system, and they are bound to be suspicious."

Deepa retrieved Adam's tracking ring from where she had hidden it and returned it to him. "Did you find anything useful on your trip?"

"The first shock is that our teacher, Alan Howard, is not dead. He is part of the terrorist gang. They must have faked his death. The second shock is that they have an informant working in the police in New Scotland Yard, so if the police discover where we are, the terrorists will be aware of that discovery. I have also discovered that the kidnapping is just part of a bigger plot, but I don't want to talk about that now until I have more information. One bit of good news is that I hope to have a laptop computer for you by tomorrow evening."

"Did you manage to find any painkillers for Darren?"

Adam slipped his hand into his pocket and pulled out the packet of tablets. "I don't know if these will help, but at least it's a start."

Deepa gave him a hug and kissed him on his cheek. "Oh, Adam, you are a genius." When she realized what she'd done, she blushed.

Adam just smiled. He did not want to show the panic he felt about the urgent need to escape and tell the authorities about Project Silver Rain. He now knew for sure that the kidnapping was just a small part of a much more serious plan and that the kidnappers would not hesitate to act to prevent the discovery of that sinister plan. If he told any of the other children about the project, there was a chance the terrorists might learn of that discovery. Many new tasks had been added to Adam's mental list of must-dos, the least of which was to find the explosives in the building. He thought that perhaps if he could find them, Sally might know how to safely disarm them. He was going to have another very busy night, and he was already feeling tired from the previous night's activities.

"Deepa, I need to get some sleep. Can you tell Sally I will wake her about midnight tonight? She and I are going up on the roof."

Adam returned to his sleeping position and tried to get some sleep. It was difficult because so many things were chasing around inside his mind.

He had just gotten to sleep when the door of the sleeping room burst open and three guards marched in. They were armed with sub-machine guns. "Everybody up now! We are doing a roll call."

The captives were lined up in the room and had to answer when their name was called. As each boy or girl replied, the guards checked that the tracking ring was present on their neck. They were then escorted to the canteen, where they were searched. After that search process, the kids were returned to their sleeping quarters, but this time, they were taken to the other room where they had first arrived. The guards left as suddenly as they had arrived. They appear to be satisfied that none of the children had whatever they were searching for. Adam tried to get back to sleep as quickly as possible.

Chapter 29 Icy Water Late at Night

The next thing he knew, Adam was being shaken into wakefulness by Sally. The room was dark as she spoke. "Adam, I think it's gone past midnight. You weren't waking up, so I thought I'd check to see if you still want to go on the roof."

Adam popped the button watch from his inhaler and checked the time. It was half an hour past midnight. "Thanks Sally, I must have been overtired. I don't normally oversleep. We had best get going. How is Darren, by the way?"

"He's not getting any worse. I think those tablets you got him have started to ease some of the pain. He doesn't seem to be bleeding anywhere, so I think he's going to be ok. Deepa will look after him while I'm away. Do I need to bring anything with me?"

"No. Just follow me as you are. I hope you are not claustrophobic. It is pretty dark and cramped where we are going."

Adam led Sally to the corner of the room and lifted the floor tile. When he disappeared under the floor, Sally followed, wriggling along under the floor behind Adam. When he could, he illuminated the way using his button LED torch. When they reached the cable duct, Adam described how to climb down. With her rock-climbing experience, Sally had no problems. He showed her the way to the stairwell and then ascended to the first floor. Once again, the corridor door was not locked, and they both crept past the office and up the ladder to the roof hatch. Adam tried the padlock. It had not been reset, so he removed it and climbed through the hatchway. Once they were on the roof, Adam pointed out to Sally the major parts of the site where they were being held captive.

He pointed out the secret building said he thought the key to the whole situation lay within the building. "I am going to try and find a way into that building and have a look around. That is why I asked you to come up here now. I need you to show me how to climb down the drainpipes, if it can be done safely. There may be some stuff in the building that will be of interest to you. Have you heard of methyl nitrate?"

"Yes, I have heard about it. It is the ugly sister of nitro glycerine. It is very unstable and quite powerful. It is the liquid those Islamic terrorists were planning to use to blow up planes in midair. I won't ask you if you think it is sensible to try and get into the building because I know you will go anyway. Show me the drainpipes you want to climb down."

Adam took Sally to the corner of the building and showed her where the drainpipes ran down the side. She hung a leg over the parapet of the flat roof and carefully lowered herself into position. She wedged her hands either side of the drainpipe within the brick surround and put her feet up against the wall and leaned back. Spider like, she moved down the wall, moving her hands and feet in sequence. She stopped and climbed back up using reverse of the previous moves.

Hooking an arm of the parapet, she swung her legs over. "It's not too difficult," she said. "Have you ever done rock climbing before?"

"No, Sally. I've never been rock climbing before, and I have a fear of heights."

"Oh, that is going to make life interesting. Learning how to climb without ropes in the dark using a relatively advanced technique? I am now convinced you are totally crazy. I don't suppose I can change your mind?"

"Sally, I am almost wetting myself here with fear, but this is just too important. Let's get on with it."

In the dim light from the car park below, Sally showed Adam the technique of arching his hand so that it jammed between the pipe and brickwork. She then told him about the need to lean back against his wedged hand with his feet against the brickwork to transfer a lot of the weight of his body on to his feet and provide grip. Sally popped over the parapet and climbed down a couple of metres. She waited for Adam.

He eased himself off the parapet feet first. He could feel the palms of his hands sweating, moistening the brickwork he desperately clung to. He was certain he was going to slip and fall the ten metres in the dark onto the concrete below.

"Adam, lean back more before you let go of the top. Bring your feet up a little higher. That's it... now lean back. Now, move one hand down and wedge it between the pipe and brickwork. Put your weight on that hand that is jammed. Now, lean back some more. Ok, Adam, release your hand at the top and jam it in between the pipe and brickwork. Release your top hand and move down about thirty cms. Now move your top foot down. Have you got it now?"

As Adam clumsily made his way down, Sally climbed just below him so that if Adam slipped, she might be able to catch him. After three terrifying minutes, he put his feet on solid ground. He was shaking his hands in the air. "That really hurts the back of your hands, but it was not as difficult as I thought it might be before I started. How do I get back up?"

"That's easy. You just reverse the process. It hurts because the back of your hands are taking a lot of pressure, and the brickwork digs into them. We'd best get away from here and go visit your building."

They ran around the edge of the car park, trying to keep to the shadows as much as possible and looking out for any guards that might be around. When they reached the building, Adam again tried the front door without success. There was no way he could overcome the electronic lock unless Deepa was able to take over the central computer controlling them. He walked right around the building, checking for windows or doors. They were all securely locked. Even the drainpipes from the roof of the building had several feet of protective razor wire coiled around them making them impossible to climb.

"This is a well-protected building. We are not going to get in here tonight. Come on, let's go. There is somewhere else I want to have a look at."

Skirting around the buildings, Adam led Sally towards the fence next to the loch. There was some light from the moon through gaps in the clouds. "Keep more than two metres away from the fence. It is electrified, and they also have a sensor wire buried under the soil. If we get too close, it will set off an alarm."

"How do you know all this stuff, Adam?"

"I'm just nosy, I guess. You see those black posts outside the fence at each corner and by the gate? They form an electronic fence using several infrared light beams. If you walk between them, it will set off an alarm in their control room."

"They have made this place like a prison or worse. We will never get out of here unless we are rescued."

"Don't worry, Sally. Their reliance on technology could be their weakness. I want to see if there is some way I can get a closer look at that boat. I don't think I can get under that fence, but there must be something. Wait here a moment and watch out for guards. Whistle if you see one."

"I can't whistle."

Adam did not hear her response as he set out to explore the length of the fence. He had taken the chance that the sensor wire did not lead under the concrete path leading to the jetty gateway in the fence. It was an old path, and he could see no recent repairs. He walked close to the inner electrified fence. It did not seem dangerous, but he could hear an occasional crackle of the high voltage. There were no gaps to be found.

When he reached the far corner, he heard the gurgle of running water beneath his feet. He was standing on a metal grid. There was a small stream running below him. Whoever had originally built the site must have covered the stream with a culvert. Looking through the fence, he could see the outline of a large pipe running into the loch. He knelt down and felt around. The metal grid was locked with a padlock. Adam smiled and got out his lock picks. He had just released the lock when he heard a *baa* like that of an agitated sheep. He looked up and saw Sally waving and pointing in the direction of the office building. Two guards had just left the building and had started a patrol of the inner fence. Adam pointed at the building and made a movement mimicking climbing and signalled to Sally that she should go and hide on the roof.

He removed the padlock and tugged at the metal grating by his feet. It was heavy, but he managed to lift it. It opened with a creaking sound. He shone his button torch down and saw some metal rungs in the wall of the manhole. With a struggle, he managed to slip through into the manhole and close the grating behind him. He clung tightly, crouching on the metal rungs of the manhole. There was a terrible smell coming from just below him. He felt below him and found the body of a dead animal wriggling with maggots. He knew it must have washed in there during a storm from outside of the site and then become caught on some obstruction. By the now dimming light of his button torch, he could see the water from the stream tumbling down a large pipe which ran away at an angle down to the loch. A bright beam of torch light flickered across the top of the grating and then went away. He could hear the guards talking as they passed by.

"I don't know why Alpha 3 wants us to inspect the whole fence on every circuit of the patrol. Nobody would survive touching that fence, and it is riddled with alarm wires."

"What he says goes, so far as I'm concerned. He's already taken £50,000 from our total bonus pool because those two kids escaped. No way am I going to let anymore of those brats get out. If he says to check the fence, that is what I'll do."

As the men continued on their patrol, Adam emerged from the manhole and carefully ran along next to the fence and back to the gate pathway. From there, he ran to the garage workshop. He tugged on the padlock, and it came open as the wedge of wood popped out. Inside the workshop, he quickly found the ropes he had seen on his previous visit. There were two of them coiled there, and they looked like climbing ropes. He pulled them from the wall and left the workshop. After re-closing the lock with the wedge of wood, he headed back to the jetty gate carrying the ropes. He waved to the roof of the office block, and Sally reappeared over the parapet. She flowed like a ghost down the wall by the drainpipe and ran across to meet Adam.

"I've found another way out, but it is a bit scary. There is a covered stream running along the edge of the site. It goes down a pipe into the loch. I think it comes out underwater. The stream level is quite low. The pipe is wide enough to crawl down. I'm going to give it a try now, but I want to be able to come back in as well. That is why I've got the rope."

"Scary? Scary? Adam, I thought you were suicidal climbing down the building when you had never done it before, but this is total madness. What if you get stuck in the pipe? What if there is a grating at the other end?"

"If there is a grating, I'll just come back. I'll be ok. By the way, I loved your sheep impression. It sounded almost real. As they say in the films 'I'll be back'. If I'm not back in half an hour, just go back with the others. Can you guard my clothes? I'm not swimming in them."

Adam slipped his trainers off his feet and then slipped out from his boiler suit, leaving only his boxer shorts.

"The night is definitely improving," Sally said with a grin. "Don't drown yourself, you stupid nutcase."

Adam picked up a rope and headed for the stream manhole. He climbed in and tied one end of the rope to one of the iron rungs and floated the rest of the rope down the sloping tunnel. He had to step barefoot onto the dead animal to reach the stream. Feet first, he partially slipped and partially lowered himself down the tube. It was total darkness, and the water felt icy cold. His body was presenting a partial blockage in the pipe, causing the flowing water to build up around him. In the total darkness, he could only feel his way along. After a couple of minutes, the flow of water along the bottom of the pipe turned into solid water. He had

266

reached the water level of the loch. He didn't know how far the pipe extended under the loch. Adam took several deep breaths ready to make the dive. He was still facing feet downwards in the pipe. Suddenly, he heard a gurgle and a sloshing noise above him. A cold wind rushed down the pipe before a heavy mass of rotting skin and bones fell on the boy's head. The pressure built up as the water from the stream backed up the pipe. Despite his best efforts to hang onto the rope, Adam could hold on no longer. A plug of boy and animal carcase was forced down the pipe into the depths of the loch. Kicking his legs free of the rope tangling around his legs, he re-orientated himself underwater and swam to the moonlit surface five metres above. "Wow, that was some ride!"

He turned in the water and saw the outline of the boat behind him. He swam around the boat, looking for some way to climb onboard. There was nothing dangling down. As he came closer to the boat, he saw in the dim moonlight an almost-submerged vessel tied alongside between the pier and the boat. He realised this was a small submarine of some kind. Adam found a rope dangling down in the water and managed to pull himself up onto the submarine. It bobbed a little in the dark, cold waters of the loch under his added weight. The top hatch to the submarine was locked, and he could see no other entrance. A wooden walkway extended from the submarine deck into the boat. The boy took that route to gain access to the boat. A few minutes of exploration revealed that all the doors and hatches of the workboat were locked. As he did not have the lock picks with him, there was nothing to be done. Lowering himself over the side of the boat, he offered his body to the icy grip of the cold, salty loch water.

It took him several dives to locate the guide rope and regain entrance to the pipe. The water pressure of the stream made it difficult to climb back up the pipe. It would have been impossible without the rope. Just when he thought he could no longer hold his breath, his face cleared of water, and he was able to gasp for precious air. He finally made it back to the manhole and pulled up the rope before securing it in a coil against one of the rungs. Lifting the heavy metal grating, he escaped and ran back to where Sally was waiting. She giggled as he took the boiler suit from her hand. Sally turned away to let him dress in privacy. He looked down and realised that at some time during the battle with the water in the pipe, he had lost his boxer shorts. The dry cloth stuck to him as he struggled to get dressed, but the thin warmth felt luxurious.

"It looks like the water was very cold, Adam."

"We'd best get back inside. I'm freezing. Can you bring the spare rope? I'll tell you what I found when we get back in the building."

When they reached the foot of the office building, Adam looked up. The building seemed very high, and he knew the cold had sapped the strength from his arms. He did not look forward to climbing back to the roof. Sally saw the hesitation in his face. She uncoiled the rope and tied it around her waist with a bowline knot. Without asking his approval, she tied a similar knot around his waist using the other end of the rope. "At least going up, you will have a rope to protect you this time. Remember to lean back to keep the weight on your feet."

Adam was still amazed at the way she could gracefully and fearlessly swarm up the wall. Her slim body hid a wiry strength. Moments later, she was at the top, calling him to follow on. He started and gritted his teeth at the pain to the back of his hands as he wedged them between the pipe and brickwork. His feet slipped a couple of times, but he immediately felt a reassuring tension on the rope as she prepared to catch him. His arms were shaking by the time he reached the roof.

Back in the sleeping area, he collapsed gratefully onto the gym mat and pulled the blanket over himself.

Simon rolled over and put a reassuring hand on Adam's shoulder. "I'm glad you are back safely, Adam."

Adam said nothing and just lay thinking they were all still in great danger. He had a lot of things to organise if he was to succeed in defeating their adversaries.

Chapter 30 Contact is Made

Prayers were said for the kidnapped school children in the early-morning assemblies of Holliston's and St Josephine's Schools. There was sombre mood amongst the pupils and teachers. Despite the instructions of the kidnappers on secrecy, rumours had spread that the families of the kidnapped pupils had received ransom demands in the post. Members of the police task force had visited the parents to get details and copies of the video DVDs to see if any clues could be gained. The whole police investigation had stalled. It was as if the kidnapped children had disappeared off the face of the planet. There were few clues left in the burned-out bus garage. Television crews and newspaper reporters cruised about the villages and towns around Amersham, trying to find related news stories. Every national newspaper carried pictures of the children. Mr. Robertson had visited the Cranford's cottage and assured them that the full resources of the Foundation would be applied to help track down their son.

In Simon's home, the Davidson's knew the only way they could possibly raise the £250,000 demanded for their son would be to sell their family home. They did not hesitate on that decision. Henry Davidson visited his local bank manager and arranged a loan facility. A *For Sale* sign had appeared on their garden fence. Henry had just arrived to work at his laboratory office when he received a phone call.

"Mr. Davidson, I'm calling you to offer assistance with the ransom payment for your son Simon. Leave the office now and drive one mile down the road to the lay-by. Park and wait. Do not inform the police or your colleagues or you will not hear from us again."

The phone connection was ended before Henry had a chance to make any response. He collected his coat and left for the meeting. When he arrived, nobody else was waiting. He turned off the engine of his car and waited patiently. Several cars passed by the lay-by, but no one stopped.

Suddenly, his passenger door opened, and a masked man climbed in beside him. The man was armed with a military handgun. "Listen carefully to what I say, and if you agree to do what we ask, we will release your son unharmed without payment of the ransom. Do you understand?"

"Yes."

The masked man pulled out a photograph and showed it to Henry. It was the picture of an upper arm with a brown birth mark shaped like the crescent of the moon. Henry recognised it immediately as his son.

"If you want to see your son alive again, you must keep this conversation secret, even if you decide not to help us. Do not tell the police or your wife. Do you agree?"

Henry balled his fists in anger. He knew this man was one of the kidnappers who had taken his innocent child and caused so many families grief and pain. He wanted to strike out but restrained himself. "Yes. What do I have to do?"

"We need your specialist skills for one day. Help us solve a technical problem, and your son will be released."

"How can my skills help you? I'm just researching global warming."

"Mr. Davidson, you and I both know you have worked on a secret biological warfare programme run by the military. We both know it is so secret that even the Prime Minister is unaware of it."

"No. I won't help you make biological weapons."

"Mr. Davidson, I give you my word that no one will be killed as the result of the work we are doing. In fact, it will help deal with global warming. If I leave the car now, your wife will receive the left hand of your son in the post tomorrow. The next day, there will be some more and so on. You will not be there to console her. Are you sure you won't help us? It is just one day's work."

Henry started the car engine. "You leave me no choice. Where do you want me to drive?"

§

Thirty miles away in London, the police task force were not despondent. It was too soon for that. They realised that they had almost no information on who was responsible for the kidnapping or indeed where they were holding the children, but it was early days. The command centre had been moved to London once it was realised that this was not some local crime. Police forces across the country were searching for places where the children may have been hidden. Police informants were dragged in for interview. Even the informal contacts with the bosses of the criminal underworld yielded no results. When the first ransom demands arrived on DVDs it had at first appeared that the messages recorded by the children had taken place in many different parts of the world. Experts soon realised that that was just technical trickery with video backgrounds added by post-editing of the video recordings.

While the police recommended against paying the ransom demands they knew the parents of the children were indeed working to raise the necessary funding. With no apparent progress by the police the parents had decided they would have to pay. The mobile phones and telephone lines of every home of a kidnapped child were tapped and constantly monitored. The Prime Minister had authorised the use of the Intelligence Services.

Detective Inspector Norris had been kept on the team. He was concentrating on the background of the teacher Alan Howard. While he had been reported shot and killed, the police had been unable to find any corpse. It also seemed that the man who acted as a teacher at the school was not the real Alan Howard. Alan Howard proper was found to be working as a volunteer in a famine relief team in North East Africa. The bus garage owner Selwyn Howell had been tracked down in South Africa and was able to supply a little information from his hospital bed.

Norris knew that the intent of the attack in Desolation Valley had been to ensure that Selwyn never spoke again. This was one of the few mistakes made by the kidnappers.

Norris was in the main control room when news broke of Henry Davidson's sudden disappearance. The whole pace of the enquiry suddenly changed when the enquiry was put under the control of the Intelligence Services. No one would speak to the police about the reason for this sudden change of control of the investigation. The senior police Commanders were told to cooperate fully or they might suddenly find themselves running police recruitment shows in northern England. He later heard rumours that Henry Davidson was on some special military watch list.

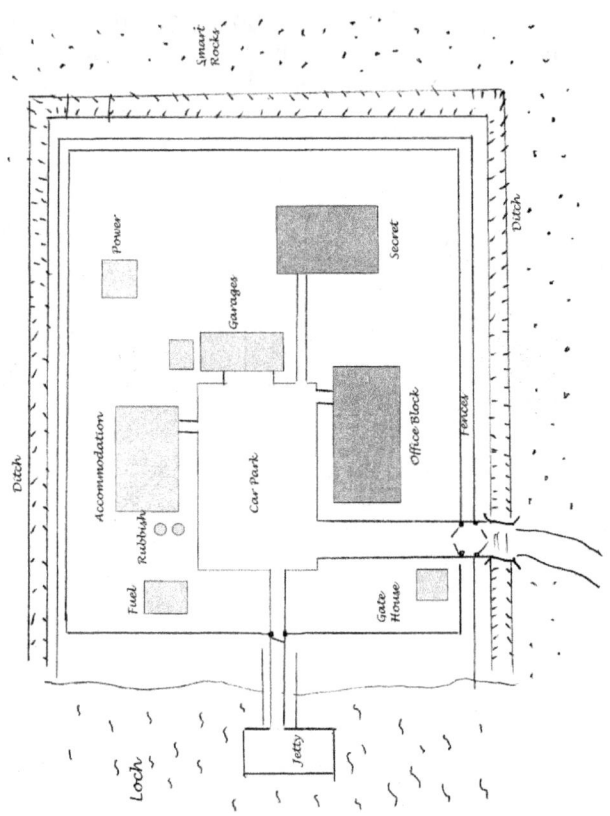

Figure 3 - Adam's sketch map of the site

Chapter 31 Time to Get Organised

In the loch side base of the terrorists, Adam decided it was time to involve more of the kidnapped children in his planned activities for escape. If Alpha 3 already suspected him as a ring leader, it would be likely that the guards would be observing him closely. Adam had also noticed that many of the children were already becoming despondent and depressed—Darren Nichols, for instance. Darren would need time to recover. Adam knew he needed the rest of them alert and ready to act as a team so there would be no delays when he needed to act.

After breakfast, he called a meeting with Simon, Deepa, and Sally. "Please sit down next to me. I need to talk."

The girls sat on the floor near Adam. Simon wriggled between Deepa and Adam.

"I just wanted you three to be aware of what I know so far. Alpha 3 has suspicions about what I'm doing. It is possible he may take me away from the group and lock me up to maintain security. If that happens, I don't want you to lose the knowledge I have gathered so far."

Adam gave them a sketched map of the compound where they were being held.

Some time was spent discussing the security measures the terrorists had put in place. He had also spent time working out their exact position on the map he had stolen earlier, so he gave his friends clear details of where they were in Scotland and the nearest local towns. Adam told them about Alan Howard being one of the terrorists and the deadline they were setting for the collection the ransom. He explained how he had been able to listen in to the conversations in the office.

They were shocked when Adam reminded them that somehow, the police had been infiltrated by the terrorists. However, Adam made no mention of the Silver Rain Project or the fact that the building had been armed with a large amount of explosives. He thought that news would be far too depressing for them at the moment.

"Last night, Sally and I found a way to get out of here. There is a stream that has been buried underground that empties out into the loch. It is possible to swim out that way, but it is very dangerous, so it is unlikely that we could use that as a major escape route for everybody. If the weather turns bad and the stream gets bigger, it would be suicidal to try and use that route."

"If you escaped the site last night, why on earth did you come back? Why didn't you try and go for help?"

"The answer to that question is laying over there on the floor. I told Darren he should not try that escape until we had more information. I'm sure at some time, the information I have gained last night about the boat and the submarine will be of some use, but we need more information. That is the second reason why I have gathered you here now."

"So what can the others do to help?" asked Deepa.

"We need to have people on the roof of this building during the day and night so we can get clear information on their security patrols and also which vehicles visit the site during the day. This place is supposed to be an operational fish research farm, so the normal things like a postman delivering letters are still going to continue. What I want to do is to ask Sally to take the lead of the group. I will stay in the background while she organises the others to watch the car park and the terrorists' movements."

"Adam, I can do that if you don't mind revealing the secret routes to the others. I think you are missing something here though. We need to keep everybody occupied. How about we run a fitness programme for everyone who is not actually involved in the watch tasks?"

"That sounds good, Sally. You could add memory training too. I will do some work on the doors to this room so the terrorists cannot unexpectedly open them when we have people out on watch. I think one of the air ducts goes right to the roof of this building. Now that we have that rope, I think we can find a way up there and not have to use the stairs past the terrorists' office. I will check that out later. Deepa, I'll need you to focus on the computer stuff. If my guess is right, we should have a delivery of your computer today or tomorrow.

"What about me, Adam?"

"Simon, I need to turn you into a thief. We'll start on that once Sally gathers the others to talk to them about the plan. Are we all agreed, then, that until we have more information, there are to be no more escape attempts?"

The other three nodded in agreement. Adam took Sally away from the other two teens.

"Sally, can I have a word before you start being the leader?"

"Sure, boss."

"I didn't mention it just now because I didn't want to worry the others, but Alpha 3 mentioned when I was listening in on them that they have armed this building with enough explosives to vaporise it. I have not the slightest doubt that Alpha 3 would not hesitate to blow up the building with us inside if anyone comes from the outside to try and rescue us. We need to find those explosives and try to disarm them. We'll do it when Simon and I get back from my explorations this morning."

"I don't think I'll mention that wonderful news to anyone else. Adam, I'm going to divide the others up into three squads and get them to choose a leader for each squad. We'll then check to see what skills each person has—like climbing or metalwork, etc. Does that sound good to you?"

"That should work. I best get going. Hey, Simon, let's go!"

Adam headed to the area behind the toilet cabin, and Simon followed with a broad grin. He was pleased he would be involved in the action against their captors. Adam led him under the raised floor and down into the basement.

They quietly moved into the base room containing the duct tunnel for the old steam heat piping. Adam removed the plywood cover and propped the wooden pallet against the wall. He climbed up into the duct and helped Simon climb in after him.

"I think this duct runs between the buildings. I have no idea what is actually at the other end, but it is worth exploring to find out. I'm afraid my little torch has just about died now, so we will have to travel in the dark most of the time. Follow me, but be sure to feel your way with your hand in the dark."

The two boys crawled along the duct. All the old piping had been removed, but there were some metal brackets along the floor. Simon had managed to graze his knees a couple of times before Adam called a halt.

"The duct branches off here. We are going to take the route that goes straight on because I think that leads to the terrorists' accommodation block and kitchen. Are you still ok, Simon?"

"Adam, you really are crazy. Why would you want to go into the one place on this site where we will find most of the terrorists? We know they sleep and eat in this building. This must be the last building in the world we should be going into right now."

"They won't be expecting us, Simon. If we are careful, they won't catch us. This building is the one most likely to have useful supplies. The first thing I want to do is explore the building and find out what is in each room. We can then go about getting some supplies to make our lives easier."

They crawled along the brick-lined duct until they came to a sheet of plywood blocking their way. Adam pushed tentatively with his foot against one of the upper corners. With a slight screeching of rusty nails against the cement, the plywood began to ease open.

"Simon, fit your hand around the corner of the plywood and hold onto it. I don't want it to fall to the ground and make a noise when I release the rest of it, ok?"

It was a bit of a tight fit in the tunnel with the two boys working on the plywood board, but eventually they managed to release it from the wall. Adam quickly shone his little torch around to explore the room. There were some packing cases of supplies, but not much else. He slid out from the duct and walked across the room to find a light switch. He switched it on and found, to his relief, that the lights worked in this room. He called Simon into the room. When he had the chance, he checked the contents of the cases. They appeared to contain just uniforms and boots. Motioning Simon to stand by the door of the room, Adam switched off the light and tried the door handle. The room was not locked. He opened the door and cautiously crept out from the room with Simon behind him. They quietly went along the corridor, checking each room. The door on one room was locked and padlocked. Adam decided to visit that later.

"It is time for us to explore further. I want you to follow me and keep quiet. If we are going to get caught, this will be when it happens."

Adam led them both up the stairs from the basement to the ground floor. The building was quiet, and it appeared none of the terrorists were active in the building. The search of the ground floor revealed the dining room, a shower room, and a kitchen area. Adam peeked into the kitchen area and could see one of the terrorists cleaning the kitchen after the early-morning food. There was a small room next to the kitchen that was being used as a food store. They noticed that the entrance door to the building was wedged open. Adam led them up to the first floor of the building and cautiously went along the corridor, exploring each room. These rooms were clearly used as the dormitories where the terrorists slept when they were not on duty. In one room, men were asleep in their beds. The other two rooms were empty of people but contained beds and the personal equipment of the terrorists. The fourth room was a combination bedroom and office. No one was present in the room.

"Simon, I think this room must belong to Alpha 3. Let's start stirring up some trouble amongst them. While I keep guard, can you go in and see if you can find a clock or watch, a torch, some batteries, some painkillers for Darren, and anything else valuable?"

The boy stepped into the room, switched on the light, and looked around. He was careful not to disturb the appearance of any items but soon came out of the room carrying the things Adam had requested. "I could only find one torch and some batteries, but I guess that will do for a start. I found a small alarm clock and an Omega watch. These tablets should be ok for Darren. I've also found about £150 in cash."

"Good. Give me the watch and the cash and then wait here for a while."

Adam disappeared into one of the dormitories for a couple of minutes and then came out holding a penknife, a roll of strong fabric adhesive tape, and an additional torch.

"They are soon going to think one of their team is a thief, particularly when they find the watch and the cash hidden in his rucksack. We had better get going before we are discovered. I need to explore the rest of the tunnel."

They carefully made their way down to the basement and found a way to secure the plywood panel so that it hung over the entrance to the duct after they had left. Crawling along the tunnel was a lot easier now that they had torches, and since they were LED torches, there was little chance of the batteries running down very quickly. At the junction of the tunnel, Adam turned left and headed into unknown territory. Before long, they came to the end of the tunnel, once again barred by a sheet of plywood. Simon was ready to hold the corner of plywood when Adam gently eased it from the wall with his feet.

The basement room they entered was full of dust-covered empty packing cases. It looked as though this rubbish had been here for many years. Adam tried the door handle, but it was locked. He looked at the lock and realised it was not the type he could pick with the lock picks contained in his inhaler.

"I don't think we can do much more in here at the moment. I am going to have to make some more lock picks before I can open this door. We need to get back to the others now anyway."

When the two boys returned to the sleeping area, they found that Sally had organised all of the remaining teenagers into three squads. Each squad had elected a leader. She had given each of the squads some small tasks to undertake, including fitness training and memory training.

She looked up as Adam approached. "Hi, Adam! How did it go? We have just about got everybody here organised. We should now be able to start the watch rota."

"Good. Give me a few minutes to recover, and I will lead them up to the roof. We had a successful trip, and we now have a route to the terrorists' accommodation block. As they don't guard that very well, it will provide an easy route to the rest of the compound. When you have a moment, get Simon to show you and Deepa the route to their accommodation block. The tunnel is quite clean and dry, and we now have some extra torches."

"I have appointed Conrad Jones as the Quartermaster. When we get moving properly, he will help coordinate the requests for any supplies or materials. I have told him to talk to you if he gets stuck for any ideas. At present, everybody thinks I am the person in command and that you are just assisting me."

"Thanks. I need to talk to Deepa first, and then I will take people up to the roof. How is Darren coming along?"

"He is still very stiff from the beating they gave him, but I think he is getting better. We will soon need some more painkillers. I am making him rest for the time being. When he is a bit better, I'll get him involved in the activities, but he is still feeling very down."

"Simon found some extra painkillers on our trip. They should be ok for Darren."

Adam walked over to Deepa, who was sitting with one of the new squads, training them on the layout of the buildings in the site where they were held captive. She looked up and smiled when she saw Adam approaching. "You got back safely then?"

"Yes. It went as expected, and we had the added bonus that we have been able to stoke some trouble amongst the terrorists. I will soon go and get your laptop computer. Are there any particular attachments you need?"

"If you could get a power supply, a mouse, and an audio headset, that would be useful. Did you happen to see how they connect their computers to the network?"

"I think they have a wireless network that spreads across the whole site. When Alpha 3 was connecting our tracker collars, there was no wired network connection to his laptop. I will see what I can do about those items you have added to the list. Do you know who is first on the rota for taking part in the roof watch?"

Deepa pointed to two people who were in the squad she was instructing. "This is

Kate, and as you know, that is Harry."

"You two follow me, and I will take you up to the roof of the building. Follow my instructions carefully and keep quiet and you should be ok. Do either of you need to go to the toilet before we go to the roof? You will be up there for a couple of hours."

Adam retrieved the climbing rope and tools from their hiding place and then led the two students through the building up to the roof. They were very nervous when they had to pass by the door to the terrorists' office. When they were on the roof, Adam asked them to give him a hand in removing the cover to the air duct, which came out onto the roof. The cover had been used in the past to stop rainfall from entering the air inlet duct to the building. Using a screwdriver to loosen some screws and a lot of effort, the three were able to lift the heavy metal dome off the top of the air duct. The air duct itself was about sixty cms. wide and dropped vertically down to the basement of the building. Adam was able to bend over the shop metal edges of the duct by using a pair of pliers. He put a knot in the climbing rope at about every metre. Securely fastening the rope on the roof, he dropped the rest of it down the duct.

"Your task is a bit boring but very important. I want you to watch all of the movements that take place down below in the car park and the other buildings and keep a record. I will leave this clock with you so you can note the accurate time. I will get Sally to send a relief for you in two hours. Meanwhile, be careful that you do not get seen by any of the guards from below."

Adam returned to the basement of the building by the usual route of the stairs. However, instead of turning to the sleeping quarters, he located the bottom of the air duct and opened the inspection hatch. He was pleased to note that the climbing rope had reached the bottom of the duct shaft. Using the rope, he climbed up the duct shaft to the roof. The two watchers had heard him coming, so they were not surprised by his sudden appearance.

"This rope will now be the normal way to get to the roof and return to the basement. It is a bit of a tough climb and not too tricky, but it is a lot less risky than going past the terrorists' office."

Adam returned to the basement using the rope and then crawled back to the sleeping quarters. He explained the roof rope arrangement to Sally, Deepa, and Simon.

Chapter 32 Sally Wants Revenge

Sally took Adam to one side to speak out of earshot of the other hostages. "Adam, we need to go and check that stuff we were talking about earlier. Simon and Deepa can take charge while we are away. We will need to be back soon in case the guards do a midday headcount."

Adam looked puzzled for a while and then realised what Sally was talking about. The pair of them disappeared under the floor in the direction of the basement.

As they wriggled along, Sally suggested to Adam where the explosives might have been hidden by the terrorists. "The most obvious place is down in the basement. They could have hidden it in the ceiling below the ground floor. It probably won't all be in one place. There will probably be several clusters that would be exploded in sequence to destroy the strong points of the building. If they used what I think they would, the explosives will be in olive green blocks about 30 by 5 by 4 cms. and joined by olive green Det cord. If it is green, it means they have access to military supplies."

"What's Det cord?"

"It's really just a long, thin rope of flexible explosives wrapped in a protective sheath. It's about one centimetre thick or a bit thinner. The detonation travels along it at about four miles a second. It spreads the explosion between the blocks of explosives in a tiny fraction of a second. You strap a detonator on one end, and the bang travels along the cord in an instant."

They searched the basement room where the cabling duct emerged. Adam now had the stronger torch he had stolen from the terrorists. He shone it upwards towards the ceiling closest to the corridor. "Oops! Look above you, Sally. Do you see what I see?"

She looked up and saw a cluster of grey-green blocks. A thin green cord disappeared in either direction through a hole that had been crudely bashed in the wall near the ceiling. The blocks were suspended out of reach on a large nail that protruded from the wall.

"All we need now is a long stepladder, some duct tape, and a knife, and I can fix this so it will be safe," she said.

"We'll come back and fix it tonight, Sally. Getting a stepladder in here unnoticed might be a bit difficult. If you stand on my shoulders, would you be able to reach?"

"Yes, I reckon so... if you can take my weight, that is."

Adam smiled. Sally did not have fifty grams of unnecessary fat on her lithe body. "You may be a bit of a walrus, but I reckon I can cope. Are you just going to cut the Det cord? Won't it explode?"

"It should be ok if I do it properly. It is much less dangerous than trying to pull detonators out. If I get it wrong, we won't have to worry about anything else ever again. Let's explore the rest of the basement. There is probably more in the other rooms."

They explored the other rooms and found other similar clusters of explosives dangling from the ceiling.

"Adam, they have installed much more explosive than they need to demolish this building. It looks like they really do want to get rid of any evidence if things go wrong. I'm sure we could remove some blocks of it without them noticing and just blast open the gates of the compound when we are ready to escape. If you show me the way to their accommodation block, I could set up the explosives inside there—probably at night, when most of them are asleep. If we demolish it, then that would just leave a couple of guards to deal with in this building."

"If you did that, Sally, it would be murder. You could go to jail for a very long time. They won't harm us if the ransom is paid, so you can hardly call it self-defence if you kill them all in cold blood. You have to trust me. There are more subtle ways of doing this. I want them alive so there is a chance of catching the people who are behind the whole plot."

Sally grabbed Adam's shoulder and turned him to face her, shining the torch in his face. The grip on his shoulder was iron hard from the strength built from many days of climbing rock faces. Her eyes sparkled with anger. "You are such a wimp at times. You have seen what they did to Darren and John. These guys deserve to be punished. Even if the police did prosecute me, no jury in the land would ever convict me given the circumstances. We have got the ideal tool here, yet you still dither with your complex plotting. We could be out of here tonight and free. We have got the tools now, and I know how to use them."

Adam paused for a moment. He knew he had to keep Sally working with him. He thought about telling her about Project Silver Rain and the catastrophe that would occur if the virus was released. He knew if he did, in her anger she would probably try and blow up that secret building as well.

"There's an old Chinese saying, by Confucius, I think. It goes along the lines of 'Before you embark on a journey of revenge, dig two graves'. Sally, I understand your anger, but killing these people is not going to deal with the bigger problem. It still leaves two or three angry guards with machine guns. How does blowing up the building deal with these tracker rings around our necks? That might destroy the transmitter that prevents the rings from exploding. Please trust me. I will make sure everyone is safe and that we get to the bottom of why they are doing this. There must be a deeper reason for all of these complex arrangements. It can't be just the kidnapping behind this."

"You know something else, don't you, Adam? What are you holding back from us?"

"I need more information before I can tell you that."

"Is this what you call trust, Adam? You are asking me to trust you, but you are not

280

being open and honest with me." She angrily stormed off with the torch, leaving Adam in the dark room.

He sighed, knowing it was pointless arguing until she had calmed down a little. He decided to get on with the work he had planned for himself for this morning. He knew the basement rooms quite well now, so he had no problem feeling his way in the darkness to the air-conditioning duct that fed the rooms in the building. He swiftly and quietly climbed to the level of the first floor and wriggled along until he reached the air vent overlooking the terrorists' office.

Not much was happening. Two terrorists were in the room below, idly chatting.

Alpha 3 entered the office about thirty minutes later. Adam could see he was carrying a stack of large cardboard boxes. He dumped them on the desk and said, "This is the replacement laptop PC. I have had a special courier to deliver it to the Police Station from Glasgow. I hope you gave the correct specifications when you ordered the replacement. Are you sure you can transfer all of the information from the old laptop to this new one?"

"Yes, Alpha 3. We are still not sure what caused the failure in your old laptop, but hopefully the disk itself was not damaged. It should be no great problem to copy the data and programs to this new machine. What do you want us to do with the old machine?"

"You might as well dump it in my room in the accommodation block. I don't want to throw it away just yet in case we need it again, but I don't want to leave it lying around in this office. Please let me know when the new one is ready because I urgently need to check my emails."

"Right, sir. I will put all of the parts for the old one in a box and leave it in your room. I will need about an hour at the most to complete the work."

"Good. I am off for a while. I'll check the perimeter fence first, but I think it is about time we give the kids a surprise shakedown just to remind them who is in control."

Alpha 3 left the room as the men sat at the desk started to work on the laptop PC. Adam wriggled back along the air-conditioning duct and returned to the basement. He swiftly climbed to the roof using the knotted rope and called the watch team to return with him to the hostages' room. As he entered the room, he received an angry glare from Sally, which he promptly ignored.

"Sally, we are going to get a surprise inspection any moment now. Is anybody missing?"

"No."

Realising Sally was still angry, he left her alone and went to chat with Darren, who was resting on a sleeping mat. "Hi. How are you feeling today?"

"I'm a bit better but still sore. All my body and muscles aches like hell. Thanks for finding those painkillers. Sally's very angry with you. She wouldn't tell me why though."

"It's the same argument you and I had really. We've seen a way of ending this, but I'm saying not yet."

"I will talk to her, Adam, but she can be very strong willed sometimes. You were right when you told me not to try and escape. We'd thought we'd got away, but these terrorists seem to have thought of everything."

"No, don't get yourself between Sally and me on this argument. She will cool down after a while when she thinks through the problems in what she had wanted to do. If you are feeling up to it, you can help me on some stuff later today. Meanwhile, just chill. The terrorists are going to do a surprise inspection in a few minutes."

"Adam, how do you discover all of this stuff?"

"Like I said before, I'm just nosy, Darren."

The hostages were lying around listlessly when the terrorists burst through doors. As usual, they were masked, but unusually this time, they were armed. "Everybody get up now!" one of them commanded. "Walk through to the next room one at a time when we call your name."

Sally made sure Darren was assisted by two other boys when he limped away. As she was leaving the room, she turned to Alpha 3. "He's getting worse, and he needs to see a doctor. You guys did some real damage to him."

"I've got a doctor on site who can check him out. He's learned his lesson, and we don't gain anything if he dies on us. It was his own fault for trying to escape. It is not like you weren't told to behave."

Sally launched herself in anger at the terrorist. He just sidestepped and hit her on the side of the head with the butt of his gun. Her knees crumpled, and she fell to the ground.

Alpha 3 pointed at two of the other girls. "Pick her up and take her through to the other room." He then turned to the three men who had accompanied him and issued a command. "Search this room. Properly."

The uniformed and masked men shifted the bedding piece by piece, checking for any hidden items. They even lifted the floor tiles and had a quick look under the floor. They found nothing. Sally had arranged that the items the hostages had been collecting had been hidden above the tiles of the suspended ceiling. They had formed a human pyramid to reach that high.

In the next room, Adam and Deepa were tending to Sally. She had regained consciousness but was feeling dizzy and had a monster headache starting. Darren had tried to help, but Adam had Simon sit with the injured boy.

Adam stood and gathered the elected leaders of the three squads. "While Sally is out of action, I'm going to assume control. As soon as she has recovered enough, I'll let her take over again. Does anyone have any problems with that?"

He looked between the people. They all made a slight shake of their heads to show that no one had objections to Adam's proposal.

"Good. Please remind your people that these terrorists are serious. They will not hesitate to use violence. We must do nothing that causes direct aggravation to them. Sally and I are looking at ways of getting you all out of here safely. Be patient and ready to act. We have already found a couple of ways to escape, but we cannot use these without endangering the rest of you."

"Why can't you just have one person escape and go and get help?"

"If the terrorists thought help was on the way, there is a serious chance we would either be moved to a backup location or they would just dispose of us. Anyway, you have all seen what happened with Darren. Please go and rejoin your squads and get them back into fitness training."

No mention was made of John Nelson, but they all knew his name should have been included at the same time as Darren's.

Adam spoke with Deepa. "Deepa, I have to go on another expedition. Can you keep everybody calm? I'll be back soon."

"Adam, these people are terrible. Is there nothing we can do to strike back at them?"

"As much as I'd like too, we cannot. We must not show them any resistance, or the violence will only get worse. I'll be back soon."

Chapter 33 A Present for Deepa

Adam moved to a corner of the room and lifted a floor tile. Following the now-familiar route, he climbed down to the basement. Using the steam pipe duct, he moved over to the terrorists' accommodation block. Men were moving around the building, but Adam knew he had to take a risk for this part of his plan. He made his way up to Alpha 3's room. Once inside, he closed the door and searched around but could not find the laptop he was trying to steal. There was a knock on the door. Adam dived under the bed to hide. After a brief pause, the door opened, and one of the terrorists entered with a cardboard box in his hands. Adam watched the man's boots as he looked around the room for a suitable place to store the cardboard box. The boots turned and walked towards the bed. The man dropped a box on the floor and kicked it under the bed. The box bashed Adam's face, but he was able to avoid making a noise.

After the man left the room, Adam swiftly slid out from under the bed, dragging the box with him. A quick look inside confirmed that the computer was there. He dashed out of the room, taking the box with him. The terrorist had not reassembled the laptop computer after he extracted the data from the hard disk. Adam hoped all of components were there.

In the basement room, he removed the battery from the laptop computer and entered the terrorists' shower room. It was steamy and hot. One of the cubicles was occupied by someone having a shower. Adam entered the next shower cubicle and turned on the water. There was a shout of complaint from the next cubicle at the sudden change in water temperature. Adam did not reply but just held the motherboard of the laptop computer under the spray of the shower for a few seconds. Turning off the water, he dashed out of the room down to the basement. He knew washing a laptop under a shower would not gain him great praise if he was at home.

Deepa looked up in surprise a few minutes later when Adam walked towards her carrying a laptop computer and a bundle of wires. His hair and clothes were soaked. "I believe this is what you have been looking for? It is a bit wet at present, so I think it will need drying out before you can use it."

"Adam, why are you soaking wet? I thought you already had a shower this morning."

Adam explained how he had sabotaged the laptop computer with a fine silver powder that caused short-circuits on the motherboard. He had to use the water spray to remove the silver powder from the laptop.

Deepa tutted as she checked through the equipment. "I think you have only got the motherboard wet. I think we can dry this out, but it might take a couple of hours. Who owns the computer?"

"We own it now, but it used to belong to Alpha 3. I'm sure it will be password protected. Do you think you can get past that password? "

Deepa took the silver locket from her neck and opened it. After a little fiddling with the contents, she removed a small memory chip from the locket and showed it to Adam. "This will be all I need. I have a complete set of hacker software loaded on this memory chip. The locket was a gift from the Guild. With the motherboard exposed, I think I can bypass the power-on password. When it is dried out, I should be able to crack this computer within an hour or so. I'll give you a shout as soon as I have gained access."

Adam realised he had been dismissed by Deepa. She had switched into geek mode. From the expression on her face, he knew he had committed a serious geek sin by washing a laptop computer.

He was now feeling very weary. He walked over to his sleeping position, lay down, and pulled a blanket over himself. He was soon asleep.

§

His dreams were disturbed three hours later when Deepa shook him into wakefulness. "Adam, I've got it working. I even have it connecting to the network. Their security is pretty poor—so poor, in fact, that I don't think they have an expert running their IT systems."

"Can you get access to the Internet? Alpha 3 was talking about wanting to collect his emails."

"Yes, I can. Do you want me to set it up so you can send emails too? We could just email the police and tell them where we are, or we can even send emails to our parents to let them know we are ok."

"Deepa, we must make no contact with the police. I know the terrorists have their own spies and informants in the police force. If we contact the police, I'm afraid the terrorists will learn we have access to the Internet. The same goes for sending email messages to our parents. If that happens, the police are bound to learn about it. Please don't tell anyone you can access the Internet. You have to trust me on this."

"If you say so, boss."

"Can you see if you can gain access to any of the terrorists' control systems? I am really interested in any systems that control the electric fence, their radar system, and also a system they call Smart Rocks. He said something about them being a meshed network of sensors outside of the fences. We need to be able to find some way to take command of their security systems. You will have to do it discreetly so they do not realise we can control their systems."

"At long last, you've given me something interesting to do. Hacking into these types of systems is what I've been trained for. Give me a couple more hours, and I should have some good news for you. I will run a network sniffer program that can watch out for the passwords when they log on to their security systems."

"That is great. I'm going to go back to sleep because I'm still feeling very tired, and I think I will be up most of the night tonight. I need to sneak out of the compound tonight to make some phone calls. It is going to be a long walk to the nearest phone box."

"Why do you need to go outside the compound to make phone calls, Adam?"

"They only have one phone line coming into the site, and I know they record and monitor all of the phone calls on that one line."

"You really are not very good at IT, are you? Did you not know you can make phone calls from a laptop computer over the Internet?"

"I'd heard about it, but can't they just monitor that as well?"

"No. There is a system called Ghostfone. All of its messages are encrypted, including voice. They will not be able to detect it or monitor the calls. You can use it to talk to other computer users, or if you have a credit card, you can make a call to any telephone. The problem is, none of us have a credit card."

Adam delved into his pockets and pulled out his black credit card. "Do you think this might work? If we use this, is there any danger the authorities can track the call back to this location?"

"No. I can fix it so the call appears as though it is coming from the USA. I just need to download the Ghostfone software from the Internet, and I could have a working solution in thirty minutes or so. Do you want me to do that?"

"Yes, I do, but remember you must tell nobody—including Sally—that we can access the phone system. You have probably realised I have not told you everything happening here, but you must trust me. There are very good reasons why I don't want the authorities to attempt to try to rescue us at the moment. If I can get the phone calls made tonight, we are as good as home, but we just have to be patient a little bit longer."

"That would be good. Perhaps when you have made your phone calls, you can relax a bit instead of always being the Foundation Officer. Then we can maybe get to know each other a bit better. I'll give you an update later, once I have got a few more things working. Are you going to talk to Sally? She seems a lot calmer now, although she does have a terrible headache."

Adam moved across the room to sit with Simon and Sally. Darren was lying next to them. He was not moving even though he was awake.

"How is your head, Sally? He gave you quite a crack on the side of your head there."

"I've taken some painkillers, but I still have a terrible headache. My vision is a bit blurred, and I think I might be getting a black eye too. The barrel of his gun caught me under the eye. You were right... we shouldn't try and take them on."

"I got Deepa a laptop computer. I asked her to try and hack into their security systems. If we can do that, we can maybe get some advantage over them."

"Adam, I haven't done that work I said I would down in the basement. Give me a couple of hours and I'll go and do that task."

"Not yet you won't, Sally. You need rest before doing that. Look at your hands! They are still shaking. It can wait until tomorrow or longer if necessary."

"You know I'm not going to let them get away with this, don't you, Adam? They must be punished. I will wait until you say it is ok, but I'm going to get my revenge."

"Let's talk about that later. Meanwhile, you had best get some rest. You, too, Simon for we have got a busy night ahead of us. Come over and chat with me for a bit, and then I want to try and get some more sleep if I can."

The two boys moved away from Darren and Sally and then went and laid down where they normally slept. Adam noticed that Simon looked really weary. Most of the hostages were now showing signs of depression and tiredness, as they had begun to accept the reality of their imprisonment. It was no longer an adventure—just a continuing horror.

"How is Darren really, Simon? I haven't had much chance to watch him today."

"He's better than he was this morning. I think it is more inside his head than his body. I don't know what they did to him, but they have broken his spirit. I've tried asking him about it, but he just clams up, and so does Sally. You are taking too many risks, Adam. I'm worried you will get caught and get the same treatment as Darren did or worse. I would hate that to happen to you."

Adam rested a reassuring hand on Simon's shoulder. "Simon, I'm sorry, but I just have to get more information about what is going on here. I'm very careful, but sometimes you have to break eggs if you want to make an omelette. I try and use other people when I can, but a lot of it I have to do myself."

There was no response. Adam listened to Simon's breathing. His friend had fallen asleep. Soon, Adam drifted into sleep laying next to Simon.

§

The sleeping children were woken by the sound of guards unravelling the chain that locked the swing doors to their room. It was time for their evening meal. Once again, the food was meat stew and boiled vegetables. It was not appetising, and much of the food was left uneaten. A consequence of Sally's attempted attack on Alpha 3 was that there was to be no film shown that evening. The hostages were herded back to their sleeping area with the exception of Simon and Darren.

Once the others had left the canteen, a lady entered the room. She looked somewhat Chinese. Taking one look at Darren, she walked over carrying a black leather doctor's bag. "I am the doctor. It is some time since I practiced medicine, but I remember the basics. Take your boiler suit off and let me examine you."

Darren awkwardly slipped off his outer clothing and stood as the doctor examined him.

"Sit on the chair."

The doctor checked his temperature using an ear thermometer. She wrapped a pressure cuff around his arm and took his blood pressure and then examined his chest with a stethoscope.

"Now, lay on your back on the floor."

She continued the examination, pressing various parts of his torso with stiff, cold fingers. "Roll over on to your stomach."

She asked various medical questions as the examination proceeded and then finally nodded her head.

"Walk forward about ten paces then come back."

Darren followed her request.

"Get dressed. You are lucky. There are no outward signs of serious injury, but you do have some nasty bruising. Whoever gave you this beating knew what they were doing. Did they do anything else?"

Darren just hung his head and did not answer.

"Hmm, well, when you get out of here, you should go to a hospital and have a thorough check-up. Are you allergic to antibiotics?"

"No."

"I'm going to give you an injection of antibiotics. I think you might have an infection, but I would need blood tests to be sure. We don't have those facilities."

She unpackaged a preloaded antibiotic hypodermic syringe. "Lean against the chair." The doctor slipped the waist band of Darren's boxers down a little and swabbed the top of his buttock with an alcohol wipe before plunging the needle in deep. After removing the hypodermic, she returned to her bag and pulled out two foil strips of capsules. "This one is antibiotic. Take one four times a day starting in the morning. Make sure you complete the whole treatment. These are painkillers. Take one four times a day. If you do not start feeling better in two days, tell the guard you need to see me again. You are not seriously ill. You may get dressed now and return to the others."

With that, she turned and left the room. The remaining guard escorted the two boys to join the rest of the hostages. Assisted by Simon, Darren sat painfully next to Sally and showed her the antibiotics.

Chapter 34 Adam Makes Some Calls

Following Darren's return, Adam waited until the chain had been rattled back into position to securely lock the door, and then he went over to see Deepa. She looked up and smiled when she saw Adam approaching. She rose from the floor and walked over to stand by a wall. "Let me stand on your shoulders so I can get the laptop down from the ceiling."

Adam helped her climb up and stand on his shoulders. She lifted a ceiling tile and retrieved the laptop computer from where it had been hidden from the terrorists. She passed the computer and a bundle of wires down to Adam and then gracefully jumped down to the floor.

She switched it on and entered a password. "I have set the password to DORFN-ARC. You should be able to remember that."

He looked puzzled. "What's a 'dorfnarc'? That just sounds like a random jumble of letters."

"Oh, you really are not a geek, are you. I would have thought you would have recognised your own name spelled backwards."

Adam grinned sheepishly. "Oh, yeah."

"I have been able to hack into their security system. I will show you how to access it a little bit later. They have one system that controls radar, another that controls the Smart Rocks, and one that controls the fence detector system. They have been stupid and not set a password on those systems. There are some other systems which they have password protected, but I hope to get hold of those passwords by running sniffer programs on the network."

"Do you think it is possible to make the radar system and the Smart Rocks system a bit forgetful so they ignore parts of the terrain outside? I don't want to turn off their systems completely because they might detect that from their office."

"Adam, why don't you ask the impossible? That might be easier. I would have to find some way of capturing their tracking signals and changing them on the fly, overcoming sequence checks. There are all kinds of problems."

He just smiled. "You will enjoy this. It is just the sort of geeky problem you love. Anyway, you have three days to complete the task. That must be loads of time for a genius like you. Have you got the phone thingy working?"

"Yes, master, I have worked my fingers to the bone as per your command. It is all working now, but if you need to make phone calls, I will need to buy some credit. Let me have that credit card of yours."

Adam handed over the credit card, and Deepa set to work. After a few minutes of concentrated work, she handed the card back. "There we go. You now have £25 phone credit, and I should have a sixty-inch plasma TV being delivered to my own home. I have set your user ID to 'adam.cranford'."

"Ha ha, very funny. Can you just show me how to make calls from here? I'll need to find somewhere quiet where people cannot overhear me. Is there any problem if I take the laptop out of this room?"

"No. The wireless network signal is very strong, so I would imagine the laptop will be fine in any of the rooms in this floor. I have taken care to set it up so nobody can easily trace the calls back to this laptop." She took him through the routine for making calls over the Internet using Ghostfone.

"Ok, I had better get moving. There are a lot of things I need to do this evening. You should have this laptop back in half an hour or so."

Adam retrieved the map he had stolen earlier and then picked up the laptop. He moved to the place where he normally exited the room and wriggled through under the floor into the next room. He checked carefully that the room was empty before he fully emerged. Placing the laptop on the floor, he tried the web browser. It worked well, and Adam spent a few minutes running Google searches.

Next, he signed onto the telephone system. After few seconds of delay, the program displayed a green connected symbol. He made the first phone call. After a few seconds, the call was answered.

"Mike Bates speaking. Can I help you?"

"Sergeant Bates, this is Captain Cranford speaking. I am sorry to disturb you, but I need your help on a couple of things."

"Captain Cranford? I think I recognise your voice, but could you possibly give me some details that might give me reason to recognise you?"

"I looked in the eye of the dragon and then crossed the bridge to the gold. Also, my father says thank you for the bottle of Puligny Montrachet from the Dorchester."

"There are an awful lot of people looking for you at present. Are you ok, sir?"

"Yes. We are all ok, except for one person who may have been a casualty. They have very extensive defences. I cannot risk a rescue by the authorities because that would probably result in further casualties, so I'm not going to tell you the exact location of the site. I have information that the police have been infiltrated by these terrorists. I think it is probably best that you do not tell anybody about this phone call, even within the Foundation. I am taking command of the situation, but a few resources would be helpful."

"Yes, sir. I'm at home, but I have a pencil and paper ready if you would just give me the details, and I will see what I can arrange."

"I need one and half tons of gold packed in tough wooden waterproof crates that have no exterior dimensions of less than seventy cms. Each crate should be light enough that it can be lifted by two people and should have strong rope handles for lifting purposes. One of those crates should have inside it a bag of gold sovereigns. That crate should be marked on the outside with a red circle. All of the other crates should not be marked."

"That represents a substantial amount of money, sir. I presume it is the ransom payment. Will we be having that gold returned?"

"Yes. The Foundation will get that back provided all of my plans work out. I also need to stop any of the parents from paying the ransom to the kidnappers, so I need a Foundation member to go and visit each of the families and offer them an insurance policy. That policy, for 10 percent of the ransom demand for their child, will guarantee that the ransom is paid in full and that their child will be rescued unharmed. I was wondering if you might speak to Hermes about the job. He would fit the part exactly. Hermes could then act as the negotiator with the kidnappers."

"When and where do you need the gold?"

Adam gave him a date and time and a map reference number.

"I also need to have a small Foundation base camp set up to temporarily store and guard the gold. I need two squads of Foundation cadets in their No. 3 uniforms to be based in the camp. They should be in place two days before the gold is delivered. They should also set up tents, hot showers, and food to provide initial shelter for the hostages after the rescue. We will need thirty spare sets of outdoor clothes for the hostages. We should also have an emergency medic in place in case there are any injuries. No one is to be told the purpose of the camp in advance, nor should they explore the surrounding areas. I will visit the camp before the rescue and give them detailed instructions."

"Ok. I can do that."

"I will also need to have a fuel tanker on site with sufficient load of Jet A-1 to refuel a Sea King helicopter at least four times. I will also need half a dozen 100-metre, ten-mm maritime ropes."

"Do you need me to arrange for the provision of a helicopter?"

"No, I don't think so. I will handle that, but if I have any problems, I will let you know. Oh yes... before I forget, I will also need three aluminium fifteen-m. flagpoles painted olive green, a pair of bolt cutters, a waterproof mobile phone with a built-in camera, some walkie talkie handsets, 500 bright green rescue light sticks, some karabiners, and a fishing rod with 100 metres of ten-kg. breaking strain line."

"Is that it, sir?"

"No, Sergeant. I also need the floor plan of someone's house and details of their alarm system."

"Who might that be, sir?"

Adam told him.

"Ah, well, that might be difficult, but I think I can pull a few strings. I can have that waiting for you at the base camp."

"Thank you, Sergeant Bates. I have to go now."

"Good luck, sir. Be safe."

Adam ended the call and dialled the next number. It took a while for the other end to answer, and when they did, there was loud music playing in the background.

"Hi. Is Stella there please?"

"Hang on... I can't hear you. I'll turn the music down. Now, who is this calling me?"

"It's Adam Cranford. Do you remember me from the paintball battle wipe-out a couple of months ago?"

"Oh, yeah. Hang on... aren't you one of the one of those school kids who got kidnapped? Have you been rescued? They have said nothing on the news."

"I'm still a hostage, but I don't have time to go into that now. Is old Ben around? If he is, can you bring him to the phone? Please don't tell anyone else it is me on the phone."

"I think he is. I'll go and get him. Hang on a tick."

Adam waited for a few minutes, listening to silence. Then he heard someone walk up to the phone and pick up the handset. An old man's voice spoke. "This is Ben. Well, lad, it seems you are good at attracting trouble. Do you want us to contact the police for you?"

"Hi, Ben. The police are the last people I want involved. The local police are tied up in this kidnapping, and I also suspect there are some senior ones too. The site where they are holding us is well guarded with loads of approach detectors. They will blow us up if anyone tries to rescue us. I've sorted out the ransom so that we will be let go, but I just want to take some precautions in case things go wrong."

"How many are them of there?

"As far as I can tell, there are twenty, and I think they are military trained. The buildings are mined with explosives."

"I don't think Stella and I can really help. There are too many for us to deal with. Why don't you just wait until the ransom is paid?"

"No, I don't want you to attack them. I just want to hire you and Stella for a few days with some of your equipment. You are still fit enough to do a bit of mountain camping, aren't you, Ben?"

"Fit enough? Cheeky lad. I'm still as fit as I was when you were still pooing in nappies."

Adam continued the conversation to explain what it was he wanted Stella and Ben to undertake and when they should perform the task.

"It sounds like a walk in the park, young man. I thought for a moment you were going to ask something difficult. Even an old fogey like me should be able to cope. Stella, here, is nodding her head and bouncing around a lot."

"How much will it cost?"

"For you, there will be no charge."

"Ben, this is business, and I'm calling on your specialist skills."

"Oh, ok then. In that case, £5,000 should cover it if you agree to pay for any lost equipment."

"Superb. There will be a 100 percent completion bonus as well on top of that. Do you take credit cards?"

Adam and Ben finalised the payment and arrangements, and Adam prepared to make the next call. He knew this might be trickier, but it was an essential part of his plan. He dialled the next number on his mental list.

"Hello. Duty Officer speaking."

"Hi. Could I speak with Flight Lieutenant Terry Hewitt please?"

"One moment, sir."

"Hewitt. How can I help you?"

"Trevor, I don't know if you remember me. I'm Adam Cranford. You gave my squad a lift to my base camp after rescuing our leader from a mineshaft. Ring any bells?"

"Oh, yes, I remember it well. A tricky rescue, but it was helped by your good preparation work. What can I do for you? Are you calling to arrange a visit to our base?"

"Actually, I called to ask if you wouldn't mind doing me a favour. I don't know if you realised that I am one of the thirty school children who have been kidnapped. I am still a hostage, but I have been able to get access to a phone. Please don't contact the police."

Adam heard the sound of a muffled crumpling as Hewitt's hand covered the microphone of his telephone handset. He could just make out the command the Flight Lieutenant was making to one of his staff. "Benson, get me that newspaper from yesterday, would you please?"

Adam heard the hand removed from the phone handset and the rustling of newspaper as pages were turned.

"Good Lord! So you are... and no, I hadn't realised. You do seem to have a habit of getting in sticky places."

"Yes. And you're not the first person to say that. Can you please be careful not to let anybody around you know you are talking to me on the phone? It is very important. There is a rescue taking place, but we cannot involve the police because we know they have been infiltrated by the terrorists who kidnapped us."

"So why are you calling me?"

"I was wondering if in a few days, you wouldn't mind taking two or three days leave and doing a spot of helicopter flying for me. I need something about the size of the Sea King to complete my plan."

"As much as I would like to help you, I can't go and just borrow a military helicopter for three days without telling people a reason why I need it. That type of thing would have to go right up the chain of command before I could do that. I'm not some kind of royal prince."

"No, you don't understand. I want to *rent* a helicopter for the three days and pay you a fee for flying it. I have access to plenty of money."

"You do know that if we use a military Sea King helicopter for private purposes, the Ministry of Defence charges about £3,000 an hour, right? I do have some friends in the oil industry that might be able to rent something for a lower cost. If you call back in five minutes, I might be to give you an answer."

"Ok, I'll do that, but please remember not to let any of the authorities know. There are lives at stake here."

"Fair enough, Adam. I will trust you on this one. Call back on the same number in five minutes."

While Adam was waiting for Terry Hewitt to make his enquiries, he decided to make one more phone call.

"...1209. Hello"

"Mr. Uddin, this is Adam Cranford. May I speak with Ali please?"

"Surely you have escaped? My family has been very worried about you."

"No, I have not escaped. I am still a captive, but I have been able to get to a phone. I am arranging an escape, but my parents and the police must not know, or it will all go wrong."

"Arranging an escape?" The phone went quiet for a moment as Mr. Uddin thought over what Adam had just said. "You are a special young man, Adam. I am now sure you did not break my window with that cricket ball by any accident. Are you sure you do not want me to tell anyone where you are?"

"No, Mr. Uddin. I have things under control here."

"I will bring my son to the phone. Please wait a moment."

"Hi, Adam! Are you safe? We have all been so worried about you."

"Hi, Ali. No, I'm not safe just yet, but I'm working on a plan to fix it. I want you to play an important part in it."

"How can I do that? You know I still find it difficult to leave my house."

"Everybody can help in their own way, Ali. I need someone I can trust to do this small but important task."

"I will do it if I can. What do you want me to do?"

Adam explained to his younger friend what he needed doing and the exact time when it should be done. "Is your father still there, Ali? I need to have a quick word with him."

Mr. Uddin's voice came on the phone. "Adam, you wished to speak with me?"

"Yes, Mr. Uddin. I will need your help after the rescue. I cannot pay for this in advance, but I will arrange payment the day we get back."

"I am sure I will find a way, Adam. You have shown great kindness to my family. What do you want me to do?"

Adam explained what it was he needed and the need for secrecy.

"Is that all? Consider it done. I will pray for your success in the escape. I still don't understand why you need to keep it a secret from the police, but I will respect your wishes."

"I must finish this phone call, as I have others to make. Thank you for your help."

Adam finished the call and then called back the airbase where Terry Hewitt was located.

"Hi, Adam. I have just finished talking with my friend. His company actually has two spare helicopters because one of their major clients has temporarily closed its offshore platform. They would welcome renting out their helicopter for a few days, but I must warn you that you are looking at around £15,000 a day for that rental. The other condition is that I have to be the pilot of the helicopter. I am sure I can take a few days leave if that would help you. I have another friend who I am sure would not mind being a navigator at the same time. Do you want to go ahead with this?"

"Does he take credit cards? I will need it for three days, and I can arrange the fuel."

"Are you really serious about this, Adam? That will cost you £45,000!"

Adam's response was to tell Terry the number on the front of his credit card and the days when he needed the helicopter.

"I will just call him back, hang on a moment."

Adam waited while the Flight Lieutenant contacted his friend again.

"Adam, my friend just needs to talk to you on the phone. I will transfer him over."

"So, you are the young man who wants to rent my helicopter. Terry tells me this needs to be done in secret. It is nothing illegal, I hope?"

"No, sir. It is for the public good, but the need is urgent, and it has to be kept secret because lives depend on it."

"Fair enough, young man. Can you tell me the security code from the strip on the back of your credit card and the date of expiry?"

He gave the man the information requested.

"Hang on for a couple minutes. I will just call the credit card company to confirm the payment."

Adam waited anxiously for news on whether the payment would be accepted.

"Wow, you must have some massive credit limit. They accepted that transaction without a query. The helicopter is yours for three days on the condition that Terry is the pilot. You will look after it for me, won't you?"

"Yes, sir, I will. I will treat it as if it is my very own bicycle."

The man hung up the phone with a parting chuckle.

The line automatically reconnected to Terry Hewitt, who was waiting to speak with Adam. "How did that go, Adam?"

"It's cool. We have the helicopter for three days. It is all paid for. Now I need to talk about some payment for you and your navigator."

"As a serving pilot in the military, I cannot take payment for this type of work. Clearly, it is important, so I am quite prepared to do this work for free."

"Flight Lieutenant Hewitt, this is business. How about I pay you £2,000 in cash per day plus expenses per person, and then I will leave it to you to donate the money to charity?"

"That seems fair to me. Now, you had better tell me where you need this helicopter, because I will need to file flight plans."

Adam spent the next few minutes discussing the exact locations and timings of where he would need the helicopter to fly. Terry Hewitt was quite surprised when he discovered that Adam had already arranged a fuel tanker at the base camp.

"Adam, now that you are my employer for a few days, you had best start calling me Terry. Is there any way I can contact you if things go wrong?"

"No. I am, after all, still a hostage, so I doubt the terrorists would want to take incoming phone calls for me. I will try and call you again closer to the day if I get chance. Otherwise, just assume the plans go ahead as I have told you. I must go now. I cannot thank you enough for your help."

Adam terminated the call and shut down the laptop computer. He returned it to Deepa. She smiled at him. "I trust you have finished all your plotting and scheming, oh great slave master? I presume now that you want me to get on and start hacking into their security systems?"

"Yes, slave, it worked really well... and if you are very good, I will let you have some of my scrambled eggs tomorrow morning at breakfast."

"Yuck. You really know how to show a girl a good time, don't you?"

Adam smiled and walked away. His busy evening had only just started.

Chapter 35 A Visit to the Secret Building

It was just getting dark outside when Adam emerged, followed by Simon, from the back of the terrorists' accommodation block. He looked towards the top of the office block where the two watchers were located. They signalled that it was all clear for him to proceed. The two boys stealthily made their way to the garage workshop. The padlock to the door of the garage workshop was still wedged closed with the piece of wood. They quickly slipped inside the building and closed the door behind them. Simon carried a bundle of old blankets and the adhesive tape they had stolen earlier. Working swiftly, they taped the blankets over the windows that looked out of the workshop.

"Simon, can you keep a lookout for guards? Also keep an eye on the watchers to see if they signal that someone is coming. What I need to do now is going to make a lot of noise and bright sparks."

"Ok. I shall throw something at you if you need to stop."

Adam found some old hacksaw blades in a box lying on one of the workbenches. He snapped them in half and then turned on an electric grindstone. Working as quickly as he could safely go, he applied the blades to the spinning grindstone and started cutting a new shape in the thin black steel. The noise it generated was agonisingly loud, and the bright shower of sparks lit up the room they were in. Adam worked on several pieces of the hacksaw blades before he was satisfied with the results. Searching around in the room, he found a gas blowtorch and a carton of unused gas cartridges. He inserted a new cartridge in the blowtorch and then used the flying sparks from the grindstone to ignite the blowtorch. Adam had finished with the grindstone, so he turned off the motor. The noise level in the room suddenly reduced, leaving just the quiet roar of the gas blowtorch. He heated the metal shapes he had cut from the hacksaw blades in the flame of the blowtorch. When the metal changed to the right colour, he quickly dropped each item into a can containing cold motor oil.

He turned off the blowtorch and turned to Simon. "We are done in here. We had best get moving onto the next part of the plan."

"What were you making? I was really scared with all the noise you were making with that grindstone."

Adam held up several metal blades that had been cut into thin, oddly curved, hooked, and wriggly shapes. "These are new lock picks. The ones I have in my inhaler were not big enough for the job I want to do next. The hacksaw blades make a very good springy metal after they have been heat treated. We had best get the blankets down from the windows and move on."

They carefully tidied up and exited the workshop and reset the padlock before making their way back to the terrorists' accommodation block. They had to wait for one of the terrorists to move out of the corridor before they could get back down to the basement of the building. Adam led them back into the tunnel between the buildings and turned left when they reached the junction. He was heading toward the secret building. Simon knew he should keep quiet as they approached their destination. The door of the room in the basement of the secret building was still locked when the boys arrived. Adam tried his new lock picks on the door. After some fiddling, he was rewarded with success, and the door latch clunked back into the unlocked position.

"Simon, be very careful and quiet for this next bit. I have no idea what we are going to find. I know Alpha 3 guards this room very carefully and doesn't let any of his other guards in this building. I think this building contains the key to why we have been kidnapped. Whatever you see in here, please do not tell anyone else about it. I suspect that if Alpha 3 finds us in here or knows we've been here, we really will be dead men."

Adam switched off the light in the basement room and cautiously opened the door, listening for the presence of anybody else outside. There was a dark corridor with a set of stairs leading upwards at one end. They crept as quietly as they could up the stairs and found they had come out into a dimly lit reception area. The exit doors from the building were locked with large magnetic locks at the top of the door. Adam checked around the door that led into the rest of the building and could find no sign of an alarm contact. He carefully pulled on the door and eased it open. There was a bright, harsh glare of fluorescent light the other side of the door. They found themselves in a broad corridor. The floor was covered in a smooth grey plastic with curves instead of sharp corners where the walls met the floor. The walls were covered in a similar grey plastic, and except for the light fittings, the ceiling mirrored the floor in shape and colour. At the end of the corridor was a double-glazed window looking out into the rest of the building.

Beyond the window, they could see a large laboratory where a single person was working. That person was encased in a biological protection suit pressurised by an air hose trailing across the floor. The worker sat at a bench, peering into some scientific equipment. Keeping low to avoid being seen from the laboratory, the two boys explored the rooms at the side of the corridor. The doors were unlocked; presumably, the terrorists were confident that the external security of the building was sufficient. On the left-hand side of the corridor, the rooms were an office, a storeroom, and a cloakroom. The cloakroom contained several spare sets of biological protection clothing. On the right-hand side of the corridor, they found one room containing animal cages, a toilet room, and a combined shower and airlock entering in to the laboratory. The door to the airlock room had soft rubber seals that closed firmly and airtight when the door was shut.

"Simon, I have seen enough for tonight. We can't go in the laboratory just yet. Even if we did, I think we would have to wear those protective suits. We will have to come back later. Have you seen this type of laboratory before?"

"Yes, I have been—"

The boys heard somebody entering the building by the lobby behind them. Adam grabbed Simon by the shoulder and dashed into the storage room at the side of the corridor. The two boys hid behind some benches, fearing they would be discovered. In his rush, Adam had left the storeroom door slightly ajar. Two men were standing outside talking about some scientific process. One of the men noticed the door was not closed. He walked over to it and pulled it shut. The two men then entered the cloakroom and started changing into the protective suits.

Adam heaved a sigh of relief but then noticed the sound of his friend quietly crying next to him. Adam put his arm around the shoulders of his friend and gave him a hug. He spoke quietly. "Wow, Simon, that was close. We will wait until they've gone inside the laboratory, and then we can get out of this building."

Simon was still sobbing quietly as Adam led him back down to the basement and back into "their" room where the old steam pipe duct entered the building.

Tears were still streaming down Simon's face. Adam tried to console him. "It's ok. We will be safe down here. That is all I need to do at the moment. We can go back and join the others in the sleeping area."

"Adam, you don't understand. I recognised the voice of one of those men. His voice is unmistakable. It was my father. He must be involved in this. He is one of the terrorists. I cannot believe it—my own father."

"No. You have got it wrong. I overheard the terrorists talking a couple of days ago. They are blackmailing your father to take part. They have probably told him you will get hurt or killed if he does not cooperate fully."

Simon stared through watery eyes at his friend. "You knew? You heard my father would be blackmailed, and you didn't tell me? What kind of friend are you?"

"There are many things I know about this kidnapping that I have not told you or the others. One of those things was about your father. I did not know for certain that they would get him here. I decided not to tell you to avoid worrying you."

Simon wiped his eyes with the sleeve of his boiler suit. "What is going to happen to him? He must be a prisoner too. They won't let him go. What do you mean you know many things about this kidnapping? Are you involved with the kidnappers as well? Is that how you know so much?"

"No. I am a hostage just like you. I know only what I've overheard. Some of it is really bad news, and I didn't want to upset people anymore than they are already. I don't know what will happen to your father. I haven't heard that bit."

"Adam, I'm not going to get out of this alive, am I? There is no way my parents can afford the ransom set for me. With my father captured, too, they really won't keep us alive."

"Don't worry about that side of things. I can't tell you how, but I have made sure there is enough money to pay the ransom—for everybody. We will be out of here in a few days, I promise you."

"But why my father? Why do they need him? He only does research into global warming. They know he has seen their faces."

Adam decided to trust Simon. He told him about Project Silver Rain and the virus being developed. His friend just sat shocked on the floor, not saying anything. After re-locking the door to the basement room, he guided the shocked boy into the duct tunnel between the buildings and gently led him back to the office block where the hostages were held.

When they reached the other basement room Simon finally began to talk again. "We have to get out of here and warn people. This is much bigger than just us school children. It could be a world catastrophe."

"The problem with that, Simon, is that if we escape, there is nothing to stop the terrorists from escaping with the virus. If the police find us after the escape, they might just bring us back like they did with Darren and John. We don't know who to trust outside. There may be loads of people who think this type of population control is needed to stop the world population from growing. If you think about it, it would be one answer to global warming."

"What are we going to do? What is to stop them from infecting us and releasing us when the ransom is paid? We could be the people who carry the infection to the rest of the world. There is one thing we could do to stop them from using us as their germ carriers."

"Don't even think about going down that route. We are going to get out of this situation unharmed, and we are going to defeat them. I have a lot of plans in action, and the more we can discover about these people, the more likely we are to win. It is not just the terrorists at this site we should worry about. It is the people supporting them that we need to try and catch. We are fighting for the lives of millions of unborn children. You just have to trust me. And please... please don't tell any of the others about Project Silver Rain! If they find out about it and panic, the terrorists could discover that we know. If that happens, we are dead, and the terrorists will find some other way of spreading the virus."

"Adam, there is no way I will be able to sleep tonight. I just do not know how you can cope with this."

"If you can't sleep, that is some good news, because I have decided I'm going back to the laboratory later tonight when the terrorists have gone to sleep. You can come with me if you want."

"Just try and stop me!"

The two boys rejoined the rest of the hostages. Adam went over to Sally and Darren to see how they were feeling. "Hi, Sally. How is it going?"

"I'm feeling a bit better, I've taken some painkillers, and my vision is returning to normal, though my head is still very sore. How did your expedition go?"

He got Sally to move away from the others before continuing the discussion and then held up the lock picks he had manufactured over in the garage. "I had some success. These new lock picks will make life a lot easier. I even managed to get into the secret building. I think I have found the place where they store their methyl nitrate. If we get some of that, would you be able to use it as an explosive?"

"Yes, I could, but I don't see the point, as we have kilograms of high explosive dangling below us. Anyway, I still need to have some detonators, otherwise it will be difficult to set off the explosives. You can make methyl nitrate explode by heating it over fifty degrees Celsius or giving it a shock like a heavy hammer blow. Are you telling me you need me to blow something up for you?"

"Yes. There are a couple of things where it would be useful if I could demolish them when the time is right. I will talk to you about them tomorrow and see if you are fit to work on them. Meanwhile, you should get some more rest. If you are fit tomorrow, you and I will be going for a swim. Can you tell me what detonators look like? I will see if we can find some. They must have some lying around here leftover from when they mined this building." Sally told Adam what they looked like and how he had to be very careful in handling them.

"How is Darren feeling?"

"He seems to be getting better. The injection the doctor gave him must be working."

"That's cool. I'll leave you to get to sleep. If you are fit, it will be a busy day. If not, don't worry. I can wait a couple of days. I'll be going out investigating the site again later tonight."

Deepa was working on the laptop when Adam arrived. She patted the floor beside her to indicate that Adam should sit there. "Hello, Secret Agent 007. How did your expedition go?"

"It was ok, I found out some more information that will be useful."

She leaned against him. "Come on, Adam. Why all this secrecy and keeping information from your loyal slave? I bet Simon knows."

"I need to find out more before I can share it. It is helping me to understand why we were kidnapped, and that will help me plan how to get out of here."

"You know perfectly well you could give me the exact map reference, and I could send an email now... and we would be released by the morning."

"Yes, but we might also all be found dead in the morning, and the terrorists might escape to do this—or worse—to someone else."

"Doesn't it worry you playing God with twenty-eight people's lives? If you get it wrong, we could all suffer for your curiosity."

"It is not that simple, Deepa. How are you getting on with the computer and the security system?"

"I see. Change the subject and hope Deepa doesn't follow that line of questioning." She turned her head to look Adam straight in the eye. "You know I trust you, Adam Cranford, don't you?"

Adam held her gaze for a while before tapping his hand on the side of the laptop computer. "Ahem... the computer?"

"Slave driver."

She broke the gaze and turned her attention to the computer.

"It's going well. It is fascinating how the Smart Rocks communicate with each other. They constantly reach out to make sure that their 'friends' are nearby and send short messages to each other. Something moved close to one of the Smart Rocks while I was watching their messages, and they all cooperated to try and find the intruder."

Adam noticed that Deepa's left hand rested against his knee when it was not on the keyboard. He did not move it. "So what would happen if I tried to move one of the Smart Rocks to make a pathway?"

"That would raise an alarm on the central control console. The Smart Rocks would panic that they could not find their neighbour."

"Do you think you could teach the Smart Rocks to lie to each other?"

"I don't know, Adam. It is not a style of programming I'm used to doing, and I'll have to download programming tools from the Internet. I will try though. What do you really want to do?"

"I want to have a safe pathway through the Smart Rocks from the fence out to open ground. It needs to be about ten metres wide."

"If you get the map and show me where, I'll try and work out the coordinates. The Smart Rocks use a combination of GPS signals and the proximity to their neighbour rocks. I might be able to load a data table of areas to be ignored."

Adam wandered over to where Simon was sitting. The map was hidden there.

"Hi, Adam. How's Deepa doing?"

"She is fine, Simon."

"So I can see."

"We are just working out how to get past the defences outside the fence. It is important stuff."

"I guess it must be. What time are we going out tonight?"

"Just after midnight. I'll see you in a while. I need to go finish this work with Deepa."

"I'm not going anywhere."

Adam spent about another hour working with Deepa. By the time he left, Deepa had devised a strategy for carving a path through the detection capabilities of the Smart Rocks. She also had a plan for the radar system. She had discovered that the results of the radar sweeps were delivered across the local area network. She thought there may be a way to capture the radar image when no intruders were present and then to replay it across the network when Adam wanted something hidden from the radar. She would be ready when the terrorists ran the next daily radar test.

When he returned, Simon was lying down on his side as if asleep. Adam lay down and pulled a blanket over himself. He wanted to get some sleep if he could before midnight. He knew he would wake up on time.

"Wake me at midnight, Adam."

Chapter 36 Collecting Supplies

Adam woke and checked the time on his button clock. It was a minute after midnight. He looked around and saw that everyone was asleep except for Deepa. Her face was lit by the glow from the laptop PC screen. He shook Simon's shoulder and gently whispered, "Wake up. It is time for you to go and play at being a hero."

Simon groaned and sat up, rubbing his eyes with the heel of his palms. "I am never, ever going to complain again about having to get up for school in the morning. I don't know how you keep going, Adam."

The boys made their way to the terrorists' accommodation building using the underground duct route. In the basement room, Adam explained his plan of action to Simon. "Can you go and check in their laundry room and kitchen to see if you can find any large bottles of bleach? If you can find any, bring it back here. Be careful... they may still be up and on patrol. I want to see what is behind the locked door in this basement. If the door is locked, there must be something useful in there."

"Why bleach, Adam?"

"That is rather obvious, isn't it, Simon? Think about where we were earlier today."

Adam set to work on the door while Simon crept up the stairs leading from the basement. The lock was not as complex as Adam had feared. It took him less than a minute to unlock it. He slipped into the room, closed the door behind him, and tried the light switch. He blinked in the bright light. He had found treasure! Directly in front of him was a rack containing machine pistols and some pre-loaded ammunition clips. To one side of the rack was a stack of ammunition boxes. He ignored the content of the rack and looked around. In the corner of the room, he found a tall, grey metal cabinet. The simple lock of the cabinet resisted Adam's lock picks for just a few seconds.

The cabinet was almost empty apart from a few metal shelves. On the top shelf was an open plain cardboard box. He looked inside the box. Packed in a matrix of cardboard packing, he saw about twenty detonators. They were made of plain copper tubes about the size of his finger and a pair of coiled wires that hung from each detonator. He carefully removed five of them and then put the cardboard box back into the cabinet. He re-locked the cabinet door and then looked around the room. He saw an old newspaper lying on the floor. Using the newspaper, he carefully wrapped the detonators so they did not touch each other, and then he popped the package into a pocket of his boiler suit.

Before leaving the room, he looked a second time at the sub-machine guns and wondered whether he should take one of those with him. He decided against doing that because, so far as he knew, none of the hostages were skilled in the use of such weapons. He certainly did not need any to complete his plans. He switched out the room light and left after re-locking the door behind him.

By the time he got back, Simon was waiting for him with a five-litre plastic bleach container. Before climbing back into the duct, he removed from his pocket the paper bundle containing the detonators and held it in front of him as he crawled along. When he reached the junction, he put the detonators to one side and then crawled in the direction of the secret building. Simon was not far behind. He was struggling a little to carry the bleach container and crawl at the same time. When they reached the basement room, Adam helped Simon climb down from the entrance of the duct.

"Find somewhere to hide the bleach in this room. I don't think we can use it tonight, but it will be handy to leave it in this room. I want to go and have a look around in that laboratory. I will need you to help me put a protective suit on. I have never done that before, and I don't want to make any mistakes."

When the boys crept up the stairs, they found the ground floor was in darkness. Adam was a bit surprised to find that none of the inner doors were locked but was relieved he did not have to take time to pick the locks. When they entered the inner corridor near the laboratory, the ceiling lights automatically switched on. Without hesitation, Adam went to the cloakroom and selected the protective suit he thought was closest to his size. Simon helped him into the suit and taped up the sleeves and legs so there were no gaps exposed. There were plenty of rolls of tape, presumably there for exactly that purpose. The clear plastic helmet started to mist a little from Adam's breath.

"Hang on, Adam. I think there must be an air pump in this suit. You will suffocate without it. Look around for a switch."

After a short, rushed search, they found a switch which started air pumping into the suit through a filter. Adam's hood started to clear.

"When you get inside, make sure you plug an air hose into the suit. When you come back out, shower the outside of the suit for a few minutes to wash any nasty bugs off."

Simon watched through the window as Adam passed through the airlock room and then plugged an air hose into his suit and set off to explore the laboratory. There were three large stainless steel cylinders that looked like giant pressure cookers. Adam was able to peer in through an inspection hatch. A soupy looking liquid of gently bubbled inside each steel vat. A temperature gauge told him the "soup" was kept at thirty-five degrees Celsius. The opposite wall had a bench surface running the whole length of the wall. It was laden with scientific equipment and some PCs. There were some large machines that resembled washing machines. Adam did not have a clue what they did, but he noticed that a pipe ran from them, draining a clear, slightly yellow liquid that was dripping down into a half-filled two-litre bottle. The bottle was labelled *Danger! Methyl Nitrate DO NOT expose to heat or sudden shock* and was resting in a bucket of iced water.

Further in the corner of the room was a large metal safe. It had a combination lock and a high-security key lock on its door. Adam did not think money was stored in that safe, but clearly it was something the terrorists wanted to carefully protect. He decided there was not much more information he could gain in the room, so he decided to leave. He showered the outside of his suit as Simon had advised before standing under an air blast to dry off the suit. He returned to Simon, and they moved into the storeroom to be able to hide if anyone unexpectedly arrived.

"I think they are brewing the virus in those metal cylinders. That must be a lot more than they would need to infect just us thirty kids. Maybe they want to spray it on a large football crowd."

"Adam, I think I've seen those types of thing before. My dad had a photograph taken of himself at work in his laboratory when I was very young. I remember seeing the same equipment in the background of that photograph."

"I've got to figure a way of destroying this stuff before they can spread the virus. If we tip some bleach into those brewing vats, I think that will work, though we need to find some more bleach if we can. I don't want to use the bleach until we are ready to escape in case the terrorists find out. The other thing that worries me is that security safe in the corner of the laboratory. That holds something important. I'd guess it may be the master culture of the virus."

"Can't you just jam the lock so they can't get into the safe... or maybe blow it up somehow?"

"Jamming the lock would just slow them down for a while. Blowing up the safe could just spread the virus in the air. Let's go. I need to think about what to do."

While Adam was talking, Simon had been exploring. There was a large white chest, very much like a deep freezer, positioned against the end wall of the storeroom. He lifted the lid and looked inside. There were thirty-two two-litre bottles standing upright and surrounded by what looked like a white snow. The temperature gauge on the chest was showing ten degrees Celsius. Simon dipped his hand in the snow and pulled it out. It did not feel cold, and a thin, almost invisible film of clear crystals coated his hand.

"Hey, I've seen this stuff before. My dad showed me. It is called 'frozen smoke' or 'aerogel'. It is the lightest solid in the world and is a super heat insulator. It's like the stuff on the underside of the space shuttle. You can have a gas flame on one side of a big piece of aerogel and ice on the other side, and the ice won't melt for ages. I wonder why they want to insulate these bottles. Frozen smoke is a great shock insulator too."

Before Adam could react, Simon pulled a bottle out from the chest, dropped the lid of the chest closed, and then banged the bottle with a *thump* down on the top of the chest. Adam lurched over and firmly removed Simon's hand from the bottle. Simon did not notice his friend's face suddenly go pale.

"Simon, I think you have come very close to turning us and the surrounding building into a fine vapour. The stuff in that bottle is probably called methyl nitrate. Someone recently described it to me as the ugly sister of nitro glycerine.

It is shock sensitive, and half a litre is enough to bring down an airliner. You have four times that amount standing there."

Simon turned pale and moved back. "Why have they got it here?"

"I overheard that it is a by-product from their process to make the virus. I saw a bottle being filled in the laboratory."

"Can we use this as an explosive to fight the terrorists?"

"Maybe, but not yet. It might be worth borrowing a few bottles. There are some empty ones over there. If we fill them with water, we can swap out some with those in the chests. I saw loads of spare empty bottles in the basement. The more we move, the less they can sell to other terrorists."

"Where can we hide them, Adam?"

"I know a very good place, but it means I am going to have to go for a swim. I need to find some cord to tie the bottles together. We should move the bottles into the tunnel between the buildings. I saw some cord in the terrorists' accommodation block. We can work from there."

"What happens if we drop one of the bottles?"

"If that happens, I don't think you will ever have to worry about anything again."

After some work, the two boys nervously moved ten bottles of the liquid explosive away from the cooler chest and substituted them with bottles of plain water. They moved the stolen bottles into the tunnel and on to the terrorists' accommodation block. Adam went into the dining area and cut the cords from the venetian blinds. Tying the bottles in two groups of five, they carried them out to the gate by the jetty at the edge of the loch. It was dark, and the moonlight was not strong.

Adam stripped off his clothes and neck ring and handed them to Simon. "Look after these for me and watch out for the guards. I have to go for a swim. And Simon, close your mouth. You have seen me naked loads of times before in the showers. I just don't want to have to sleep in wet clothes tonight. If I'm not back in thirty minutes or so, make your way back to the other hostages. Don't wait for me any longer than that, and take my clothes with you if you have to go. I don't want the guards finding them."

Adam made two trips along the electric fence to the manhole to the stream carrying bottles. Removing the padlock, he eased the grille open. It made a rusty creaking noise, but there were no guards around to hear the noise. They had checked earlier. He gently lowered the bottles into the stream that gurgled below. He edged down the slanting pipe with them towards the loch. He used the knotted rope to control his descent. *I guess I will soon know if they are sensitive to the increased water pressure or not,* he thought to himself as the icy water enveloped him. He was working in total darkness and could only rely on his sense of touch.

This time, his exit from the pipe was much more dignified and controlled when compared with the previous time. Adam gently kicked to the surface and then swam the bottles to the safe place he had chosen. He tied them down securely and out of sight of any inquisitive eyes. By the time he struggled back up the knotted rope to the manhole, the cold of the water had thoroughly chilled his body. His teeth were chattering from the cold by the time he got back to Simon. "That is so cold it is almost painful."

"Adam, you have been outside the fence? You knew an escape route and you didn't tell us?"

"I told you about the route earlier. The neck rings are one obstacle, and the cold of the water might kill people from exposure. We are in the middle of wild Scottish mountains, Not everyone can swim properly, and you know we have to stay to deal with the virus. Anyway, I'm cold and tired. Let's talk about it in the morning."

Their work for the night now done, they returned to join the rest of the hostages. Adam rolled against Simon to try and steal some of his body heat after they lay down. They were exhausted and soon fell asleep until they were awakened by the sound of the terrorists removing the chain from the door to their room. The routine of the next day had started.

Chapter 37 Sally in Action

Adam asked Quartermaster Conrad to see if he could get hold of a mobile phone and charger from the sleeping quarters of the terrorists. As there was no mobile phone wireless signal in the locality, it was unlikely that anyone would notice that the phone had gone missing. He also asked Conrad if he could find some waterproof sandwich boxes. Adam asked Simon to show Conrad and his team the route to the other building. He then wandered over to see Sally.

Sally was sporting a large black eye, but otherwise, she had recovered from the effects of the pistol blow she had received from Alpha 3. Adam insisted that she take back from him the lead of the other hostages. Even Darren was starting to feel better and was more active.

"Sally, are you going to be fit enough today to attempt to make those explosives in the basement safe?"

She stretched out her arm. There was no shakiness to her hand. She bent and gave Darren a quick kiss on the cheek. "I'll be back in a while, love. Don't go away."

Sally and Adam crawled under the floor down to the basement so she could start dealing with the demolition blocks hanging from the ceiling. Adam already had a torch and a sharp knife available. Sally slipped off her sports shoes and looked at Adam. "I need to stand on your shoulders now. Lean against the wall over there, make a cup for my foot with your hands, and I will climb up your body. When I'm up there, don't wriggle."

Adam moved into position. He discovered that while Sally looked slim, her muscle-packed, lithe body was actually quite heavy. As she was the lady with the sharp knife, he didn't complain or make any rude comments. Sally climbed back down within a couple of seconds of climbing up.

"What's wrong, Sally? Can't you fix it?"

She pointed upwards with the torch. The detonating cord had been cut and was dangling down close to the wall. "Is that all it takes? I could have done that."

"Yes, Adam, but would you have known what to do?"

They moved through to the other rooms and performed a similar operation in each one.

"So is that it? Is it all safe now?"

"Yes, that is it—all fixed. I presume the main detonator is located somewhere on the first floor. That will fire as the terrorists have planned, but the explosion will only travel as far as the first basement room and then find no high explosive to set off. We might hear a bit of a *bang*, but that is all. No major explosion."

"Sally, as you have done so well on this, I have a little present for you."

Adam retrieved the bundle of newspaper containing the detonators and handed them over to the girl. Her eyes lit up when she saw them. "How in the hell did you manage to get these? I really can blow them up now. I'll get Conrad to find me some batteries and some electrical wire."

"Before you make too many plans, Sally, I need you to do some work for me. There are three important tasks. I need you to mine the cliffs along the track with enough explosives to bring them down and block the road. That device needs to have an accurate timer."

"If you can get me a mobile phone, I can do that now that I have the detonators. We have plenty of explosives hanging above us."

"I've already put in a request with Conrad for a mobile phone or two. With a bit of luck, we should have one by the middle of the day. I have a soldering iron available from one of my earlier raids."

"The next two are a bit more difficult. I need a small bomb that will be activated ready for explosion when it is immersed in water but does not explode until it is lifted out of the water. The third task, I have no idea how to do, but I need something I can carry that will destroy the contents of a security safe, but it can't be a blast bomb that could damage the surrounding stuff."

"Adam, in your explorations, did you notice if the garage has any vehicle spray painting equipment stored in there?"

"Yes. There was quite a bit of equipment and paints. I think they must be planning to paint their boats or maybe a lorry."

"Did you happen to note what colours there were?"

"No. It was pretty dark. Most paints look the same colour in the dark."

"Adam, I think we need a trip to that garage workshop tonight to have a closer look. I'll need one extra thing I think even you will find difficult to steal."

"Oh? What is that?"

"I will need some magnesium ribbon, about twenty cms. in length, or something similar that burns very hot."

"I will see what I can do."

"Give me a lift up. I need to get some of that explosive from up there."

She climbed up on his shoulders again and worked on the packs of demolition charges above them. "Here... catch this."

Sally dropped a block of high explosive into Adam's hands. He fumbled and just managed to catch it, which was difficult with Sally still standing on his shoulders. "Hey! Careful, Sally. I almost dropped that."

"Don't worry. It is about as dangerous as modelling clay until the detonator is added."

She jumped down from his shoulders holding several blocks of explosives. "That should be enough for what we need. So, you are finally going to make a move, Adam Cranford, and punish these kidnappers?"

"Yes. I have a plan, and it is moving forwards. We need to go out tonight and prepare the explosives to demolish the rocky outcrop that overhangs the track."

"If we can get a mobile phone, I can do that. How do we get out? I hope it is not using the stream. I could hear you shivering for ages last night."

"How did you know I'd been in the loch?"

"I could smell the seaweed. Let's go back and join the others. Can I tell them we will escape soon?"

"No, not yet."

"Adam, we have got all we need to escape. Why wait?"

"Sally, we have been through this before. Not yet. Just trust me. I have set an effective plan in motion that will get us all out safe and also deal with the key players in the terrorists."

Sally said nothing more, which surprised Adam. He had expected more of an argument.

They returned to rejoin the rest of the hostages, who were running fitness training exercises in their sleeping area. Their system of watchers on the roof had helped them understand when the guards went on patrol and which routes they used. The watchers also recorded the reaction when animals such as wild deer approached within 100 metres of the outer fence. When that happened, a couple of guards would hurry to the site where the animals had been and search the area. A post office van visited the site around ten a.m. each morning, and a van was seen arriving at the site in the afternoon, delivering food and other parcels. The guards always kept a careful watch on the vehicles to prevent a repeat of what had happened with the rubbish collection lorry. The spirits of the watching team had been raised when they saw a police van arrive in the site, but those hopes were dashed when they saw one of the guards have a friendly conversation with the policeman driving the vehicle.

By midday, Conrad's scavengers had found a mobile phone and charger and some waterproof sandwich boxes. Sally immediately set to work, and just before the evening meal, she summoned Adam to the basement room where she had been working. She pointed to two sandwich boxes on the floor. "There you are... one timer bomb and one water-triggered bomb. Neither is particularly powerful— probably enough power to blow off a door—but they can be used to detonate larger loads of explosives."

"Sally, you are fantastic. If Darren wasn't just upstairs, I could kiss you. These are an important part of my plan. Can I set the time on the mobile phone now?"

"Yes, but for safety, I won't actually connect it to the detonator until we actually set the explosives on the rocky outcrop by the track. All you have to do is to set a calendar event on the mobile phone organiser. When the event alarm sounds, there will be a big *bang*. If you know what time to set, does that mean you know when things are going to happen?"

"Yes. It will be about five days from now, but please do not tell anyone else in case we are raising their hopes falsely." Adam programmed the date and time into the mobile phone and showed it to Sally.

"Let's go and get some food."

§

That evening, Adam set Simon to the task of swapping the remaining bottles of methyl nitrate with water-filled ones. The original bottles filled with liquid explosives were to be moved by Simon into the tunnel between the buildings. Sally and Adam decided investigating the garage workshop would be their first task of the night. Once the watchers on the roof had signalled that the way was clear, the two teenagers carefully made their way into the garage. The old blankets that had been previously used to shield the windows were still there. Adam put them back in place to cover the windows so their torchlight would not be spotted from outside. He kept guard while Sally rummaged through the paint equipment and supplies.

"Yes! They have got some. This is just what we need." Sally held up a couple of metal cans. Using a screwdriver, she pried off the lid of the cans and looked inside. She looked up with a smile and dipped her hand in one of the cans. As she lifted her hand out, a trickle of fine silver-grey powder fell back into the can. She opened the other can to reveal a soft, fine, dark red powder. "These are paint pigments. I wondered if they might have some lying around. If I mix them in the correct proportions, they will make a thermite compound. Once ignited, it will burn fiercely enough to melt through steel. If you put a can full of that compound on top of your safe, it will burn through and drip hot molten iron inside like lava from a volcano."

"Isn't that rather dangerous, Sally?"

"No. It is very stable until it is ignited with something like magnesium ribbon. We might be able to do it with a blow torch, but the magnesium would be much more effective. They use this stuff for welding railway lines together. Finding some magnesium is your job. Right, Adam?"

"Ok, yeah, I think I can sort that out in the morning. Let's take these cans back to the tunnel, and then we can do our real work for the night."

They returned to the accommodation block and temporarily stored the cans of paint pigment in the basement. While they were there, Adam opened the crate containing the spare uniforms and pulled a couple out. "I'm going to throw these over the gate by the jetty. I really don't fancy walking around the Scottish countryside at night almost naked after swimming in the loch. Let's go, Sally."

When they reached the gate by the pathway to the jetty, Adam threw the uniforms over the top of the electrified wire gate. After reminding Sally to keep at least twenty cms. from the electrified fence, he ran to the manhole gate over the stream. Adam beckoned to Sally to join him. He opened the manhole gate and then stripped off his hostage boiler suit before climbing down into the manhole. He found a dry place to wedge his clothes. He also unhooked his neck ring and hung it from one of the metal rungs in the manhole. Picking up the water-activated bomb and a bag containing blocks of explosives, he issued some instructions to Sally. "Wait here until you see me pick up the spare clothes on the other side of the gate. Then come and join me. Don't forget your timer bomb. Climb down the pipe using the knotted rope, but when the pressure from the stream gets too much, let go of the rope. Don't forget to close the metal grille of the manhole cover before you leave."

Adam crept down into the pipe and let the flow of the icy stream water take him out into the loch. He surfaced for air and then dived under the water again and fixed the water-activated detonator bomb next to his store of bottles of methyl nitrate. It would be safe until somebody tried to lift the bottles from the water. He surfaced and then swam to the shore to collect the uniforms that were lying outside of the gate. He waved to Sally, who then disappeared from sight before joining him about a minute later.

They both appreciated the warmth of the dry clothing before they picked up the bag of explosives and set off to find the track and the rocky outcrop.

"I can see what you mean, Adam. That is not a good escape route for the rest of the hostages. I didn't realise just how cold it would be. Even if we got people out through that route, you would then have the problem of getting them somewhere warm fairly quickly."

"I know, Sally. I have been often tempted, but it also leaves the problems of dealing with these neck tracker rings. I was able to get mine disarmed, but every other neck ring is still active. If your tracker ring starts beeping tonight, you will have to turn back."

They scrambled along the shore until they were out of sight of the main gatehouse. Joining the track, they walked along until the rocky outcrop was in sight. They were just 100 metres from the outcrop when Sally's neck ring started to emit a beeping sound.

"Quick, Sally, let's run back fifty metres along the track."

They both ran back, and beeping sound from her neck ring ceased.

"I am going to have to do this alone. Can you give me quick instruction as to how I should place the explosives? It might be an idea if you connected up the mobile phone to the detonator while we are here."

Sally gave Adam some basic instruction on how to lay the demolition charges. She made him practice it three times at the trackside before she was satisfied. She then connected the detonator to the mobile phone and repacked the waterproof sandwich box. "Here you are, Adam. It's all yours. Let us just hope you do not get a mobile phone signal while you are working on the outcrop. If you do, there are probably messages waiting for this phone, and you might find that rather exciting."

Sally waited while Adam went to the rocky outcrop. He spent some time looking in the dim moonlight for the features in the rocks that Sally had suggested. Eventually, he was satisfied and carefully packed demolition blocks and the sandwich box in a deep crevice behind some rocks at the top of the outcrop. He hurried back to Sally, and they made their way back to the jetty. Adam hid the stolen uniforms in a dry place under the jetty and then swam underwater back to the pipe entrance. They surfaced briefly to refill their lungs with air and then dived again. Sally was first to climb back into the pipe; Adam followed shortly afterwards. By the time Adam reached the manhole, Sally had lifted the grille and had already dressed.

"I feel so cold. Adam, I hope I never have to do that again."

"If everything goes to plan, that should be the last time you have to do that."

On their way back, Sally and Adam called in at the basement of the terrorists' accommodation block where Sally mixed the paint pigment powders in the correct proportions. "All you need to do is to take a pile of this mixture, put it into some kind of container, and stand it on top of the safe. A couple of kilograms should be enough, even for a fire safe. Put a strip of magnesium in the top and light it and then stand well back. It will create loads of smoke, but it will not explode."

Adam was freezing cold from swimming in the loch but was soon dozing off to sleep on his return to the hostages' room and hardly noticed when Simon returned from his tasks for the night. "Goodnight, Adam. It seems like I had the longer task this time. I'll speak to you in the morning."

In the morning, the noise of the rattling chain did not wake Adam. He was in deep sleep. One of the other boys shook him awake before the guard came to investigate. He didn't really wake up until the hot water from the showers hit his face. Simon was at the showerhead next to him and was grinning as Adam finally surfaced from sleep.

"You look absolutely shattered, Adam. I got all the bottles swapped out like you asked. They are in the pipe duct just after the junction on the way to the secret building. I also managed to get you a bag full of that frozen smoke you asked me for. It is amazingly light, and I have no clue what you intend using it for."

"That is brilliant, Simon. We have now got most things done that we needed to do before the escape. It will be a couple of days yet. I hope I can get some more sleep today. I have a couple of things to do tonight, but they shouldn't take too long."

After changing into clean orange boiler suits, the two boys joined the others for breakfast. As Deepa came in to the canteen, she smiled at Adam and gave a thumbs-up sign. The breakfast was monotonously the same as previous days, but Adam was pleased to note he was not selected by the guards to help perform the tidying-up chores. There were some advantages to being suspected by Alpha 3.

When all of the hostages had returned to their room. Adam went to see Deepa. "You look happy. What's up?"

"I have made a lot of progress on the computer hacking. I can now control the electric fence, the Smart Rocks, and the radar. I also have control of something in the sea entrance to the loch. I'm not quite sure what they are, but judging by the map representation, they are spread about thirty meters apart."

"I think those are sea mines they have positioned in the entrance channel to the loch. What type of control do you have over them?"

"I was watching the network traffic yesterday, and my sniffer saw some passwords for applications on the network. It took a bit of fiddling to work out which ones were involved, but I think I have sorted out the access control problems and the right protocol."

"Deepa, I am a techno-moron. Just tell me what control you have over the sea mines."

"That is what I was trying to tell you, Adam. I can turn them on or off, but I also have admin control, so I can stop other people from controlling the sea mines."

"That might be useful. What have you managed to do with the Smart Rocks?"

"For a techno-moron, you are actually quite clever. I was trying to set it up so there would be a corridor that would enable undetected approach, but that would have been obvious to the terrorists if they logged into that system. The solution was to get certain Smart Rocks to lie to the other rocks when they detect movement in their area. That way around there is nothing obvious to the terrorist operators, as the hack only shows up when somebody actually approaches the Smart Rocks. They tested their radar in the afternoon, and I was able to capture a movie of the radar image. I can play that back anytime you want. That would prevent the terrorists detecting anything on the radar during playback. I have one question though. Do you want the radar fix running when we might be using this laptop for something else? The laptop is not powerful enough to handle both things at the same time."

"Yes, that could be the case. However, I do know where there is another PC that runs all the time. It is probably connected to the network as well. I can get access to that PC tomorrow, but I won't be able to bring it here."

"That is no problem, Adam. All you need to do is just browse a webpage from the PC, and I will take over the PC remotely. I'll give you the link. Sally tells me you went rock climbing last night?"

"Yes, I did. Did she tell you why?"

"She dodged that question, so I didn't push the issue. That must mean you have a way out of the site? If that is the case, I need you to pop out tonight and test that the Smart Rocks hack I have done works properly."

Adam groaned. "I was hoping to get some rest tonight. It seems like there is no rest for the wicked. If you tell me what you need, I will go out and check out those rocks for you."

"Oh, it is quite simple. I just need you to walk towards the corridor you wanted out there and see if the terrorists shoot you or not. If they do shoot you, we will know my programming has been bad."

"Deepa, sometimes you really know how to test a guy's faith in your geekiness. If you don't mind being awake at midnight, I will perform the test for you."

The rest of the day was relatively peaceful for the hostages. Adam managed to catch up with his sleep and was feeling fully refreshed by the time of the evening meal.

Chapter 38 Hope at Last

The room was filled to capacity with tables and chairs. Some people had to stand at the back of the room. A tall, grey-haired gentleman was speaking calmly to the anxious people. "Ladies and gentlemen, thank you for attending this meeting this evening at such short notice. All of you will have already been visited by one of our representatives. May I remind you of the promise of secrecy document you have all signed? As you are now aware, our organisation provides specialist insurance for kidnapping and ransom demands. Our team is specially trained in negotiating with kidnappers and hostage takers.

"We have come to offer you a solution. The kidnappers will be paid their demanded ransom in full, and your children will be released. We charge a small fee as a percentage of the total ransom to recover our costs. In the unlikely and unhappy event that any of your children are injured or are not returned within a month, the insurance policy will pay you twice the amount of the ransom as compensation. This means that none of you will have to put your homes up for sale to rescue your children."

One of the parents gathered in the hotel ballroom spoke up. "You people are just parasites trying to take advantage of our terrible situation. The police will recover our children, and we do not need to pay your fees."

"On the contrary, we would be delighted if the police succeed in recovering your children safe and well. In that event, we would be happy to refund in full any fees you have paid to us provided we have not already paid the ransom for the release. I must warn you that in our conversations with the police, it is very clear they do not have the slightest idea where your children are being held. They do not know who is behind this kidnapping. We have received an anonymous phone call which we believe confirms that all of your children are healthy and well. There was sufficient information in that call to confirm that the caller has been in contact with the children. We have, of course, given full details of the call to the national police force who are handling this case."

The parent who had spoken before replied. "So you are sure that is it then—no ifs, ands, or buts? There must be some conditions, some fine print, that you would need to apply. How on earth does your organisation make any money out of these situations?"

"We are a very good at recovering ransom payments from the kidnappers after the hostages have been released. We will then make our money on the fee you have paid. We even offer a loan facility to those parents who cannot immediately pay a fee. The only condition to which you must all agree is that you appoint us as the sole negotiator with the kidnappers. We will give you forty-eight hours from now to make up your minds. We strongly suggest you take a copy of our terms and conditions and have your solicitors check the details. Now, are there other any more questions?"

The meeting finished about ten minutes later. By that time, all the parents had decided in their hearts that they would accept this offer. There seemed to be nothing to lose, and it greatly improved the chances of their children being returned home. Gordon and Amanda Cranford had recognised Mr. Robertson, who had been standing and speaking at the front of the room. They did not tell anybody else about his connection with the Foundation. They knew that if he was involved, this was indeed a genuine offer. For the first time in several days, their hearts felt a little lighter with the realisation that they were likely to see their son again.

As they left the room, they passed other parents who were gathered around Detective Inspector Norris, demanding to know whether police had made any real progress. He had been invited to the meeting to ensure that the police were aware of what had been said to the parents about the new ransom payment arrangements. The police had agreed to the parents meeting when they had been told they would be allowed to place hidden tracking devices in the bag containing the payment. The police would also be allowed to monitor the handover. The payment would be in untraceable bearer bonds that could be exchanged in secrecy for money at many banks around the world. Intelligence Services were planning the mounting of a major surveillance operation to track the money. That amount of money in cash would have weighed one and a half tons; the bearer bonds, on the other hand, were just a few sheets of paper.

§

In a secure basement garage of the City of London building some thirty miles from the parents' meeting, preparations were taking place to load twenty-three wooden crates into the back of a large white van. The total payload was about two tons. There were no outward signs that this van had been equipped with an upgraded police pursuit V6 supercharged engine and a specially enhanced suspension system. This vehicle and its contents would be well guarded until it began its journey early the following morning. The final destination of the van was still not known, but it would be telephoned to the driver during his trip up to Scotland.

§

While the van was being prepared in London, two squads of Foundation cadets were made busy unloading camping gear from a lorry in Scotland. Their campsite was a few miles away from the nearest village at the foot of a small mountain. The cadets had no idea of the purpose of the camp but had been provided instructions and only short notice of the event. They had been instructed to provide sleeping accommodation for fifty people, including a camp kitchen, shower facilities, and latrines. This was not an unusual request, as the Foundation cadets often planned, trained, and practiced providing disaster relief support. What they did find unusual was having to prepare a temporary helicopter landing pad and also a hard standing area for a 19,000-litre tanker lorry. Those cadets did not know they would also be working hard during the following day and night as well.

322

Chapter 39 Final Stages

Adam psyched himself up for another midnight swim in the loch. He hated the painful coldness of the water, but he knew he was the one who had to take that trip. Deepa and he had already discussed what should be done to test the Smart Rocks. She would be waiting and ready to watch the computer system to confirm that her hacking had created a safe corridor through the Smart Rocks and the radar system deployed by the terrorists.

As Adam crawled through the now-familiar tunnel to the other building, he carried a bag containing the frozen smoke Simon had obtained for him earlier. Making a small diversion, Adam retrieved a bottle of methyl nitrate from those his friend had hidden in the tunnel. Adam had decided to be alone for this trip. He winced as he sat in the cold stream water before sliding down the pipe into the depths of the loch. As he swam, he trailed the bottle of liquid explosives behind him using a piece of cord. He did not want the bottle bumping as he climbed up a mooring rope into the workboat moored next to the jetty.

Like a pale grey ghost, he slithered over the gunwale of the workboat. Pausing briefly to check that nobody was watching him, he found the cabin door of the boat. This time, he had brought his lock picks with him secured in a small bag tied around his neck. A few seconds later, he had overcome the cabin door lock. Returning briefly to the gunwale, he pulled on the cord that tracked down to the water and retrieved the bottle of methyl nitrate. He disappeared inside the boat for several minutes. Once again, he was thankful for the training he had received from Ali in working in total darkness. Making sure the cabin door was locked properly, he swam to the jetty and found the uniform he had hidden previously. Pulling this on to cover his pale body and also to retain some body heat, he set off to find the position of the Smart Rock corridor outside of the fence he had planned with Deepa.

This part of the midnight activities made Adam feel particularly nervous. He had no way of knowing whether Deepa had been successful. If she had failed in any way, Adam knew he could expect a beating at the hands of the guards, and worse still, it would mean his escape plans could be compromised. It was lonely and cold work. The moonlight was poor that night, and the ground where Adam was crawling was particularly rough. It had bracken and many hidden plants that tore at his skin. As he approached the outer fence, he saw two guards inside the inner fence walking towards him. He froze, scarcely daring to breathe for three minutes until they walked past him, casually chatting with each other. Adam reversed his path and crawled away from the fence. He sat and watched for ten minutes before deciding no alert had been raised. He steeled himself the icy swim in the loch, but fifteen minutes later, he was back under his blanket in the room with the rest of the hostages. It took him some time to get to sleep because there were so many things he was thinking of and worrying about. When the morning finally arrived, it took Simon to shake him before he woke up.

At breakfast, Deepa made a thumbs-up sign to Adam. He took that to mean the previous night's test had been successful. He smiled back and returned to chatting with Simon.

"So, what was Deepa looking so happy about just then? You two seem to be spending a lot of time together now. You didn't take me with you last night. I know you were in the loch because I could smell the sea water."

"It's not what you think. I've got Deepa doing some important work for the rescue. Me going out last night was just part of that work. She's a nice girl, but I won't be dating her or anything like that."

"Just remember I'm around too. I hate sitting around doing nothing when I could be helping. The others keep asking me questions about what's happening because I'm around you, but you don't seem to tell me everything."

"Don't be daft, Simo. In fact, you know the real secret of this place. None of the others know that—not even Sally or Deepa. Since I told you that, you have got to realise I really trust you. I'll try and find out later today what has happened to your father, but I need some rest today because I have another long night ahead of me."

§

The hostages' breakfast was interrupted by Alpha 3 entering the canteen and standing in front of them all. A silence spread across the room as the children stopped eating and talking. "Attention, everyone," he said. "I have some good news for you all. Your parents have agreed to pay the ransoms demanded for all of you. Apparently, you are collectively worth your weight in gold. You should all be going home safely in a few days from now. That is all."

He turned and left the room. The noise of chatter immediately filled the canteen as the children excitedly looked forward to getting home with their own families.

§

While the hostages finished their breakfast, a mile further north, a sixteen-year-old girl and a wiry old man were unloading a pair of quad bike ATVs and a cross-country motorbike from a trailer that had been towed from South Wales behind a Land Rover. They had already pitched camp and prepared camouflage netting to obscure their campsite from any inquisitive strangers.

§

Across the other side of Scotland, two men with military-style haircuts were driving along the Scottish coast in a dark blue Volvo estate. They had fishing equipment in the back of their car, but their destination was a helicopter support base where aviation engineers were making final checks on a Sea King helicopter.

§

Off the west coast of Cornwall, a medium-sized freighter had made an unscheduled change in course when her captain had received instructions from a country on the other side of the world. He was planning a new course to anchor the ship off the western coast of Scotland. In the London Mercantile Exchange, new computer records were set up to prove that the freighter now had business in Norway in a few days' time.

§

As the hostages were being returned to their room after breakfast, a phone call was made from a central London office. The call was to a Swiss-owned investment bank to order £25 million pounds of bearer bonds. They were to be delivered to an address in Lombard Street in the City of London by security courier the following morning. Police and Security Services were setting up a network of video surveillance of the area, ready for the planned delivery of the ransom money. A special briefcase equipped with a tiny, sophisticated, hidden and undetectable location transmitter had already been delivered to the Lombard Street address.

§

Adam knew the kidnappers would be busy planning the details of the escape now that the ransom had been agreed. He knew he had to update the information he had gathered so far. Shortly after his return from breakfast, Adam was wriggling through the air-conditioning duct above the first floor of the office building. For the first hour of waiting in the cramped metal pipe by the vent above the terrorists' office, Adam heard nothing new. Then, he heard the office door creak open.

"Their insistence on paying only in gold bars is an inconvenience, but that is all," said Alpha 3. "I have a deadline I must meet, so I have accepted payment in gold. One of the advantages of gold payment is that it is completely untraceable. Our backers have temporarily deposited £5 million in our bank account so we can pay off any operational expenses. The gold will be delivered to a remote site in the north of England. You and two of your men will be taking a truck tomorrow morning to pick up the gold bullion. Apparently, it will be packed into conveniently sized crates so that it will be easy to load the gold into the truck."

"So what is to stop us from cheating and driving off with the gold and leaving you here?"

"You have worked with me long enough now to realise that playing that type of trick would not be very good for the health of you or your family. The parents have employed a specialist negotiator, and I'm sure they will not play any tricks during the delivery of the ransom. He may be a tough negotiator, but I get the feeling he wants the whole process completed without any problems. The following day, we will evacuate from this site with the gold in the truck and leave the children here in the basement of the building. We will drive down the coast to a small port where we will be picked up by a freighter."

"What about the boat and the mini submarine?"

"Oh, I have other plans for those. You do not need to worry about them. They will be leaving late at night tomorrow. This whole thing has gone a lot smoother than I expected. In a few days, we will all be very rich, and the kids will be back at their homes. If you can leave me now, I have some work I need to do in private."

Adam heard the office door open and then close. He then heard Alpha 3 speaking on the telephone. "Doctor Gwon, this is Alpha 3. Can you give me an update on how the virus production is coming along?"

Adam could not hear what was being said on the telephone by Doctor Gwon.

"I'm sorry Doctor Gwon, but we need to move the vats containing the virus by tomorrow night, midnight at the latest. Can you achieve that? They will be travelling as we agreed on the workboat."

"Ok. It is agreed we will expose the children to the virus just before we leave. You do not have to worry about tidying the laboratory. I will make sure there are no traces of evidence. I will speak to you again later this afternoon."

Alpha 3 replaced the telephone receiver and left the room. Adam decided he had heard enough, so he wriggled back along the air duct and returned to the room holding the rest of the hostages. On his return, he found Sally listening to her watcher team, who had just returned from the roof of the building.

"Yes, Sally, there is a definite change in the pattern of activity. A new lorry we have not seen before has turned up and is parked beside the garage. We think they are getting ready to leave. What do you think? Will we be free tomorrow?"

"I will just ask the master spy standing behind you. Adam, what do you reckon?"

"I think it will probably be tomorrow or the day after, but I think we should continue with the rota of watchers."

"Tina, Helen, thank you for your report. Can you leave Adam and me alone for a while please? There are a couple of progress issues I want to discuss with him in private." After the girls departed, Sally looked at Adam. "Adam, I know what you think, but we cannot let Alpha 3 get away unpunished for what he had his men do to Darren."

"Trust me, Sally, Alpha 3 will be caught, and we will let the police deal with him. I have plans to ensure they do not get away with the ransom money. You just have to be a little patient."

"Adam, I don't know why they made you a Captain in the Foundation. I can tell you are going to do nothing. You are just going to let them get away. You are a total wimp. Well, if you are not prepared to take some action, I am. I will make sure they get punished."

"Sally, don't do anything stupid. These are ruthless people, and there is a lot at stake here. I don't want to have to stop you as well. I can't allow you to do something that might put everyone at risk."

"What do you mean, stop me *as well?* Who else have you stopped? Did that include Darren's escape attempt?" Sally noticed Adam's expression harden, and his eyes seemed to turn a slate grey colour. There was a cold-hearted look she had never seen before in his eyes.

"I just mean I'll do whatever is necessary to make sure my plans work. I won't let people get in my way."

She gasped at that and glared hard at Adam before turning on her heel and storming away towards Darren and Deepa.

There was not much for Adam to do during the day so he tried to get as much sleep as possible. Even though most of the children were cheerful at the prospect of release, they noticed the stormy tension between Sally and Adam.

For Adam, the day was one of waiting for the long hours to slowly pass by. He was feeling nervous about the activities he'd planned for the night. With the news of their planned release, the structure of the hostage teams fell apart, and people just sat around waiting. Eventually, the time for the evening meal came around. Adam moved to sit at the same table as Sally and Darren, but she made it obvious she would prefer he sat somewhere else. Adam shrugged his shoulders at Simon, and they found another table.

"What is up with Sally? She seems positively hostile toward you."

"She wants to punish the kidnappers for what they did to Darren, but I told her she shouldn't."

"She must be a bit crazy. Doesn't she remember what happened to her last time she tried something like that? Are you going out into the loch again tonight?"

"Yes. I will be gone for quite some time, so don't get worried. I will be back before breakfast tomorrow."

"I guess since you haven't asked me to help you already, there isn't much point in asking if you want me to come along tonight."

"It is good of you to offer again, but you would be outside of the safe range for your neck tracker ring. I am just going to meet some people who will help us to escape, but I will need your help tomorrow during the day."

"I don't know how you do it each time, Adam. How can you bear to come back into the site each time you manage to escape?"

"I guess I would just miss your ugly face if I didn't come back."

§

Adam waited until seven thirty p.m. before leaving the hostage room that evening. He left his neck ring with Simon. It was just beginning to get dark when he flitted across the yard of the site to reach the stream manhole. He didn't relish the cold trip in the stream water down to the loch, but he knew he couldn't delay any further. Emerging cold and dripping from the loch, he ran along the rocky beach for about twenty minutes before he reached his objective. He stubbed his toes a couple of times along the route and fell a couple of times.

Stella was waiting on the seat of a quad bike. A second quad bike stood nearby. She gave Adam some dry clothes and shoes, but most welcome of all, a mug of hot coffee from a vacuum flask. She looked at her watch.

"Where is old Ben, Stella?"

"Oh, he is up in the hills installing a few toys. He will be there before us. I'm sorry, Adam, but we had best get going. Put your helmet and gloves on. We can turn the headlights on soon."

She started the engine of the quad and waited for Adam to do the same. She had researched and practiced the route earlier in the day. At times, their speed exceeded thirty MPH across the hillside. After some initial nervousness, Adam was beginning to enjoy the ride. It was a long, circuitous route that made sure no motor noise from the quad bikes reached the guards back at the hostage site. Adam was pleased to see the Foundation campsite after about thirty minutes of hard riding following the tail light of Stella's machine.

One of the cadets emerged from the darkness as Adam and Stella parked their quad bikes. "Can I help you?"

"Is your Officer present? Can you take me to him?"

"Sure. Follow me."

The cadet led them to a tent. The interior layout was typical of the Foundation command tents Adam had seen before. A man wearing the uniform of a Foundation Lieutenant rose to meet them. As they shook hands, the Lieutenant noticed the red star flash on Adam's ring. He stepped back in amazement and then saluted. "I'm sorry, Captain. They didn't tell me you would be here. You must be—"

"No names for the moment, Lieutenant, if you please," said Adam, giving a slight nod towards the cadet.

"I am afraid I can't stay long. I need to spend ten to fifteen minutes briefing you. Has the helicopter arrived?"

"Yes, sir. The Flight Lieutenant arrived a couple of hours ago. Their Sea King is refuelled and ready to go. There is also a large white van with a load of crates waiting for you as well."

"Good. Has old Ben Bryson turned up as well?"

"A little less of the 'old' if you don't mind." Adam whirled around to find Ben standing behind him. He hadn't heard the old man approach. Ben was smiling. They shook hands. The sharp eyes of the old man noticed Adam's ring showing a red glowing star.

Adam spoke the cadet who was still hovering in the background. "Cadet, would you mind fetching the helicopter pilot? Ask him to join us here."

The eighteen-year-old cadet was a bit amazed that a boy in his early teens had wandered into the camp from the night and taken command. He saluted. "Er... yes, sir, right away."

Adam immediately reached for a map of the area that was resting on the top of the Officer's desk and started briefing the Lieutenant on the location of the hostage site and the defences.

"You are one of the hostages? I won't ask how you got out, but why not just get the police here?"

"I know for a fact that the local police are infiltrated and they might warn the kidnappers. If those kidnappers knew a rescue was underway, the lives of the other twenty-eight children would be at risk. This whole affair is much more serious than a simple kidnapping. Your squad's work here over the next couple of days is an important part of the rescue."

Ben immediately caught on the figure of twenty-eight other hostages. "Twenty-eight children?"

Adam frowned. "These kidnappers are ruthless. I think the whole affair is backed by some foreign government. We lost one of the boys soon after we arrived." Adam continued the briefing, telling those present what needed to be done and the timings that were essential. He did not explain Ben's and Stella's part in the planned activities. They already knew that information. He was just finished briefing when Flight Lieutenant Hewitt arrived in the tent.

"Good evening, young man, or should I say boss?"

Adam grinned. "Can we load the trail bike in the heli and get on the move? Stella and Ben here would not mind helping to load the bike and fastening it down. I get the feeling Ben may have done that before."

"Sure thing, boss. Give me five minutes, and we will be ready to lift off."

As they left, Adam turned to the Foundation Lieutenant. "Did you get a package and a mobile phone for me from Headquarters in London?"

"Oh, yes. Sorry, I'd forgotten them. They came up in the white van. I don't suppose you want to tell me what is in those crates?"

He found the package and mobile phone for Adam. The boy checked that they were alone before speaking. "As your guys are guarding it tonight, I might as well tell you. They contain £25 million pounds' worth of gold bars. We are giving them to the terrorists tomorrow to pay the ransom."

"Terrorists?"

"Like I said, this is a lot more serious than a simple kidnapping. Secrecy is essential. Just make sure your cadets take care and stick exactly to the route I've shown you. I had best get going. I have a helicopter waiting for me. I'll be back around five a.m. tomorrow morning."

"Before you go, sir, the Sergeant Quartermaster sent you this as well. His note said he thought you might find it useful where you are going."

The Lieutenant saluted Adam and passed him a metre-long black plastic tube with a shoulder strap. The tube was about ten cms. in diameter. Adam returned the salute as he turned to leave.

"Have a good flight, sir, and good luck."

Terry Hewitt, the helicopter pilot, had thoughtfully provided some warm clothing and travel sickness pills for the ninety-minute flight. Adam opened his package shortly after takeoff and studied the plans contained in it. It was too noisy in the cabin for Stella and Adam to hold much of a conversation. Ben was already relaxed and reading a book by the time the aircraft took off. During the trip, Adam opened the plastic tube and studied the contents. Among the contents was a full lock-picking set in a canvas wrapper. The other item was a puzzle to Adam until he read the instructions contained in the tube.

The engine note changed tune when Terry realised they were close to their destination and reduced their air speed. One of Terry's colleagues had crudely lit a landing area in a large, flat field at their destination. He stood in the field and lit a green flare to help the pilot judge the wind direction. Terry landed the large aircraft on the field. Once he was satisfied it was not going to sink into the ground, he cut the engines.

The pilot and navigator helped Ben unload the cross-country trail bike. It was configured to carry two people. Ben mounted the bike.

"Ben, these are the coordinates where we need to go. It should only take about twenty minutes."

Stella helped to program the GPS system mounted on the bike handlebars. Ben revved the motor. "Ok, Adam, hold on."

The journey only took fifteen minutes at the hands of the older man. Adam thought it was one of the scariest forms of transport ever invented. They had stopped 100 metres from Adam's destination. Out in the countryside away from streetlights, it was quite dark, but to Adam, this was not a barrier. The plans had told him that the boundary wall alarm system had infrared intrusion detector beams along the top; the main gate was alarmed with motion sensors. Adam left Ben with the motorcycle and walked closer to the building, carrying the tube. He chose what he thought was the best place on the wall to climb its two-metre height. He opened the tube and pulled out the contents and started adjusting the device to the correct shape.

A firm hand descended on his shoulder, and Adam jumped. "Those infrared beam benders can be a bit difficult to adjust correctly." Once again, Ben had crept up on him without Adam hearing his approach. Ben took the beam bender from Adam and fiddled with the adjustments. "I saw it when you opened the tube in the helicopter. If you were given one of these, you must have some seriously good friends. Kneel down on all fours so I can stand on you to reach the top of the wall. I'm not that heavy."

Adam knelt, and Ben stepped up on him with the delicacy of an expert rock climber. Adam thought he must weigh less than Sally. Ben fiddled with the equipment for a while and then delicately jumped down. "Adam, that is one clever device. It adjusts itself automatically. It bends the infrared beams in a U shape, and you can now climb over the top of the wall without triggering the alarm. Are you going to come back this way?"

"No. I'll come out through the main gate."

"Ok. When you have gone in, I will remove the beam bender. No point in leaving evidence lying around."

Ben helped Adam climb feet first over the wall through the U shape of the beam bender. Once inside the garden, he made his way to the building. He knew all of the ground-floor doors and windows were alarmed at night. In addition, there were motion sensors active in every ground-floor room. He looked around the building and found an aluminium ladder at the back of a garage. It was chained and padlocked to the wall. The padlock did not resist Adam's full lock-picking kit for long. He'd brought his homemade picks along with him, but the proper lock-smith picks made the work a lot easier. With the lock and chain out of the way, Adam removed a section of the ladder and went to the back of the house where he'd seen an open bedroom window. From his recollection of the floor plan of the house, it was the room where an on-site Security Services officer slept. Carefully opening the window and removing a shaving mirror, he still climbed in past the sleeping guard and made his way to the room he wanted.

Chapter 40 The Shell Game

Adam woke the man by sitting on the end of the end and gently shaking a foot that was poking out from under the bedding.

"I'm sorry to wake you, sir. Please do not panic or raise the alarm. You are under no threat at all."

The man sat up in bed abruptly. "Who are you? What are you doing in my bedroom?"

"If you care to switch on your bedside light, sir, you will be able to see me better. I've had to break in here because I don't know who to trust in the police on a matter of national importance."

The bedside light flared on, causing both the people in the room to blink at its brightness. Adam immediately recognised the senior politician he had seen in newspapers and on television news programmes. "Do you need your dressing gown, sir?"

"No. What I do need to know is why this young man is sitting in my bedroom late at night and who you are. Is my security guard unharmed?"

"He is ok. Call him if you wish, but I would prefer that you hear my story first. I am Adam Cranford. I am one of the thirty school children who were kidnapped that everyone is looking for."

"You've escaped? As much as I'm pleased to see you, why not go to the police instead of breaking into my house and waking me up?"

Adam quickly told him the story of the kidnapping and the discovery that the terrorists were manufacturing a virus that could cause a global catastrophe for the human race.

"So why have you come to me?"

"Even though the ransom will be paid, I don't think they will let us go without first infecting us with the virus. I think the only way to handle this is to send in the Special Armed Forces and take them by surprise." He mentioned the neck rings that prevented the hostages from leaving the site.

"Won't they know something is wrong when they find you missing?"

"No. I have some rich friends who will get me back before seven a.m. I have written the location of the site on here and the best time to mount the attack." Adam passed the man a piece of paper containing the details.

"How did you find out all this information?"

Adam described how he had climbed through the air ducts and listened to the conversation of the terrorists.

"Young man, I'm now going to wake my security officer. You need have no worries. I just want him to check your identity. If you are who you say you are, your information will be very useful in rescuing your friends and dealing with this virus problem."

The Government Minister picked up a telephone and roused his security officer from his bed.

"Please come through to my room. There is a matter that needs your attention in here. No, you do not need to be armed."

The security man soon entered the room dressed in a hastily pulled-on jacket and a pair of jeans.

"Jackson, this young man says he is one of the thirty hostages. He says his name is Adam Cranford. Can you please check that quickly? Do not tell any of your police colleagues for the time being."

The man disappeared and returned a couple minutes later. "Yes, sir, his face matches the photos."

"In that case, we appear to have a national hero standing in front of us. Please place him under arrest and lock him in the secure room downstairs. I have some urgent phone calls to make."

Adam felt the strong hand of the protection officer clamp down on his shoulder. "No! You don't understand! I have to go back tonight or the others will suffer!"

"Come along quietly now, lad. You will be safe here, but I'm afraid you are under arrest."

Adam shrugged his shoulders and let the guard lead him away. He offered no resistance as the man led him downstairs after turning off the ground-floor alarm system.

"That's good," said the guard. "I'm glad I'm not having to put you in these handcuffs."

Adam was led to a small room in the basement of the building. The guard fumbled with the lock, and Adam suddenly wriggled away and started to run. The guard chased after him. Just when he thought he'd caught the young teen, he suddenly found himself flying through the air and landing hard on his back. Before he could recover from the fall, Adam had handcuffed the guard's hands behind his back and stuffed a wedge of cloth in his mouth as a gag.

Adam took out his mobile phone and crept back up the stairs to the bedroom of the man he had come to visit. The teen did not enter but listened at the doorway. The Minister was on the phone to someone.

"Yes. I think he is genuine... No, I have had him arrested. If this is as serious as you guys think it is, we can't have him wandering around spreading the story... Yes, I agree we need to send a task force in to deal with these people. I think his intelligence is probably quite accurate, but you will be able to question him further. I know it will be terribly sad, but we cannot afford for this virus to escape. If we cannot rescue the children safely, we may have to activate Project BLEACH and destroy all life at that site. From what you tell me, it is very remote. We could issue the usual press denials about how there was an accident during the rescue attempt. Nobody needs to know what really happened... Yes, you had best send some people over to collect him."

At that point in the conversation, Adam crept away from the house and out through the front gate to meet up with Ben.

"How did it go in there, Adam?"

"There were no surprises, Ben. Let's go and catch that lift back to the base camp."

§

The flight back to the Foundation base camp was uneventful, and Adam managed to get some sleep despite the noise in the helicopter cabin. When the Sea King arrived, there was just enough time for a hot mug of tea before Stella led Adam back through the mountains to the loch side on the quad bikes.

"Are you sure you want to go back in there, Adam? With all your information, the police or military could take the place and rescue the others."

Adam was getting ready for the swim back in the loch. "No, Stella. I just can't take the risk that the terrorists get to hear about it from their contacts in the police. They can literally wipe out everybody at the touch of a button."

"Good luck anyway. You know that if you were any good as a planner, you would have asked us to bring you a wetsuit for the swim back. If the site is so secure, how can you get in and out so easily?"

Adam described the underwater entrance and the path past a lethally charged electric fence that faced him on the return trip.

"Ah!"

"I'll see you later tonight, Stella. I have to get a move-on. It will be dawn soon. You two have fun tonight, won't you?"

Adam turned and set off along the loch shore to rejoin the hostages. He slipped under a blanket and tried to sleep a little more before the security guards woke them for breakfast. When the noise of the chain rattling on the door handle started to wake the children, Simon sat up and leaned on one elbow facing Adam.

"You were gone for ages last night. Did everything go well?"

"Yes, it all went pretty much as I expected. Let's go get a shower. I'm starving and can't wait for breakfast."

The guards were getting quite lax about checking the hostages for unauthorised items at shower time. Adam had no problem hiding the mobile phone and the new lock-picking set.

Breakfast that morning was different in that while the children were eating, the terrorists were walking around with a video camera making sure all of the children were recorded. Many of the video shots included the plasma screen displaying the early-morning news program.

"Why do you think they are doing that, Adam?"

"At a guess, I would say they need proof we are all alive before the ransom money is paid."

"So, do you think we will be freed today?"

"My guess is it will probably be tomorrow morning before we get out of here. I need you to help me this morning in the secret building. It will be a bit risky, but it is work we have to do."

"You know I will help you, Adam—anything to get back at these people. Have you heard any news about my father?"

"No. I'm afraid I have seen nothing that would let me know where he is or what has happened to him. While these terrorists can be ruthless, I don't think they harm people unless they really have to."

When the meal was complete, Simon was selected by the guards to help tidy up the breakfast things. Adam returned to the sleeping room with the rest of the hostages. He approached Sally to find out what had been planned for the day for the children. She barely spoke to him and made it plain that she would prefer he went away and left her and Darren in peace. Adam was not surprised. Sally and his sister Gilly seemed to share many characteristics, including stubbornness. Darren just smiled and shrugged his shoulders at his friend. Adam was not worried and decided to speak to Deepa instead. There was still some work Adam needed Deepa to complete. She looked up and smiled when Adam approached.

"It looks like you have found out you are not Sally's favourite person at the moment. She is terrible when she gets in one of her moods. What were you up to last night? You seemed to be out all night."

"Oh, I was just making sure things will be quite interesting in the next twenty-four hours. We should all be safely out of here by tomorrow morning, but there are a couple of things I need you to do now. Can you start the laptop and log in to their access control system? I need to do something to their sea mines controls. Once we have done that, I want to turn off the electric fence. And finally, have you been able to prepare anything so we can run the radar and the Smart Rocks spoof system on another PC?"

"Ok, if you can give me a lift up so I can get to the ceiling tiles, I will get the laptop computer down."

Forming a cup with his hands, Adam allowed Deepa to step up and recover the laptop computer from the suspended ceiling.

After a few moments of tinkering with the computer Deepa looked up at Adam. "Here we go, boss... one fully functional prison camp security control system at your disposal. You wanted the sea mines first, didn't you?"

Deepa typed in a few commands, and an image of the sea entrance of the loch appeared on the screen. There were thirty sea mines marked on the map. They had been laid and anchored a few weeks earlier from the workboat captained by

Fergus McCrinnon.

"Can you tell me the status of those mines, Deepa?"

The girl moved the mouse cursor around the screen, highlighting each mine in sequence. "So far as I can tell, they are all set to passive."

"Can you change their status to active?"

Deepa worked with the PC and soon changed the green marking around the mine symbols to a red colour. "They are all now set to active."

"Is there a password for the mine control system, and can we change it?"

"Yes, Adam. What do you want as a new password?"

"Let me set the password. It is safer for you if you do not know the new password."

"Ok. Give me a moment." Deepa typed a few keys and then passed the laptop to Adam to allow him to enter the new password. They repeated a similar process with the electric fence, this time changing the status from active to off.

"What about the remote control of another PC so we can maintain the corridor for the Smart Rocks and the radar?"

Deepa opened the locket around her neck and extracted the memory chip. She passed it to Adam. "When you are standing next to the PC, plug this memory chip into the USB slot and web browse http://192.168.15.57. If it works ok, you will see a plain orange screen briefly, but you will need to let me know when, because I will need to have this laptop switched on when you are at the PC."

"Ok. That sounds easy enough, even for a jock like me."

"So what was the web address again?"

Adam told her and she smiled.

"One last thing. Can I borrow the laptop again for a moment?"

She handed it over again. Before she could react, Adam produced large knife and carved three large metal shavings from the metal frame of the laptop. She snatched it back from him. "What are you doing, Adam? You could have damaged it."

"No, it's ok. I checked it out on the web last time you lent the laptop to me. Where I carved shouldn't do any damage. The frame of that laptop is made from magnesium metal. I need some magnesium for something else I need to do today."

The expression on Deepa's face told Adam she was not best pleased with his act of IT vandalism. She checked out the laptop. It was still running ok, and the damage was superficial.

"Deepa my next action will be later this afternoon. Once I've gone, leave your laptop running for the next hour, because I'll visiting that other PC. I'm pleased you are not just a pretty face, you know. Your brain has helped us a lot."

As Adam walked away, Deepa's frown changed to a secret smile.

Chapter 41 The Payoff

After breakfast, the Foundation cadets unloaded the heavy crates from the van and loaded them into the helicopter.

"Hey, Jock, these are heavy. I wonder what is in them?"

"I don't know. The Lieutenant wouldn't say when I asked, but they must weigh at least fifty kilos each if not more. I suppose the helicopter can lift them ok."

Once the crates had been transferred, they started the process of carrying the three fifteen-metre aluminium flag poles to the top of the mountain as instructed by their officer. With six cadets combining to carry one pole at a time, the weight was just about bearable over the rough ground. It did mean, however, that the one-and-a-half-mile trip was travelled six times that morning.

"Hey, Rod, I do hope we don't have to mount these flagpoles here. Flying flags at the top of the mountain would be about the type of daft thing they'd ask us to do."

"I've done some crazy things with the Foundation before, but this just about is the limit. Jock, I wouldn't be surprised if they tell us next to carry them down the mountain again."

Once the poles were at the top of the mountain, they portaged the rest of the equipment up from their camp. The boys wished the helicopter could have been used to carry the load up the mountain. Their Officer told them the helicopter was needed to fly the crates to another site. There was excitement building in the cadets. The rumour going around the camp was that the boy who had visited them was the youngest Officer in the history of the Foundation. The secrecy of the operation and the night-time helicopter flights added to that excitement. That excitement helped overcome their tiredness.

§

At nine a.m. that morning, a lorry had left the loch-side base where the hostages were being held. The lorry was driving to a remote point in the Northumberland countryside, identified only by a GPS coordinate reference point. The lorry actually passed within one mile of the campsite where the gold was being stored. The rendezvous had been agreed as taking place at 13:00 hours. The terrorists already had an observer in place, hidden close the rendezvous site. The observer's task was to confirm it was safe for the lorry to approach. He was also armed with a sniper rifle to discourage unwanted interventions.

§

The cadets were lugging the third flagpole up the mountainside at the time when the Sea King helicopter took off heading southeast towards the rendezvous point. Trevor Hewitt swung the helicopter in a big loop as it came close to the rendezvous point to give the appearance that it had approached from the south. He kept the engines running while the twenty-three crates were unloaded and then left covered in camouflage netting.

§

Shortly after the crates were left in a field, in the City of London, a trusted courier was handed a black leather briefcase. He was asked to walk a specific route through the ancient back alleys of the city. When he reached his destination at the Waterman's Walk, he was to hand over the briefcase to a man who would present the correct credentials. The security services had arranged a team of fifteen skilled surveillance officers to follow and watch the courier along the route. Those watchers were helpless when a bicycle courier swept past the foot courier in Bengal Court and snatched the briefcase from him in one of the dark back alleys in the City of London. The ancient alley was only wide enough for two people to walk side by side. The police watched in despair from their command centre CCTV screens as the cyclist disappeared into another narrow alleyway hidden from the sight of their surveillance cameras. Three cyclists emerged from the other end of the alley, each carrying a similar black briefcase. Those three cyclists split and went in three different directions. When they reached other covered places, three more cyclists emerged for the one that went in. The police were trying to track nine different cyclists at the same time, all transporting a black briefcase. The commanding officer quickly gave the instruction to send the signal to switch on the hidden tracking device. There was no response from the tracking unit. The security personnel had to report to their bosses that they had lost sight of the briefcase containing the ransom in less than five minutes.

Thirty minutes later, a snowy-haired, elderly man in a dark uniform with three stripes on his arm entered a vault seventy metres under the London clay. He laid a black briefcase on top of a row of gold bars. He would deal with that later. He had to get a move-on if he was to get to City Airport in time to catch his plane to Scotland.

§

No one took any notice of the plane flying 10,000 metres above the west coast of Scotland. Unsurprisingly, nobody saw the ten soldiers jumping from the plane in a HALO free-fall. They were ten miles from their objective when they started, but when they opened their parachutes at 1,000 metres, they had only three miles to hike over the Scottish moorland to reach their objective. In the sparsely populated countryside, no one saw their descent. Their task was to observe and rescue the hostages if possible. By two p.m., they were in their initial observation position on the mountainside overlooking the buildings.

Chapter 42 Disaster

Adam waited until the late afternoon before making his next move. "Come on, Simon. We've got work to do."

Retrieving the mobile phone from its hiding place, Adam led his friend under the floor into the tunnel between the buildings.

As soon as Adam had left the hostages' room, Sally sprang in to action. She wriggled under the floor into the basement of the building where she had made her cache of supplies.

"Simon, be careful not to kick those bottles as you crawl past. We are going to the secret building. We need to make sure they cannot use the virus. Wait in the tunnel while I retrieve something from the terrorists' accommodation block."

Adam quickly exited into the basement of the accommodation block and found the can containing the mixture of paint pigments. He then returned to his friend in the tunnel. "This is something Sally prepared earlier. If it works, it will help us deal with the security safe in the laboratory. Let's get going to the other building. We will have to be careful because there may be people around during the day."

"Adam, is it really worth taking the risk during the day? Can't we wait until night time?"

"I'm sorry, Simon, but we have to get this done now just in case things go wrong later tonight when all the fireworks start."

Once in the basement of the secret building, Adam performed his magic on the lock of the basement door. "Simon, bring your bottle of bleach."

They crept up onto the ground floor and carefully opened the door from the reception area. They went to look through the windows overlooking the laboratory. So far as they could see, the area was deserted.

Adam took some photographs through the window of the equipment using the mobile phone camera and then said, "We both need to get a protective suit on this time."

"Ok, Adam. You first and then you help me."

The boys went into the cloakroom, and Adam took out his inhaler and disasssembled it and rested some of the contents on top of the paint pigment mixture. They then wriggled into the protective suits and helped each other dress in the plastic suits. The process went a lot more smoothly this time, having done it once before.

Adam touched his plastic helmet against Simon's helmet. "When you are inside, tip the bleach into the stainless steel vats. They have inspection hatches at the top that you can open. Use it all up... don't skimp. Remember to close the hatches when you're done. I don't want them to guess immediately what has happened. I have to deal with the safe."

They passed through the airlock room into the main laboratory. Simon immediately set to work on the vats. He tipped about a litre of bleach into each one. He didn't know if it was enough to kill the virus, but that was all they had.

While Simon was doing that, Adam first visited the desktop PC that was running on the laboratory workbench. Following Deepa's instructions, he inserted the tiny memory chip into the USB socket on the back of the PC. He managed to find the web browser and typed in the address Deepa had specified. After a few seconds, the screen flashed just a solid orange colour and then reverted to the browser screen. Adam closed the browser and left the PC. He took a laboratory stool and climbed onto it so he could reach the top of the safe in the corner of the room. He stood the can of paint pigment mixture on top and poked the slivers of magnesium from the laptop into the top of the powder. He thought hard and recalled the instructions he'd received with the inhaler. He mixed some of the potassium permanganate crystals with the silver dust and the magnesium shavings from his inhaler and then placed his mixture around the base of magnesium slivers in the paint pigment. Nothing happened.

He frantically looked around for something to ignite the magnesium, but he could see nothing. It looked like Simon had just about finished with the bleach in the vats. He rushed over to his friend. "I've got a real problem. I need to ignite some magnesium."

"Why, Adam?"

Adam told him about the improvised thermite mix and what he'd tried to do with the potassium permanganate and the silver.

"Put a drop of water on it, Adam."

"Water? I want to set it alight, not put it out."

"Trust me, Adam."

He decided to take a chance. He found a ballpoint pen, dipped it into some water, and moistened his mixture. Nothing happened. After a few seconds, though, the mixture started bubbling. Tiny flashes of bright light appeared, and then the magnesium caught with a bright, crackling light. Adam watched, mesmerised. He felt Simon tugging his arm.

"Come on, Adam! We can't hang around. They might have smoke detectors."

Adam jerked out of his entranced state, and both boys rushed out of the laboratory. In a final glance towards the safe, Adam could see a roaring bright flame on top and clouds of smoke filling the laboratory. They stood for an agonisingly slow thirty seconds under the decontamination shower before stripping out of their protective suits. When they looked through the window into the laboratory, they could see nothing. The room was full of smoke. They rushed down the stairs to the basement of the building. Adam fumbled a little with the lock picks as he re-locked the door of their room. Climbing back into the tunnel, they carefully pulled the hardboard back into place to hide the duct entrance.

"Wow, Adam, that was subtle. I bet they don't notice anything wrong in their lab after that set of fireworks. I think that will burn their building down."

"I didn't know it was going to be that strong. Come on. We had best get back with the others and try and look innocent."

They crawled back to their building as quickly as they could. When they reached the basement, Adam told Simon to go on ahead. Adam climbed up the knotted rope in the air duct to call the watchers down and told them to return to the main room.

"Adam, they've just caught Sally! She sneaked into their garage. Smoke started coming out from the building over there, and the terrorists rushed out from their accommodation block. They saw Sally just when she was leaving the garage."

"Ok. You two had best go down and join the others. I'll follow in a minute."

Once they had disappeared out of sight, Adam emptied his pockets and put the items on top of the small brick room that housed the entrance hatch to the roof. So far as he could tell, they were out of sight.

He climbed back down the shaft using the knotted rope to the basement and then joined the others. They had all heard Sally had been caught outside.

Adam went to Darren. "Darren, what was she doing out there?"

"I told her not to do it, but she wanted to take revenge on the terrorists. I don't know what she has done. I begged her not to go. She was waiting for you to leave because she knew you would stop her."

"I'm afraid I don't know what will happen next, Darren. We will just have to wait and see."

About an hour later, the doors to their room were unchained, and Alpha 3 strode in. As usual, his face was masked. "I want all of you to go to the canteen now. You are going to eat early tonight—but not you, Cranford. You and I are going to have a little chat upstairs."

A guard took Adam and led him away. When the other hostages entered the canteen area, they saw Sally sitting on a chair. Her face was bruised and red, and her hair was dishevelled.

Alpha 3 held his hand up for silence. "I strongly suggest you all listen to what Sally Busby here has to say. This is your last chance to behave. If you can manage that for the next few hours, you will all leave here safely. Meanwhile, I need to have a discussion with Master Cranford."

The terrorist leader turned and left them with just one guard in place.

They all looked at Sally, wondering what had happened. She lifted her head defiantly and spoke to them. "I did something stupid, ok, and I got caught. I admit it. It was my fault and nobody else's. These guys are not so bad. They have got their money. There is a lorry load of crates containing gold. They showed me. All the terrorists want to do is just escape now with their money, and we will be released unharmed. Adam is some kind of traitor. He gave away Darren and John when they tried to escape earlier."

"No, Sally, you've got it all wrong!" shouted a shocked Simon.

"Look, I know that you are a bit soft on Adam, but Alpha 3 showed me the note Adam wrote. I recognised the handwriting. It told them how and when Darren and John planned to escape. He is evil, Simon. He's responsible for John's death."

"You don't know the whole story, Sally. You have made a terrible mistake. We have just come back from burning down their secret laboratory where they were brewing some awful virus. This was not just a simple kidnapping. He was out last night arranging a rescue."

Tears were streaming down Simon's face.

§

At that moment, upstairs in the corridor, Alpha 3 was speaking to Adam, who was held on each arm by two guards and handcuffed. "You have been a very destructive young man, and you have caused me a great deal of trouble and expense. Fortunately, you only destroyed the contents of the safe. Your fire was soon put out. Young Sally was most cooperative when she discovered you are a traitor. I have men fixing the explosives right now, and we have found the laptop you stole. Your tunnels are being sealed as we speak. She thinks I will let you all go free and unharmed now we have the money."

He raised his pistol and fired two shots, then instructed his men. "Throw him in that room. We have got some work to do."

§

Downstairs in the canteen, all the hostages were staring at Simon after what he had just revealed. Sally looked shocked. And just then, they all heard the sound of the two pistol shots above them.

"I hope you can live with yourself, Sally Busby, if we actually live to get out of here," Simon blurted out before he collapsed, sobbing on a canteen bench. Deepa, tears streaming down her face, moved to try and comfort the sobbing boy.

The remainder of the hostages stood around in shocked horror, scarcely able to take in what had just happened so suddenly.

§

On the mountain behind the fish-breeding research base, unaware of the events inside, the Foundation cadets were putting on full camouflage uniforms as they prepared to move the flagpoles down the mountain towards the fence of the research station. Dusk was just starting, and the land was all turning grey. They found it a lot easier to move the fifteen-metre poles downhill. They knew they had to be careful to avoid noise.

The Special Forces soldiers who had parachuted in earlier started moving closer to their objective. They could see the occasional person moving around, and their portable thermal imaging cameras spotted the heat of other people by the buildings. The gentle throb from a diesel generator confirmed there was some activity around the buildings. Using throat microphones, they reported back to their Commanders using satellite radio links.

§

At the research station, the terrorists were carefully carrying the heavy insulated stainless steel vats from the laboratory and strapping them down on the desk of the workboat. They also loaded the insulated chest containing the methyl nitrate bottles on to the workboat. Dr. Gwon was supervising the transfer. Much of the equipment had to be left behind. Alpha 3 could not spare men to perform sentry duties around the site. The radar system was switched on and would give early warning of any unwanted visitors.

The terrorists' personal equipment and clothing had been loaded into the back of the lorry containing the crates, and their accommodation building had then been thoroughly soaked with diesel fuel, ready to be set alight by timer after they left the site. Alpha 3 had one of the men take a bottle of methyl nitrate and prime it with a timer detonator. That was placed against the liquid propane gas fuel tank. The timer was set for midnight, by which time they would be about 100 miles away and their cargo loaded on the freighter that would be waiting for them. A similar time had been set for the detonators for explosives in the office block where the hostages were held captive. The terrorists had soon repaired the detonator cord that Sally had previously cut. The pipe and air ducts in the building had been filled with expanded polyurethane foam that had by now set hard.

The hostages were locked in a room with no new information. All they could do was wait for rescue. Sally had told them they would be safe. None of the hostages noticed the fine mist descending on them from a small nozzle in the ceiling.

The terrorists had quickly found and defused the crude bomb Sally had left in Alpha 3's Land Rover. By seven p.m., they were all loaded in the vehicles and boats, ready and waiting to go, leaving the hostages behind.

Exactly two minutes later, the Foundation cadets on the hillside heard the signal for which they were waiting. There was an explosion by the side of the loch. They started moving down close to the fence in the corridor that was carefully marked on the map. They carried the flagpoles the final 100 metres and started work.

On hearing the explosion, Alpha 3 despatched a man along the track. He came back with grim news. "The track is totally blocked by a rock fall caused by an explosion. We would need a bulldozer to get through. If we try to use explosives to clear it, we would destroy the road."

Alpha 3 cursed. He had underestimated the Cranford boy. He knew there was no other route out for the lorry carrying the gold. The isolation of the site was one of the selection criteria for the research station site. The crates would have to go out by sea on the workboat. He heard the faint crackle of gunfire in the distance. Cursing again, he returned to the office, taking his laptop computer with him. The first thing he did was to make an urgent phone call to his leader.

§

On the mountainside, the soldiers crept closer to their objective. They did not notice the tripwire until too late. A rocket flare suddenly erupted from beside them, marking their position on the mountainside. Almost immediately, they saw gunfire erupt from their objective at the bottom of the mountain. The soldiers were out of gunfire range, but they knew they had been discovered.

They withdrew back up the mountain and made a report to their Commander. They did so with a heavy heart because they knew the consequences. "Tango team has made hostile contact. The bad guys are now aware we are here."

"Understood. Await orders."

The grim faced Special Forces soldiers knew the next order would be for them to illuminate the target buildings with an infrared targeting laser when the next phase of the operation commenced. A decision had been made at senior government levels that Project BLEACH should take place. A flight of bombers would drop smart bombs on the target and completely obliterate and incinerate it. The sudden disappearance of Henry Davidson, one of the hostages' parents and an expert on germ warfare, combined with the information from Adam Cranford, meant there must be no risk that the virus would survive. They had hoped to get samples for future research, but that was a lower priority. With the terrorists aware of intruders and them firing at the troops, decisive action had to be taken.

Chapter 43 The Escape

Adam felt a hand on his body trying to turn him to see if he was injured. Adam was lying face down with his hands handcuffed behind his back. He recognised the voice.

"Are you alright? You've been unconscious for a while."

"John? John Nelson? Is that you?"

"Yeah, it's me. Who are you?"

"It's me, Adam Cranford. I thought they had killed you!"

"No. They just did the trick with the pistol like just did with you—to scare the other hostages. They beat me up and broke my arm, but their doctor has reset it. Simon's dad is here too. He's chained to other end of the room and can't reach you."

"Mr. Davidson? Are you ok?"

"Hi, Adam. Yes, I'm ok, given the circumstances. Have you got any news? Is my son alright?"

"Simon is still a hostage, but I think he's ok. He just helped me burn out their laboratory. That's why they threw me in here, I think."

"You know about their laboratory? You know what they are doing, Adam? We have got to stop them. I didn't want to help them, but they said—"

"I know all about it, sir. There is going to a rescue soon, but I have to get out of here to help guide people in."

"We are both chained to the wall, and they've locked the door. I don't think we can help, Adam."

"They handcuffed me, but John, if you can reach in my pocket and find the long thin thing and put it in my left hand, I think I can get out. My face feels a bit sore. I think they broke my nose when I landed in here."

Adam felt John's hand searching his body, patting down the pockets until he found the lock pick. After a bit of a struggle, John managed to pull the lock pick out and put it into Adam's hand. After ten minutes of difficult work, Adam suddenly felt a *click*, and the pressure released on his right wrist. He wriggled his hand free and then quickly released his other hand from the handcuffs. Standing, he made his way to the door and looked for a light switch. He found it and tried the switch. The light did not work. Feeling around the door, he found the door handle and lock. After some experimentation with the lock, he realised the keyhole had been filled. It would not be possible to pick that lock.

He returned to John to release the chain around the boy's ankle. It was not possible without a spanner or some sort of wrench. The chain had been locked in place with a tightened nut and bolt. Henry Davidson's chain was the same.

"I don't think I can get you guys free without tools. Is there any other way out of this room?"

"They have bricked up most of the window, but the top bit does open if you can reach it, Adam."

Adam found the window. They were right; he could feel the brickwork blocking the window opening except for a gap at the top. The mortar smelled as though it had been recently laid.

"Mr. Davidson, can you give me a boost so I can reach the top?"

"I'll give it a go. Call me Henry if you like. It is none too formal in here."

After some fumbling in the dark, Henry managed to lift Adam upwards. The boy grabbed the top of the brickwork and pulled himself up. By stretching his arm down inside between the bricks and the window, he was able to release a catch, and the window swung open. "I'm going out through the window. I'll be back with some help."

It was a tight fit, but he managed to wriggle through the gap at the top of the brickwork. An eight-metre drop onto hard concrete was facing Adam. He wriggled further and was able to reach the thin outer window ledge. He was upside down with his hand resting on the bottom window frame when suddenly gravity took over and the remaining part of his body slid out into the air. He managed to grab onto the window frame with one hand and stopped himself from falling. Pulling his free hand up to the window frame, he managed to dangle by both hands from the first-floor window ledge.

Slowly, he pulled himself back up and used a mantle-shelf move to lift one foot onto the window ledge. By bracing and bridging his feet against the brickwork on either side of the window frame and leaning back with his hands inside it, he was able to climb upwards. By the time he reached the top of the window, his legs were beginning to shake violently from the stress. In a desperate move, he threw one hand upwards and managed to curl his finger around the brick parapet of the flat roof of the office building. That lunge cost him the grip on his feet, and they slipped off the brickwork. He was dangling by one hand over the drop. In increasing desperation, he managed to fling his other hand onto the edge of the parapet and gradually pull himself up on to the roof.

Looking across the parking area, he could see some of the terrorists transferring items from the lorry to the workboat.

Adam ran across to the air vent at the other end of the roof. He grabbed the knotted rope and started to climb down. He had almost reached the bottom when his feet touched an obstacle. Adam put some weight on the obstacle, but it would not move. He worked his hand down and felt what was blocking his way—a dome of hard foam plastic. The terrorists had found that route and blocked it. He climbed back up to the roof of the building and paused while he considered what to do next. It was the thing he dreaded most. He was going to have to climb down the drainpipe of the building and find some way of breaking into the building again.

He tried the roof hatch, but that was locked from the inside.

As he sat thinking about what he should do next, he heard the roof hatch doorway open. In the dim light, he saw a figure climbing out onto the roof.

A man dressed in dark clothing walked across to Adam. "I thought we might find you up here. It was unlikely the room would have held you for long."

It was Alpha 3. Adam started to panic but decided to act calmly. "So, have you come up here to negotiate surrender, Alpha 3?"

"I hardly think so, Cranford. After all, I am the man with the gun, and you are the hostage sitting on the building loaded with explosives."

At that moment, they heard jet planes flying overhead, and then the sky glowed with the light of explosions the other side of the mountain. Shortly afterwards, the rumble of multiple explosions rolled like distant thunder down the mountainside to the roof where they were standing.

"My contact has just told me you have given this location to the military. Clearly, they do not know at this point that you gave them a slightly wrong map reference. I presume you have made arrangements for them to be given the correct reference if you do not contact somebody outside real soon?"

"Yes, Alpha 3. I did not think they would resort to bombing so soon, but I guess that means you do not have too long to make up your mind as to what you want to do. As you have not sailed away on your boats, I presume you have realised I have activated the minefield at the entrance to the loch?"

"Yes, young man. That was particularly sneaky. The young Indian girl was sensible enough to tell us it was you who had set the password. She laughed at us and said that since we had killed you, we would never escape. What do we need to do to persuade you to tell us that password so we can deactivate the mines?"

"I am a trader, not a warrior. How about we do a trade? You release all of the hostages first and pay me £1 million, and I will let you go."

"Given your efforts in the laboratory, Cranford, I presume you know about Project Silver Rain?"

"Yes, I do. In a way, it doesn't seem such a bad idea. It would certainly bring down the world population. I just disagree with the way you are doing it and using us as hostages. What puzzles me is why you need to come to Scotland to do this and why you need to involve Henry Davidson in this."

"The original virus that was used can only be sourced in this part of Scotland, and when the disease is 'discovered', it will be traced back to here. Add to that the fact that we have photographs of a leading British scientist involved in the manufacture of the virus. A lot of people are going to blame Britain for the outbreak. That will make my sponsors very happy, and I will be well paid for that."

"I knew this kidnapping was about more than just the money. The whole thing was so you could get Henry Davidson here and force him to work without alerting the authorities. I presume you asked him before and he refused?"

"You are a very clever young man. Are you sure you don't want to swap sides and work for me? It would be very profitable."

"No, thanks. You guys are losers, and I don't want to work for losers."

"Time is getting short. Will you give me the password, or do I have to shoot some of the hostages to persuade you?"

"They are only rich kids who wouldn't think twice about betraying me. They would not be a great loss to the world. I am quite prepared to sacrifice all of them to make sure I win. I have already told you the terms. Take it or leave it."

Alpha 3 paused before answering. "You really mean that, don't you?"

"You have heard the terms, Alpha 3. Like I said before, time is getting short. Surely you don't think the military are the only people I have lined up to help me?"

"Ok. I will pay you £1 million and will leave you all here unharmed if you give me the password."

"You have a deal. I hope you have a laptop with Internet connection, because I will not accept payment in gold. It is to be direct deposited to my overseas bank account."

"You know about the gold as well?"

"Yup. Let's go."

Alpha 3 led Adam down to the office. The man powered up his laptop and connected it to his bank's web site. He had to authenticate his access using a special code key-fob as well. Within five minutes, £1 million had been transferred to a bank account whose details Adam had supplied.

Alpha 3 started the site security system on his laptop and then turned the screen to face Adam. "The password, if you please?"

Adam typed in the correct password to control the sea mines.

Alpha 3 took control of the laptop and deactivated the sea mines. Having completed that, he switched off the laptop and then smashed the keyboard and the screen with the butt of his automatic pistol. "I'm leaving you, young man. I doubt we'll ever meet again. By the way, I suppose I should let you know we have activated the electric fence again, and your neck ring has also been activated. As we agreed, I am leaving you all here unharmed. However, once we are a safe distance away from the loch, the explosives in the building will detonate. When that happens, the transmitter controlling your neck rings will cease to work, and you know what happens then. Cheerio! Have a nice day now. And oh, before I go, you should know the explosives are also connected to the alarm system. If anyone tries to get past the fence, it will suddenly get very unhealthy in here." With a snide smile of victory on his face, the terrorist turned and left the office.

Adam waited on the flat roof until the last terrorist had left the jetty before he reached on the top of the water tank and hatch building on the roof. He found the torch he had secured there earlier in the day. He went to the side of the building nearest the fence and flashed a signal in Morse code towards the waiting Foundation cadet—dot dot dot dash. There was no immediate response, so he repeated the letter. This time, there was a flashed response of two letters: dash dash dash... dash dot dash.

He stood upright with the torch shining on his face. The cadets worked fast to erect the tripod made from the flagpoles they had laboriously carried down the mountainside in the dark. Once the tripod had been secured, one of the cadets climbed to the top where the poles crossed, carrying a fishing rod on his back. When he was in place, he carefully cast the fishing line weighted with a lead weight towards Adam. The lead weight landed on the roof behind Adam, who heard the noise of it landing. He found the line by walking the length of the roof. He gave the line a few gentle tugs. The cadet on the tripod responded similarly.

Adam pulled a rope attached to the fishing line across from the tripod. It stretched high over the double wire fences. When he had enough rope, he secured his end by tying it around the base of the brick hatch building. Once the rope was secure and tight, he saw the LED headlight of a cadet progressing across the rope. There was a downward slope towards the tripod from the roof, so the cadet had to work quite hard as he climbed across. Adam helped him over the final obstacle of the parapet.

The cadet had pulled a second rope with him, along with some climbing slings and carabiners. "Good evening, Captain," he said. "Nice evening for a spot of rope climbing. Cadet David Thomas at your service."

"I'm pleased to see you, Cadet. We have to work fast. There are thirty people downstairs that we need to get up here quickly and across the rope. Make sure they do not touch the inner fence, as it is electrified and both fences are alarmed. Setting the alarm off would be very bad news. Warn people to stay within the marked pathway."

Across the fences, Adam could see a pathway being marked out up the mountainside with bright green light sticks. "Did you bring the bolt cutters, walkie talkie, and some extra light sticks with you?" he asked the cadet.

David reached behind him in his rucksack and pulled out a large heavy pair of bolt cutters. From his pockets, he pulled out about a dozen light sticks and a walkie talkie radio.

Adam bent the light sticks to activate them and scattered a few on the roof to provide some light. Then, he switched on the walkie talkie, changed to Channel 15, and pressed the transmit key. "Attention! This is Charlie Alpha. You may now break radio silence. Please relay the message to base camp. The birds are leaving the nest. Acknowledge? Roger."

"Charlie Alpha, this is Delta Bravo. Relay request acknowledged. Roger."

"David, I have a job for you. Can you cut this neck ring with the bolt cutters? Just here."

The neck ring fell onto the flat roof. Picking up the rest of light sticks and the bolt cutters, Adam turned to go down the hatch into the building. "I'm going to send people up to you now, David. Send them out over the rope as quickly as you can. Once thirty people have gone through, get off the roof yourself and leave the rope in place. This place is wired with explosives. I need people to be at least 500 metres away from the building. Don't hang around for me, but leave me a sling and your rucksack."

§

A couple miles away in the cadet base camp, a snowy-haired old man in a black Foundation Sergeant's uniform smiled as he heard the relayed message. He picked up his mobile phone and dialled a number. The call was answered quickly. "Mr. Uddin, can you please pass a message to Ali from Adam? He says it is time to change the fielders' positions."

"Yes, I certainly will do that."

The call ended.

The father passed the mobile phone over to his son. Ali pressed the fast-dial button for a prerecorded number. It took about twenty seconds for the call to be answered.

"Hello. Detective Inspector Norris speaking."

"Hello, Inspector. I'm a friend of Adam Cranford. He tells me you were right about Stilson's window. He asked me to tell you he made a mistake with the map reference for his location. Please tell your bosses the correct one."

Ali recalled from memory the six-digit number Adam had asked him to remember and told the policeman. Norris repeated the number, and Ali terminated the call. That mobile phone had not been used before that evening and would never be used again.

§

By the time that call was completed, Adam had cut through the chain to the door of the hostages' room and had burst in. "Everyone, there is no time for explanations. You have to leave the building now. After you have had your neck ring removed, follow the green light sticks to the roof. Follow the instructions of the person waiting for you there. Your lives depend on this. Let's hope the fitness training has worked!"

He pointed to two of the bigger boys. "You two, kneel down and I will cut off your neck rings."

The rings were swiftly removed and fell harmlessly to the floor.

"Ok, now you cut off the others' rings and then come up to the first floor with the bolt cutters and find me. I will be in the middle room. You have seen the safe place to cut the rings?"

"Yeah, Adam."

"Simon, come with me as soon as you are free."

The hostages had formed a line by the time Adam left the room. He dashed up to the first floor to find Henry Davidson and John Nelson. Their door was locked, and it took Adam a few minutes to pick the stiff lock. By the time he had finished, Simon and the other two boys had arrived with the bolt cutters.

"Quick! Cut the chains off John and Mr. Davidson and then help them up to the roof. Is everyone gone from downstairs?"

"Yes, Adam. We followed the last one."

Adam dashed out of the room downstairs to check the rooms to ensure the building really was empty. Then he made his way into the office that had been used by the terrorists. He searched around for any paperwork, but the desks were empty. They had been careful to remove any evidence. He saw the wreckage of the laptop on the desk and smiled. He searched around to see if he could find the detonator or Det cord to disable the explosives, but he could not find it. Grabbing the laptop, he hurried to the roof. As he stepped onto the roof, he heard the last person departing down the rope slide. He found the rucksack and bundled the, torch, radio set, and laptop into it before launching himself along the rope. At the tripod end of the rope, he found another rope tied and dangling down to the ground.

On the ground, he took the walkie talkie and pressed the send button. "This is Charlie Alpha. Please relay message to Bravo Bravo. Meet me at position Charlie. Acknowledge? Roger"

"Charlie Alpha. Bravo Bravo to meet you at position Charlie. Roger."

"Roger and out."

§

While Adam was sliding across the rope, the workboat and the mini submarine were getting close to the entrance channel of the loch. Inside the engine compartment of the workboat, the vibration of the motor had been causing particles of frozen smoke to fall free through a hole in the package containing the insulating material. When the bottle of methyl nitrate, strapped there by Adam, no longer had a protective thermal insulating layer, the heat and vibration from the exhaust pipe detonated the liquid. The explosion massively damaged the engine, causing it to seize, and made a large bulge and an underwater split in the metal hull of the vessel. It started to sink.

Fergus McCrinnon knew the water of the loch was deep where they were. "Right, boys. I think we have hit one of the mines. This boat is going to sink in deep water. We are going to have to abandon her. Get in the life raft I'm about to release."

He climbed on top of the cabin of the workboat and unclipped a large white plastic cylinder and rolled it over the edge of the boat. It immediately started inflating on the water to form a rescue life raft. Meanwhile, Alpha 3 had signalled to the mini submarine to come over and join them. When it came alongside, he jumped from the workboat onto the mini submarine. Opening the main hatch, he climbed inside and signalled to the pilot to pull away, leaving his men to rescue themselves. Most of the terrorists managed to get inside the life raft before Fergus McCrinnon climbed in and cut the tether rope. The wind across the loch started to blow the life raft back in the direction they had just sailed. One minute later, the workboat sank in more than forty metres of water.

§

As Adam ran along the track past the pile of boulders blocking the roadway and towards position Charlie, he heard the explosion further along the loch. In the distance, he heard the *thwop thwop* of the rotor blades of the Sea King helicopter as it crested the mountain to join him at position Charlie. The teen boy and the helicopter arrived at the rendezvous point at almost the same time. It landed, and the cabin door was opened. Adam was helped in by the navigator. Inside the rear cabin of the helicopter, he found two old men and a couple of cadets waiting to greet him.

"Sergeant Bates, I think it is about time we put the air sea rescue skills of our pilot to the test while we go and rescue twenty-three wooden crates that will be now floating in the loch. I hope they are all watertight."

§

A couple miles away to the north, the squad of special service soldiers had just received new instructions that they were to proceed southwards towards the valley containing the loch.

§

Back at the Foundation base camp, the freed hostage school children were just beginning to arrive. They were greeted with warm, dry clothing, hot drinks, and hot showers. The Foundation Lieutenant had changed out of uniform to greet the incoming people. Part of Adam's instructions had been that the Foundation's part in this rescue should not be known by the hostages. The last of the hostages had just crested the mountain, guided by the Foundation cadets when an explosion lit the loch side behind them. The office building suddenly ceased to exist. A second explosion followed almost simultaneously as the bottles of methyl nitrate hidden in the tunnel exploded in sympathy to the initial shock wave.

§

The last of the cadets had returned from the hillside when the navigation lights of the Sea King helicopter appeared over the base camp. The weary cadets had one last task for that night, and that was to move twenty-three heavy wooden crates from the helicopter to the waiting white van. They were aided in this by the boys who had been hostages. Adam spotted the crate with the red circle on the outside and asked the cadets to bring it inside the command tent. He waited for the cadets to leave. With a borrowed screwdriver, he unscrewed the lid and opened one of the bags contained inside. He counted out 110 gold sovereigns in the presence of Sergeant Bates and then closed up the crate. From the gold sovereigns, he walked over to the helicopter and handed the pile of coins to the Flight Lieutenant.

"I believe you now have to decide on a suitable charity?"

"Adam, you really don't need to pay for us to take part in this rescue. However, I'm sure the local lifeboat station next to our base would welcome these coins in their collection box. It has been a long day, but a day I will never forget. I must go and get some sleep now, or I will not be allowed to fly the helicopter back to its owners in the morning. Don't forget we have promised to allow your squad to visit our base. I'll be expecting a phone call from you."

Adam shook hands with the pilot and the navigator, and they headed off to their tent to sleep.

The teen heard a voice behind him. He spun and found Sergeant Bates behind him. "In my view, sir, I now fully agree with the Council of Elders that you deserve the red star on your collar. Ben Bryson was telling me about the other fireworks show you had arranged in the valley not too far from here. I rather suspect there will be some annoyed officials tomorrow, but they won't be able to argue with the fact that there are now thirty rescued hostages."

"Sergeant, if the officials had been nice to me instead of trying to arrest me, I might have told them the truth."

"I daresay you're right, sir. The van is now loaded with the gold, so with your permission, I had best go and accompany it on its trip back to London."

"I'd be grateful if you could arrange one more thing, Sergeant. I know the Foundation needs to cover its expenses on this, but can you make sure the poorer families are never actually charged for the ransom insurance? After all, we did get the gold back."

"We would not have charged them anyway, sir."

Even though Adam was not in Foundation uniform, the Sergeant broke protocol, smiled, and saluted the teenage officer. Adam returned the salute and left the Sergeant to go and join the other freed school children.

Simon was chatting with his father, and they did not notice Adam immediately. However, Deepa had seen him approach and came out of the crowd to greet him with a smile. "Hello, Mister Hero." She gestured with her hand at the tents and the helicopter. "I can see now why the Foundation gave you the red star. It is a real shame we can't tell the others about it. Simon told us about the virus. I now know why you didn't let us escape earlier. Sally told me about the explosives in the building. They really weren't going to let us leave alive, were they?"

"That is all in the past now, so there is no point in worrying about it."

"Did the terrorists get away?"

"Alpha 3 managed to get away from the loch, but the virus didn't. The others will probably be rounded up by the police tomorrow. They will be wet and cold. I had the pilot radio details to the police. Talking about getting away... here is our ride just arriving."

A large coach had just arrived at the base camp. A man stepped out from the passenger door and helped his blind son step down before handing him his crutch. Adam walked over and greeted the new arrivals. "Mr. Uddin, thank you for arranging this. It means we will be able to deliver everyone home without the newspaper and TV reporters mobbing us back in Buckinghamshire when we arrive. Hi, Ali. How are you? You look a bit sleepy."

"Adam, you just do not know how much my son can talk when he is excited. He talked all the way up here. His is very excited to meet you again."

"Mr. Uddin, the drivers, you, and Ali must have some food and drink, and then we should get back. I would imagine the others are keen to get home to their own beds after their ordeal. Ali, I'll come talk as soon as I'm free."

Adam found a cadet and asked him to look after the four people from the coach. He went in search of Stella and Ben. He found them in the middle of a bunch of cadets, examining the quad bikes. The cadets dispersed when Adam asked for some privacy.

"Adam, those were some spectacular fireworks back there in the valley. It is good job you had warned us to get clear after the initial contact. Ben was a bit disappointed he had to leave because he had arranged a few surprises to greet his old regiment."

"It was worth it, though, Stella. I have to really thank you two for taking the risks you did. That air strike really convinced the terrorists it was time to go."

Ben put a firm hand on Adam's shoulder and looked him in the eye. "You see? I was right. Even though you are a Rupert, I knew you would do good."

"I've been meaning to ask you Ben. how did you know about my promotion?"

They were interrupted when a squad of cadets marched up and picked up Adam and carried him on their shoulders to a large campfire and sat him in a large throne made of branches in front of the fire. The rest of the ex-hostages were gathered around, seated on the benches. The Squad Leader stepped back and saluted. "This chair is yours by Right of Valour, Sir." Loud cheering erupted from around the campfire.

§

Half an hour later, the rescued school children were drifting off to sleep as their coach headed southward on the ten-hour journey to their homes. The weary Foundation cadets were sleeping in their tents. Stella and Ben were staying as guests at the camp. It was not the first time they had seen Foundation uniforms.

§

As the children were on their journey home, off the Scottish coast, a mini submarine was being winched out of the sea. It was to going to be stowed on the deck of the freighter hidden under canvas sheets to protect it from the prying eyes of satellites. None of the crew noticed the bottles tied securely under the hull of the submarine, nor did they notice the sea water draining out from the plastic sandwich box. The detonation of the C4 explosive triggered the methyl nitrate in the bottles. After the explosion, the freighter capsized and sank so quickly that the crew only had chance to send out a brief distress call. The call went unheeded.

§

The ex-hostages all slept well on the journey home, none more so than Adam. However, about six a.m., he was woken by the relief driver. "I'm sorry to wake you, but that Mr. Bates suggested an alteration to your plan for delivering everyone home. He thought one coach dropping off people at each house might attract the attention of the press."

The man told Adam of the new plan, and he smiled. "That sounds good to me."

The relief driver left, and his place was taken by a slim, blonde-haired girl. "Adam, I'm sorry. I should have trusted you. I almost wrecked the whole plan, didn't I?"

"It doesn't matter, Sally. We got out safe, and really that is all that matters. If I'd told you more of the story, you probably would not have done what you did."

"We are all going to throw you a mega party when we get back."

"No. As much as I'd like that, my part in all of this has to remain secret to protect the Foundation. Please thank the others, but I'm just a normal school boy."

"I'm just sad Alpha 3 got away unpunished."

Adam chose to say nothing more.

Ten minutes later, the coach pulled into a motorway service station. Awaiting them in the car park was a fleet of fifteen executive limousines. The children split up from the coach with two people to a car. As she was driven home, Deepa noticed her driver wore a gold signet ring on the little finger of his right hand.

Order Form

Alaric Adair Books
Oaksys Tech Ltd
41 Chalsey Road
Brockley
London SE4 1YN
United Kingdom
http://www.alaricadair.com

Please send (   ) copies of Teen Valour to:

Name: ....

Address: ....

               ....

               ....

               ....

I enclose a cheque for the full amount payable to Oaksys Tech Ltd. The recommended retail price is £9.99 per book and £3.00 postage and packing per parcel in the UK.

Extra copies of Teen Valour may be ordered by post direct from the publishers. They can be easily ordered through the Internet at the publishers website on: http://shop.alaricadair.com

or from the websites of Tesco, Amazon, WH Smith, Waterstones, Barnes & Noble, Lulu.

Your local book shop should be able to order a copy of the book. Check the publisher website for discount offers and other Adam Cranford goods.

Membership of the Adam Cranford Fan Club is free and gives access to special offers, adavance releases and branded Adam Cranford goods. Check out the Alaric Adair website (http://www.alaricadair.com).

Order Form

Alaric Adair Books
Oaksys Tech Ltd
41 Chalsey Road
Brockley
London SE4 1YN
United Kingdom
http://www.alaricadair.com

Please send ( ) copies of Teen Valour to:

Name: ....
Address: ....
           ....
           ....
           ....

I enclose a cheque for the full amount payable to Oaksys Tech Ltd. The recommended retail price is £9.99 per book and £3.00 postage and packing per parcel in the UK.

Extra copies of Teen Valour may be ordered by post direct from the publishers. They can be easily ordered through the Internet at the publishers website on: http://shop.alaricadair.com

or from the websites of Tesco, Amazon, WH Smith, Waterstones, Barnes & Noble, Lulu.

Your local book shop should be able to order a copy of the book. Check the publisher website for discount offers and other Adam Cranford goods.

Membership of the Adam Cranford Fan Club is free and gives access to special offers, adavance releases and branded Adam Cranford goods. Check out the Alaric Adair website (http://www.alaricadair.com).

www.ingramcontent.com/pod-product-compliance
Lightning Source LLC
Chambersburg PA
CBHW061310170626
46817CB00001B/128